THE BEST
CRIME
STORIES
EVER TOLD

THE BEST
CRIME
STORIES
EVER TOLD

EDITED BY **DOROTHY L. SAYERS**

INTRODUCTION BY **OTTO PENZLER**

Skyhorse Publishing

Skyhorse Publishing books may be purchased in bulk at special discounts for sales promotion, corporate gifts, fund-raising, or educational purposes. Special editions can also be created to specifications. For details, contact the Special Sales Department, Skyhorse Publishing, 307 West 36th Street, 11th Floor, New York, NY 10018 or info@skyhorsepublishing.com.

www.skyhorsepublishing.com

10 9 8 7 6 5

Library of Congress Cataloging-in-Publication Data is available on file.
ISBN: 978-1-62087-049-5

Printed in the United States of America

CONTENTS

INTRODUCTION
OTTO PENZLER

If there is a universal truth to the compiling of an anthology, it is that it is a subjective undertaking. It is almost unthinkable that two people, given the freedom to choose whatever they wanted to include in what attempts to be a definitive collection, would ever select precisely the same stories, just as different folks reach for different chocolates in the big deluxe assortment of sweets.

I probably would not have named exactly the same stories that Dorothy L. Sayers assembled in a book that is comprised of stories from the massive 1932 volume, *The Second Omnibus of Crime*. As the title so conspicuously announces, she had edited a prior volume four years earlier titled, perhaps not surprisingly, *The Omnibus of Crime*, which proved so successful that it prompted this sequel, which also enjoyed brisk sales and the affection of readers, leading to still another volume, this one titled, informatively, if not very creatively, *The Third Omnibus of Crime*.

Sayers was English—as English as one can get. Born and raised in Oxford, she was one of the first female graduates from the venerable university in that beautiful city, and she lived in England for the rest of her life. Perhaps, then, she may be excused for her prejudice in favor of British detective stories. All six of the stories defined by Sayers as "Detection and Mystery" were written by fellow Brits, as if Melville Davisson Post, Mark Twain, Thomas Bailey Aldrich, Frank Stockton, Richard Harding Davis, Jacques Futrelle, O. Henry, and the other superb American writers of crime fiction who had been producing distinguished novels and short stories had never been born. And don't even *think* about finding anyone who wrote in a language other than English.

On the other hand, it would be difficult to argue that the authors she selected don't belong in the pantheon of the greatest mystery writers of all time. Robert Barr and his deliciously twisted plots, E. C. Bentley's subtle, sly humor, Freeman Wills Crofts dismantling the perfect alibi, J. S. Fletcher and his mastery of mood, and Baroness Orczy with her outstanding characterizations all have produced irresistible stories.

An even richer vein has been opened for the stories defined by Sayers as "Mystery and Horror." Once you have read Ambrose Bierce's "The Damned Thing," you will never forget it. Fortunately American writers made it into this section or else you would have been denied the excruciating horror (though nothing supernatural here) of "The Open Boat," as well as Edgar Allan Poe's little-known but haunting "Berenice."

Not that English writers, who deserve their reputation of being particularly good at this sort of thing, have been ignored. One need merely hear the names Algernon Blackwood, J. S. Le Fanu, H. G. Wells, and W. W. Jacobs to shudder. And if you've never before read Saki's dazzling short-short story "Sredni Vashtar" you are in for a memorable moment.

In addition to being one of the most accomplished and revered detective writers of the twentieth century, mainly for her novels about Lord Peter Wimsey, Sayers was a serious scholar of the genre and was instrumental, both by example and by her perceptive analyses of other authors' works, in changing this important literary form, helping to imbue it with many of the elements that readers quickly came to expect and appreciate as a more modern form of storytelling.

The Second Omnibus of Crime was published in the middle of what is referred to nowadays as the Golden Age of the detective story, that period between the two World Wars when mystery fiction flourished and began to be treated as serious literature by influential critics. Such masters as Agatha Christie, R. Austin Freeman, Anthony Berkeley, Crofts, Sayers, S. S. Van Dine, Ellery Queen, G. K. Chesterton, and John Dickson Carr all wrote during those years, and they helped elevate what had been mere puzzles into the realm of the fully developed novel.

Although not as well-remembered today as some of his more illustrious colleagues, Berkeley was respected and admired by them for his ingenuity and his dedication to improving detective fiction. He presciently wrote the following in his introduction to his acclaimed mystery novel, *The Second Shot* (published in 1930):

I personally am convinced that the days of the old crime-puzzle pure and simple, relying entirely on plot and without any added attractions of character, style, or even humor, are, if not numbered, at any rate in the hands of the auditors; and that the detective story is in process of developing into the novel with a detective or crime interest, holding its reader less by mathematical than by psychological ties. The puzzle element will no doubt remain, but it will become a puzzle of character rather than a puzzle of time, place, motive and opportunity. There is a complication of emotion, drama, psychology and adventure behind the most ordinary murder in real life, the possibilities of which for fictional purposes the conventional detective story misses completely.

Of course he was entirely correct. The detective fiction written during the past half-century or more has, for the most part, focused on character development far more than ingenious murder methods, clues, red herrings, tight alibis, and the other accoutrements of early detective fiction. Today, it is far more concerned with the "why" a crime was committed than the "how."

The stories in *The Best Crime Stories Ever Told* were mainly written during the first three decades of the twentieth century and there are certain elements of which you may be certain.

The detective stories will be fair, otherwise Sayers would not have selected them. There are no secret doors or passageways, nor are there long-lost twin brothers who committed the crime. You will be expected to think along with the protagonist of the story and perhaps beat him to the solution. Written in the changing time of which Berkeley wrote, you will see well-executed plots but you will also encounter interesting characters. What you will *not* encounter is gratuitous, brain-and-blood-spattering violence, nor will you be permitted to voyeuristically spy on characters engaging in sexual activity that was, in the era in which the stories were written, regarded as private.

In all the stories you will experience the battle between Good and Evil. There are wicked people here. In the detective stories, you may regard it as a certainty that they will be caught and punished. In the others, those loosely connected as "Mystery and Horror," well, nothing can be regarded as a certainty.

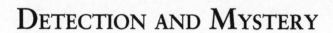

DETECTION AND MYSTERY

DETECTION AND MYSTERY

LORD CHIZELRIGG'S
MISSING FORTUNE

ROBERT BARR

The name of the late Lord Chizelrigg never comes to my mind without instantly suggesting that of Mr. T. A. Edison. I never saw the late Lord Chizelrigg, and I have met Mr. Edison only twice in my life, yet the two men are linked in my memory, and it was a remark the latter once made that in great measure enabled me to solve the mystery which the former had wrapped round his actions.

There is no memorandum at hand to tell me the year in which those two meetings with Edison took place. I received a note from the Italian Ambassador in Paris requesting me to wait upon him at the Embassy. I learned that on the next day a deputation was to set out from the Embassy to one of the chief hotels, there to make a call in state upon the great American inventor, and formally present to him various insignia accompanying certain honors which the King of Italy had conferred upon him. As many Italian nobles of high rank had been invited, and as these dignitaries would not only be robed in the costumes pertaining to their orders, but in many cases would wear jewels of almost inestimable value, my presence was desired in the belief that I might perhaps be able to ward off any attempt on the part of the deft-handed gentry who might possibly make an effort to gain these treasures, and I may add, with perhaps some little self-gratification, no *contretemps* occurred.

Mr. Edison, of course, had long before received notification of the hour at which the deputation would wait upon him, but when we entered the large parlor assigned to the inventor, it was evident to me at a glance that the celebrated man had forgotten all about the function. He stood by a bare table, from which the cloth had been jerked and flung into a corner, and upon that table were placed several bits of black and greasy machinery—cog-wheels, pulleys, bolts, etc. These seemingly belonged to a French workman who stood on the other side of the table, with one of the parts in his grimy hand. Edison's own hands were not too clean, for he had palpably been examining the material, and conversing with the workman, who wore the ordinary long blouse of an iron craftsman in a small way. I judged him to be a man with a little shop of his own in some back street, who did odd jobs of engineering, assisted, perhaps, by a skilled helper or two, and a few apprentices. Edison looked sternly toward the door as the solemn procession filed in, and there was a trace of annoyance on his face at the interruption, mixed with a shade of perplexity to what this gorgeous display all meant. The Italian as ceremonious as the Spaniard where a function is concerned and the official who held the ornate box which contained the jewelry resting on a velvet cushion stepped slowly forward, and came to a stand in front of the bewildered American. Then the Ambassador, in sonorous voice, spoke some gracious words regarding the friendship existing between the United States and Italy, expressed a wish that their rivalry should ever take the form of benefits conferred upon the human race, and instanced the honored recipient as the most notable example the world had yet produced of a man bestowing blessings upon all nations in the arts of peace. The eloquent Ambassador concluded by saying that, at the command of his royal master, it was both his duty and his pleasure to present, and so forth and so forth.

Mr. Edison, visibly ill at ease, nevertheless made a suitable reply in the fewest possible words, and the *étalage* being thus at an end, the noblemen, headed by their Ambassador, slowly retired, myself forming the tail of the procession. Inwardly I deeply sympathized with the French workman who thus unexpectedly found himself confronted by so much magnificence. He cast one wild look about him, but saw that his retreat was cut off, unless he displaced some of these gorgeous grandees. He tried then to shrink into himself, and finally stood helpless, like one paralyzed. In spite of republican institutions, there is deep down in every Frenchman's heart a respect and awe for official pageants, sumptuously staged and costumed as this one was. But he likes to view it from afar, and supported by his fellows, not thrust incongruously into the midst of things, as was the case with this panic-stricken engineer. As I passed out, I cast glance over my shoulder at the humble artisan content with a profit of a few francs a day, and at the millionaire inventor opposite him. Edison's face, which during the address had been cold and impassive, reminding me vividly of a bust of Napoleon, was now all aglow with enthusiasm as he turned to his humble visitor. He cried joyfully to the workman:

"A minute's demonstration is worth an hour's explanation. I'll call round to-morrow at your shop, about ten o'clock, and show you how to make the thing work."

I lingered in the hall until the Frenchman came out, then, introducing myself to him, asked the privilege of visiting his shop next day at ten. This was accorded with that courtesy which you will always find among the industrial classes of France, and next day I had the pleasure of meeting Mr. Edison. During our conversation I complimented him on his invention of the incandescent electric light, and this was the reply that has ever remained in my memory:

"It was not an invention, but a discovery. We knew what we wanted: a carbonized tissue, which would withstand the electric current in a vacuum for, say, a thousand hours. If no such tissue existed, then the incandescent light, as we know it, was not possible. My assistants started out to find this tissue, and we simply carbonized everything we could lay our hands on, and ran the current through it in a vacuum. At last we struck the right thing, as we were bound to do if we kept on long enough, and if the thing existed. Patience and hard work will overcome any obstacle."

This belief has been of great assistance to me in my profession. I know the idea is prevalent that a detective arrives at his solutions in a dramatic way through following clues invisible to the ordinary man. This doubtless frequently happens, but, as a general thing, the patience and hard work which Mr. Edison commends is a much safer guide. Very often the following of excellent clues has led me to disaster, as was the case with my unfortunate attempt to solve the mystery of the five hundred diamonds.

As I was saying, I never think of the late Lord Chizelrigg without remembering Mr. Edison at the same time, and yet the two were very dissimilar. I suppose Lord Chizelrigg was the most useless man that ever lived, while Edison is the opposite.

One day my servant brought in to me a card on which was engraved "Lord Chizelrigg."

"Show his lordship in," I said, and there appeared a young man of perhaps twenty-four or twenty-five, well dressed, and of most charming manners, who, nevertheless, began his interview by asking a question such as had never before been addressed to me, and which, if put to a solicitor or other professional man, would have been answered with some indignation. Indeed, I believe it is a written or unwritten law of the legal profession that the acceptance of such a proposal as Lord Chizelrigg made to me would, if proved, result in the disgrace and ruin of the lawyer.

"Monsieur Valmont," began Lord Chizelrigg, "do you ever take up cases on speculation?"

"On speculation, sir? I do not think I understand you."

His lordship blushed like a girl, and stammered slightly as he attempted an explanation.

"What I mean is, do you accept a case on a contingent fee? That is to say, monsieur—er—well, not to put too fine a point upon it, no results, no pay."

I replied somewhat severely: "Such an offer has never been made to me, and I may say at once that I should be compelled to decline it were I favored with the opportunity. In the cases submitted to me, I devote my time and attention to their solution. I try to deserve success, but I cannot command it, and as in the interim I must live, I am reluctantly compelled to make a charge for my time, at least. I believe the doctor sends in his bill, though the patient dies."

The young man laughed uneasily, and seemed almost too embarrassed to proceed, but finally he said: "Your illustration strikes home with greater accuracy than probably you imagined when you uttered it. I have just paid my last penny to the physician who attended my late uncle, Lord Chizelrigg, who died six months ago. I am fully aware that the suggestion I made may seem like a reflection upon your skill, or, rather, as implying a doubt regarding it.

But I should be grieved, monsieur, if you fell into such an error. I could have come here and commissioned you to undertake some elucidation of the strange situation in which I find myself, and I make no doubt you would have accepted the task if your numerous engagements had permitted. Then, if you failed, I should have been unable to pay you, for I am practically bankrupt. My whole desire, therefore, was to make an honest beginning, and to let you know exactly how I stand. If you succeed, I shall be a rich man; if you do not succeed, I shall be what I am now, penniless. Have I made it plain now why I began with a question which you had every right to resent?"

"Perfectly plain, my lord, and your candor does you credit."

I was very much taken with the unassuming manners of the young man, and his evident desire to accept no service under false pretenses. When I had finished my sentence the pauper nobleman rose to his feet and bowed.

"I am very much your debtor, monsieur, for your courtesy in receiving me, and can only beg pardon for occupying your time on a futile quest. I wish you good morning, monsieur."

"One moment, my lord," I rejoined, waving him to his chair again. "Although I am unprepared to accept a commission on the terms you suggest, I may, nevertheless, be able to offer a hint or two that will prove of service to you. I think I remember the announcement of Lord Chizelrigg's death. He was somewhat eccentric, was he not?"

"Eccentric?" said the young man, with a slight laugh, seating himself again. "Well, *rather!*"

"I vaguely remember that he was accredited with the possession of something like twenty thousand acres of land?"

"Twenty-seven thousand, as a matter of fact," replied my visitor.

"Have you fallen heir to the lands as well as to the title?"

"Oh, yes; the estate was entailed. The old gentleman could not divert it from me if he would, and I rather suspect that fact must have been the cause of some worry to him."

"But surely, my lord, a man who owns, as one might say, a principality in this wealthy realm of England, cannot be penniless?"

Again the young man laughed.

"Well, no," he replied, thrusting his hand in his pocket and bringing to light a few brown coppers and a white silver piece. "I possess enough money to buy some food to-night, but not enough to dine at the Hotel Cecil. You see, it is like this. I belong to a somewhat ancient family, various members of whom went the pace, and mortgaged their acres up to the hilt. I could not raise a further penny on my estates were I to try my hardest, because at the time the money was lent, land was much more valuable than it is to-day. Agricultural depression and all that sort of thing, have, if I may put it so, left me a good many thousands worse off than if I had no land at all. Besides this, during my late uncle's life, Parliament, on his behalf, intervened once or twice, allowing him in the first place to cut valuable timber, and in the second place to sell the pictures of Chizelrigg Chase at Christie's for figures which make one's mouth water."

"And what became of the money?" I asked; whereupon once more this genial nobleman laughed.

"That is exactly what I came up in the lift to learn if Monsieur Valmont could discover."

"My lord, you interest me," I said, quite truly, with an uneasy apprehension that I should take up his case after all, for I liked the young man already. His lack of pretense appealed to me, and that sympathy which is so universal among my countrymen enveloped him, as I may say, quite independent of my own will.

"My uncle," went on Lord Chizelrigg, "was somewhat of an anomaly in our family. He must have been a reversal to a very, very ancient type; a type of which we have no record. He was as miserly as his forefathers were prodigal. When he came into the title and estate some twenty years ago, he dismissed the whole retinue of servants, and, indeed, was defendant in several cases at law where retainers of our family brought suit against him for wrongful dismissal, or dismissal without a penny compensation in lieu of notice. I am pleased to say he lost all his cases, and when he pleaded poverty, got permission to sell a certain number of heirlooms, enabling him to make compensation, and giving him something on which to live.

These heirlooms at auction sold so unexpectedly well, that my uncle acquired a taste, as it were, of what might be done. He could always prove that the rents went to the mortgagees, and that he had nothing on which to exist, so on several occasions he obtained permission from the courts to cut timber and sell pictures, until he denuded the estate and made an empty barn of the old manor house. He lived like any laborer, occupying himself sometimes as a carpenter, sometimes as a blacksmith; indeed, he made a blacksmith's shop of the library, one of the most noble rooms in Britain, containing thousands of valuable books which again and again he applied for permission to sell, but this privilege was never granted to him. I find, on coming into the property, that my uncle quite persistently evaded the law, and depleted this superb collection, book by book, surreptitiously, through dealers in London. This, of course, would have got him into deep trouble if it had been discovered before his death, but now the valuable volumes are gone, and there is no redress. Many of them are doubtless in America or in museums and collections of Europe."

"You wish me to trace them, perhaps?" I interpolated.

"Oh, no; they are past praying for. The old man made tens of thousands by the sale of the timber, and other tens of thousands by disposing of the pictures. The house is denuded of its fine old furniture, which was immensely valuable, and then the books, as I have said, must have brought in the revenue of a prince, if he got anything like their value, and you may be sure he was shrewd enough to know their worth. Since the last refusal of the courts to allow him further relief, as he termed it, which was some seven years ago, he had quite evidently been disposing of books and furniture by a private sale, in defiance of the law. At that time I was under age, but my guardians opposed his application to the courts, and demanded an account of the moneys already in his hands. The judges upheld the opposition of my guardians, and refused to allow a further spoliation of the estate, but they did not grant the accounting my guardians asked, because the proceeds of the former sales were entirely at the disposal of my uncle, and were sanctioned by the law to permit him to live as befitted his station. If he lived meagerly instead of lavishly, as my guardians contended, that, the judges said, was his affair, and there the matter ended.

My uncle took a violent dislike to me on account of this opposition to his last application, although, of course, I had nothing whatever to do with the matter. He lived like a hermit, mostly in the library, and was waited upon by an old man and his wife, and these three were the only inhabitants of a mansion that could comfortably house a hundred. He visited nobody, and would allow no one to approach Chizelrigg Chase. In order that all who had the misfortune to have dealings with him should continue to endure trouble after his death, he left what might be called a will, but which rather may be termed a letter to me. Here is a copy of it:

'My Dear Tom,—You will find your fortune between a couple of sheets of paper in the library.

Your affectionate uncle,

REGINALD MORAN, EARL OF CHIZELRIGG.'"

"I should doubt if that were a legal will," said I. "It doesn't need to be," replied the young man with a smile. "I am next of kin, and heir to everything he possessed, although, of course, he might have given his money elsewhere if he had chosen to do so. Why he did not bequeath it to some institution, I do not know. He knew no man personally except his own servants, whom he misused and starved; but, as he told them, he misused and starved himself, so they had no cause to grumble. He said he was treating them like one of the family. I suppose he thought it would cause me more worry and anxiety if he concealed the money, and put me on the wrong scent, which I am convinced he has done, than to leave it openly to any person or charity."

"I need not ask if you have searched the library?"

"Searched it? Why, there never was such a search since the world began!"

"Possibly you put the task into incompetent hands?"

"You are hinting, Monsieur Valmont, that I engaged others until my money was gone, then came to you with a speculative proposal. Let me assure you such is not the case. Incompetent hands, I grant you, but the hands were my own. For the past six months I have lived practically as my uncle lived. I have rummaged that library from floor to ceiling. It was left in a frightful state, littered with old newspapers, accounts, and what not. Then, of course, there were the books re-maining in the library, still a formidable collection."

"Was your uncle a religious man?"

"I could not say. I surmise not. You see, I was unacquainted with him, and never saw him until after his death. I fancy he was not religious, otherwise he could not have acted as he did. Still, he proved himself a man of such twisted mentality that anything is possible."

"I knew a case once where an heir who expected a large sum of money was bequeathed a family Bible, which he threw into the fire, learning afterwards, to his dismay, that it contained many thousands of pounds in Bank of England notes, the object of the devisor being to induce the legatee to read the good Book or suffer through the neglect of it."

"I have searched the scriptures," said the youthful earl with a laugh, "but the benefit has been moral rather than material."

"Is there any chance that your uncle has deposited his wealth in a bank, and has written a check for the amount, leaving it between two leaves of a book?"

"Anything is possible, monsieur, but I think that highly improbable. I have gone through every tome, page by page, and I suspect very few of the volumes have been opened for the last twenty years."

"How much money do you estimate he accumulated?"

"He must have cleared more than a hundred thousand pounds, but speaking of banking it, I would like to say that my uncle evinced a deep distrust of banks, and never drew a check in his life, so far as I am aware. All accounts were paid in gold by his old steward, who first brought the receipted bill in to my uncle, and then received the exact amount, after having left the room, and waited until he was rung for, so that he might not learn the repository from which my uncle drew his store. I believe if the money is ever found it will be in gold, and I am very sure that this will was written, if we may call it a will, to put us on the wrong scent."

"Have you had the library cleared out?"

"Oh, no; it is practically as my uncle left it. I realized that if I were to call in help, it would be well that the newcomer found it undisturbed."

"You were quite right, my lord. You say you examined all the papers?"

"Yes; so far as that is concerned, the room has been very fairly gone over, but nothing that was in it the day my uncle died has been removed, not even his anvil."

"His anvil?"

"Yes; I told you he made a blacksmith's shop, as well as bedroom, of the library. It is a huge room, with a great fireplace at one end which formed an excellent forge. He and the steward built the forge in the eastern fireplace, of brick and clay, with their own hands, and erected there a secondhand blacksmith's bellows."

"What work did he do at his forge?"

"Oh, anything that was required about the place. He seems to have been a very expert ironworker. He would never buy a new implement for the garden or the house so long as he could get one secondhand, and he never bought anything secondhand while at his forge he might repair what was already in use. He kept an old cob, on which he used to ride through the park, and he always put the shoes on this cob himself, the steward informs me, so he must have understood the use of blacksmith's tools. He made a carpenter's shop of the chief drawing-room and erected a bench there. I think a very useful mechanic was spoiled when my uncle became an earl."

"You have been living at the Chase since your uncle died?"

"If you call it living, yes. The old steward and his wife have been looking after me, as they looked after my uncle, and, seeing me day after day, coatless, and covered with dust, I imagine they think me a second edition of the old man."

"Does the steward know the money is missing?"

"No; no one knows it but myself. This will was left on the anvil, in an envelope addressed to me."

"Your statement is exceedingly clear, Lord Chizelrigg, but I confess I don't see much daylight through it. Is there a pleasant country around Chizelrigg Chase?"

"Very; especially at this season of the year. In autumn and winter the house is a little draughty. It needs several thousand pounds to put it in repair."

"Draughts do not matter in the summer. I have been long enough in England not to share the fear of my countrymen for a *courant d'air.* Is there a spare bed in the manor house, or shall I take down a cot with me, or let us say a hammock?"

"Really," stammered the earl, blushing again, "you must not think I detailed all these circumstances in order to influence you to take up what may be a hopeless case. I, of course, am deeply interested, and, therefore, somewhat prone to be carried away when I begin a recital of my uncle's eccentricities. If I receive your permission, I will call on you again in a month or two. To tell you the truth, I borrowed a little money from the old steward, and visited London to see my legal advisers, hoping that in the circumstances I may get permission to sell something that will keep me from starvation. When I spoke of the house being denuded, I meant relatively, of course. There are still a good many antiquities which would doubtless bring me in a comfortable sum of money. I have been borne up by the belief that I should find my uncle's gold. Lately I have been beset by a suspicion that the old gentleman thought the library the only valuable asset left, and for this reason wrote his note, thinking I would be afraid to sell anything from that room. The old rascal must have made a pot of money out of those shelves. The catalogue shows that there was a copy of the first book printed in England by Caxton, and several priceless Shakespeares, as well as many other volumes that a collector would give a small fortune for. All these are gone. I think when I show this to be the case, the authorities cannot refuse me the right to sell something, and, if I get this permission, I shall at once call upon you."

"Nonsense, Lord Chizelrigg. Put your application in motion, if you like. Meanwhile, I beg of you to look upon me as a more substantial banker than your old steward. Let us enjoy a good dinner together at the Cecil to-night, if you will do me the honor to be my guest. To-morrow we can leave for Chizelrigg Chase. How far is it?"

"About three hours," replied the young man, becoming as red as a new Queen Anne villa.

"Really, Monsieur Valmont, you overwhelm me with your kindness, but nevertheless I accept your generous offer."

"Then that's settled. What's the name of the old steward?"

"Higgins."

"You are certain he has no knowledge of the hiding-place of this treasure?"

"Oh, quite sure. My uncle was not a man to make a confidant of anyone, least of all an old babbler like Higgins."

"Well, I should like to be introduced to Higgins as a benighted foreigner. That will make him despise me, and treat me like a child."

"Oh, I say," protested the earl, "I should have thought you'd lived long enough in England to have got out of the notion that we do not appreciate the foreigner. Indeed, we are the only nation in the world that extends a cordial welcome to him, rich or poor."

"*Certainement*, my lord, I should be deeply disappointed did you not take me at my proper valuation, but I cherish no delusions regarding the contempt with which Higgins will regard me. He will look upon me as a sort of simpleton to whom the Lord has been unkind by not making England my native land. Now, Higgins must be led to believe that I am in his own class; that is, a servant of yours. Higgins and I will gossip over the fire together, should these spring evenings prove chilly, and before two or three weeks are past I shall have learned a great deal about your uncle that you never dreamed of. Higgins will talk more freely with a fellow-servant than with his master, however much he may respect that master, and then, as I am a foreigner, he will babble down to my comprehension, and I shall get details that he never would think of giving to a fellow-countryman."

The young earl's modesty in such description of his home as he had given me left me totally unprepared for the grandeur of the mansion, one corner of which he inhabited. It is such a place as you read of in romances of the Middle Ages; not a pinnacled or turreted French chateau of that period, but a beautiful and substantial stone manor house of a ruddy color, whose warm hue seemed to add a softness to the severity of its architecture. It is built round an outer and an inner courtyard, and could house a thousand, rather than the hundred with which its owner had accredited it. There are many stone-mullioned windows, and one at the end of the library might well have graced a cathedral. This superb residence occupies the center of a heavily timbered park, and from the lodge at the gates we drove at least a mile and a half under the grandest avenue of old oaks I have ever seen. It seemed incredible that the owner of all this should actually lack the ready money to pay his fare to town!

Old Higgins met us at the station with a somewhat rickety cart, to which was attached the ancient cob that the late earl used to shoe. We entered a noble hall, which probably looked the larger because of the entire absence of any kind of furniture, unless two complete suits of venerable armor which stood on either hand might be considered as furnishing. I laughed aloud when the door was shut, and the sound echoed like the merriment of ghosts from the dim timbered roof above me.

"What are you laughing at?" asked the earl.

"I am laughing to see you put your modern tall hat on that mediaeval helmet."

"Oh, that's it! Well, put yours on the other. I mean no disrespect to the ancestor who wore this suit, but we are short of the harmless, necessary hatrack, so I put my topper on the antique helmet, and thrust the umbrella (if I have one) in behind here, and down one of his legs. Since I came in possession, a very crafty-looking dealer from London visited me, and attempted to sound me regarding the sale of these suits of armor. I gathered he would give enough money to keep me in new suits, London made, for the rest of my life, but when I endeavored to find out if he had had commercial dealings with my prophetic uncle, he became frightened and bolted. I imagine that if I had possessed presence of mind enough to have lured him into one of our most uncomfortable dungeons, I might have learned where some of the family treasures went to. Come up these stairs, Monsieur Valmont, and I will show you your room."

We had lunched on the train coming down, so after a wash in my own room I proceeded at once to inspect the library. It proved, indeed, a most noble apartment, and it had been scandalously used by the old reprobate, its late tenant. There were two huge fireplaces, one in the middle of the north wall and the other at the eastern end. In the latter had been erected a rude brick forge, and beside the forge hung a great black bellows, smoky with usage. On a wooden block lay the anvil, and around it rested and rusted several hammers, large and small. At the western end was a glorious window filled with ancient stained glass, which, as I have said, might have adorned a cathedral. Extensive as the collection of books was, the great size of this chamber made it necessary that only the outside wall should be covered with bookcases, and even these were divided by tall windows. The opposite wall was blank, with the exception of a picture here and there, and these pictures offered a further insult to the room, for they were cheap prints, mostly colored lithographs that had appeared in Christmas numbers of London weekly journals, incased in poverty-stricken frames, hanging from nails ruthlessly driven in above them. The floor was covered with a litter of papers, in some places knee-deep, and in the corner farthest from the forge still stood the bed on which the ancient miser had died.

"Looks like a stable, doesn't it?" commented the earl, when I had finished my inspection. "I am sure the old boy simply filled it up with this rubbish to give me the trouble of examining it. Higgins tells me that up to within a month before he died the room was reasonably clear of all this muck. Of course it had to be, or the place would have caught fire from the sparks of the forge. The old man made Higgins gather all the papers he could find anywhere about the place, ancient accounts, newspapers, and what not, even to the brown wrapping paper you see, in which parcels came, and commanded him to strew the floor with this litter, because, as he complained, Higgins's boots on the boards made too much noise, and Higgins, who is not in the least of an inquiring mind, accepted this explanation as entirely meeting the case."

Higgins proved to be a garrulous old fellow, who needed no urging to talk about the late earl; indeed, it was almost impossible to deflect his conversation into any other channel. Twenty years' intimacy with the eccentric nobleman had largely obliterated that sense of deference with which an English servant usually approaches his master. An English underling's idea of nobility is the man who never by any possibility works with his hands. The fact that Lord Chizelrigg had toiled at the carpenter's bench; had mixed cement in the drawing-room; had caused the anvil to ring out till midnight, aroused no admiration in Higgins's mind. In addition to this, the ancient nobleman had been penuriously strict in his examination of accounts, exacting the uttermost farthing, so the humble servitor regarded his memory with supreme contempt. I realized before the drive was finished from the station to Chizelrigg Chase that there was little use of introducing me to Higgins as a foreigner and a fellow-servant. I found myself completely unable to understand what the old fellow said. His dialect was as unknown to me as the Choctaw language would have been, and the young earl was compelled to act as interpreter on the occasions when we set this garrulous talking machine going.

The new Earl of Chizelrigg, with the enthusiasm of a boy, proclaimed himself my pupil and assistant, and said he would do whatever he was told. His thorough and fruitless search of the library had convinced him that the old man was merely chaffing him, as he put it, by leaving such a letter as he had written. His lordship was certain that the money had been hidden somewhere else; probably buried under one of the trees in the park. Of course, this was possible, and represented the usual method by which a stupid person conceals treasure, yet I did not think it probable. All conversations with Higgins showed the earl to have been an extremely suspicious man; suspicious of banks, suspicious even of Bank of England notes, suspicious of every person on earth, not omitting Higgins himself. Therefore, as I told his nephew, the miser would never allow the fortune out of his sight and immediate reach.

From the first the oddity of the forge and anvil being placed in his bedroom struck me as peculiar, and I said to the young man,—

"I'll stake my reputation that that forge or anvil, or both, contain the secret. You see, the old gentleman worked sometimes till midnight, for Higgins could hear his hammering. If he used hard coal on the forge, the fire would last through the night, and being in continual terror of thieves, as Higgins says, barricading the castle every evening before dark, as if it were a fortress, he was bound to place the treasure in the most unlikely spot for a thief to get at it. Now, the coal fire smoldered all night long, and if the gold was in the forge underneath the embers, it would be extremely difficult to get at. A robber rummaging in the dark would burn his fingers in more senses than one. Then, as his lordship kept no less than four loaded revolvers under his pillow, all he had to do, if a thief entered his room, was to allow the search to go on until the thief started at the forge, then, doubtless, as he had the range with reasonable accuracy, night or day, he might sit up in bed and blaze away with revolver after revolver. There were twenty-eight shots that could be fired in about double as many seconds, so you see the robber stood little chance in the face of such a fusillade. I propose that we dismantle the forge."

Lord Chizelrigg was much taken by my reasoning, and one morning early we cut down the big bellows, tore it open, found it empty, then took brick after brick from the forge with a crowbar, for the old man had builded better than he knew with Portland cement. In fact, when we cleared away the rubbish between the bricks and the core of the furnace we came upon one cube of cement which was as hard as granite. With the aid of Higgins, and a set of rollers and levers, we managed to get this block out into the park, and attempted to crush it with the sledge hammers belonging to the forge, in which we were entirely unsuccessful. The more it resisted our efforts, the more certain we became that the coins would be found within it. As this would not be treasure-trove in the sense that the Government might make a claim upon it, there was no particular necessity for secrecy, so we had up a man from the mines near by with drills and dynamite, who speedily shattered the block into a million pieces, more or less. Alas! there was no trace in its debris of "pay dirt," as the western miner puts it. While the dynamite expert was on the spot, we induced him to shatter the anvil as well as the block of cement, and then the workman, doubtless thinking the new earl was as insane as the old one had been—shouldered his tools and went back to his mine.

The earl reverted to his former opinion that the gold was concealed in the park, while I held even more firmly to my own belief that the fortune rested in the library.

"It is obvious," I said to him, "that if the treasure is buried outside, some one must have dug the hole. A man so timorous and so reticent as your uncle would allow no one to do this but himself. Higgins maintained the other evening that all picks and spades were safely locked up by himself each night in the tool house. The mansion itself was barricaded with such exceeding care that it would have been difficult for your uncle to get outside even if he wished to do so. Then such a man as your uncle is described to have been would continually desire ocular demonstration that his savings were intact, which would be practically impossible if the gold had found a grave in the park I propose now that we abandon violence and dynamite, and proceed to an intellectual search of the library."

"Very well," replied the young earl; "but as I have already searched the library very thoroughly, your use of the word 'intellectual,' Monsieur Valmont, is not in accord with your customary politeness. However, I am with you. 'Tis for you to command, and me to obey."

"Pardon me, my lord," I said, "I used the word 'intellectual' in contradistinction to the word 'dynamite.' It had no reference to your former search. I merely propose that we now abandon the use of chemical reaction, and employ the much greater force of mental activity. Did you notice any writing on the margins of the newspapers you examined?"

"No, I did not."

"Is it possible that there may have been some communication on the white border of a newspaper?"

"It is, of course, possible."

"Then will you set yourself to the task of glancing over the margin of every newspaper, piling them away in another room when your scrutiny of each is complete? Do not destroy anything, but we must clear out the library completely. I am interested in the accounts, and will examine them."

It was exasperatingly tedious work; but after several days my assistant reported every margin scanned without result, while I had collected each bill and memorandum, classifying them according to date. I could not get rid of a suspicion that the contrary old beast had written instructions for the finding of the treasure on the back of some account, or on the flyleaf of a book, and as I looked at the thousands of volumes still left in the library, the prospect of such a patient and minute search appalled me. But I remembered Edison's words to the effect that if a thing exists, search, exhaustive enough, will find it. From the mass of accounts I selected several; the rest I placed in another room, alongside the heap of the earl's newspapers.

"Now," said I to my helper, "if it please you, we will have Higgins in, as I wish some explanation of these accounts."

"Perhaps I can assist you," suggested his lordship, drawing up a chair opposite the table on which I had spread the statements. "I have lived here for six months, and know as much about things as Higgins does. He is so difficult to stop when once he begins to talk. What is the first account you wish further light upon?"

"To go back thirteen years, I find that your uncle bought a secondhand safe in Sheffield. Here is the bill. I consider it necessary to find that safe."

"Pray forgive me, Monsieur Valmont," cried the young man, springing to his feet and laughing; "so heavy an article as a safe should not slip readily from a man's memory, but it did from mine. The safe is empty, and I gave no more thought to it."

Saying this, the earl went to one of the bookcases that stood against the wall, pulled it round as if it were a door, books and all, and displayed the front of an iron safe, the door of which he also drew open, exhibiting the usual empty interior of such a receptacle.

"I came on this," he said, "when I took down all these volumes. It appears that there was once a secret door leading from the library into an outside room which has long since disappeared; the walls are very thick. My uncle doubtless caused this door to be taken off its hinges, and the safe placed in the aperture, the rest of which he then bricked up."

"Quite so," said I, endeavoring to conceal my disappointment. "As this strong box was bought secondhand and not made to order, I suppose there can be no secret crannies in it?"

"It looks like a common or garden safe," reported my assistant, "but we'll have it out if you say so."

"Not just now," I replied; "we've had enough of dynamiting to make us feel like housebreakers already."

"I agree with you. What's the next item on the programme?"

"Your uncle's mania for buying things at secondhand was broken in three instances so far as I have been able to learn from a scrutiny of these accounts. About four years ago he purchased a new book from Denny Co., the well-known booksellers of the Strand. Denny Co. deal only in new books. Is there any comparatively new volume in the library?"

"Not one."

"Are you sure of that?"

"Oh, quite; I searched all the literature in the house. What is the name of the volume he bought?"

"That I cannot decipher. The initial letter looks like 'M,' but the rest is a mere wavy line. I see, however, that it cost twelve-and-sixpence, while the cost of carriage by parcel post was sixpence, which shows it weighed something under four pounds. This, with the price of the book, induces me to think it was a scientific work, printed on heavy paper and illustrated."

"I know nothing of it," said the earl.

"The third account is for wall paper; twenty-seven rolls of an expensive wall paper, and twenty-seven rolls of a cheap paper, the latter being just half the price of the former. This wall paper seems to have been supplied by a tradesman in the station road in the village of Chizelrigg."

"There's your wall paper," cried the youth, waving his hand; "he was going to paper the whole house, Higgins told me, but got tired after he had finished the library, which took him nearly a year to accomplish, for he worked at it very intermittently, mixing the paste in the boudoir, a pailful at a time, as he needed it. It was a scandalous thing to do, for underneath the paper is the most exquisite oak paneling, very plain, but very rich in color."

I rose and examined the paper on the wall. It was dark brown, and answered the description of the expensive paper on the bill.

"What became of the cheap paper?" I asked.

"I don't know."

"I think," said I, "we are on the track of the mystery. I believe that paper covers a sliding panel or concealed door."

"It is very likely," replied the earl. "I intended to have the paper off, but I had no money to pay a workman, and I am not so industrious as was my uncle. What is your remaining account?"

"The last also pertains to paper, but comes from a firm in Budge Row, London, E.C. He has had, it seems, a thousand sheets of it, and it appears to have been frightfully expensive. This bill is also illegible, but I take it a thousand sheets were supplied, although, of course, it may have been a thousand quires, which would be a little more reasonable for the price charged, or a thousand reams, which would be exceedingly cheap."

"I don't know anything about that. Let's turn on Higgins."

Higgins knew nothing of this last order of paper either. The wallpaper mystery he at once cleared up. Apparently the old earl had discovered by experiment that the heavy, expensive wall paper would not stick to the glossy paneling, so he had purchased a cheaper paper, and had pasted that on first. Higgins said he had gone all over the paneling with a yellowish-white paper, and after that was dry he pasted over it the more expensive rolls.

"But," I objected, "the two papers were bought and delivered at the same time; therefore he could not have found by experiment that the heavy paper would not stick."

"I don't think there is much in that," commented the earl; "the heavy paper may have been bought first, and found to be unsuitable, and then the coarse, cheap paper bought afterwards. The bill merely shows that the account was sent in on that date. Indeed, as the village of Chizelrigg is but a few miles away, it would have been quite possible for my uncle to have bought the heavy paper in the morning, tried it, and in the afternoon sent for the commoner lot; but, in any case, the bill would not have been presented until months after the order, and the two purchases were thus lumped together."

I was forced to confess that this seemed reasonable.

Now, about the book ordered from Denny's. Did Higgins remember anything regarding it? It came four years ago.

Ah, yes, Higgins did; he remembered it very well indeed. He had come in one morning with the earl's tea, and the old man was sitting up in bed reading this volume with such interest that he was unaware of Higgins's knock, and Higgins himself, being a little hard of hearing, took for granted the command to enter. The earl hastily thrust the book under the pillow, alongside the revolvers, and rated Higgins in a most cruel way for entering the room before getting permission to do so. He had never seen the earl so angry before, and he laid it all to this book. It was after the book had come that the forge had been erected and the anvil bought. Higgins never saw the book again, but one morning, six months before the earl died, Higgins, in raking out the cinders of the forge, found what he supposed was a portion of the book's cover. He believed his master had burned the volume.

Having dismissed Higgins, I said to the earl: "The first thing to be done is to inclose this bill to Denny Co., booksellers, Strand. Tell them you have lost the volume, and ask them to send another. There is likely some one in the shop who can decipher the illegible writing.

I am certain the book will give us a clue. Now, I shall write to Braun Sons, Budge Row. This is evidently a French company; in fact, the name as connected with paper making runs in my mind, although I cannot at this moment place it. I shall ask them the use of this paper that they furnished to the late earl."

This was done accordingly, and now, as we thought, until the answers came, we were two men out of work. Yet the next morning, I am pleased to say, and I have always rather plumed myself on the fact, I solved the mystery before replies were received from London. Of course, both the book and the answer of the paper agents, by putting two and two together, would have given us the key.

After breakfast I strolled somewhat aimlessly into the library, whose floor was now strewn merely with brown wrapping paper, bits of string, and all that. As I shuffled among this with my feet, as if tossing aside dead autumn leaves in a forest path, my attention was suddenly drawn to several squares of paper, unwrinkled, and never used for wrapping. These sheets seemed to me strangely familiar. I picked one of them up, and at once the significance of the name Braun Sons occurred to me. They are paper makers in France, who produce a smooth, very tough sheet, which, dear as it is, proves infinitely cheap compared with the fine vellum it deposed in a certain branch of industry. In Paris, years before, these sheets had given me the knowledge of how a gang of thieves disposed of their gold without melting it. The paper was used instead of vellum in the rougher processes of manufacturing gold leaf. It stood the constant beating of the hammer nearly as well as the vellum, and here at once there flashed on me the secret of the old man's midnight anvil work. He was transforming his sovereigns into gold leaf, which must have been of a rude, thick kind, because to produce the gold leaf of commerce he still needed the vellum as well as a "crutch" and other machinery, of which we had found no trace.

"My lord," I called to my assistant (he was at the other end of the room), "I wish to test a theory on the anvil of your own fresh common sense."

"Hammer away," replied the earl, approaching me with his usual good-natured, jocular expression.

"I eliminate the safe from our investigations because it was purchased thirteen years ago, but the buying of the book, of wall covering, of this tough paper from France, all group themselves into a set of incidents occurring within the same month as the purchase of the anvil and the building of the forge; therefore, I think they are related to one another. Here are some sheets of paper he got from Budge Row. Have you seen anything like it? Try to tear this sample."

"It's reasonably tough," admitted his lordship, fruitlessly endeavoring to rip it apart.

"Yes. It was made in France, and is used in gold beating. Your uncle beat his sovereigns into gold leaf. You will find that the book from Denny's is a volume on gold beating, and now as I remember that scribbled word which I could not make out, I think the title of the volume is 'Metallurgy.' It contains, no doubt, a chapter on the manufacture of gold leaf."

"I believe you," said the earl; "but I don't see that the discovery sets us any farther forward. We're now looking for gold leaf instead of sovereigns."

"Let's examine this wall paper," said I.

I placed my knife under a corner of it at the floor, and quite easily ripped off a large section. As Higgins had said, the brown paper was on top, and the coarse, light-colored paper underneath. But even that came from the oak panelling as easily as though it hung there from habit, and not because of paste.

"Feel the weight of that," I cried, handing him the sheet I had torn from the wall.

"By Jove!" said the earl, in a voice almost of awe.

I took it from him, and laid it, face downward, on the wooden table, threw a little water on the back, and with a knife scraped away the porous white paper. Instantly there gleamed up at us the baleful yellow of the gold. I shrugged my shoulders and spread out my hands. The Earl of Chizelrigg laughed aloud and very heartily.

"You see how it is," I cried. "The old man first covered the entire wall with this whitish paper. He heated his sovereigns at the forge and beat them out on the anvil, then completed the process rudely between the sheets of this paper from France. Probably he pasted the gold to the wall as soon as he shut himself in for the night, and covered it over with the more expensive paper before Higgins entered in the morning."

We found afterwards, however, that he had actually fastened the thick sheets of gold to the wall with carpet tacks.

His lordship netted a trifle over a hundred and twenty-three thousand pounds through my discovery, and I am pleased to pay tribute to the young man's generosity by saying that his voluntary settlement made my bank account swell stout as a City alderman.

THE ORDINARY HAIR-PINS

E. C. BENTLEY

A small committee of friends persuaded Lord Aviemore to sit for a presentation portrait, and the painter to whom they gave the commission was Philip Trent. It was a task that fascinated him, for he had often seen and admired in public places the high, half-bald skull, vulture nose, and grim mouth of the peer who was said to be deeper in theology than any other layman, and whose devotion to charitable work had brought him national honour. It was only at the third sitting that Lord Aviemore's sombre taciturnity was laid aside.

"I believe, Mr. Trent," he remarked, abruptly, "that you used to have a portrait of my late sister-in-law here. I was told that it hung in this studio."

Trent continued his work quietly. "It was just a rough drawing I made, after seeing her in 'Carmen' before her marriage. It used to hang here. Before your first visit I removed it."

The sitter nodded slowly. "Very thoughtful of you. Nevertheless, I should much like to see it, if I may."

"Of course." And Trent drew the framed sketch from behind a curtain. Lord Aviemore gazed long in silence at Trent's very spirited likeness of the famous singer, while the artist worked busily to capture the first expression of feeling that he had so far seen on that impassive face. Lighted and softened by melancholy, it looked for the first time noble.

At last the sitter turned to him. "I would give a good deal," he said, simply, "to possess that drawing."

Trent shook his head. "I don't want to part with it." He laid a few strokes carefully on the canvas and went on: "You would like to know why, I dare say. I will tell you. It is my personal memory of a woman whom I found more admirable than any other I ever saw. Lillemor Wergeland's beauty and physical perfection were a marvel. Her voice was a miracle. Her spirit matched them. I never spoke to her; but everybody in my world talked about her, and many of them knew her."

Lord Aviemore said nothing for a few minutes. Then he spoke slowly. "I do not think you were far wrong about Lady Aviemore. Once I thought differently. When I heard that my elder brother was about to marry a *prima donna*, a woman whose portrait was sold all over the world, who was famous for extravagance in dress and what seemed to me undignified, self-advertising conduct—I was appalled when I heard from him of this engagement. I will not deny that I was also shocked at the idea of a marriage with the daughter of plain Norwegian peasants. She was an orphan of only ten years old when Colonel Stamer and his wife went to lodge at her brother's farm for the fishing. They fell in love with the child, and, having none of their own, they adopted her. All this my brother told me. He knew, he wrote, just what I would think; he only asked me to meet her, and then to judge. Of course, I did so at the first opportunity."

Lord Aviemore paused and stared thoughtfully at the portrait. "She charmed everyone who came near her," he went on presently. "I resisted the spell, but before they had been long married she had vanquished all my prejudice. Her life was all generous impulses and frank enjoyment. But she was not childish. It was not that she was what is called intellectual; but she had a singular spaciousness of mind in which nothing little or mean could live; it had, I used to fancy, some kinship with her Norwegian landscapes of mountain and sea. She was, as you say, extremely beautiful, with the vigorous purity of the fair-haired northern race. All sorts of men were at her feet; but my brother's marriage was the happiest I have ever known."

Trent worked busily upon his canvas, and soon the low, meditative voice resumed.

"It was almost this time six years ago—the middle of March—that I received the terrible news from Taormina. I had just returned from Canada, and I went out there at once. When I saw her she showed no emotion; but there was in her calmness the most unearthly sense of desolation that I have ever perceived. She believed, I found, that she was to blame. You have heard that a slight shock of earthquake caused the villa to collapse, and that my brother and his child were found dead in the ruins; you have heard that Lady Aviemore was sailing in the bay at the time. But you have probably not heard that my brother had a presentiment that their visit to Sicily would end in death, and wished to abandon it; that his wife laughed away his forebodings with her strong modern common sense. But we are of Highland blood and tradition, Mr. Trent, and such interior warnings are no trifles to us. . . . On the tenth day her husband and son were killed. She did not think, as you may suppose, that there was merely coincidence here. The shock changed her whole mental being; she believed then, as I believed, that my brother inwardly foreknew that death awaited him if he went to that place."

He said no more, until Trent remarked, "I know slightly a man called Selby, a solicitor, who was with Lady Aviemore just after her husband's death."

Lord Aviemore said that he remembered Mr. Selby. He said it with such a total absence of expression of any kind that the subject of Selby was killed instantly; and he did not resume that of the tragedy of her whom all the world remembered still as Lillemor Wergeland.

A few months later, when the portrait of Lord Aviemore was to be seen at the show of the N.S.P.P., Trent received a friendly note from Arthur Selby, who asked if Trent would do him the favour of calling at his office by appointment for a private talk. "I should like," he wrote, "to put a certain story before you, a story with a problem in it. I gave it up as a bad job long ago myself; but seeing your portrait of A. at the show reminded me of your reputation as an unraveller."

Thus it happened that, a few days later, Trent was closeted with Selby in one of the rooms of the firm in which that very capable, somewhat dandified, lawyer was a partner. Selby, who never wasted words, came quickly to the point.

"The story I referred to," he said, "is the Aviemore story. I was with her at the time of her suicide. I am an executor of her will. In the strictest confidence, I should like to tell you that story as I know it." He folded his arms upon the broad writing-table between them, and went on: "You know all about the accident. I will start with March 10th, when Lord Aviemore and his son were buried in the cemetery at Taormina. His widow left the villa next day, discharging all the servants except her maid, with whom she went to the Hotel Cavour. There, as I gathered, she seldom left her rooms. She was undoubtedly quite overwhelmed by what had happened, though she seems never to have lost her grip on herself. Her brother-in-law, the present peer, arrived on the 15th. He had only just returned from Canada." Selby raised his finger and repeated, "From Canada, you will remember. He had gone out to get ideas about the emigration prospect."

I understood. He remained at the hotel, meaning to accompany her home, when she should feel equal to the journey. It was not until the 18th that we received a long telegram from her, asking if we could send someone representing the firm to her at Taormina; she stated that she wished to discuss business matters, but did not yet feel able to travel. You understand that Lady Aviemore, who already possessed considerable means of her own, came into a large income under her husband's will. She was a client who could afford to indulge her whims.

"I went out to Taormina. On my arrival Lady Aviemore saw me and told me quite calmly that she was acquainted with the provisions of her late husband's will, and that she now wished to make her own. I took her instructions and prepared the will. The next day I and the British Consul witnessed her signature. You may remember, Trent, that when the provisions of that will became public after her death, they attracted a good deal of attention. You don't remember? Well, to put it simply, she left two thousand pounds to her brother, Knut Wergeland, of Myklebostad, in Norway, and fifty to her maid, Maria Krogh, also a Norwegian, who had been with her some years. The whole of the rest of her property she left to her brother-in-law unconditionally. That surprised me, because he had disapproved bitterly of the marriage, and he hadn't concealed his opinion. But she said to me that she could think of nobody who would do so much good with her money as her brother-in-law. From that point of view she was justified. Lord Aviemore is said to spend most of his income in charitable work. Anyhow, she made him her heir."

"And what did he say to it?"

Selby coughed. "There is no evidence that he knew anything about it before her death. No evidence," he repeated, slowly. "But now let me get on with my story. Lady Aviemore asked me to remain to transact business for her until she should leave Taormina. This she did at last on March 30th, accompanied by Lord Aviemore, myself, and her maid. To shorten the railway journey, as she told us, she planned to go by boat first to Brindisi, then to Venice, and from Venice home by rail. The boats from Brindisi to Venice all go in the day-time, except once a week, when a boat from Corfu arrives in the evening, and goes on about eleven. It happened we could get across from Taormina in time to catch that boat, and Lady Aviemore decided to go by it. We had a few hours in Brindisi, dined there, and about ten o'clock went on board. Lady Aviemore complained of a headache. She went at once to her cabin, which was a deck-cabin, asking me to send someone to collect her ticket at once, as she wanted to sleep as soon as possible, and not to be awakened again. That was done. Shortly before the boat left the maid came to me and told me her mistress was then lying down, and had said she wished to be called at half-past seven in the morning. The maid then went to her own cabin in the second class. Soon after we were out of the harbour I turned in myself. At that time Lord Aviemore was still up. He was leaning over the rail on the promenade deck, upon which Lady Aviemore's cabin opened, and at some distance from the cabin. His own was on the other side of the same deck. I think only two or three other people still remained on the deck, looking out over the sea. It was beginning to blow. I thought we should very likely have some bad weather in an hour or two, and so it turned out. It didn't trouble me, however, and I slept very well.

"It was a quarter to eight when Lord Aviemore woke me by coming into the cabin. He was pale and agitated. He told me that his sister-in-law could not be found, that the maid had gone to her cabin at half-past seven and found it empty!

"I got up in a hurry and went to the cabin. The dressing-case Lady Aviemore had taken with her was there, and her small velvet bag lay on the bed, with her fur coat. Her purse, full of notes and silver, and her jewel-case were on the table, and by them lay a note, folded up, but without address, which you can see presently. To make a long story short, she had disappeared in the night, and there is not the slightest doubt that she found her grave in the Adriatic. The body was never recovered."

Selby paused, and unlocked a drawer in the table before him. He took out a lady's black velvet bag and a folded sheet of thin ruled paper.

"It was Lord Aviemore," he said, "who found this note in the cabin, and was the first to read it. While I read it, he sat on the cabin-bed with his face in his hands. All through what followed—the official inquiries and so forth—he seemed scarcely awake to what was happening, and I had to do most of the talking. When I had brought him back to London, the firm wrote telling him about the will, which I had not mentioned to him for fear of upsetting him yet more during the journey. Later on, when I saw him about the disposal of Lady Aviemore's personal effects and valuables, I mentioned that there was a handkerchief bag, with a few trifles in it. 'Give it away,' he said. 'Do what you like with it.' Well I kept it," said Selby, with an air of slight embarrassment, "as a sort of memento. And I kept the note too. Here it is."

Selby ceased, and handed the note to Trent. He read these words, written in a large, firm, rounded hand:

I have loved more, and been more happy, than is good for anyone. And it was through me that they died. Such an ending to such a marriage as ours has been is far worse than death to me. This is not sorrow that I feel; it is destruction, absolute ruin. My soul is quite empty. I have been kept up this month past only by the resolution I took on the day when I lost them, by the thought of what I am going to do now. I take my leave of a world I cannot bear any more.

There followed the initials "L.A." Trent read and re-read the pitiful message, so full of the awful egoism of grief. He asked at length, "Is this her usual handwriting?"

"Except that it seems to have been written with a bad pen it is just like her usual writing. But now listen, Trent. I asked you here today because of your reputation for getting at the truth of things. Soon after the suicide I got an idea into my head, and I have puzzled over these relics of Lady Aviemore a good many times without much result. I did find out a fact or two, though; and it struck me that if I could discover something, you would probably do much better."

Trent, studying the paper, ignored this tribute. "Well," he said, finally, "what is your idea?"

"I'd rather not state it, Trent. But I can tell you a fact or two, as I said. That sheet, as you see, is a sheet torn from an ordinary ruled writing-pad. Now here is a point. I have taken that sheet to a friend of mine who is in the paper business. He has told me that it is a make of paper never sold in Europe at all, but sold a good deal in Canada. Next, Lady Aviemore never was in Canada. And the pad from which the sheet was torn was not in her dressing-case or anywhere in the cabin. Nor was there any pen and ink there, or any fountain-pen. The ink, you see, is a nasty-looking grey ink."

"Continental hotel ink, in fact. She wrote it in the hotel, then, with an hotel pen. But not on hotel paper. Yes, I see," remarked Trent, gazing at the other thoughtfully. "And the other things?" he inquired, suddenly.

"Suggest nothing to me," remarked Selby. "But you have a look at them." He turned the little bag out upon the table, "Here you are—handkerchief, powder-box and puff, mirror, nail-file, hairpins—"

"Of course," Trent murmured, "hair-pins." He took them in his hand, "Four hair-pins—quite new, I should say. Do they tell a story, Selby?"

"I don't see how. They're just ordinary black hair-pins—as you say, they look too fresh and bright to have been used."

"And that last thing?"

"This is a box of Ixtil, the anti-seasick stuff. Two doses are gone, I believe it's very good."

"I didn't know," Trent remarked, idly, turning the box about, "that you could buy it abroad."

"I was with Lady Aviemore when she bought it at Brindisi, just before going on board."

"Did she buy anything else?"

"I really can't tell you," Selby replied, with a touch of pique. Trent seemed to be asking aimless questions while he stared at the capsules in their tiny box. "She went shopping for an hour or so before dinner, but she was alone, and I didn't see her again until she came down to dinner."

"And so you noticed nothing curious at all," mused Trent, "except this about the paper, and the note having been prepared in advance—which is certainly queer enough. Just cast your mind back beyond the last day. All through the time you were with them nothing came under your notice that seemed strange in the circumstances?"

Selby fingered his chin. "If you put it like that, I can remember a rather funny thing that I never thought of again until now. But I can't see how it could possibly—"

"Yes, I know. But you asked me here to consider the case in my own way, didn't you?"

"You are so jolly professional, Trent," Selby complained. "It was simply this. Two or three days before we left Taormina I was standing in the hotel office when the mail arrived. As I was waiting to see if there was anything for me, the porter put down on the counter a rather smart-looking package that had just come— done up the way they do it at a really first-class shop, if you know what I mean. It looked like a biggish book, or box of chocolates, or something—about twelve inches by ten, at a guess—and it had French stamps on it, but the postmark I didn't notice. And this, I saw, was addressed to Mile. Maria Krogh, if you please—Lady Aviemore's Norwegian maid, about the plainest and stodgiest-looking girl in the world, I should say. Well, Maria was there waiting, too, and presently the man handed it to her. She showed no surprise, but went off with it, and just then her mistress came down the big stairs. She saw the parcel and just held out her hand for it as if it was a matter of course; and Maria handed it over in the same way, and the Countess went upstairs with it. But her name wasn't on the parcel, that I'll swear; and Maria hadn't even cut the string. I thought it was quaint, but I forgot it almost at once, because Lady Aviemore decided that evening to leave the place, and I had plenty to attend to. And if you want to know," added Selby, with a hint of irritation, as Trent opened his lips to speak, "where Maria Krogh is, all I can tell you is that I took her ticket for her in London to Christiansand, where her home is, because she was too much upset to do things for herself; and I never thought of her again until we sent her the fifty pounds that was left her, which she acknowledged. Now, then!"

Trent laughed at the solicitor's tone, and Selby laughed also. His friend walked to the fireplace and pensively adjusted his tie. "Well, I must be off," he announced, suddenly. "What do you say to dining with me on Friday? If by that time I've anything to suggest about this thing, I will tell you then. You will? That's splendid." And he hastened away.

But on Friday, Trent seemed to have nothing to suggest. He was so reluctant to approach the subject that Selby supposed him to be chagrined at his failure to accomplish anything, and did not press the matter.

It was some months later, on a day in September, that Trent walked up the valley road at Myklebostad, looking farewell at the mountain at the end of the valley, the whitecapped father of the torrent that roared down a twenty-foot fall beside him. He had been a week at this most remote backwater of Europe, three hours by steamer from the nearest place that ranked as a town, and with full sixty miles of rugged hills between him and a railway station. The savage beauty of that watery landscape, where sun and rain worked together daily to achieve an unearthly purity in the scene, had justified far better than he had hoped his story that he had come there in search of matter for his brush.

He had painted busily while the light lasted, and he had learned in the evenings as much as he could of his neighbours. It was little enough, for the postmaster, in whose cottage he had a room, spoke only an indifferent German; and no one else, so far as he could discover, had anything but Norwegian, of which Trent knew scarcely a dozen traveller's phrases. But he had seen, he thought every man, woman, and child in the valley, and he had closely attended to the household of Knut Wergeland, the rich man of the place, who had the largest farm. He and his wife, both elderly and grim-faced peasants, lived with two servants in an old turf-roofed steading. Not another person, Trent was certain, inhabited the house. They had two sons, he learned, in America.

He had decided at length that his voyage of curiosity to Myklebostad had been ill-inspired. Knut and his wife were no more than a thrifty peasant pair. They had given him a meal at their house one day when he was sketching near the place, and they had refused with gentle firmness to take any payment. Both produced upon him an impression of illimitable trustworthiness and competency in the life they led so utterly out of the world.

That day, as Trent gazed up to the mountain, his eye was caught by a flash of the sunlight against the dense growth of birches that ran from bottom to top of the precipitous height that was the valley wall to his left.

It was a bright blink, about half a mile from where he stood; it remained steady, and at several points above and below he saw the same bright appearance. Considering it, he perceived that there must be a wire somehow led up the steep hill-face, among the trees. A merely idle curiosity drew his steps towards the spot on the road whence the wire seemed to be taken upwards. In a few minutes he came to the opening among the trees of a rough track leading upwards among rocks and roots, at such an angle that only a vigorous climber could attempt it. Close by, in the edge of the thicket, stood a tall post, from the top of which a bright wire stretched upwards through the branches in the same direction as the path.

Trent slapped the post with a sounding blow. "Heavens and earth!" he exclaimed. "I had forgotten the saeter!"

At once he began to climb.

A thicket carpet of rich pasture began where the deep birchbelt ended at the top of the height. It stretched away for miles over a gently-sloping upland. As Trent came into the open, panting, after a strenuous forty-minute climb, the heads of a few browsing cattle were sleepily turned towards him. Beyond them wandered many more, and a hundred yards away stood a tiny wooden hut, turf-roofed. This plateau was the saeter, a thing of which Trent had read in some guide-book, and never thought since; the high grass-land attached to some valley farm. The wire he had seen was stretched from bottom to top, the fall being very steep, so that the bales of the hay-crop could be slid down to the valley without carrying. At the summer's end, cows were led by an easier detour to the uplands, there to remain grazing for six weeks or more, attended by some robust peasant-woman who lived solitary with the herd.

And there, at the side of the hut, bending over a rough table, a woman stood. Trent, as he slowly approached, noted her short, rough skirt and coarse, sack-like upper garment, her thick grey stockings and clumsy clogs. About her bare head her pale gold hair was fastened in tight plaits. As she looked up on hearing Trent's footfall, two heavy silver ear-rings dangled about the tanned and toil-worn face of this very type of the middle-aged peasant-woman of the region.

She ceased her task of scraping a large cake of chocolate into a bowl, and straightened her tall body; smiling, with her lean hands on her hips, she spoke in Norwegian, greeting him. Trent made the proper reply. "And that," he added, in English, "is almost all of the language I know. Perhaps, madam, you speak English?"

Her light blue eyes looked puzzlement, and she spoke again in Norwegian, pointing downward to the valley. He nodded, and she began to talk pleasantly in her unknown tongue. From within the hut she brought two thick mugs; she pointed rapidly to the chocolate in the bowl, to himself and herself, then downward again to the village.

"I should like it of all things," he said; "you are most kind and hospitable, like all your people. What a pity it is we have no language in common!" She brought him a stool and gave him the chocolate cake and a knife, making signs that he should continue the scraping; then within the hut she kindled a fire of twigs, and began to boil water in a black pot. Plainly it was her dwelling, the roughest Trent had ever seen. On two small shelves against the rough planks of the wall were ranged a few pieces of earthenware, coarse and chipped, but clean. A wooden bedplace, with straw and two neatly-folded blankets, filled a third of the space of the hut. All the carpentering was of the rudest. From a small chest in a corner she drew a biscuit-tin, half-full of flat cakes of stale bread. There seemed to be nothing else in the tiny place save a heap of twigs for firing.

She made chocolate in the two mugs, and then, on Trent's insistence, sat upon the only stool at the little table outside the hut, while he made a seat of an upturned milk-pail. She continued to talk amiably, while he finished with difficulty one of the bread-cakes.

"I believe," he said, at last, setting down his empty mug, "you are talking merely to hear the sound of your own voice, madam. It is excusable in you. You don't understand English, so I will tell you to your face it is a most beautiful voice. I should say," he went on, thoughtfully, "that you ought, with training, to have been one of the greatest soprano singers who ever lived."

She heard him calmly, and shook her head, as not understanding.

"Well, don't say I didn't break it gently,"Trent protested. He rose to his feet. "Madam, I know that you are Lady Aviemore. I have broken in upon your solitude, and I ask your pardon for that; but I could not be sure unless I saw you. I give you my word that no one knows, and no one shall know from me, what I know."

He made as if to return by the way he came. But the woman held up her hand. A singular change had come over her brown face. An open and lively spirit now looked out of her desolate blue eyes, and she smiled another and much more intelligent smile. After a few minutes she spoke in English, fluent but quaintly pronounced. "Sir," she said, "you have behaved very nicely up till now. It has been amusing for me; there is not much comedy on the sater. Now will you have the goodness to explain."

He told her in a few words that he had suspected she was still alive; that he had thought over the facts which had come to his knowledge; and that he had been led to think she was probably in that place. "I thought you might guess that I had recognised you," he added. "So it seemed best to assure you that your secret was safe. Was it wrong to speak?"

She shook her head, gazing at him with her chin on her hand. Presently she said, "I think you are not against me. But I do not understand why you kept my secret from others when you had found it out."

"I sought for it because I am curious," he answered. "I kept it, and I will always keep it, because—oh, well! because to me Lillemor Wergeland is a sort of divinity."

She laughed suddenly. "Incense! And I in these rags, in this place, with what I can see in this little spotty piece of cheap looking-glass! Ah, well! You have come a long way. Monsieur le Curieux, and it would be a cruelty not to confide in you. After all, it was simple.

"It was only a day or two after the disaster that the resolve came to me. I never hesitated a moment. It was through me that they were in that place—you have heard that? I felt I must leave the world I knew, and that knew me. Suicide never occurred to me—what is there more contemptible? As for a convent, unhappily there is none for people with minds like mine. I meant simply to disappear, and the only way to succeed was to get the reputation of being dead. I thought it out for some days and nights. Then I wrote, in the name of my maid, to an establishment in Paris where I used to buy things for the stage. I sent money, and ordered a dark brown transformation—that is a lady's word for a wig—some stuff for darkening the skin, various pigments and pencils, et tout le bazar. My maid did not know what I had sent for; she only handed the parcel to me when it arrived. She would have thrown herself in the fire for me, I think, my maid Maria. The day the things came I announced that I would return home by the route you know."

"Then it was as I guessed!" Trent exclaimed. "You disguised yourself on the steamer at Brindisi, and slipped off in the dark before it started."

"I was no such imbecile, indeed," returned the lady, with a hint of sharpness. "How if my absence had been discovered somehow before the starting? That could happen; and then what? No; when we reached Brindisi from Taormina, I knew we had some hours there. I put on a thick veil and went out alone. At the office by the harbour I took a second-class berth for myself, Miss Julia Simms, travelling from Brindisi to Venice. I found the boat was already alongside the quay. Then I went into the poorer streets of the town and bought some clothes, very ugly ones, some shoes, some cheap toilet things."

"Some black hair-pins," murmured Trent.

"Naturally, black," she assented. She looked at him inquiringly, then resumed. "I bought also a melancholy little cheap portmanteau-thing, and put my purchases in it. I took it on a cab to the harbour, and gave one of the ship's stewards a lira to put it in Miss Simms's cabin to await her. After that I bought two other things, a long mackintosh coat and a funny little cap, the very things for Miss Simms, and at the hotel I pushed them under the things my maid had already packed in my dressing case. On the steamer, when I was locked in my cabin without danger of disturbance, I took off my fur coat, I arranged a dark, rather catty sort of face for myself, and fitted on Miss Simms's hair. I put on her mackintosh and cap. When the boat began to move away from the quay, and people on deck were looking over the rail, I just stepped out of my cabin, shut the door, and walked straight to Miss Simms's berth at the other end of the ship. There is not much more to say. When we reached Venice I did not look for the others, and I never saw them. I went straight on to Paris, and wrote to my brother Knut that I was alive, and told him just what I meant to do if he would help me. Such things do not seem so mad to a true child of Norway."

"What things?" Trent asked.

"Things of deep sorrow, malady of soul, escape from the world. He and his wife have been true and good to me. I am supposed to be her cousin, Hilda Bjornstad. I left them money, more than enough to pay for me, but they did not know that when they welcomed me here."

She ceased, and smiled vaguely at Trent, who was considering her tale with eyes that gazed fixedly at the sky-line. "Yes, of course," he remarked, presently, in an abstracted manner. "That was it. So simple! And now may I tell you," he went on, with a sudden change of tone, "one or two details you have forgotten?

"At Brindisi you bought, just before going on the boat, a box of the stuff called Ixtil, to prevent sea-sickness. You took a dose before going on board and another just after, as the directions prescribed. Then, as Mr. Selby happened to know you had it, you thought it best to leave it behind when you vanished. Also you left behind you, in your hurry, four black hair-pins, quite new, which had somehow, I suppose, got loose inside your little bag, and which were found there by Selby. You see, Lady Aviemore, it was Selby who brought me into this. He told me all the facts he knew. And he showed me the velvet bag and its contents. But he did not attach any importance to the two things I have just mentioned."

Lady Aviemore raised her eyebrows perceptibly. "I cannot see why he should. And I cannot see why he should bring in anybody."

"Because he had some vague idea of your brother-in-law having caused your death, or, at any rate, having known your intention to commit suicide. He never said it outright, but it was plain that that was in his mind. You see, Lord Aviemore stood to benefit enormously by your death; and then there was the matter of your note announcing your suicide."

"It announced," she remarked, "the truth: that I was leaving a world I could not bear. The words might mean one thing or another. But what of the note?"

"That truthful note," said Trent, "was written with pen and ink, of which there was none in your cabin. It was written on paper which had been torn from a block, and no block was found. Also it was discovered that that particular make of paper is sold in Canada, but has never been sold in Europe. You had never been in Canada. Lord Aviemore had just come back from Canada. You see?"

"But did not Mr. Selby perceive that my brother-in-law is a saint?" inquired the lady, with a touch of impatience. "Surely that was plain! An evident saint!"

"In my slight knowledge of him," admitted Trent, "he struck me in that way. But Selby is a lawyer, and lawyers don't understand saints. Besides, Lord Aviemore disliked him, I fancy, and perhaps he felt the same way about Lord Aviemore."

"It is true he did not approve of Mr. Selby, because he disliked all men who were smart and worldly. But now I will tell you. That evening in the hotel at Brindisi I wanted to write the note, and I asked my brother-in-law for a sheet from a block he had in his hand and was about to write upon. That is all. I wrote it in the hotel writing-room, and took it afterwards in my bag to the cabin."

"We supposed you had written it beforehand," Trent observed, "and that was one of the things that led me to feel morally certain that you were still alive. I'll explain. If, as we thought, you had written the note in the hotel, your suicide was a premeditated act. Yet Selby afterwards saw you buying that medicine, and it was plain that you had taken two doses. Now, it struck me that it was ridiculous for anyone already determined on drowning herself at sea to begin treating herself against sea-sickness. Then there were those new black hair-pins. The sight of them was a revelation to me. They meant disguise. For I knew, of course, that with that hair you had probably never used a dark hair-pin in your life."

The Countess felt at her pale-gold plaits, and gravely extended a black hair-pin. "In the valley we all use them."

"It is very different in the valley, I know," he said, quietly.

The lady regarded her guest with something of respect. "It still remains," she said, "to explain how you knew it was in Norway, and here, as a poor farm-servant, that I should hide myself. It seemed to me the last thing in the world—your world—that a woman who had lived my life would be expected to do."

"There was no certainty about it," he answered. "It was a strong possibility, that's all. Your problem, you see, was just what you say—to hide yourself. And you had another, I think. You had to get your living somehow. Everything you possessed—except some small sum in cash, I suppose—you left behind you when you disappeared. Now, a woman cannot very well go on acting and disguising herself for ever. A man can grow hair on his face or shave it off; for a woman, disguise must be a perpetual anxiety. If she has to get employment, and especially if she has no references, it's an impossibility."

She nodded gravely. "That was how I saw it."

"So," he pursued, "it came to this: that Lillemor Wergeland had to come to the surface again somewhere, and in no long time; Lillemor Wergeland, whose type of beauty and general appearance were so marked and unmistakable, and whose photograph had gone all over the world. The fact is that for some time I didn't see how it could possibly have been done. There were only a few countries, I supposed, of which you knew enough of the language to make any attempt to live and work in them. In those countries you would always attract attention by your physical type and your accent; and if you attracted attention, discovery might follow at any moment. The more I thought of it the more difficult it seemed.

"And then the idea came. There was one country in which your looks and speech would not betray you as a foreigner—your own country. And among those corners of the world where Lillemor Wergeland could go with a fair certainty of being unrecognised, the remoter villages of Norway would be. And at Myklebostad, on the Langfjord, which the map told me was thirty miles from the nearest town and sixty from the nearest railway, Lillemor Wergeland had a brother, who was also the richer by two thousand pounds for her supposed death.

"You see, then, how I formed the theory which brought me to this place on a sketching holiday," Trent stood up and gazed across the valley to the sunlit white peaks beyond. "I have visited Norway before, but I have never had such an interesting time. And now, before I return to the haunts of men, let me say again that I shall forget at once all that has happened to-day. Don't think it was a vulgar curiosity that brought me here. There was once a supreme artiste called Lillemore Wergeland, whose gifts made me her debtor and servant. Anything that happened to her touched me; I had a sort of right to go seeking what it really was that had happened."

She stood before him in her coarse and stained clothes, her hands clasped behind her, with a face and attitude of perfect dignity.

"Very well. You stand on your right, and I on mine—to arrange my own life, since I am alone in it. And I will spend it here, where it began. My soul was born here, before it went out to have adventures, and it has crept home again for comfort. Believe me, it is not only as you say, that I am safe from discovery here. That counts very much; but it is the truth that I felt I must go out of the world, and live out my life where it began, in this far-away, lonely place, where everything is humble, and there is no wealth or luxury at all, and the hills and the fjords are severe and grand, just as God made them before there were any men. Some people used to have that impulse, you know, long ago, when something had happened to make them tired of the world, or to stain their souls so that they must go apart and wash their wickedness away. And this, all this is my own, own land! And now," she ended, suddenly, "we understand one another."

She extended her hand, saying, "I do not know your name."

"Why should you?" he asked, bending over it; then went quickly from her. At the beginning of the descent he glanced back once; she waved her hand with a quick gesture.

Half-way down the rugged climb Trent stopped. Far above a wonderful voice was singing to the glory of the Norse land, whose mountains (it sang) not even the storm that should rive the globe itself would be able to shake.

"Ja! Herligt er mit Fodeland,
Der ewig trodser Tidens Tand,"

sang the voice.

Trent looked out upon the wild landscape.

"Her Fatherland!" he soliloquised. "Well, well! They say the strictest parents have the most devoted children."

THE BITER BIT

WILLIAM WILKIE COLLINS

FROM CHIEF INSPECTOR THEAKSTONE, OF THE
DETECTIVE POLICE, TO SERGEANT BULMER OF
THE SAME FORCE

LONDON, *4th July, 18—.*

SERGEANT BULMER,—

    This is to inform you that you are wanted to assist in looking up
a ease of importance, which will require all the attention of an experienced member of the force. The matter of the robbery on which you
are now engaged, you will please to shift over to the young man who
brings you this letter. You will tell him all the circumstances of the
case, just as they stand; you will put him up to the progress you have

made (if any) towards detecting the person or persons by whom the money has been stolen; and you will leave him to make the best he can of the matter now in your hands. He is to have the whole responsibility of the case, and the whole credit of his success, if he brings it to a proper issue.

So much for the orders that I am desired to communicate to you.

A word in your ear, next, about this new man who is to take your place. His name is Matthew Sharpin; and he is to have the chance given him of dashing into our office at a jump—supposing he turns out strong enough to take it. You will naturally ask me how he comes by this privilege. I can only tell you that he has some uncommonly strong interest to back him in certain high quarters which you and I had better not mention except under our breaths. He has been a lawyer's clerk; and he is wonderfully conceited in his opinion of himself, as well as mean and underhand to look at. According to his own account, he leaves his old trade, and joins ours, of his own free will and preference. You will no more believe that than I do. My notion is, that he has managed to ferret out some private information in connexion with the affairs of one of his master's clients, which makes him rather an awkward customer to keep in the office for the future, and which, at the same time, gives him hold enough over his employer to make it dangerous to drive him into a corner by turning him away. I think the giving him this unheard-of chance among us, is, in plain words, pretty much like giving him hush-money to keep him quiet. However that may be, Mr. Matthew Sharpin is to have the case now in your hands; and if he succeeds with it, he pokes his ugly nose into our office, as sure as fate. I put you up to this, Sergeant, so that you may not stand in your own light by giving the new man any cause to complain of you at headquarters, and remain yours,

FRANCIS THEAKSTONE.

FROM MR. MATTHEW SHARPIN TO CHIEF INSPECTOR THEAKSTONE

LONDON, 5th July, 18——.

DEAR SIR,—

Having now been favoured with the necessary instructions from Sergeant Bulmer, I beg to remind you of certain directions which I have received, relating to the report of my future proceedings which I am to prepare for examination at headquarters.

The object of my writing, and of your examining what I have written, before you send it in to the higher authorities, is, I am informed, to give me, as an untried hand, the benefit of your advice, in case I want it (which I venture to think I shall not) at any stage of my proceedings. As the extraordinary circumstances of the case on which I am now engaged, make it impossible for me to absent myself from the place where the robbery was committed, until I have made some progress towards discovering the thief, I am necessarily precluded from consulting you personally. Hence the necessity of my writing down the various details, which might, perhaps, be better communicated by word of mouth. This, if I am not mistaken, is the position in which we are now placed. I state my own impressions on the subject, in writing, in order that we may clearly understand each other at the outset; and have the honour to remain, your obedient servant,

MATTHEW SHARPIN.

FROM CHIEF INSPECTOR THEAKSTONE TO MR. MATTHEW SHARPIN

LONDON, *5th July, 18——.*

SIR,——

You have begun by wasting time, ink, and paper. We both of us perfectly well knew the position we stood in towards each other, when I sent you with my letter to Sergeant Bulmer. There was not the least need to repeat it in writing. Be so good as to employ your pen, in future, on the business actually in hand.

You have now three separate matters on which to write to me. First, You have to draw up a statement of your instructions received from Sergeant Bulmer, in order to show us that nothing has escaped your memory, and that you are thoroughly acquainted with all the circumstances of the case which has been entrusted to you. Secondly, You are to inform me what it is you propose to do. Thirdly, You are to report every inch of your progress (if you make any) from day to day, and, if need be, from hour to hour as well. This is *your* duty. As to what *my* duty may be, when I want you to remind me of it, I will write and tell you so. In the meantime, I remain, yours,

FRANCIS THEAKSTONE.

FROM MR. MATTHEW SHARPIN TO CHIEF INSPECTOR THEAKSTONE

LONDON, *6th July, 18——.*

SIR,——

You are rather an elderly person, and, as such, naturally inclined to be a little jealous of men like me, who are in the prime of their lives and their faculties. Under these circumstances, it is my duty to be considerate towards you, and not to bear too hardly on your small failings. I decline, therefore, altogether, to take offence at the tone of your letter; I give you the full benefit of the natural generosity of my nature; I sponge the very existence of your surly communication out of my memory—in short, Chief Inspector Theakstone, I forgive you, and proceed to business.

My first duty is to draw up a full statement of the instructions I have received from Sergeant Bulmer. Here they are at your service, according to my version of them.

At number 13, Rutherford Street, Soho, there is a stationer's shop. It is kept by one Mr. Yatman. He is a married man, but has no family. Besides Mr. and Mrs. Yatman, the other inmates in the house are a young single man named Jay, who lodges in the front room on the second floor—a shopman, who sleeps in one of the attics,—and a servant-of-all-work, whose bed is in the back-kitchen. Once a week a charwoman comes for a few hours in the morning only, to help this servant. These are all the persons who, on ordinary occasions, have means of access to the interior of the house, placed, as a matter of course, at their disposal.

Mr. Yatman has been in business for many years, carrying on his affairs prosperously enough to realise a handsome independence for a person in his position. Unfortunately for himself, he endeavoured to increase the amount of his property by speculating. He ventured boldly in his investments, luck went against him, and rather less than two years ago he found himself a poor man again. All that was saved out of the wreck of his property was the sum of two hundred pounds.

Although Mr. Yatman did his best to meet his altered circumstances, by giving up many of the luxuries and comforts to which he and his wife had been accustomed, he found it impossible to retrench so far as to allow of putting by any money from the income produced by his shop. The business has been declining of late years—the cheap advertising stationers having done it injury with the public. Consequently, up to the last week the only surplus property possessed by Mr. Yatman consisted of the two hundred pounds which had been recovered from the wreck of his fortune. This sum was placed as a deposit in a joint-stock bank of the highest possible character.

Eight days ago, Mr. Yatman and his lodger, Mr. Jay, held a conversation on the subject of the commercial difficulties which are hampering trade in all directions at the present time. Mr. Jay (who lives by supplying the newspapers with short paragraphs relating to accidents, offences, and brief records of remarkable occurrences in general—who is, in short, what they call a penny-a-liner) told his landlord that he had been in the city that day, and had heard unfavourable rumours on the subject of the joint-stock banks. The rumours to which he alluded had already reached the ears of Mr. Yatman from other quarters; and the confirmation of them by his lodger had such an effect on his mind—predisposed as it was to alarm by the experience of his former losses—that he resolved to go at once to the bank and withdraw his deposit.

It was then getting on towards the end of the afternoon; and he arrived just in time to receive his money before the bank closed.

He received the deposit in bank-notes of the following amounts;—one fifty-pound note, three twenty-pound notes, six ten-pound notes, and six five-pound notes. His object in drawing the money in this form was to have it ready to lay out immediately in trifling loans, on good security, among the small tradespeople of his district, some of whom are sorely pressed for the very means of existence at the present time. Investments of this kind seemed to Mr. Yatman to be the most safe and the most profitable on which he could now venture.

He brought the money back in an envelope placed in his breast-pocket; and asked his shopman, on getting home, to look for a small flat tin cash-box, which had not been used for years, and which, as Mr. Yatman remembered it, was exactly of the right size to hold the bank-notes. For some time the cash-box was searched for in vain. Mr. Yatman called to his wife to know if she had any idea where it was. The question was overheard by the servant-of-all-work, who was taking up the tea-tray at the time, and by Mr. Jay, who was coming downstairs on his way out to the theatre. Ultimately the cash-box was found by the shopman. Mr. Yatman placed the bank-notes in it, secured them by a padlock, and put the box in his coat-pocket. It stuck out of the coat-pocket a very little, but enough to be seen. Mr. Yatman remained at home, upstairs, all the evening. No visitors called. At eleven o'clock he went to bed, and put the cash-box along with his clothes, on a chair by the bedside.

When he and his wife woke the next morning, the box was gone. Payment of the notes was immediately stopped at the bank of England; but no news of the money has been heard of since that time.

So far, the circumstances of the case are perfectly clear. They point unmistakably to the conclusion that the robbery must have been committed by some person living in the house. Suspicion falls, therefore, upon the servant-of-all-work, upon the shopman, and upon Mr. Jay. The two first knew that the cash-box was being inquired for by their master, but did not know what it was he wanted to put into it. They would assume, of course, that it was money. They both had opportunities (the servant, when she took away the tea-and the shopman, when he came, after shutting up, to give the keys of the till to his master) of seeing the cash-box in Mr. Yatman's pocket, and of inferring naturally, from its position there, that he intended to take it into his bedroom with him at night.

Mr. Jay, on the other hand, had been told, during the afternoon's conversation on the subject of joint-stock banks, that his landlord had a deposit of two hundred pounds in one of them. He also knew that Mr. Yatman left him with the intention of drawing that money out; and he heard the inquiry for the cash-box, afterwards, when he was coming downstairs. He must, therefore, have inferred that the money was in the house, and that the cash-box was the receptacle intended to contain it. That he could have had any idea, however, of the place in which Mr. Yatman intended to keep it for the night, is impossible, seeing that he went out before the box was found, and did not return till his landlord was in bed. Consequently, if he committed the robbery, he must have gone into the bedroom purely on speculation.

Speaking of the bedroom reminds me of the necessity of noticing the situation of it in the house, and the means that exist of gaining easy access to it at any hour of the night.

The room in question is the back-room on the first floor. In consequence of Mrs. Yatman's constitutional nervousness on the subject of fire (which makes her apprehend being burnt alive in her room, in case of accident, by the hampering of the lock if the key is turned in it) her husband has never been accustomed to lock the bedroom door. Both he and his wife are, by their own admission, heavy sleepers. Consequently the risk to be run by any evil-disposed persons wishing to plunder the bedroom, was of the most trifling kind. They could enter the room by merely turning the handle of the door; and if they moved with ordinary caution, there was no fear of their waking the sleepers inside. This fact is of importance. It strengthens our conviction that the money must have been taken by one of the inmates of the house, because it tends to show that the robbery, in this case, might have been committed by persons not possessed of the superior vigilance and cunning of the experienced thief.

Such are the circumstances, as they were related to Sergeant Bulmer, when he was first called in to discover the guilty parties, and, if possible, to recover the lost bank-notes. The strictest inquiry which he could institute, failed of producing the smallest fragment of evidence against any of the persons on whom suspicion naturally fell. Their language and behaviour, on being informed of the robbery, was perfectly consistent with the language and behaviour of innocent people. Sergeant Bulmer felt from the first that this was a case for private inquiry and secret observation. He began by recommending Mr. and Mrs. Yatman to affect a feeling of perfect confidence in the innocence of the persons living under their roof; and he then opened the campaign by employing himself in following the goings and comings, and in discovering the friends, the habits, and the secrets of the maid-of-all-work.

Three days and nights of exertion on his own part, and on that of others who were competent to assist his investigations, were enough to satisfy him that there was no sound cause for suspicion against the girl.

He next practised the same precaution in relation to the shopman. There was more difficulty and uncertainty in privately clearing up this person's character without his knowledge, but the obstacles were at last smoothed away with tolerable success; and though there is not the same amount of certainty, in this case, which there was in that of the girl, there is still fair reason for supposing that the shopman has had nothing to do with the robbery of the cash-box.

As a necessary consequence of these proceedings, the range of suspicion now becomes limited to the lodger, Mr. Jay.

When I presented your letter of introduction to Sergeant Bulmer, he had already made some inquiries on the subject of this young man. The result, so far, has not been at all favourable. Mr. Jay's habits are irregular; he frequents public houses, and seems to be familiarly acquainted with a great many dissolute characters; he is in debt to most of the tradespeople whom he employs; he has not paid his rent to Mr. Yatman for the last month; yesterday evening he came home excited by liquor, and last week he was seen talking to a prize-fighter. In short, though Mr. Jay does call himself a journalist, in virtue of his penny-a-line contributions to the newspapers, he is a young man of low tastes, vulgar manners, and bad habits. Nothing has yet been discovered in relation to him, which redounds to his credit in the smallest degree.

I have now reported, down to the very last details, all the particulars communicated to me by Sergeant Bulmer. I believe you will not find an omission anywhere; and I think you will admit, though you are prejudiced against me, that a clearer statement of facts was never laid before you than the statement I have now made. My next duty is to tell you what I propose to do, now that the case is confided to my hands.

In the first place, it is clearly my business to take up the case at the point where Sergeant Bulmer has left it. On his authority, I am justified in assuming that I have no need to trouble myself about the maid-of-all-work and the shopman. Their characters are now to be considered as cleared up. What remains to be privately investigated is the question of the guilt or innocence of Mr. Jay. Before we give up the notes for lost, we must make sure, if we can, that he knows nothing about them.

This is the plan that I have adopted, with the full approval of Mr. and Mrs. Yatman, for discovering whether Mr. Jay is or is not the person who has stolen the cash-box:—

I propose, to-day, to present myself at the house in the character of a young man who is looking for lodgings. The back-room on the second floor will be shown to me as the room to let; and I shall establish myself there to-night, as a person from the country who has come to London to look for a situation in a respectable shop or office.

By this means I shall be living next to the room occupied by Mr. Jay. The partition between us is mere lath and plaster. I shall make a small hole in it, near the cornice, through which I can see what Mr. Jay does in his room, and hear every word that is said when any friend happens to call on him. Whenever he is at home, I shall be at my post of observation. Whenever he goes out, I shall be after him. By employing these means of watching him, I believe I may look forward to the discovery of his secret—if he knows anything about the lost bank-notes—as to a dead certainty.

What you may think of my plan of observation I cannot undertake to say. It appears to me to unite the invaluable merits of boldness and simplicity. Fortified by this conviction, I close the present communication with feelings of the most sanguine description in regard to the future, and remain your obedient servant,

MATTHEW SHARPIN.

FROM THE SAME TO THE SAME

7th July.

SIR,—

As you have not honoured me with any answer to my last communication, I assume that, in spite of your prejudices against me, it has produced the favourable impression on your mind which I ventured to anticipate. Gratified beyond measure by the token of approval which your eloquent silence conveys to me, I proceed to report the progress that has been made in the course of the last twenty-four hours.

I am now comfortably established next door to Mr. Jay; and I am delighted to say that I have two holes in the partition, instead of one. My natural sense of humour has led me into the pardonable extravagance of giving them appropriate names. One I call my peep-hole, and the other my pipe-hole. The name of the first explains itself; the name of the second refers to a small tin pipe, or tube, inserted in the hole, and twisted so that the mouth of it comes close to my ear, while I am standing at my post of observation. Thus, while I am looking at Mr. Jay through my peep-hole, I can hear every word that may be spoken in his room through my pipe-hole.

Perfect candour—a virtue which I have possessed from my childhood—compels me to acknowledge, before I go any further, that the ingenious notion of adding a pipe-hole to my proposed peep-hole originated with Mrs. Yatman. This lady—a most intelligent and accomplished person, simple, and yet distinguished, in her manners—has entered into all my little plans with an enthusiasm and intelligence which I cannot too highly praise. Mr. Yatman is so cast down by his loss, that he is quite incapable of affording me any assistance. Mrs. Yatman, who is evidently most tenderly attached to him, feels her husband's sad condition of mind even more acutely than she feels the loss of the money; and is mainly stimulated to exertion by her desire to assist in raising him from the miserable state of prostration into which he has now fallen.

"The money, Mr. Sharpin," she said to me yesterday evening, with tears in her eyes, "the money may be regained by rigid economy and strict attention to business. It is my husband's wretched state of mind that makes me so anxious for the discovery of the thief. I may be wrong, but I felt hopeful of success as soon as you entered the house; and I believe, if the wretch who has robbed us is to be found, you are the man to discover him." I accepted this gratifying compliment in the spirit in which it was offered—firmly believing that I shall be found, sooner or later, to have thoroughly deserved it.

Let me now return to business; that is to say, to my peep-hole and my pipe-hole.

I have enjoyed some hours of calm observation of Mr. Jay. Though rarely at home, as I understand from Mrs. Yatman, on ordinary occasions, he has been indoors the whole of this day. That is suspicious, to begin with. I have to report, further, that he rose at a late hour this morning (always a bad sign in a young man), and that he lost a great deal of time, after he was up, in yawning and complaining to himself of headache. Like other debauched characters, he ate little or nothing for breakfast. His next proceeding was to smoke a pipe—a dirty clay pipe, which a gentleman would have been ashamed to put between his lips. When he had done smoking, he took out pen, ink, and paper, and sat down to write with a groan—whether of remorse for having taken the bank-notes, or of disgust at the task before him, I am unable to say. After writing a few lines (too far away from my peep-hole to give me a chance of reading over his shoulder), he leaned back in his chair, and amused himself by humming the tunes of certain popular songs. Whether these do, or do not, represent secret signals by which he communicates with his accomplices remains to be seen. After he had amused himself for some time by humming, he got up and began to walk about the room, occasionally stopping to add a sentence to the paper on his desk. Before long, he went to a locked cupboard and opened it. I strained my eyes eagerly, in expectation of making a discovery. I saw him take something carefully out of the cupboard—he turned round—and it was only a pint bottle of brandy! Having drunk some of the liquor, this extremely indolent reprobate lay down on his bed again, and in five minutes was fast asleep.

After hearing him snoring for at least two hours, I was recalled to my peep-hole by a knock at his door. He jumped up and opened it with suspicious activity.

A very small boy, with a very dirty face, walked in, said, "Please, sir, they're waiting for you," sat down on a chair, with his legs a long way from the ground, and instantly fell asleep! Mr. Jay swore an oath, tied a wet towel round his head, and going back to his paper, began to cover it with writing as fast as his fingers could move the pen. Occasionally getting up to dip the towel in water and tie it on again, he continued at this employment for nearly three hours; then folded up the leaves of writing, woke the boy, and gave them to him, with this remarkable expression—"Now, then, young sleepyhead, quick—march! If you see the governor, tell him to have the money ready when I call for it." The boy grinned, and disappeared. I was sorely tempted to follow "sleepy-head," but, on reflection, considered it safest still to keep my eye on the proceedings of Mr. Jay.

In half an hour's time, he put on his hat and walked out. Of course, I put on my hat and walked out also. As I went downstairs, I passed Mrs. Yatman going up. The lady has been kind enough to undertake, by previous arrangement between us, to search Mr. Jay's room, while he is out of the way, and while I am necessarily engaged in the pleasing duty of following him wherever he goes. On the occasion to which I now refer, he walked straight to the nearest tavern, and ordered a couple of mutton chops for his dinner. I placed myself in the next box to him, and ordered a couple of mutton chops for my dinner. Before I had been in the room a minute, a young man of highly suspicious manners and appearance, sitting at a table opposite, took his glass of porter in his hand and joined Mr. Jay. I pretended to be reading the newspaper, and listened, as in duty bound, with all my might.

"Jack has been here inquiring after you," says the young man.

"Did he leave any message?" asks Mr. Jay.

"Yes," says the other. "He told me, if I met with you, to say that he wished very particularly to see you to-night; and that he would give you a look-in, at Rutherfold Street, at seven o'clock."

"All right," says Mr. Jay. "I'll get back in time to see him."

Upon this, the suspicious-looking young man finished his porter, and saying that he was rather in a hurry, took leave of his friend (perhaps I should not be wrong if I said his accomplice) and left the room.

At twenty-five minutes and a half past six—in these serious cases it is important to be particular about time—Mr. Jay finished his chops and paid his bill. At twenty-six minutes and three-quarters I finished my chops and paid mine. In ten minutes more I was inside the house in Rutherford Street, and was received by Mrs. Yatman in the passage. That charming woman's face exhibited an expression of melancholy and disappointment which it quite grieved me to see.

"I am afraid, Ma'am," says I, "that you have not hit on any little criminating discovery in the lodger's room?"

She shook her head and sighed. It was a soft, languid, fluttering sigh;—and, upon my life, it quite upset me. For the moment I forgot business, and burned with envy of Mr. Yatman.

"Don't despair, Ma'am," I said, with an insinuating mildness which seemed to touch her. "I have heard a mysterious conversation— I know of a guilty appointment—and I expect great things from my peep-hole and my pipe-hole to-night. Pray, don't be alarmed, but I think we are on the brink of a discovery."

Here my enthusiastic devotion to business got the better of my tender feelings. I looked—winked—nodded—left her.

When I got back to my observatory, I found Mr. Jay digesting his mutton chops in an armchair, with his pipe in his mouth. On his table were two tumblers, a jug of water, and the pint bottle of brandy. It was then close upon seven o'clock. As the hour struck, the person described as "Jack" walked in.

He looked agitated—I am happy to say he looked violently agitated. The cheerful glow of anticipated success diffused itself (to use a strong expression) all over me, from head to foot. With breathless interest I looked through my peep-hole, and saw the visitor—the "Jack" of this delightful case—sit down, facing me, at the opposite side of the table to Mr. Jay. Making allowance for the difference in expression which their countenances just now happened to exhibit, these two abandoned villains were so much alike in other respects as to lead at once to the conclusion that they were brothers. Jack was the cleaner man and the better dressed of the two. I admit that, at the outset. It is, perhaps, one of my failings to push justice and impartiality to their utmost limits. I am no Pharisee; and where Vice has its redeeming point, I say, let Vice have its due—yes, yes, by all manner of means, let Vice have its due.

"What's the matter now, Jack?" says Mr. Jay.

"Can't you see it in my face?"says Jack.

"My dear fellow, delays are dangerous. Let us have done with suspense, and risk it the day after to-morrow."

"So soon as that?" cried Mr. Jay, looking very much astonished. "Well, I'm ready, if you are. But, I say, Jack, is Somebody Else ready too? Are you quite sure of that?"

He smiled as he spoke—a frightful smile—and laid a very strong emphasis on those two words, "Somebody Else." There is evidently a third ruffian, a nameless desperado, concerned in the business.

"Meet us to-morrow," says Jack, "and judge for yourself. Be in the Regent's Park at eleven in the morning, and look out for us at the turning that leads to the Avenue Road."

"I'll be there," says Mr. Jay. "Have a drop of brandy and water? What are you getting up for? You're not going already?"

"Yes, I am," says Jack. "The fact is, I'm so excited and agitated that I can't sit still anywhere for five minutes together. Ridiculous as it may appear to you, I'm in a perpetual state of nervous flutter. I can't, for the life of me, help fearing that we shall be found out. I fancy that every man who looks twice at me in the street is a spy—"

At those words, I thought my legs would have given way under me. Nothing but strength of mind kept me at my peep-hole—nothing else, I give you my word of honour.

"Stuff and nonsense!" cried Mr. Jay, with all the effrontery of a veteran in crime. "We have kept the secret up to this time, and we will manage cleverly to the end. Have a drop of brandy and water, and you will feel as certain about it as I do."

Jack steadily refused the brandy and water, and steadily persisted in taking his leave.

"I must try if I can't walk it off," he said. "Remember to-morrow morning—eleven o'clock, Avenue Road side of the Regent's Park."

With those words he went out. His hardened relative laughed desperately, and resumed the dirty clay pipe.

I sat down on the side of my bed, actually quivering with excitement.

It is clear to me that no attempt has yet been made to change the stolen bank-notes; and I may add that Sergeant Bulmer was of that opinion also, when he left the case in my hands. What is the natural conclusion to draw from the conversation which I have just set down? Evidently, that the confederates meet to-morrow to take their respective shares in the stolen money, and to decide on the safest means of getting the notes changed the day after. Mr. Jay is, beyond a doubt, the leading criminal in this business, and he will probably run the chief risk—that of changing the fifty-pound note. I shall, therefore, still make it my business to follow him—attending at the Regent's Park to-morrow, and doing my best to hear what is said there. If another appointment is made for the day after, I shall, of course, go to it. In the meantime, I shall want the immediate assistance of two competent persons (supposing the rascals separate after their meeting) to follow the two minor criminals. It is only fair to add, that, if the rogues all retire together, I shall probably keep my subordinates in reserve. Being naturally ambitious, I desire, if possible, to have the whole credit of discovering this robbery to myself.

8th July.

I have to acknowledge, with thanks, the speedy arrival of my two subordinates—men of very average abilities, I am afraid; but, fortunately, I shall always be on the spot to direct them.

My first business this morning was, necessarily, to prevent mistakes by accounting to Mr. and Mrs. Yatman for the presence of two strangers on the scene. Mr. Yatman (between ourselves, a poor feeble man) only shook his head and groaned. Mrs. Yatman (that superior woman) favoured me with a charming look of intelligence.

"Oh, Mr. Sharpin!" she said, "I am so sorry to see those two men! Your sending for their assistance looks as if you were beginning to be doubtful of success."

I privately winked at her (she is very good in allowing me to do so without taking offence), and told her, in my facetious way, that she laboured under a slight mistake.

"It is because I am sure of success, Ma'am, that I send for them. I am determined to recover the money, not for my own sake only, but for Mr. Yatman's sake—and for yours."

I laid a considerable amount of stress on those last three words. She said, "Oh, Mr. Sharpin!" again—and blushed of a heavenly red—and looked down at her work. I could go to the world's end with that woman, if Mr. Yatman would only die.

I sent off the two subordinates to wait, until I wanted them, at the Avenue Road gate of the Regent's Park. Half an hour afterwards I was following the same direction myself, at the heels of Mr. Jay.

The two confederates were punctual to the appointed time, I blush to record it, but it is nevertheless necessary to state, that the third rogue—the nameless desperado of my report, or if you prefer it, the mysterious "Somebody Else" of the conversation between the two brothers—is a Woman! and, what is worse, a young woman! and what is more lamentable still, a nice-looking woman! I have long resisted a growing conviction, that, wherever there is mischief in this world, an individual of the fair sex is inevitably certain to be mixed up in it. After the experience of this morning, I can struggle against that sad conclusion no longer.—I give up the sex—excepting Mrs. Yatman, I give up the sex.

The man named "Jack" offered the woman his arm. Mr. Jay placed himself on the other side of her. The three then walked away slowly among the trees. I followed them at a respectful distance. My two subordinates, at a respectful distance also, followed me.

It was, I deeply regret to say, impossible to get near enough to them to overhear their conversation, without running too great a risk of being discovered. I could only infer from their gestures and actions that they were all three talking with extraordinary earnestness on some subject which deeply interested them. After having been engaged in this way a full quarter of an hour, they suddenly turned round to retrace their steps. My presence of mind did not forsake me in this emergency. I signed to the two subordinates to walk on carelessly and pass them, while I myself slipped dexterously behind a tree. As they came by me, I heard "Jack" address these words to Mr. Jay:—

"Let us say half-past ten to-morrow morning. And mind you come in a cab. We had better not risk taking one in this neighbourhood."

Mr. Jay made some brief reply, which I could not overhear. They walked back to the place at which they had met, shaking hands there with an audacious cordiality which it quite sickened me to see. They then separated. I followed Mr. Jay. My subordinates paid the same delicate attention to the other two.

Instead of taking me back to Rutherford Street, Mr. Jay led me to the Strand. He stopped at a dingy, disreputable-looking house, which, according to the inscription over the door, was a newspaper office, but which, in my judgment, had all the external appearance of a place devoted to the reception of stolen goods.

After remaining inside for a few minutes, he came out, whistling, with his finger and thumb in his waistcoat pocket. A less discreet man than myself would have arrested him on the spot. I remembered the necessity of catching the two confederates, and the importance of not interfering with the appointment that had been made for the next morning. Such coolness as this, under trying circumstances, is rarely to be found, I should imagine, in a young beginner, whose reputation as a detective policeman is still to make.

From the house of suspicious appearance, Mr. Jay betook himself to a cigar-divan, and read the magazines over a cheroot. I sat at a table near him, and read the magazines likewise over a cheroot. From the divan he strolled to the tavern and had his chops. I strolled to the tavern and had my chops. When he had done, he went back to his lodging. When I had done, I went back to mine. He was overcome with drowsiness early in the evening, and went to bed. As soon as I heard him snoring, I was overcome with drowsiness, and went to bed also.

Early in the morning my two subordinates came to make their report.

They had seen the man named "Jack" leave the woman near the gate of an apparently respectable villa-residence, not far from the Regent's Park. Left to himself, he took a turning to the right, which led to a sort of suburban street, principally inhabited by shopkeepers. He stopped at the private door of one of the houses, and let himself in with his own key—looking about him as he opened the door, and staring suspiciously at my men as they lounged along on the opposite side of the way. These were all the particulars which the subordinates had to communicate. I kept them in my room to attend on me, if needful, and mounted to my peep-hole to have a look at Mr. Jay.

He was occupied in dressing himself, and was taking extraordinary pains to destroy all traces of the natural slovenliness of his appearance. This was precisely what I expected. A vagabond like Mr. Jay knows the importance of giving himself a respectable look when he is going to run the risk of changing a stolen bank-note. At five minutes past ten o'clock, he had given the last brush to his shabby hat and the last scouring with bread-crumb to his dirty gloves. At ten minutes past ten he was in the street, on his way to the nearest cab-stand, and I and my subordinates were close on his heels.

He took a cab, and we took a cab. I had not overheard them appoint a place of meeting, when following them in the Park on the previous day; but I soon found that we were proceeding in the old direction of the Avenue Road gate.

The cab in which Mr. Jay was riding turned into the Park slowly. We stopped outside, to avoid exciting suspicion. I got out to follow the cab on foot. Just as I did so, I saw it stop, and detected the two confederates approaching it from among the trees. They got in, and the cab was turned about directly. I ran back to my own cab, and told the driver to let them pass him, and then to follow as before.

The man obeyed my directions, but so clumsily as to excite their suspicions. We had been driving after them about three minutes (returning along the road by which we had advanced) when I looked out of the window to see how far they might be ahead of us. As I did this, I saw two hats popped out of the windows of their cab, and two faces looking back at me. I sank into my place in a cold sweat;—the expression is coarse, but no other form of words can describe my condition at that trying moment.

"We are found out!" I said faintly to my two subordinates. They stared at me in astonishment. My feelings changed instantly from the depth of despair to the height of indignation.

"It is the cabman's fault. Get out, one of you," I said, with dignity—"get out and punch his head."

Instead of following my directions (I should wish this act of disobedience to be reported at headquarters) they both looked out of the window. Before I could pull them back, they both sat down again. Before I could express my just indignation, they both grinned, and said to me, "Please to look out, sir!"

I did look out. The thieves' cab had stopped.

Where?

At a church door!!!

What effect this discovery might have had upon the ordinary run of men, I don't know. Being of a strong religious turn myself, it filled me with horror. I have often read of the unprincipled cunning of criminal persons; but I never before heard of three thieves attempting to double on their pursuers by entering a church! The sacrilegious audacity of that proceeding is, I should think, unparalleled in the annals of crime.

I checked my grinning subordinates by a frown. It was easy to see what was passing in their superficial minds. If I had not been able to look below the surface, I might, on observing two nicely-dressed men and one nicely-dressed woman enter a church before eleven in the morning on a week day, have come to the same hasty conclusion at which my inferiors had evidently arrived. As it was, appearances had no power to impose on *me*. I got out, and, followed by one of my men, entered the church. The other man I sent round to watch the vestry door. You may catch a weasel asleep—but not your humble servant, Matthew Sharpin!

We stole up the gallery stairs, diverged to the organ loft and peered through the curtains in front. There they were all three, sitting in a pew below—yes, incredible as it may appear, sitting in a pew below!

Before I could determine what to do, a clergyman made his appearance in full canonicals, from the vestry door, followed by a clerk. My brain whirled, and my eyesight grew dim. Dark remembrances of robberies committed in vestries floated through my mind. I trembled for the excellent man in full canonicals—I even trembled for the clerk.

The clergyman placed himself inside the altar rails. The three desperadoes approached him. He opened his book, and began to read. What?—you will ask.

I answer, without the slightest hesitation, the first lines of the Marriage Service.

My subordinate had the audacity to look at me, and then to stuff his pocket-handkerchief into his mouth. I scorned to pay any attention to him. After I had discovered that the man "Jack" was the bridegroom, and that the man Jay acted the part of father, and gave away the bride, I left the church, followed by my man, and joined the other subordinate outside the vestry door. Some people in my position would now have felt rather crestfallen, and would have begun to think that they had made a very foolish mistake. Not the faintest misgiving of any kind troubled me. I did not feel in the slightest degree depreciated in my own estimation. And even now, after a lapse of three hours, my mind remains, I am happy to say, in the same calm and hopeful condition.

As soon as I and my subordinates were assembled together outside the church, I intimated my intention of still following the other cab, in spite of what had occurred. My reason for deciding on this course will appear presently. The two subordinates were astonished at my resolution. One of them had the impertinence to say to me:—

"If you please, sir, who is it that we are after? A man who has stolen money, or a man who has stolen a wife?"

The other low person encouraged him by laughing. Both have deserved an official reprimand; and both, I sincerely trust, will be sure to get it.

When the marriage ceremony was over, the three got into their cab; and once more our vehicle (neatly hidden round the corner of the church, so that they could not suspect it to be near them) started to follow theirs.

We traced them to the terminus of the South-Western Railway. The newly-married couple took tickets for Richmond—paying their fare with a half-sovereign, and so depriving me of the pleasure of arresting them, which I should certainly have done, if they had offered a bank-note. They parted from Mr. Jay, saying, "Remember the address,—14 Babylon Terrace. You dine with us to-morrow week." Mr. Jay accepted the invitation, and added, jocosely, that he was going home at once to get off his clean clothes, and to be comfortable and dirty again for the rest of the day. I have to report that I saw him home safely, and that he is comfortable and dirty again (to use his own disgraceful language) at the present moment.

Here the affair rests, having by this time reached what I may call its first stage.

I know very well what persons of hasty judgment will be inclined to say of my proceedings thus far. They will assert that I have been deceiving myself all through, in the most absurd way; they will declare that the suspicious conversations which I have reported, referred solely to the difficulties and dangers of successfully carrying out a runaway match; and they will appeal to the scene in the church, as offering undeniable proof of the correctness of their assertions. So let it be. I dispute nothing up to this point. But I ask a question, out of the depths of my own sagacity as a man of the world, which the bitterest of my enemies will not, I think, find it particularly easy to answer.

Granted the fact of the marriage, what proof does it afford me of the innocence of the three persons concerned in that clandestine transaction? It gives me none. On the contrary, it strengthens my suspicions against Mr. Jay and his confederates, because it suggests a distinct motive for their stealing the money. A gentleman who is going to spend his honeymoon at Richmond wants money; and a gentleman who is in debt to all his tradespeople wants money. Is this an unjustifiable imputation of bad motives? In the name of outraged morality, I deny it. These men have combined together, and have stolen a woman. Why should they not combine together, and steal a cash-box? I take my stand on the logic of rigid virtue; and I defy all the sophistry of vice to move me an inch out of my position.

Speaking of virtue, I may add that I have put this view of the case to Mr. and Mrs. Yatman. That accomplished and charming woman found it difficult, at first, to follow the close chain of my reasoning. I am free to confess that she shook her head, and shed tears, and joined her husband in premature lamentation over the loss of the two hundred pounds. But a little careful explanation on my part, and a little attentive listening on hers, ultimately changed her opinion. She now agrees with me, that there is nothing in this unexpected circumstance of the clandestine marriage which absolutely tends to divert suspicion from Mr. Jay, or Mr. "Jack," or the runaway lady. "Audacious hussy" was the term my fair friend used in speaking of her, but let that pass. It is more to the purpose to record that Mrs. Yatman has not lost confidence in me and that Mr. Yatman promises to follow her example, and do his best to look hopefully for future results.

I have now, in the new turn that circumstances have taken, to await advice from your office. I pause for fresh orders with all the composure of a man who has got two strings to his bow. When I traced the three confederates from the church door to the railway terminus, I had two motives for doing so. First, I followed them as a matter of official business, believing them still to have been guilty of the robbery. Secondly, I followed them as a matter of private speculation, with a view of discovering the place of refuge to which the runaway couple intended to retreat, and of making my information a marketable commodity to offer to the young lady's family and friends. Thus, whatever happens, I may congratulate myself beforehand on not having wasted my time. If the office approves of my conduct, I have my plan ready for further proceedings. If the office blames me, I shall take myself off, with my marketable information, to the genteel villa-residence in the neighbourhood of the Regent's Park. Any way, the affair puts money into my pocket, and does credit to my penetration as an uncommonly sharp man.

I have only one word more to add, and it is this:—If any individual ventures to assert that Mr. Jay and his confederates are innocent of all share in the stealing of the cash-box, I, in return, defy that individual— though he may even be Chief Inspector Theakstone himself—to tell me who has committed the robbery at Rutherford Street, Soho.

I have the honour to be,

Your very obedient servant,

MATTHEW SHARPIN.

FROM CHIEF INSPECTOR THEAKSTONE TO SERGEANT BULMER

BIRMINGHAM, *9th July.*

SERGEANT BULMER,—

That empty-headed puppy, Mr. Matthew Sharpin, has made a mess of the case at Rutherford Street, exactly as I expected he would. Business keeps me in this town; so I write to you to set the matter straight. I enclose, with this, the pages of feeble scribble-scrabble which the creature, Sharpin, calls a report. Look them over; and when you have made your way through all the gabble, I think you will agree with me that the conceited booby has looked for the thief in every direction but the right one. You can lay your hand on the guilty person in five minutes, now. Settle the case at once; forward your report to me at this place; and tell Mr. Sharpin that he is suspended till further notice. Yours,

FRANCIS THEAKSTONE.

FROM SERGEANT BULMER TO CHIEF INSPECTOR THEAKSTONE

LONDON, *10th July.*

INSPECTOR THEAKSTONE,—

Your letter and enclosure came safe to hand. Wise men, they say, may always learn something, even from a fool. By the time I had got through Sharpin's maundering report of his own folly, I saw my way clear enough to the end of the Rutherford Street case, just as you thought I should. In half an hour's time I was at the house. The first person I saw there was Mr. Sharpin himself.

"Have you come to help me?" says he.

"Not exactly," says I. "I've come to tell you that you are suspended till further notice."

"Very good," says he, not taken down, by so much as a single peg, in his own estimation, "I thought you would be jealous of me. It's very natural; and I don't blame you. Walk in, pray, and make yourself at home. I'm off to do a little detective business on my own account, in the neighbourhood of the Regent's Park. Ta-ta, sergeant, ta-ta!"

With those words he took himself out of the way—which was exactly what I wanted him to do.

As soon as the maid-servant had shut the door, I told her to inform her master that I wanted to say a word to him in private. She showed me into the parlour behind the shop; and there was Mr. Yatman, all alone, reading the newspaper.

"About this matter of the robbery, sir," says I.

He cut me short, peevishly enough—being naturally a poor, weak, womanish sort of man. "Yes, yes, I know," says he. "You have come to tell me that your wonderfully clever man, who has bored holes in my second-floor partition, has made a mistake, and is off the scent of the scoundrel who has stolen my money."

"Yes, sir," says I. "That *is* one of the things I came to tell you. But I have got something else to say, besides that."

"Can you tell me who the thief is?" says he, more pettish than ever.

"Yes, sir," says I, "I think I can."

He put down the newspaper, and began to look rather anxious and frightened.

"Not my shopman?" says he. "I hope, for the man's own sake, it's not my shopman."

"Guess again, sir," says I.

"That idle slut, the maid?" says he.

"She is idle, sir," says I, "and she is also a slut; my first inquiries about her proved as much as that. But she's not the thief."

"Then in the name of heaven, who is?" says he.

"Will you please to prepare yourself for a very disagreeable surprise, sir?" says I. "And in case you lose your temper, will you excuse my remarking that I am the stronger man of the two, and that, if you allow yourself to lay hands on me, I may unintentionally hurt you, in pure self-defence?"

He turned as pale as ashes, and pushed his chair two or three feet away from me.

"You have asked me to tell you, sir, who has taken your money," I went on. "If you insist on my giving you an answer—"

"I do insist," he said, faintly. "Who has taken it?"

"Your wife has taken it," I said very quietly, and very positively at the same time.

He jumped out of the chair as if I had put a knife into him, and struck his fist on the table, so heavily that the wood cracked again.

"Steady, sir," says I. "Flying into a passion won't help you to the truth."

"It's a lie!" says he, with another smack of his fist on the table—"a base, vile, infamous lie! How dare you—"

He stopped, and fell back into the chair again, looked about him in a bewildered way, and ended by bursting out crying.

"When your better sense comes back to you, sir," says I, "I am sure you will be gentleman enough to make an apology for the language you have just used. In the meantime, please to listen, if you can, to a word of explanation. Mr. Sharpin has sent in a report to our inspector, of the most irregular and ridiculous kind; setting down, not only all his own foolish doings and sayings, but the doings and sayings of Mrs. Yatman as well. In most cases, such a document would have been fit for the waste-paper basket; but, in this particular case, it so happens that Mr. Sharpin's budget of nonsense leads to a certain conclusion, which the simpleton of a writer has been quite innocent of suspecting from the beginning to the end. Of that conclusion I am so sure, that I will forfeit my place, if it does not turn out that Mrs. Yatman has been practising upon the folly and conceit of this young man, and that she has tried to shield herself from discovery by purposely encouraging him to suspect the wrong persons. I tell you that confidently; and I will even go further. I will undertake to give a decided opinion as to why Mrs. Yatman took the money, and what she has done with it, or with a part of it. Nobody can look at that lady, sir, without being struck by the great taste and beauty of her dress—"

As I said those last words, the poor man seemed to find his powers of speech again. He cut me short directly, as haughtily as if he had been a duke instead of a stationer.

"Try some other means of justifying your vile calumny against my wife," says he. "Her milliner's bill for the past year, is on my file of receipted accounts at this moment."

"Excuse me, sir," says I, "but that proves nothing. Milliners, I must tell you, have a certain rascally custom which comes within the daily experience of our office. A married lady who wishes it, can keep two accounts at her dressmaker's; one is the account which her husband sees and pays; the other is the private account, which contains all the extravagant items, and which the wife pays secretly, by instalments, whenever she can. According to our usual experience, these instalments are mostly squeezed out of the housekeeping money. In your case, I suspect no instalments have been paid; proceedings have been threatened; Mrs. Yatman, knowing your altered circumstances, has felt herself driven into a corner; and she has paid her private account out of your cash-box."

"I won't believe it," says he. "Every word you speak is an abominable insult to me and to my wife."

"Are you man enough, sir," says I, taking him up short, in order to
save time and words, "to get that receipted bill you spoke of just now
off the file, and come with me at once to the milliner's shop where
Mrs. Yatman deals?"

He turned red in the face at that, got the bill directly, and put on
his hat. I took out of my pocket-book the list containing the numbers
of the lost notes, and we left the house together immediately.

Arrived at the milliner's (one of the expensive West-end houses,
as I expected), I asked for a private interview, on important business,
with the mistress of the concern. It was not the first time that she and
I had met over the same delicate investigation. The moment she set
eyes on me, she sent for her husband. I mentioned who Mr. Yatman
was, and what we wanted.

"This is strictly private?" inquires her husband. I nodded my head.

"And confidential?" says the wife. I nodded again.

"Do you see any objection, dear, to obliging the sergeant with a
sight of the books?" says the husband.

"None in the world, love, if you approve of it," says the wife.

All this while poor Mr. Yatman sat looking the picture of astonishment and distress, quite out of place at our polite conference. The books were brought—and one minute's look at the pages
in which Mrs. Yatman's name figured was enough, and more than
enough, to prove the truth of every word I had spoken.

There, in one book, was the husband's account, which Mr. Yatman
had settled. And there, in the other, was the private account, crossed
off also; the date of settlement being the very day after the loss of
the cash-box. This said private account amounted to the sum of a
hundred and seventy-five pounds, odd shillings; and it extended over
a period of three years. Not a single instalment had been paid on it.

Under the last line was an entry to this effect: "Written to for the third time, June 23rd." I pointed to it, and asked the milliner if that meant "last June." Yes, it did mean last June; and she now deeply regretted to say that it had been accompanied by a threat of legal proceedings.

"I thought you gave good customers more than three years' credit?" says I.

The milliner looks at Mr. Yatman, and whispers to me—"Not when a lady's husband gets into difficulties."

She pointed to the account as she spoke. The entries after the time when Mr. Yatman's circumstances became involved were just as extravagant, for a person in his wife's situation, as the entries for the year before that period. If the lady had economised in other things, she had certainly not economised in the matter of dress.

There was nothing left now but to examine the cash-book, for form's sake. The money had been paid in notes, the amounts and numbers of which exactly tallied with the figures set down in my list.

After that, I thought it best to get Mr. Yatman out of the house immediately. He was in such a pitiable condition, that I called a cab and accompanied him home in it. At first he cried and raved like a child: but I soon quieted him—and I must add, to his credit, that he made me a most handsome apology for his language, as the cab drew up at his house door. In return, I tried to give him some advice about how to set matters right, for the future, with his wife. He paid very little attention to me, and went upstairs muttering to himself about a separation. Whether Mrs. Yatman will come cleverly out of the scrape or not, seems doubtful. I should say, myself, that she will go into screeching hysterics, and so frighten the poor man into forgiving her. But this is no business of ours. So far as we are concerned, the case is now at an end; and the present report may come to a conclusion along with it.

I remain, accordingly, yours to command,

THOMAS BULMER.

P.S.—I have to add, that, on leaving Rutherford Street, I met Mr. Matthew Sharpin coming to pack up his things.

"Only think!" says he, rubbing his hands in great spirits, "I've been to the genteel villa-residence; and the moment I mentioned my business, they kicked me out directly. There were two witnesses of the assault; and it's worth a hundred pounds to me, if it's worth a farthing."

"I wish you joy of your luck," says I.

"Thank you," says he. "When may I pay you the same compliment on finding the thief?"

"Whenever you like," says I, "for the thief is found."

"Just what I expected," says he. "I've done all the work; and now you cut in, and claim all the credit—Mr. Jay of course?"

"No," says I.

"Who is it then?" says he.

"Ask Mrs. Yatman," says I. "She's waiting to tell you."

"All right! I'd much rather hear it from that charming woman than from you," says he, and goes into the house in a mighty hurry.

What do you think of that, Inspector Theakstone? Would you like to stand in Mr. Sharpin's shoes? I shouldn't, I can promise you!

FROM CHIEF INSPECTOR THEAKSTONE TO MR. MATTHEW SHARPIN

12th July.

SIR,—

Sergeant Bulmer has already told you to consider yourself suspended until further notice. I have now authority to add, that your services as a member of the Detective Police are positively declined. You will please to take this letter as notifying officially your dismissal from the force.

I may inform you, privately, that your rejection is not intended to cast any reflections on your character. It merely implies that you are not quite sharp enough for our purpose. If we are to have a new recruit among us, we should infinitely prefer Mrs. Yatman.

Your obedient servant,

FRANCIS THEAKSTONE.

NOTE ON THE PRECEDING CORRESPONDENCE, ADDED BY MR. THEAKSTONE

The Inspector is not in a position to append any explanations of importance to the last of the letters. It has been discovered that Mr. Matthew Sharpin left the house in Rutherford Street five minutes after his interview outside of it with Sergeant Bulmer—his manner expressing the liveliest emotions of terror and astonishment, and his left cheek displaying a bright patch of red, which might have been the result of a slap on the face from a female hand. He was also heard, by the shopman at Rutherford Street, to use a very shocking expression in reference to Mrs. Yatman; and was seen to clench his fist vindictively, as he ran round the corner of the street. Nothing more has been heard of him; and it is conjectured that he has left London with the intention of offering his valuable services to the provincial police.

On the interesting domestic subject of Mr. and Mrs. Yatman still less is known. It has, however, been positively ascertained that the medical attendant of the family was sent for in a great hurry, on the day when Mr. Yatman returned from the milliner's shop. The neighbouring chemist received, soon afterwards, a prescription of a soothing nature to make up for Mrs. Yatman. The day after, Mr. Yatman purchased some smelling-salts at the shop, and afterwards appeared at the circulating library to ask for a novel, descriptive of high life, that would amuse an invalid lady. It has been inferred from these circumstances that he has not thought it desirable to carry out his threat of separating himself from his wife—at least in the present (presumed) condition of that lady's sensitive nervous system.

THE MYSTERY OF THE SLEEPING-CAR EXPRESS

FREEMAN WILLS CROFTS

No one who was in England in the autumn of 1909 can fail to remember the terrible tragedy which took place in a Northwestern express between Preston and Carlisle. The affair attracted enormous attention at the time, not only because of the arresting nature of the events themselves, but even more for the absolute mystery in which they were shrouded.

Quite lately a singular chance has revealed to me the true explanation of the terrible drama, and it is at the express desire of its chief actor that I now take upon myself to make the facts known. As it is a long time since 1909, I may, perhaps, be pardoned if I first recall the events which came to light at the time.

One Thursday, then, early in November of the year in question, the 10:30 p.m. sleeping-car train left Euston as usual for Edinburgh, Glasgow, and the North. It was generally a heavy train, being popular with business men who liked to complete their day's work in London, sleep while travelling, and arrive at their northern destination with time for a leisurely bath and breakfast before office hours. The night in question was no exception to the rule, and two engines hauled behind them eight large sleeping-cars, two firsts, two thirds, and two vans, half of which went to Glasgow, and the remainder to Edinburgh.

It is essential to the understanding of what follows that the composition of the rear portion of the train should be remembered. At the extreme end came the Glasgow van, a long, eight-wheeled, bogie vehicle, with Guard Jones in charge. Next to the van was one of the third-class coaches, and immediately in front of it came a first-class, both labelled for the same city. These coaches were fairly well filled, particularly the third-class. In front of the first-class came the last of the four Glasgow sleepers. The train was corridor throughout, and the officials could, and did, pass through it several times during the journey.

It is with the first-class coach that we are principally concerned, and it will be understood from the above that it was placed in between the sleeping-car in front and the third-class behind, the van following immediately behind the third. It had a lavatory at each end and six compartments, the last two, next the third-class, being smokers, the next three non-smoking, and the first, immediately beside the sleeping car, a "Ladies Only." The corridors in both it and the third-class coach were on the left-hand side in the direction of travel—that is, the compartments were on the side of the double line.

The night was dark as the train drew out of Euston, for there was no moon and the sky was overcast. As was remembered and commented on afterwards, there had been an unusually long spell of dry weather, and, though it looked like rain earlier in the evening, none fell till the next day, when, about six in the morning, there was a torrential downpour.

As the detectives pointed out later, no weather could have been more unfortunate from their point of view, as, had footmarks been made during the night, the ground would have been too hard to take good impressions, while even such traces as remained would more than likely have been blurred by the rain.

The train ran to time, stopping at Rugby, Crewe and Preston. After leaving the latter station Guard Jones found he had occasion to go forward to speak to a ticket-collector in the Edinburgh portion. He accordingly left his van in the rear and passed along the corridor of the third-class carriage adjoining.

At the end of this corridor, beside the vestibule joining it to the first class, were a lady and gentleman, evidently husband and wife, the lady endeavouring to soothe the cries of a baby she was carrying. Guard Jones addressed some civil remark to the man, who explained that their child had been taken ill, and they had brought it out of their compartment as it was disturbing the other passengers.

With an expression of sympathy, Jones unlocked the two doors across the corridor at the vestibule between the carriages, and, passing on into the first-class coach, re-closed them behind him. They were fitted with spring locks, which became fast on the door shutting.

The corridor of the first-class coach was empty, and as Jones walked down it he observed that the blinds of all the compartments were lowered, with one exception—that of the "Ladies Only." In this compartment, which contained three ladies, the light was fully on, and the guard noticed that two out of the three were reading.

Continuing his journey, Jones found that the two doors at the vestibule between the first-class coach and the sleeper were also locked, and he opened them and passed through, shutting them behind him. At the sleeping-car attendant's box, just inside the last of these doors, two car attendants were talking together. One was actually inside the box, the other standing in the corridor. The latter moved aside to let the guard pass, taking up his former position as, after exchanging a few words, Jones moved on.

His business with the ticket-collector finished, Guard Jones returned to his van. On this journey he found the same conditions obtaining as on the previous—the two attendants were at the rear end of the sleeping-car, the lady and gentleman with the baby in the front end of the third-class coach, the first-class corridor deserted, and both doors at each end of the latter coach locked. These details, casually remarked at the time, became afterwards of the utmost importance, adding as they did to the mystery in which the tragedy was enveloped.

About an hour before the train was due at Carlisle, while it was passing through the wild moorland country of the Westmorland highlands, the brakes were applied—at first gently, and then with considerable power. Guard Jones, who was examining parcel waybills in the rear end of his van, supposed it to be a signal check, but as such was unusual at this place, he left his work and, walking down the van, lowered the window at the left-hand side and looked out along the train.

The line happened to be in a cutting, and the railway bank for some distance ahead was dimly illuminated by the light from the corridors of the first and third-class coaches immediately in front of his van. As I have said, the night was dark, and, except for this bit of bank, Jones could see nothing ahead. The railway curved away to the right, so, thinking he might see better from the other side, he crossed the van and looked out of the opposite window, next the up line.

There were no signal lights in view, nor anything to suggest the cause of the slack, but as he ran his eye along the train he saw that something was amiss in the first-class coach. From the window at its rear end figures were leaning, gesticulating wildly, as if to attract attention to some grave and pressing danger. The guard at once ran through the third-class to this coach, and there he found a strange and puzzling state of affairs. The corridor was still empty, but the centre blind of the rear compartment—that is, the first reached by the guard—had been raised. Through the glass Jones could see that the compartment contained four men. Two were leaning out of the window on the opposite side, and two were fumbling at the latch of the corridor door, as if trying to open it. Jones caught hold of the outside handle to assist, but they pointed in the direction of the adjoining compartment, and the guard, obeying their signs, moved on to the second door.

The centre blind of this compartment had also been pulled up, though here, again, the door had not been opened. As the guard peered in through the glass he saw that he was in the presence of a tragedy.

Tugging desperately at the handle of the corridor door stood a lady, her face blanched, her eyes starting from her head, and her features frozen into an expression of deadly fear and horror. As she pulled she kept glancing over her shoulder, as if some dreadful apparition lurked in the shadows behind. As Jones sprang forward to open the door his eyes followed the direction of her gaze, and he drew in his breath sharply.

At the far side of the compartment, facing the engine and huddled down in the corner, was the body of a woman. She lay limp and inert, with head tilted back at an unnatural angle into the cushions and a hand hanging helplessly down over the edge of the seat. She might have been thirty years of age, and was dressed in a reddish-brown fur coat with toque to match. But these details the guard hardly glanced at, his attention being riveted to her forehead. There, above the left eyebrow, was a sinister little hole, from which the blood had oozed down the coat and formed a tiny pool on the seat. That she was dead was obvious.

But this was not all. On the seat opposite her lay a man, and, as far as Guard Jones could see, he also was dead.

He apparently had been sitting in the corner seat, and had fallen forward so that his chest lay across the knees of the woman and his head hung down towards the floor. He was all bunched and twisted up—just a shapeless mass in a grey frieze overcoat, with dark hair at the back of what could be seen of his head. But under that head the guard caught the glint of falling drops, while a dark, ominous stain grew on the floor beneath.

Jones flung himself on the door, but it would not move. It stood fixed, an inch open, jammed in some mysterious way, imprisoning the lady with her terrible companions. As she and the guard strove to force it open, the train came to a standstill. At once it occurred to Jones that he could now enter the compartment from the opposite side.

Shouting to reassure the now almost frantic lady, he turned to the end compartment, intending to pass through it on to the line and so back to that containing the bodies. But here he was again baffled, for the two men had not succeeded in sliding back their door. He seized the handle to help them, and then he noticed their companions had opened the opposite door and were climbing out on to the permanent way.

It flashed through his mind that an up-train passed about this time, and, fearing an accident, he ran down the corridor to the sleeping-car, where he felt sure he would find a door that would open. That at the near end was free, and he leaped out on to the track. As he passed he shouted to one of the attendants to follow him, and to the other to remain where he was and let no one pass. Then he joined the men who had already alighted, warned them about the up-train, and the four opened the outside door of the compartment in which the tragedy had taken place.

Their first concern was to get the uninjured lady out, and here a difficult and ghastly task awaited them. The door was blocked by the bodies, and its narrowness prevented more than one man from working. Sending the car attendant to search the train for a doctor, Jones clambered up, and, after warning the lady not to look at what he was doing, he raised the man's body and propped it back in the corner seat.

The face was a strong one with clean-shaven but rather coarse features, a large nose, and a heavy jaw. In the neck, just below the right ear, was a bullet hole which, owing to the position of the head, had bled freely. As far as the guard could see, the man was dead. Not without a certain shrinking, Jones raised the feet, first of the man, and then of the woman, and placed them on the seats, thus leaving the floor clear except for its dark, creeping pool. Then, placing his handkerchief over the dead woman's face, he rolled back the end of the carpet to hide its sinister stain.

"Now, ma'am, if you please," he said; and keeping the lady with her back to the more gruesome object on the opposite seat, he helped her to the open door, from where willing hands assisted her to the ground.

By this time the attendant had found a doctor in the third-class coach, and a brief examination enabled him to pronounce both victims dead. The blinds in the compartment having been drawn down and the outside door locked, the guard called to those passengers who had alighted to resume their seats, with a view to continuing their journey.

The fireman had meantime come back along the train to ascertain what was wrong, and to say the driver was unable completely to release the brake. An examination was therefore made, and the tell-tale disc at the end of the first-class coach was found to be turned, showing that someone in that carriage had pulled the communication chain. This, as is perhaps not generally known, allows air to pass between the train pipe and the atmosphere, thereby gently applying the brake and preventing its complete release. Further investigation showed that the slack of the chain was hanging in the end smoking-compartment, indicating that the alarm must have been operated by one of the four men who travelled there. The disc was then turned back to normal, the passengers reseated, and the train started, after a delay of about fifteen minutes.

Before reaching Carlisle, Guard Jones took the name and address of everyone travelling in the first and third-class coaches, together with the numbers of their tickets. These coaches, as well as the van, were thoroughly searched, and it was established beyond any doubt that no one was concealed under the seats, in the lavatories, behind luggage, or, in fact, anywhere about them.

One of the sleeping-car attendants having been in the corridor in the rear of the last sleeper from the Preston stop till the completion of the search, and being positive no one except the guard had passed during that time, it was not considered necessary to take the names of the passengers in the sleeping-cars, but the numbers of their tickets were noted.

On arrival at Carlisle the matter was put into the hands of the police. The first-class carriage was shunted off, the doors being locked and sealed, and the passengers who had travelled in it were detained to make their statements. Then began a most careful and searching investigation, as a result of which several additional facts became known.

The first step taken by the authorities was to make an examination of the country surrounding the point at which the train had stopped, in the hope of finding traces of some stranger on the line.

The tentative theory was that a murder had been committed and that the murderer had escaped from the train when it stopped, struck across the country, and, gaining some road, had made good his escape.

Accordingly, as soon as it was light, a special train brought a force of detectives to the place, and the railway, as well as a tract of ground on each side of it, were subjected to a prolonged and exhaustive search. But no traces were found. Nothing that a stranger might have dropped was picked up, no footsteps were seen, no marks discovered. As has already been stated, the weather was against the searchers. The drought of the previous days had left the ground hard and unyielding, so that clear impressions were scarcely to be expected, while even such as might have been made were not likely to remain after the downpour of the early morning.

Baffled at this point, the detectives turned their attention to the stations in the vicinity. There were only two within walking distance of the point of the tragedy, and at neither had any stranger been seen. Further, no trains had stopped at either of these stations; indeed, not a single train, either passenger or goods, had stopped anywhere in the neighbourhood since the sleeping-car express went through. If the murderer had left the express, it was, therefore, out of the question that he could have escaped by rail.

The investigators then turned their attention to the country roads and adjoining towns, trying to find the trail—if there was a trail—while it was hot. But here, again, no luck attended their efforts. If there were a murderer, and if he had left the train when it stopped, he had vanished into thin air. No traces of him could anywhere be discovered.

Nor were their researches in other directions much more fruitful.

The dead couple were identified as a Mr. and Mrs. Horatio Llewelyn, of Gordon Villa, Broad Road, Halifax. Mr. Llewelyn was the junior partner of a large firm of Yorkshire ironfounders. A man of five-and-thirty, he moved in good society and had some claim to wealth. He was of kindly though somewhat passionate disposition, and, so far as could be learnt, had not an enemy in the world. His firm was able to show that he had had business appointments in London on the Thursday and in Carlisle on the Friday, so that his travelling by the train in question was quite in accordance with his known plans.

His wife was the daughter of a neighbouring merchant, a pretty girl of some seven-and-twenty. They had been married only a little over a month, and had, in fact, only a week earlier returned from their honeymoon. Whether Mrs. Llewelyn had any definite reason for accompanying her husband on the fatal journey could not be ascertained. She also, so far as was known, had no enemy, nor could any motive for the tragedy be suggested.

The extraction of the bullets proved that the same weapon had been used in each case—a revolver of small bore and modern design. But as many thousands of similar revolvers existed, this discovery led to nothing.

Miss Blair-Booth, the lady who had travelled with the Llewelyns, stated she had joined the train at Euston, and occupied one of the seats next the corridor. A couple of minutes before starting the deceased had arrived, and they sat in the two opposite corners. No other passengers had entered the compartment during the journey, nor had any of the three left it; in fact, except for the single visit of the ticket-collector shortly after leaving Euston, the door into the corridor had not been even opened.

Mr. Llewelyn was very attentive to his young wife, and they had conversed for some time after starting, then, after consulting Miss Blair-Booth, he had pulled down the blinds and shaded the light, and they had settled down for the night. Miss Blair-Booth had slept at intervals, but each time she wakened she had looked round the compartment, and everything was as before. Then she was suddenly aroused from a doze by a loud explosion close by.

She sprang up, and as she did so a flash came from somewhere near her knee, and a second explosion sounded. Startled and trembling, she pulled the shade off the lamp, and then she noticed a little cloud of smoke just inside the corridor door, which had been opened about an inch, and smelled the characteristic odour of burnt powder. Swinging round, she was in time to see Mr. Llewelyn dropping heavily forward across his wife's knees, and then she observed the mark on the latter's forehead and realized they had both been shot.

Terrified, she raised the blind of the corridor door which covered the handle and tried to get out to call assistance. But she could not move the door, and her horror was not diminished when she found herself locked in with what she rightly believed were two dead bodies. In despair she pulled the communication chain, but the train did not appear to stop, and she continued struggling with the door till, after what seemed to her hours, the guard appeared, and she was eventually released.

In answer to a question, she further stated that when her blind went up the corridor was empty, and she saw no one till the guard came.

The four men in the end compartment were members of one party travelling from London to Glasgow. For some time after leaving they had played cards, but, about midnight, they, too, had pulled down their blinds, shaded their lamp, and composed themselves to sleep. In this case also, no person other than the ticket-collector had entered the compartment during the journey. But after leaving Preston the door had been opened. Aroused by the stop, one of the men had eaten some fruit, and having thereby soiled his fingers, had washed them in the lavatory. The door then opened as usual. This man saw no one in the corridor, nor did he notice anything out of the common.

Some time after this all four were startled by the sound of two shots. At first they thought of fog signals, then, realising they were too far from the engine to hear such, they, like Miss Blair-Booth, unshaded their lamp, raised the blind over their corridor door, and endeavoured to leave the compartment. Like her they found themselves unable to open their door, and, like her also, they saw that there was no one in the corridor. Believing something serious had happened, they pulled the communication chain, at the same time lowering the outside window and waving from it in the hope of attracting attention. The chain came down easily as if slack, and this explained the apparent contradiction between Miss Blair-Booth's statement that she had pulled it, and the fact that the slack was found hanging in the end compartment. Evidently the lady had pulled it first, applying the brake, and the second pull had simply transferred the slack from one compartment to the next.

The two compartments in front of that of the tragedy were found to be empty when the train stopped, but in the last of the non-smoking compartments were two gentlemen, and in the "Ladies Only," three ladies. All these had heard the shots, but so faintly above the noise of the train that the attention of none of them was specially arrested, nor had they attempted any investigation. The gentlemen had not left their compartment or pulled up their blinds between the time the train left Preston and the emergency stop, and could throw no light whatever on the matter.

The three ladies in the end compartment were a mother and two daughters, and had got in at Preston. As they were alighting at Carlisle they had not wished to sleep, so they had left their blinds up and their light unshaded. Two of them were reading, but the third was seated at the corridor side, and this lady stated positively that no one except the guard had passed while they were in the train.

She described his movements—first, towards the engine, secondly, back towards the van, and a third time, running, towards the engine after the train had stopped—so accurately in accord with the other evidence that considerable reliance was placed on her testimony. The stoppage and the guard's haste had aroused her interest, and all three ladies had immediately come out into the corridor, and had remained there till the train proceeded, and all three were satisfied that no one else had passed during that time.

An examination of the doors which had jammed so mysteriously revealed the fact that a small wooden wedge, evidently designed for the purpose, had been driven in between the floor and the bottom of the framing of the door, holding the latter rigid. It was evident therefore that the crime was premeditated, and the details had been carefully worked out beforehand. The most careful search of the carriage failed to reveal any other suspicious object or mark.

On comparing the tickets issued with those held by the passengers, a discrepancy was discovered. All were accounted for except one. A first single for Glasgow had been issued at Euston for the train in question, which had not been collected. The purchaser had therefore either not travelled at all, or had got out at some intermediate station. In either case no demand for a refund had been made.

The collector who had checked the tickets after the train left London believed, though he could not speak positively, that two men had then occupied the non-smoking compartment next to that in which the tragedy had occurred, one of whom held a Glasgow ticket, and the other a ticket for an intermediate station. He could not recollect which station nor could he describe either of the men, if indeed they were there at all.

But the ticket collector's recollection was not at fault, for the police succeeded in tracing one of these passengers, a Dr. Hill, who had got out at Crewe. He was able, partially at all events, to account for the missing Glasgow ticket. It appeared that when he joined the train at Euston, a man of about five and thirty was already in the compartment. This man had fair hair, blue eyes, and a full moustache, and was dressed in dark, well-cut clothes. He had no luggage, but only a waterproof and a paper-covered novel. The two travellers had got into conversation, and on the stranger learning that the doctor lived at Crewe, said he was alighting there also, and asked to be recommended to an hotel. He then explained that he had intended to go on to Glasgow and had taken a ticket to that city, but had since decided to break his journey to visit a friend in Chester next day. He asked the doctor if he thought his ticket would be available to complete the journey the following night, and if not, whether he could get a refund.

When they reached Crewe, both these travellers had alighted, and the doctor offered to show his acquaintance the entrance to the Crewe Arms, but the stranger, thanking him, declined, saying he wished to see to his luggage. Dr. Hill saw him walking towards the van as he left the platform.

Upon interrogating the staff on duty at Crewe at the time, no one could recall seeing such a man at the van, nor had any inquiries about luggage been made. But as these facts did not come to light until several days after the tragedy, confirmation was hardly to be expected.

A visit to all the hotels in Crewe and Chester revealed the fact that no one in any way resembling the stranger had stayed there, nor could any trace whatever be found of him.

Such were the principal facts made known at the adjourned inquest on the bodies of Mr. and Mrs. Llewelyn. It was confidently believed that a solution to the mystery would speedily be found, but as day after day passed away without bringing to light any fresh information, public interest began to wane, and became directed into other channels.

But for a time controversy over the affair waxed keen. At first it was argued that it was a case of suicide, some holding that Mr. Llewelyn had shot first his wife and then himself; others that both had died by the wife's hand. But this theory had only to be stated to be disproved.

Several persons hastened to point out that not only had the revolver disappeared, but on neither body was there powder blackening, and it was admitted that such a wound could not be self-inflicted without leaving marks from this source. That murder had been committed was therefore clear.

Rebutted on this point, the theorists then argued that Miss Blair–Booth was the assassin. But here again the suggestion was quickly negatived. The absence of motive, her known character and the truth of such of her statements as could be checked were against the idea. The disappearance of the revolver was also in her favour. As it was not in the compartment nor concealed about her person, she could only have rid herself of it out of the window. But the position of the bodies prevented access to the window, and, as her clothes were free from any stain of blood, it was impossible to believe she had moved these grim relics, even had she been physically able.

But the point that finally demonstrated her innocence was the wedging of the corridor door. It was obvious she could not have wedged the door on the outside and then passed through it. The belief was universal that whoever wedged the door fired the shots, and the fact that the former was wedged an inch open strengthened that view, as the motive was clearly to leave a slot through which to shoot.

Lastly, the medical evidence showed that if the Llewelyns were sitting where Miss Blair-Booth stated, and the shots were fired from where she said, the bullets would have entered the bodies from the direction they were actually found to have done.

But Miss Blair-Booth's detractors were loath to recede from the position they had taken up. They stated that of the objections to their theory only one—the wedging of the doors—was overwhelming. And they advanced an ingenious theory to meet it.

They suggested that before reaching Preston Miss Blair-Booth had left the compartment, closing the door after her, that she had then wedged it, and that, on stopping at the station, she had passed out through some other compartment, re-entering her own through the outside door.

In answer to this it was pointed out that the gentleman who had eaten the fruit had opened his door after the Preston stop, and if Miss Blair-Booth was then shut into her compartment she could not have wedged the other door. That two people should be concerned in the wedging was unthinkable. It was therefore clear that Miss Blair-Booth was innocent, and that some other person had wedged both doors, in order to prevent his operations in the corridor being interfered with by those who would hear the shots.

It was recognised that similar arguments applied to the four men in the end compartment—the wedging of the doors cleared them also.

Defeated on these points the theorists retired from the field. No further suggestions were put forward by the public or the daily Press. Even to those behind the scenes the case seemed to become more and more difficult the longer it was pondered.

Each person known to have been present came in turn under the microscopic eye of New Scotland Yard, but each in turn had to be eliminated from suspicion, till it almost seemed proved that no murder could have been committed at all. The prevailing mystification was well summed up by the chief at the Yard in conversation with the inspector in charge of the case.

"A troublesome business, certainly," said the great man, "and I admit that your conclusions seem sound. But let us go over it again. There must be a flaw somewhere."

"There must, sir. But I've gone over it and over it till I'm stupid, and every time I get the same result."

"We'll try once more. We begin, then, with a murder in a railway carriage. We're sure it was a murder, of course?"

"Certain, sir. The absence of the revolver and of powder blackening and the wedging of the doors prove it."

"Quite. The murder must therefore have been committed by some person who was either in the carriage when it was searched, or had left before that. Let us take these two possibilities in turn. And first, with regard to the searching. Was that efficiently done?"

"Absolutely, sir. I have gone into it with the guard and attendants. No one could have been overlooked."

"Very good. Taking first, then, those who were in the carriage, There were six compartments. In the first were the four men, and in the second Miss Blair-Booth. Are you satisfied these were innocent?"

"Perfectly, sir. The wedging of the doors eliminated them."

"So I think. The third and fourth compartments were empty, but in the fifth there were two gentlemen. What about them?"

"Well, sir, you know who they were. Sir Gordon M'Clean, the great engineer, and Mr. Silas Hemphill, the professor of Aberdeen University. Both utterly beyond suspicion."

"But, as you know, inspector, no one is beyond suspicion in a case of this kind."

"I admit it, sir, and therefore I made careful inquiries about them. But I only confirmed my opinion."

"From inquiries I also have made I feel sure you are right. That brings us to the last compartment, the 'Ladies Only.' What about those three ladies?"

"The same remarks apply. Their characters are also beyond suspicion, and, as well as that, the mother is elderly and timid, and couldn't brazen out a lie. I question if the daughters could either.

I made inquiries all the same, and found not the slightest ground for suspicion."

"The corridors and lavatories were empty?"

"Yes, sir."

"Then everyone found in the coach when the train stopped may be definitely eliminated?"

"Yes. It is quite impossible it could have been any that we have mentioned."

"Then the murderer must have left the coach?"

"He must; and that's where the difficulty comes in."

"I know, but let us proceed. Our problem then really becomes—how did he leave the coach?"

"That's so, sir, and I have never been against anything stiffer."

The chief paused in thought, as he absently selected and lit another cigar. At last he continued:

"Well, at any rate, it is clear he did not go through the roof or the floor, or any part of the fixed framing or sides. Therefore he must have gone in the usual way—through a door. Of these, there is one at each end and six at each side. He therefore went through one of these fourteen doors. Are you agreed, inspector?"

"Certainly, sir."

"Very good. Take the ends first. The vestibule doors were locked?"

"Yes, sir, at both ends of the coach. But I don't count that much. An ordinary carriage key opened them and the murderer would have had one."

"Quite. Now, just go over again our reasons for thinking he did not escape to the sleeper."

"Before the train stopped, sir. Miss Bintley, one of the three in the 'Ladies Only,' was looking out into the corridor, and the two sleeper attendants were at the near end of their coach. After the train stopped, all three ladies were in the corridor, and one attendant was at the sleeper vestibule. All these persons swear most positively that no one but the guard passed between Preston and the searching of the carriage."

"What about these attendants? Are they reliable?"

"Wilcox has seventeen years' service, and Jeffries six, and both bear excellent characters. Both, naturally, came under suspicion of the murder, and I made the usual investigation. But there is not a scrap of evidence against them, and I am satisfied they are all right."

"It certainly looks as if the murderer did not escape towards the sleeper."

"I am positive of it. You see, sir, we have the testimony of two separate lots of witnesses, the ladies and the attendants. It is out of the question that these parties would agree to deceive the police. Conceivably one or other might, but not both."

"Yes, that seems sound. What, then, about the other end—the third-class end?"

"At that end," replied the inspector, "were Mr. and Mrs. Smith with their sick child. They were in the corridor close by the vestibule door, and no one could have passed without their knowledge. I had the child examined, and its illness was genuine. The parents are quiet persons, of exemplary character, and again quite beyond suspicion. When they said no one but the guard had passed I believed them. However, I was not satisfied with that, and I examined every person that travelled in the third-class coach, and established two things: first, that no one was in it at the time it was searched who had not travelled in it from Preston; and secondly, that no one except the Smiths had left any of the compartments during the run between Preston and the emergency stop. That proves beyond question that no one left the first-class coach for the third after the tragedy."

"What about the guard himself?"

"The guard is also a man of good character, but he is out of it, because he was seen by several passengers as well as the Smiths running through the third-class after the brakes were applied."

"It is clear, then, the murderer must have got out through one of the twelve side doors. Take those on the compartment side first. The first, second, fifth and sixth compartments were occupied, therefore he could not have passed through them. That leaves the third and fourth doors. Could he have left by either of these?"

The inspector shook his head.

"No, sir," he answered, "that is equally out of the question. You will recollect that two of the four men in the end compartment were looking out along the train from a few seconds after the murder until the stop. It would not have been possible to open a door and climb out on to the footboard without being seen by them. Guard Jones also looked out at that side of the van and saw no one. After the stop these same two men, as well as others, were on the ground, and all agree that none of these doors were opened at any time."

"H'm," mused the chief, "that also seems conclusive, and it brings us definitely to the doors on the corridor side. As the guard arrived on the scene comparatively early, the murderer must have got out while the train was running at a fair speed. He must therefore have been clinging on to the outside of the coach while the guard was in the corridor working at the sliding doors. When the train stopped all attention was concentrated on the opposite, or compartment, side, and he could easily have dropped down and made off. What do you think of that theory, inspector?"

"We went into that pretty thoroughly, sir. It was first objected that the blinds of the first and second compartments were raised too soon to give him time to get out without being seen. But I found this was not valid. At least fifteen seconds must have elapsed before Miss Blair-Booth and the men in the end compartment raised their blinds, and that would easily have allowed him to lower the window, open the door, pass out, raise the window, shut the door, and crouch down on the footboard out of sight. I estimate also that nearly thirty seconds passed before Guard Jones looked out of the van at that side. As far as time goes he could have done what you suggest. But another thing shows he didn't. It appears that when Jones ran through the third-class coach, while the train was stopping, Mr. Smith, the man with the sick child, wondering what was wrong, attempted to follow him into the first-class. But the door slammed after the guard before the other could reach it, and, of course, the spring lock held it fast. Mr. Smith therefore lowered the end corridor window and looked out ahead, and he states positively no one was on the footboard of the first-class. To see how far Mr. Smith could be sure of this, on a dark night we ran the same carriage, lighted in the same way, over the same part of the line, and we found a figure crouching on the footboard was clearly visible from the window. It showed a dark mass against the lighted side of the cutting. When we remember that Mr. Smith was specially looking out for something abnormal, I think we may accept his evidence."

"You are right. It is convincing. And, of course, it is supported by the guard's own testimony. He also saw no one when he looked out of his van."

"That is so, sir. And we found a crouching figure was visible from the van also, owing to the same cause—the lighted bank."

"And the murderer could not have got out while the guard was passing through the third-class?"

"No, because the corridor blinds were raised before the guard looked out."

The chief frowned.

"It is certainly puzzling," he mused. There was silence for some moments, and then he spoke again.

"Could the murderer, immediately after firing the shots, have concealed himself in a lavatory and then, during the excitement of the stop, have slipped out unperceived through one of these corridor doors and, dropping on the line, moved quietly away?"

"No, sir, we went into that also. If he had hidden in a lavatory he could not have got out again. If he had gone towards the third-class the Smiths would have seen him, and the first-class corridor was under observation during the entire time from the arrival of the guard till the search. We have proved the ladies entered the corridor immediately the guard passed their compartment, and two of the four men in the end smoker were watching through their door till considerably after the ladies had come out."

Again silence reigned while the chief smoked thoughtfully.

"The coroner had some theory, you say?" he said at last.

"Yes, sir. He suggested the murderer might have, immediately after firing, got out by one of the doors on the corridor side—probably the end one—and from there climbed on the outside of the coach to some place from which he could not be seen from a window, dropping to the ground when the train stopped. He suggested the roof, the buffers, or the lower step. This seemed likely at first sight, and I tried therefore the experiment. But it was no good. The roof was out of the question. It was one of those high curved roofs—not a flat clerestory—and there was no handhold at the edge above the doors. The buffers were equally inaccessible. From die handle and guard of the end door to that above the buffer on the corner of the coach was seven feet two inches. That is to say, a man could not reach from one to the other, and there was nothing he could hold on to while passing along the step. The lower step was not possible either. In the first place it was divided—there was only a short step beneath each door—not a continuous board like the upper one—so that no one could pass along the lower while holding on to the upper, and secondly, I couldn't imagine anyone climbing down there, and knowing that the first platform they came to would sweep him off."

"That is to say, inspector, you have proved the murderer was in the coach at the time of the crime, that he was not in it when it was searched, and that he did not leave it in the interval. I don't know if that that is a very creditable conclusion."

"I know, sir. I regret it extremely, but that's the difficulty I have been up against from the start."

The chief laid his hand on his subordinate's shoulder.

"It won't do," he said kindly. "It really won't do. You try again. Smoke over it, and I'll do the same, and come in and see me again to-morrow."

But the conversation had really summed up the case justly. My Lady Nicotine brought no inspiration, and, as time passed without bringing to light any further facts, interest gradually waned till at last the affair took its place among the long list of unexplained crimes in the annals of New Scotland Yard.

And now I come to the singular coincidence referred to earlier whereby I, an obscure medical practitioner, came to learn the solution of this extraordinary mystery. With the case itself I had no connection, the details just given being taken from the official reports made at the time, to which I was allowed access in return for the information I brought. The affair happened in this way.

One evening just four weeks ago, as I lit my pipe after a long and tiring day, I received an urgent summons to the principal inn of the little village near which I practised. A motor-cyclist had collided with a car at a cross-roads and had been picked up terribly injured. I saw almost at a glance that nothing could be done for him, in fact, his life was a matter of a few hours. He asked coolly how it was with him, and, in accordance with my custom in such cases, I told him, inquiring was there anyone he would like sent for. He looked me straight in the eyes and replied:

"Doctor, I want to make a statement. If I tell it you will you keep it to yourself while I live and then inform the proper authorities and the public?"

"Why, yes," I answered; "but shall I not send for some of your friends or a clergyman?"

"No," he said, "I have no friends, and I have no use for parsons. You look a white man; I would rather tell you."

I bowed and fixed him up as comfortably as possible, and he began, speaking slowly in a voice hardly above a whisper.

"I shall be brief for I feel my time is short. You remember some few years ago a Mr. Horatio Llewelyn and his wife were murdered in a train on the North-Western some fifty miles south of Carlisle?"

I dimly remembered the case.

"'The sleeping-car express mystery,' the papers called it?" I asked.

"That's it," he replied. "They never solved the mystery and they never got the murderer. But he's going to pay now. I am he."

I was horrified at the cool, deliberate way he spoke. Then I remembered that he was fighting death to make his confession and that, whatever my feelings, it was my business to hear and record it while yet there was time. I therefore sat down and said as gently as I could:

"Whatever you tell me I shall note carefully, and at the proper time shall inform the police."

His eyes, which had watched me anxiously, showed relief.

"Thank you. I shall hurry. My name is Hubert Black, and I live at 24, Westbury Gardens, Hove. Until ten years and two months ago I lived at Bradford, and there I made the acquaintance of what I thought was the best and most wonderful girl on God's earth— Miss Gladys Wentworth. I was poor, but she was well off. I was diffident about approaching her, but she encouraged me till at last I took my courage in both hands and proposed. She agreed to marry me, but made it a condition our engagement was to be kept secret for a few days. I was so mad about her I would have agreed to anything she wanted, so I said nothing, though I could hardly behave like a sane man from joy.

"Some time before this I had come across Llewelyn, and he had been very friendly, and had seemed to like my company. One day we met Gladys, and I introduced him. I did not know till later that he had followed up the acquaintanceship.

"A week after my acceptance there was a big dance at Halifax. I was to have met Gladys there, but at the last moment I had a wire that my mother was seriously ill, and I had to go. On my return I got a cool little note from Gladys saying she was sorry, but our engagement had been a mistake, and I must consider it at an end. I made a few inquiries, and then I learnt what had been done. Give me some stuff, doctor; I'm going down."

I poured out some brandy and held it to his lips.

"That's better," he said, continuing with gasps and many pauses: "Llewelyn, I found out, had been struck by Gladys for some time. He knew I was friends with her, and so he made up to me. He wanted the introduction I was fool enough to give him, as well as the chances of meeting her he would get with me. Then he met her when he knew I was at my work, and made hay while the sun shone. Gladys spotted what he was after, but she didn't know if he was serious. Then I proposed, and she thought she would hold me for fear the bigger fish would get off. Llewelyn was wealthy, you understand. She waited till the ball, then she hooked him, and I went overboard. Nice, wasn't it?"

I did not reply, and the man went on:

"Well, after that I just went mad. I lost my head and went to Llewelyn, but he laughed in my face. I felt I wanted to knock his head off, but the butler happened by, so I couldn't go on and finish him then. I needn't try to describe the hell I went through—I couldn't, anyway. But I was blind mad, and lived only for revenge. And then I got it. I followed them till I got a chance, and then I killed them. I shot them in that train. I shot her first and then, as he woke and sprang up, I got him too."

The man paused.

"Tell me the details," I asked; and after a time he went on in a weaker voice:

"I had worked out a plan to get them in a train, and had followed them all through their honeymoon, but I never got a chance till then. This time the circumstances fell out to suit. I was behind him at Euston and heard him book to Carlisle, so I booked to Glasgow. I got into the next compartment. There was a talkative man there, and I tried to make a sort of alibi for myself by letting him think I would get out at Crewe. I did get out, but I got in again, and travelled on in the same compartment with the blinds down. No one knew I was there. I waited till we got to the top of Shap, for I thought I could get away easier in a thinly populated country. Then, when the time came, I fixed the compartment doors with wedges, and shot them both. I left the train and got clear of the railway, crossing the country till I came on a road. I hid during the day and walked at night till after dark on the second evening I came to Carlisle. From there I went by rail quite openly. I was never suspected."

He paused, exhausted, while the Dread Visitor hovered closer.

"Tell me," I said, "just a word. How did you get out of the train?"

He smiled faintly.

"Some more of your stuff," he whispered; and when I had given him a second dose of brandy he went on feebly and with long pauses which I am not attempting to reproduce:

"I had worked the thing out beforehand. I thought if I could get out on the buffers while the train was running and before the alarm was raised, I should be safe. No one looking out of the windows could see me, and when the train stopped, as I knew it soon would, I could drop down and make off. The difficulty was to get from the corridor to the buffers. I did it like this:

"I had brought about sixteen feet of fine, brown silk cord, and the same length of thin silk rope. When I got out at Crewe I moved to the corner of the coach and stood close to it by way of getting shelter to light a cigarette. Without anyone seeing what I was up to I slipped the end of the cord through the bracket handle above the buffers. Then I strolled to the nearest door, paying out the cord, but holding on to its two ends. I pretended to fumble at the door as if it was stiff to open, but all the time I was passing the cord through the handle-guard, and knotting the ends together.

"If you've followed me you'll understand this gave me a loop of fine silk connecting the handles at the corner and the door. It was the colour of the carriage, and was nearly invisible. Then I took my seat again.

"When the time came to do the job, I first wedged the corridor doors. Then I opened the outside window and drew in the end of the cord loop and tied the end of the rope to it. I pulled one side of the cord loop and so got the rope pulled through the corner bracket handle and back again to the window. Its being silk made it run easily, and without marking the bracket. Then I put an end of the rope through the handle-guard, and after pulling it tight, knotted the ends together. This gave me a loop of rope tightly stretched from the door to the corner.

"I opened the door and then pulled up the window. I let the door close up against a bit of wood I had brought. The wind kept it to, and the wood prevented it from shutting.

"Then I fired. As soon as I saw that both were hit I got outside. I kicked away the wood and shut the door. Then with the rope for handrail I stepped along the footboard to the buffers. I cut both the cord and the rope and drew them after me, and shoved them in my pocket. This removed all traces.

"When the train stopped I slipped down on the ground. The people were getting out at the other side so I had only to creep along close to the coaches till I got out of their light, then I climbed up the bank and escaped."

The man had evidently made a desperate effort to finish, for as he ceased speaking his eyes closed, and in a few minutes he fell into a state of coma which shortly preceded his death.

After communicating with the police I set myself to carry out his second injunction, and this statement is the result.

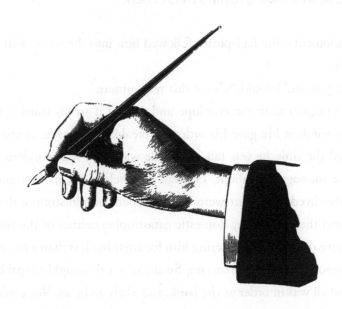

BLIND GAP MOOR

J. S. FLETCHER

I

Etherington, manager of the Old Bank at Leytonsdale, in Northshire,
was in the first week of his annual month's holiday, and he was celebrating
his freedom from the ordinary routine of life by staying in bed an hour
longer than usual every morning. Consequently, on this particular—and
as fate would have it, eventful—morning, it was 10 o'clock when he came
down to breakfast in the coffee-room of the Grand Hotel at Scarbor-
ough, in which place he meant to stay a fortnight before going on for
a similar period to Whitby. It would not have mattered to him if the
hands of the clock had pointed to 11, for he had no plans for the day.
His notion of a perfect holiday was to avoid plans of any sort, and to
let things come. And something quite unexpected was coming to him

at that moment—the hall-porter followed him into the room with a telegram.

"For you, sir," he said. "Come this very minute."

Etherington took the envelope and carried it to his usual seat near the window. He gave his order for breakfast before he opened it, but all the time he was talking to the waiter he was wondering what the message was about. He was a bachelor—his mother and sister who lived with him were such excellent administrators that he scouted the idea of any domestic catastrophe; neither of the two would have dreamed of bothering him for anything less than a fire or an explosion. His under-manager, Swale, was a thoroughly capable man, and all was in order at the bank, and likely to be so. Nor could he think of anyone who could have reason to wire him about business outside the bank affairs, nor about pleasure, nor about engagements. But just then the waiter retired, and Etherington opened the buff envelope, unfolded the flimsy sheet within, and read the message in one glance.

> "Swale found shot on Blind Gap Moor at 6 o'clock this morning. Believed to be a case of murder. Police would like you to return. Please wire time arrival—
> LEVER."

It was characteristic of Etherington, always a calm, self-possessed man, that he folded up the message, put it carefully in his pocket-book, and ate steadily through his substantial breakfast before asking the waiter to get him a railway time-table. But he was thinking all the time he ate and drank.

Murder? who would wish to murder Swale? He mentally figured Swale—a quiet, inoffensive fellow of thirty, who had been in the service of the Leytonsdale Old Bank ever since his schooldays, and had lived the life of a mouse. And what could have taken Swale, a man of fixed habits, to a wild desolate spot like Blind Gap Moor before 6 o'clock of a May morning? He knew Swale and his habits very well and he had never heard that the sub-manager was fond of getting up to see the sun, rise—and yet Blind Gap Moor was a good hour's walk from the town. Perhaps he had been shot during the night, or during the previous evening—in that case, what was he doing there ? For Swale was not a fellow to take long, country walks— he was a bookworm, a bit of a scribbler, in an amateur fashion, given to writing essays and papers on the antiquities of the town, and he accordingly liked to spend his evenings and burn the midnight oil at home. Odd—the whole thing! But—murder? That was a serious business, murder! Still, no one who ever knew Swale would ever have dreamed of connecting him with suicide.

As for himself, he must act. He beckoned the head waiter to his side with a nod.

"You'll have to get me my bill," he said. "I am called home— unexpectedly. But first—a railway guide and a telegram form."

It was a long journey across country to Leytonsdale, involving three changes and two tedious waitings for connections, and 5 o'clock had struck before Etherington got out of the branch train at the little station of his small market town. Lever, the junior clerk who had wired to him that morning, was awaiting him; together they walked out into the road which led to the centre of the place.

"Well?" asked Etherington, in his usual laconic fashion. "Anything fresh since morning?"

"Nothing," replied Lever. "But the police are now certain it's a case of murder; they say there's no doubt about it."

"Give me the facts," said the manager. "Bare facts."

"One of Lord Selwater's gamekeepers found him," answered the clerk. "Just before 6 this morning. He was lying dead near that cairn of stones on the top of Blind Gap Moor—shot through the heart.

The doctors say he would die at once, and that he was shot at close quarters. And—he'd been robbed."

Etherington made a little sound which denoted incredulity.

"Robbed!" he exclaimed. "Bless me! Why, what could Swale have on him that would make anybody go to the length of murder?"

"His watch and chain were gone," began Lever, "and—"

"Worth three pounds at the outside!" interrupted Etherington.

"Yes; but he'd a lot of money on him," proceeded the clerk. "It turns out that for this last year or two he's collected the rents for those two farms up on the moor—Low Flatts and Quarry Hill. He'd been there last night. Marshall, the farmer at Low Flatts, says he paid him £56; Thomson, at Quarry Hill, paid him £48. So he'd have over £100 on him."

"All missing?" asked the manager.

"There wasn't anything on him but some coppers," replied Lever. "Watch, chain, purse, pocket-book—all gone. That ring, that he used to wear, was gone."

"How had those men paid him?" asked Etherington. "Cheque or cash?"

"Notes and gold," answered Lever.

The manager walked on in silence for a while. Certainly this seemed like murder preceding robbery.

"Do they suspect anybody?" he asked. Lever shook his head.

"They haven't said so to me if they do," he replied. "The superintendent wants to see you at once."

Etherington went straight to the police station. The superintendent shook his grizzled head at the sight of him.

"Bad business this, Mr. Etherington," he said as the manager sat down. "First murder case we've had in my thirty years' experience of this district."

"Are you sure it's murder?" asked Etherington quietly.

"What else?" demanded the superintendent. "If it had been suicide the revolver that killed him would have been lying close by. No, sir—it's murder! And we haven't the shadow of a clue."

"I've heard the main facts from our clerk, Lever," remarked Etherington. "Is there anything you haven't told him?"

"There's precious little to tell, Mr. Etherington," answered the superintendent. "I've got at everything connected with his doings yesterday. He was at the bank all day, as usual. Nothing happened out of the common, according to your staff. He left the bank at 5 o'clock and went home to his lodgings. All was as usual there. His landlady says he had his dinner at 6 o'clock—just as usual. He went out at 7— didn't say anything. He called on Matthew Marshall at Low Flatts Farm at a quarter past 8. Marshall paid him half a year's rent. He was at James Thomson's, at Quarry Hill, just before 9; Thomson paid him a half year's rent, too. He stopped talking a bit with Thomson, and left there about 9.20.

"Thomson walked out to his gate with him, and saw him strike across the moor; it was getting darkish by that time, of course, but he saw him going towards that old cairn, near which he was found this morning. There was naught on him—he'd been robbed as well as murdered, sir."

"How far," asked Etherington, "is this place where he was found from these two farms?"

"A good mile from Quarry Hill—mile and a half from Low Flatts," replied the superintendent.

"Everything is very quiet on those moors at night," observed Etherington. "Did no one hear the sound of a shot?"

"I thought of that and inquired into it," answered the superintendent. "Nobody heard any shot. If somebody had heard a shot, you know, they'd only have thought it was one of Lord Selwater's keepers shooting at something. But so far I've heard of nobody who noticed aught of that sort. You see, except those two farms, there isn't a house on that part of the moors."

"There's Mr. Charlesworth's place—up above that cairn," suggested Etherington.

"Ay, but it's over the brow of the hill," said the superintendent. "That 'ud prevent the sound being heard there. I called at Charlesworth's; they'd heard nothing."

"Any suspicious characters about?" asked Etherington.

"My men haven't heard of any," answered the superintendent. "There were some gypsies in the neighbourhood a fortnight ago, but they cleared out."

"Poachers, now??" suggested the manager. "There are men in this town who poach on those moors."

"Just so. But we've no reason to suspect any particular one of 'em," said the superintendent. "I know of two men who do go up there after what they can get, but I've found out they were both safe in the town all yesterday evening and last night. No, sir, I think the whole thing'll go deeper than that."

"How?" asked Etherington.

"Somebody must have known Mr. Swale was going to collect those rents last night," said the superintendent meaningly. "He was laid in wait for. And yet, so far as I can make out, there wasn't a soul knew he collected them except Marshall and Thompson."

"I didn't know," remarked Etherington.

"Just so. According to the two farmers he's collected them ever since old Mr. Sellers died," continued the superintendent. "Those farms belong to Mrs. Hodgson, a London lady. Now, if somebody had got to know that Mr. Swale would have £100 in cash after he'd been to these farms last night—eh?"

"You don't suspect either of the two farmers?" asked the manager.

The superintendent shook his head firmly.

"No, sir; both decent, honest, straightforward fellows," he replied. "Oh, no! No, it's a deeper job than that, Mr. Etherington."

Etherington rose to go. After all, in this particular matter he could do nothing.

"Of course, there'll be an inquest?" he asked.

"To-morrow, at 10," answered the superintendent. "But, beyond what I've told you we've no evidence. It'll be a case of 'Wilful murder against some person or persons unknown,' you know, unless something comes out, and where it is to come from I don't know."

Nor did Etherington know, and he said so and went away. And after he had dined with his mother and sister, and discussed with them the tragic affair which had interrupted his holiday, he took his walking-stick and set off out of town to the scene of the murder. And there, in the gathering dusk, he met Charlesworth, the man who lived at an old house called Hill Rise, on the edge of the moor, well above the cairn near which Swale's body had been found. Etherington knew Charlesworth well; he was an old customer of the bank, a man who did a big trade in timber. He was evidently on his way home at that moment, and was glancing inquisitively at the cairn when Etherington came up.

"Nothing to see," he remarked, as the manager advanced. "They were looking for footmarks all day, but they found none. The grass is too close and wiry for that."

"I didn't expect to see anything," said Etherington. "It's some years since I was up this way. I came now to look around, to try to make out how it was nobody heard that shot last night. I understand nothing was heard at your place?"

Charlesworth, a big, athletic man, turned and pointed to the top of the moor above him.

"My place is just three-quarters of a mile over there," he answered. "There's all this rise between it and us, and a thickish belt of wood between, too. We couldn't hear a pistol shot from here. We heard nothing."

"What about those farms?" asked the manager. Charlesworth pointed in another direction.

"You can't see Low Flatts," he said. "It's down in that hollow yonder. And you can only see a chimney of Quarry Hill—that's it, peeping up behind that line in the moor. They'd hear nothing. It's an easy thing to try, as I told the police. Whoever killed Swale selected a good place. It isn't once in a month there's anybody about here o' nights—at this time of the year."

Etherington made no answer for the moment. He stood staring about him in the fast-gathering dusk. A wild and lonely place, indeed! Miles upon miles of ling and heather, and, beyond the chimney of Quarry Hill Farm, not a sign of human habitation.

"I wonder who did kill him?" he muttered absent-mindedly at last.

Charlesworth turned towards the hill-top with a nod of farewell.

"There's only one man living who knows that," he said; and went away.

II

No evidence was brought forward at the inquest on this unfortunate sub-manager's body which threw any light on the mystery of his murder or incriminating any person. Yet one small, possible clue was produced. A booking clerk from an obscure wayside station in a neighbouring dale came forward, and said that, at 5:30 o'clock on the morning of the discovery of the body, he, on going to his station to issue tickets for the first train, then about due, found walking up and down the platform a rough, sailorlike man, a perfect stranger, who presently took a ticket for Northport.

As he could give no very particular description of him, and as Northport was a town of some 250,000 inhabitants, the chances of finding this man were small. Nevertheless, there was the fact that such an individual, a stranger to the district, was within five miles of the cairn on Blind Gap Moor within a few hours of the time at which Swale was probably murdered.

Nothing came of this. Nothing came of anything that was brought forward in evidence. Only one matter seemed strange. The Leytonsdale Old Bank was one of the very few country banks which issued notes of their own; both the farmers had paid their rents to Swale in these local bank-notes. At the end of a month none of these notes had reached the bank, where a careful lookout had been kept for them, each man having been able to furnish Etherington with particulars of their numbers.

And the manager came to the conclusion that the thief-murderer was a man sharp enough to know that there would be danger in dealing with those notes, and was making himself content with the small amount of gold, and the watch, chain and ring, which he had secured, or was so much more sharp as to change notes at some far off place, whence they would reach the bank slowly and at long intervals.

Six weeks passed, and one day Etherington, entering the bank after his luncheon hour, asked Lever, now promoted to the sub-managership, if anything had happened during his absence.

"Nothing," replied Lever, "except that Mr. Charlesworth retired the first of those bills drawn on Folkingham & Greensedge. It was due next week. He said he'd take it up now, as he had cash of theirs in hand."

"That's the second time he's done that, isn't it?" asked Etherington, glancing at a memorandum which Lever put before him.

"Third," answered Lever. "He retired one in April and one in January. We hold three more yet. One August, October, December."

The manager made no further remark. He went into his own room and sat down to his desk. But he began to think, and his thoughts centred on a question. Why had Charlesworth got into a practice of taking up the bills of his drawn on Folkingham & Greensedge a few days before they were due for presentation? Why, as in the case of the last three, did he come to the bank and retire them by paying cash, instead of following the usual course of having them presented on maturity to their acceptors? Once in a way this might have been done without remark, but it was becoming a practice. Charlesworth was a timber merchant in a biggish way of business. He did a lot of business with a firm in Northport—Folkingham & Greensedge, agents and exporters. For twelve or fifteen years, to Etherington's knowledge, Charlesworth had been in the habit of drawing upon this firm for large amounts against consignments of timber. Up to about six months before this the bills so drawn had always been allowed to mature and to be presented in due course for payment, which had always been prompt. But, as Lever just said, Charlesworth had himself retired the last three before they could be presented. Why?

That question began to bother Etherington. Why should a man bother himself to retire a bill which would fully mature in a week, and would be promptly met? It was a strange course—and since the New Year it had been repeated three times. Again—why?

Etherington waited until Lever had gone to his lunch, then he possessed himself of certain books and documents. He carried them into his own room, and jotted some dates and figures down on a slip of paper. In October of the previous year Charlesworth had brought in six acceptances of Folkingham & Greensedge's. They were of various terms as regards length; each one was for a considerable amount—the one, for instance, which Charlesworth had taken up that very day was for over £1,500. And the whole lot—representing a sum of about £7,000 to £8,000—had, of course, been discounted by Etherington as soon as they were paid in by their drawer. There was nothing unusual in that—Etherington had been discounting similar acceptances, drawn by Charlesworth, accepted by Folkingham & Greensedge, for many years. What was unusual—and in the manager's opinion, odd—was that, mostly, Charlesworth had taken up these bills before they became due. And for the third time Etherington asked himself the one pertinent question—why?

He took the books and papers back to their places presently, and got out a lot of bills which were waiting to mature. It was easy work to pick out the three of Charlesworth's to which Lever had referred as being still in their hands. He took them to his room and laid them on his desk, and examined each carefully. The first, due in August, was for £950; the second, due in October, for £800; the third, due in December, for £1,175. But Etherington was not concerned, he was not even faintly interested, in the amounts. What he was looking at was the signatures in each case. And presently, remembering that he had letters of Folkingham & Greensedge's in his possession, he looked for and found them, and began to make a minute comparison, letter by letter, stroke by stroke, between the signatures on that firm's correspondence paper and those written across the face of the bills. It was a close, meticulously close, examination that he made—first with the naked eye, secondly with the aid of a magnifying glass. And, though he was no expert in caligraphy, he came to the conclusion, at the end of ten minutes' careful inspection, that the signature of Folkingham & Greensedge had in each case been carefully forged.

Etherington remained looking at those oblong slips of blue stamped paper for a long time. Then he put them, folded, into an envelope, in his pocket-book. And when Lever came back he went out to him.

"I must leave earlier than usual," he remarked. "There's nothing that needs my attention, I think. See that all's right. And be here at 9 sharp in the morning. Lever; I want to see you then."

He walked quickly away to his own house, made ready for a short journey, and set off. It was only a two hours' run to Northport, and he must go there at once. Such a doubt as that which had arisen in his mind could not be allowed to await solution—he must settle it. If he was right in his belief that he had discovered a forgery, what might not arise out of it?

The Greensedge, who had given part of its name to the firm with which Charlesworth did such extensive business, had been dead some years; so had the original Folkingham. There was no Greensedge now—the entire business belonged to one, Stephen Folkingham, a middle-aged man, who kept up the old style of the firm in spite of the fact that he was its sole proprietor. When Etherington arrived at his office in the famous shipping town, Stephen Folkingham had gone home. The bank manager followed him to his house outside the town, and was presently closeted with him in private.

"You are surprised to see me?" said Etherington.

"Frankly, yes!" replied Folkingham. "Something important of course."

"And as private as it is important—for the moment at any rate," said Etherington. He drew out his pocket-book, produced the three bills, and spread them on his host's desk. He pointed to the accepting signatures across the fronts. "Are these signatures yours?"

Folkingham started. He bent down, glanced at the dates, and let out a surprised exclamation.

"Good heavens, no!" he answered. "I haven't accepted a bill of Charlesworth's for—oh, eighteen months. I've dropped all trade with him for quite that time."

"Then, those signatures, to be plain, are forged?" said the manager.

Folkingham shrugged his shoulders.

"So far as I'm concerned, yes," he replied, "I know nothing whatever about them—nothing! I've dropped that particular line of trade—some time ago. You don't mean to say that Charlesworth—"

Etherington sat down and told Folkingham all about it. There had been six bills. Three had been retired. Probably the other three would have been similarly retired. And—nobody would have known of the forgery. The two men stared at each other when the story came to an end. Each was thinking. But Etherington was thinking of something that was not in the other man's thoughts—something worse than forgery.

"What's to be done?" asked Folkingham at last. "Or, rather, what do you intend to do?"

"I should be greatly obliged to you if you'd come over to Leytonsdale in the morning," answered the manager. "He must be confronted. And your denial to his face—is precisely what I do want."

"All right," agreed Folkingham, after thinking this proposal over. "I'll be with you by noon. Now stop and have some dinner—you can get a train back at 8:30. Dear, dear, this is extraordinary! What on earth's behind it?"

Etherington did not discuss that. He was still thinking of his other idea; he thought of it all the way home in the train; he thought of it during the night; he was thinking of it at 9 o'clock next morning when he went to the bank and found Lever there and took him into his private room.

"Lever," he said, "you remember that last day that Swale was alive; just stir your memory. Can you remember anything special that he did—here? Anything relating to bank business? Think!"

Lever, a somewhat slow-going young man, thought for some time before he replied.

"I can't think of anything except that, during the afternoon, he got all the acceptances out and went through them," he answered. "There was nothing else, I'm sure, out of the ordinary."

"Did he make any remark to you about any of those acceptances?" asked Etherington.

"No," replied Lever. "None!"

Etherington nodded, intimating that he had no more to ask. But as soon as Lever had left the room he, himself, went out again and walked around to the police station.

III

Etherington remained closeted with Campbell, the superintendent of police, until after 10 o'clock. When he returned to the bank the doors had been opened to the public, and two or three customers had already entered. In one of them, a big, raw-boned countryman, the manager recognised Matthew Marshall, the tenant of Low Flatts Farm.

Marshall, who had evidently cashed a small cheque, was standing in front of the counter with a little pile of gold and silver between himself and Lever, who was leaning forward from the other side to look intently at something which the farmer held in his big hand.

"A' but doan't tell me!" Marshall was saying, in his broad vernacular. "I'm none one to forget owt o' t' sovereigns 'at I paid to poor Mestur Swale t' very neet 'at he wor done for—it is! I tell yer—'im an' me, an' my wife an' all, lewked at that theer mark."

Etherington went directly to the farmer's side and looked at the sovereign, on the upper side of which somebody had stamped two deeply-incised letters—X. M. And Marshall turned to him with a wide smile.

"I'm tellin' Mestur Lever theer 'at this here sovereign is one—" he began.

"I heard what you said," interrupted Etherington, taking the coin and examining it. "Are you sure of what you say?"

"Ay, shure as I am 'at I'm speakin' to you, Mestur Etherington," answered the farmer promptly. "I'd noticed them letters on that coin afore iver I paid it away to Mestur Swale yon neet 'at t' poor feller was murdered. Him an' me had a bit o' talk about it. Oh, ay, that's t' very identical coin 'at I gev him! Now, isn't it queer 'at it should turn up at yor bank—what?"

"Leave it with me," said Etherington, putting the marked sovereign in his pocket. "Mr. Lever will give you another in its place, Marshall," he went on, leading the man towards the door; "don't say anything about this in the town this morning. Come back here for a few minutes at 12 o'clock."

The farmer opened his mouth, gave the manager a shrewd nod, and went off in silence; and Etherington went behind the counter to Lever.

"Did Charlesworth pay any of that money which he brought yesterday in gold?" he asked quietly.

"Twenty pounds or so," answered Lever. He, too, suddenly looked shrewdly at the manager, and his professional stolidity broke down. "Good heavens," he exclaimed. "You don't think—"

"Hush!" said Etherington. "Listen! Charlesworth will be coming here just after 12. I've telephoned him. He won't suspect anything from my message. Bring him straight into the private room."

There was no one but Etherington in the private room when Charlesworth walked into it at a quarter past 12. And there was nothing remarkable in the manager's surroundings, except that on his blotting-pad lay a sovereign and a closed envelope.

"Just a question or two," said Etherington, in his calmest and iciest manner. "You paid some money in yesterday—to retire one of those acceptances. That sovereign was amongst others which you paid in."

"Well?" said Charlesworth. He glanced at the coin unconsciously; and the manager, watching him closely, failed to see any sign of alarm. "What of it?"

Etherington put the point of his pen to the coin.

"That sovereign," he said, "is marked. It's one which Marshall handed to Swale—the night Swale was murdered. How did it come into your possession?"

Charlesworth's face flushed a little at that, and he bent forward, looking at the coin.

"How on earth can I tell that?" he demanded. "You know how money changes hands!"

"I should like," remarked Etherington, "to know if that sovereign has changed hands more than once since Marshall gave it to Swale. But—here is another question. What did Swale tell you when you met him that night at Blind Gap Moor? Come!"

He rose to his feet as he spoke, picking up the envelope and beginning to take three strips of blue paper from it. And Charlesworth rose, too, and stepped back a little, staring almost incredulously at his questioner.

"Come!" repeated Etherington. "What's the use of denial? Didn't Swale tell you that he had found out that the supposed signature of Folkingham and Greensedge on your acceptances were—forgeries? And didn't you—eh? You know what you did then, Mr. Charlesworth, I think. But—"

He tapped a bell as he spoke, and the door of an inner room opened and revealed Folkingham and the police superintendent, and behind them the round, staring amazed face of the farmer. Etherington laughed.

"You see?" he said, indicating Folkingham. "Hadn't you better confess and be done with it? Come—"

"Look at him!" shouted Campbell, as he sprang into the room. "The revolver! Look out!"

But the room was a big one, and Charlesworth was at the further side. And before any of them could reach him he had turned the revolver on himself and sent a bullet through his brain.

Etherington made a little, half-articulate sound of vexation.

"I hurried him too much!" he muttered. "But, then, I never thought he'd do that!" He turned to the startled superintendent. "Get him taken away, will you?" he said quietly. "The affair is—over."

THE REGENT'S PARK MURDER

BARONESS ORCZY

By this time Miss Polly Burton had become quite accustomed to her extraordinary *vis-à-vis* in the corner.

He was always there, when she arrived, in the selfsame corner, dressed in one of his remarkable check tweed suits; he seldom said good morning, and invariably when she appeared he began to fidget with increased nervousness, with some tattered and knotty piece of string.

"Were you ever interested in the Regent's Park murder?" he asked her one day.

Polly replied that she had forgotten most of the particulars connected with that curious murder, but that she fully remembered the stir and flutter it had caused in a certain section of London society.

"The racing and gambling set, particularly, you mean," he said. "All the persons implicated in the murder, directly or indirectly, were of the type commonly called 'Society men,' or 'men about town,' whilst the Harewood Club in Hanover Square, round which centered all the scandal in connection with the murder, was one of the smartest clubs in London.

Probably the doings of the Harewood Club, which was essentially a gambling club, would for ever have remained 'officially' absent from the knowledge of the police authorities but for the murder in the Regent's Park and the revelations which came to light in connection with it.

"I dare say you know the quiet square which lies between Portland Place and the Regent's Park and is called Park Crescent at its south end, and subsequently Park Square East and West. The Marylebone Road, with all its heavy traffic, cuts straight across the large square and its pretty gardens, but the latter are connected together by a tunnel under the road; and of course you must remember that the new tube station in the south portion of the Square had not yet been planned.

"February 6th, 1907, was a very foggy night, nevertheless Mr. Aaron Cohen, of 30, Park Square West, at two o'clock in the morning, having finally pocketed the heavy winnings which he had just swept off the green table of the Harewood Club, started to walk home alone. An hour later most of the inhabitants of Park Square West were aroused from their peaceful slumbers by the sounds of a violent altercation in the road. A man's angry voice was heard shouting violently for a minute or two, and was followed immediately by frantic screams of 'Police' and 'Murder.' Then there was the double sharp report of fire-arms, and nothing more.

"The fog was very dense, and, as you no doubt have experienced yourself, it is very difficult to locate sound in a fog. Nevertheless, not more than a minute or two had elapsed before Constable F 18, the point policeman at the corner of Marylebone Road, arrived on the scene, and, having first of all whistled for any of his comrades on the beat, began to grope his way about in the fog, more confused than effectually assisted by contradictory directions from the inhabitants of the houses close by, who were nearly falling out of the upper windows as they shouted out to the constable.

"'By the railings, policeman.'

"'Higher up the road.'

"'No, lower down.'

"'It was on this side of the pavement I am sure.'

"'No, the other.'

"At last it was another policeman, F 22, who, turning into Park Square West from the north side, almost stumbled upon the body of a man lying on the pavement with his head against the railings of the Square. By this time quite a little crowd of people from the different houses in the road had come down, curious to know what had actually happened.

"The policeman turned the strong light of his bull's-eye lantern on the unfortunate man's face.

"'It looks as if he had been strangled, don't it?' he murmured to his comrade.

"And he pointed to the swollen tongue, the eyes half out of their sockets, bloodshot and congested, the purple, almost black, hue of the face.

"At this point one of the spectators, more callous to horrors, peered curiously into the dead man's face. He uttered an exclamation of astonishment.

"'Why, surely, it's Mr. Cohen from No. 30!'

"The mention of a name familiar down the length of the street had caused two or three other men to come forward and to look more closely into the horribly distorted mask of the murdered man.

"Our next-door neighbour, undoubtedly,' asserted Mr. Ellison, a young barrister, residing at No. 31.

"What in the world was he doing this foggy night all alone, and on foot?' asked somebody else.

"He usually came home very late. I fancy he belonged to some gambling club in town. I dare say he couldn't get a cab to bring him out here. Mind you, I don't know much about him. We only knew him to nod to.'

"Poor beggar! it looks almost like an old-fashioned case of garrotting.'

"Anyway, the blackguardly murderer, whoever he was, wanted to make sure he had killed his man!' added Constable F 18, as he picked up an object from the pavement. 'Here's the revolver, with two cartridges missing. You gentlemen heard the report just now?'

"He don't seem to have hit him though. The poor bloke was strangled, no doubt.'

"And tried to shoot at his assailant, obviously,' asserted the young barrister with authority.

"If he succeeded in hitting the brute, there might be a chance of tracing the way he went.'

"But not in the fog.'

"Soon, however, the appearance of the inspector, detective, and medical officer, who had quickly been informed of the tragedy, put an end to further discussion.

"The bell at No. 30 was rung, and the servants—all four of them women—were asked to look at the body.

"Amidst tears of horror and screams of fright, they all recognized in the murdered man their master, Mr. Aaron Cohen. He was therefore conveyed to his own room pending the coroner's inquest.

"The police had a pretty difficult task, you will admit; there were so very few indications to go by, and at first literally no clue.

"The inquest revealed practically nothing. Very little was known in the neighbourhood about Mr. Aaron Cohen and his affairs. His female servants did not even know the name or whereabouts of the various clubs he frequented.

"He had an office in Throgmorton Street and went to business every day. He dined at home, and sometimes had friends to dinner. When he was alone he invariably went to the club, where he stayed until the small hours of the morning.

"The night of the murder he had gone out at about nine o'clock. That was the last his servants had seen of him. With regard to the revolver, all four servants swore positively that they had never seen it before, and that, unless Mr. Cohen had bought it that very day, it did not belong to their master.

"Beyond that, no trace whatever of the murderer had been found, but on the morning after the crime a couple of keys linked together by a short metal chain were found close to a gate at the opposite end of the Square, that which immediately faced Portland Place. These were proved to be, firstly, Mr. Cohen's latchkey, and, secondly, his gate-key of the Square.

"It was therefore presumed that the murderer, having accomplished his fell design and ransacked his victim's pockets, had found the keys and made good his escape by slipping into the Square, cutting under the tunnel, and out again by the further gate. He then took the precaution not to carry the keys with him any further, but threw them away and disappeared in the fog.

"The jury returned a verdict of wilful murder against some person or persons unknown, and the police were put on their mettle to discover the unknown and daring murderer. The result of their investigations, conducted with marvellous skill by Mr. William Fisher, led, about a week after the crime, to the sensational arrest of one of London's smartest young bucks.

"The case Mr. Fisher had got up against the accused briefly amounted to this:

"On the night of February 6th, soon after midnight, play began to run very high at the Harewood Club, in Hanover Square. Mr. Aaron Cohen held the bank at roulette against some twenty or thirty of his friends, mostly young fellows with no wits and plenty of money. 'The Bank' was winning heavily, and it appears that this was the third consecutive night on which Mr. Aaron Cohen had gone home richer by several hundreds than he had been at the start of play.

"Young John Ashley, who is the son of a very worthy county gentleman who is M.F.H. somewhere in the Midlands, was losing heavily, and in his case also it appears that it was the third consecutive night that Fortune had turned her face against him.

"Remember," continued the man in the corner, "that when I tell you all these details and facts, I am giving you the combined evidence of several witnesses, which it took many days to collect and to classify.

"It appears that young Mr. Ashley, though very popular in society, was generally believed to be in what is vulgarly termed 'low water'; up to his eyes in debt, and mortally afraid of his dad, whose younger son he was, and who had on one occasion threatened to ship him off to Australia with a £5 note in his pocket if he made any further extravagant calls upon his paternal indulgence.

"It was also evident to all John Ashley's many companions that the worthy M.F.H. held the purse-strings in a very tight grip. The young man, bitten with the desire to cut a smart figure in the circles in which he moved, had often recourse to the varying fortunes which now and again smiled upon him across the green tables in the Harewood Club.

"Be that as it may, the general consensus of opinion at the Club was that young Ashley had changed his last 'pony' before he sat down to a turn of roulette with Aaron Cohen on that particular night of February 6th.

"It appears that all his friends, conspicuous among whom was Mr. Walter Hatherell, tried their very best to dissuade him from pitting his luck against that of Cohen, who had been having a most unprecedented run of good fortune. But young Ashley, heated with wine, exasperated at his own bad luck, would listen to no one; he tossed one £5 note after another on the board, he borrowed from those who would lend, then played on parole for a while. Finally, at half-past one in the morning, after a run of nineteen on the red, the young man found himself without a penny in his pockets, and owing a debt—a gambling debt—a debt of honour of £1500 to Mr. Aaron Cohen.

"Now we must render this much maligned gentleman that justice which was persistently denied to him by press and public alike; it was positively asserted by all those present that Mr. Cohen himself repeatedly tried to induce young Mr. Ashley to give up playing. He himself was in a delicate position in the matter, as he was the winner, and once or twice the taunt had risen to the young man's lips, accusing the holder of the bank of the wish to retire on a competence before the break in his luck.

"Mr. Aaron Cohen, smoking the best of Havanas, had finally shrugged his shoulders and said: 'As you please!'

"But at half-past one he had had enough of the player, who always lost and never paid—never could pay, so Mr. Cohen probably believed. He therefore at that hour refused to accept Mr. John Ashley's 'promissory' stakes any longer. A very few heated words ensued, quickly checked by the management, who are ever on the alert to avoid the least suspicion of scandal.

"In the meanwhile Mr. Hatherell, with great good sense, persuaded young Ashley to leave the Club and all its temptations and go home; if possible to bed.

"The friendship of the two young men, which was very well known in society, consisted chiefly, it appears, in Walter Hatherell being the willing companion and helpmeet of John Ashley in his mad and extravagant pranks. But to-night the latter, apparently tardily sobered by his terrible and heavy losses, allowed himself to be led away by his friend from the scene of his disasters. It was then about twenty minutes to two.

"Here the situation becomes interesting," continued the man in the corner in his nervous way. "No wonder that the police interrogated at least a dozen witnesses before they were quite satisfied that every statement was conclusively proved.

"Walter Hatherell, after about ten minutes' absence, that is to say at ten minutes to two, returned to the club room. In reply to several inquiries, he said that he had parted with his friend at the corner of New Bond Street, since he seemed anxious to be alone, and that Ashley said he would take a turn down Piccadilly before going home—he thought a walk would do him good.

"At two o'clock or thereabouts Mr. Aaron Cohen, satisfied with his evening's work, gave up his position at the bank and, pocketing his heavy winnings, started on his homeward walk, while Mr. Walter Hatherell left the club half an hour later.

"At three o'clock precisely the cries of 'Murder' and the report of fire-arms were heard in Park Square West, and Mr. Aaron Cohen was found strangled outside the garden railings."

"Now at first sight the murder in the Regent's Park appeared both to police and public as one of those silly, clumsy crimes, obviously the work of a novice, and absolutely purposeless, seeing that it could but inevitably leading perpetrators, without any difficulty, to the gallows.

"You see, a motive had been established. 'Seek him whom the crime benefits,' say our French *confrères*. But there was something more than that.

"Constable James Funnell, on his beat, turned from Portland Place into Park Crescent a few minutes after he had heard the clock at Holy Trinity Church, Marylebone, strike half-past two. The fog at that moment was perhaps not quite so dense as it was later on in the morning, and the policeman saw two gentlemen in overcoats and top-hats leaning arm in arm against the railings of the Square, close to the gate. He could not, of course, distinguish their faces because of the fog, but he heard one of them saying to the other:

"'It is but a question of time, Mr. Cohen. I know my father will pay the money for me, and you will lose nothing by waiting.'

"To this the other apparently made no reply, and the constable passed on; when he returned to the same spot, after having walked over his beat, the two gentlemen had gone, but later on it was near this very gate that the two keys referred to at the inquest had been found.

"Another interesting fact," added the man in the corner, with one of those sarcastic smiles of his which Polly could not quite explain, "was the finding of the revolver upon the scene of the crime. That revolver, shown to Mr. Ashley's valet, was sworn to by him as being the property of his master.

"All these facts made, of course, a very remarkable, so far quite unbroken, chain of circumstantial evidence against Mr. John Ashley. No wonder, therefore, that the police, thoroughly satisfied with Mr. Fisher's work and their own, applied for a warrant against the young man, and arrested him in his rooms in Clarges Street exactly a week after the committal of the crime.

"As a matter of fact, you know, experience has invariably taught me that when a murderer seems particularly foolish and clumsy, and proofs against him seem particularly damning, that is the time when the police should be most guarded against pitfalls.

"Now in this case, if John Ashley had indeed committed the murder in Regent's Park in the manner suggested by the police, he would have been a criminal in more senses than one, for idiocy of that kind is to my mind worse than many crimes.

"The prosecution brought its witnesses up in triumphal array one after another. There were the members of the Harewood Club—who had seen the prisoner's excited condition after his heavy gambling losses to Mr. Aaron Cohen; there was Mr. Hatherell, who, in spite of his friendship for Ashley, was bound to admit that he had parted from him at the corner of Bond Street at twenty minutes to two, and had not seen him again till his return home at five a.m.

"Then came the evidence of Arthur Chipps, John Ashley's valet. It proved of a very sensational character.

"He deposed that on the night in question his master came home at about ten minutes to two. Chipps had then not yet gone to bed. Five minutes later Mr. Ashley went out again, telling the valet not to sit up for him. Chipps could not say at what time either of the young gentlemen had come home.

"That short visit home—presumably to fetch the revolver—was thought to be very important, and Mr. John Ashley's friends felt that his case was practically hopeless.

"The valet's evidence and that of James Funnell, the constable, who had overheard the conversation near the park railings, were certainly the two most damning proofs against the accused. I assure you I was having a rare old time that day. There were two faces in court to watch which was the greatest treat I had had for many a day. One of these was Mr. John Ashley's.

"Here's his photo—short, dark, dapper, a little 'racy' in style, but otherwise he looks a son of a well-to-do farmer. He was very quiet and placid in court, and addressed a few words now and again to his solicitor. He listened gravely, and with an occasional shrug of the shoulders, to the recital of the crime, such as the police had reconstructed it, before an excited and horrified audience.

"Mr. John Ashley, driven to madness and frenzy by terrible financial difficulties, had first of all gone home in search of a weapon, then waylaid Mr. Aaron Cohen somewhere on that gentleman's way home. The young man had begged for delay. Mr. Cohen perhaps was obdurate; but Ashley followed him with his importunities almost to his door.

"There, seeing his creditor determined at last to cut short the painful interview, he had seized the unfortunate man at an unguarded moment from behind, and strangled him; then, fearing that his dastardly work was not fully accomplished, he had shot twice at the already dead body, missing it both times from sheer nervous excitement. The murderer then must have emptied his victim's pockets, and, finding the key of the pardon, thought that it would be a safe way of evading capture by cutting across the squares, under the tunnel, and so through the more distant gate which faced Portland Place.

"The loss of the revolver was one of those unforeseen accidents which a retributive Providence places in the path of the miscreant, delivering him by his own act of folly into the hands of human justice.

"Mr. John Ashley, however, did not appear the least bit impressed by the recital of his crime. He had not engaged the services of one of the most eminent lawyers, expert at extracting contradictions from witnesses by skilful cross-examinations—oh, dear me, no! he had been contented with those of a dull, prosy, very second-rate limb of the law, who, as he called his witnesses, was completely innocent of any desire to create a sensation.

"He rose quietly from his seat, and, amidst breathless silence, called the first of three witnesses on behalf of his client. He called three—but he could have produced twelve—gentlemen, members of the Ashton Club in Great Portland Street, all of whom swore that at three o'clock on the morning of February 6th, that is to say, at the very moment when the cries of 'Murder' roused the inhabitants of Park Square West, and the crime was being committed, Mr. John Ashley was sitting quietly in the clubrooms of the Ashton playing bridge with the three witnesses. He had come in a few minutes before three—as the hall porter of the Club testified—and stayed for about an hour and a half.

"I need not tell you that this undoubted, this fully proved, *alibi* was a positive bomb-shell in the stronghold of the prosecution. The most accomplished criminal could not possibly be in two places at once, and though the Ashton Club transgresses in many ways against the gambling laws of our very moral country, yet its members belong to the best, most unimpeachable classes of society. Mr. Ashley had been seen and spoken to at the very moment of the crime by at least a dozen gentlemen whose testimony was absolutely above suspicion.

"Mr. John Ashley's conduct throughout this astonishing phase of the inquiry remained perfectly calm and correct. It was no doubt the consciousness of being able to prove his innocence with such absolute conclusion that had steadied his nerves throughout the proceedings.

"His answers to the magistrate were clear and simple, even on the ticklish subject of the revolver.

"'I left the club, sir,' he explained, 'fully determined to speak with Mr. Cohen alone in order to ask him for a delay in the settlement of my debt to him. You will understand that I should not care to do this in the presence of other gentlemen. I went home for a minute or two—not in order to fetch a revolver, as the police assert, for I always carry a revolver about with me in foggy weather—but in order to see if a very important business letter had come for me in my absence.

"'Then I went out again, and met Mr. Aaron Cohen not far from the Harewood Club, I walked the greater part of the way with him, and our conversation was of the most amiable character. We parted at the top of Portland Place, near the gate of the Square, where the policeman saw us. Mr. Cohen then had the intention of cutting across the Square, as being a shorter way to his own house. I thought the

Square looked dark and dangerous in the fog, especially as Mr. Cohen was carrying a large sum of money.

"'We had a short discussion on the subject, and finally I persuaded him to take my revolver, as I was going home only through very frequented streets, and moreover carried nothing that was worth stealing. After a little demur Mr. Cohen accepted the loan of my revolver, and that is how it came to be found on the actual scene of the crime; finally I parted from Mr. Cohen a very few minutes after I had heard the church clock striking a quarter before three. I was at the Oxford Street end of Great Portland Street at five minutes to three, and it takes at least ten minutes to walk from where I was to the Ashton Club.'

"This explanation was all the more credible, mind you, because the question of the revolver had never been very satisfactorily explained by the prosecution. A man who has effectually strangled his victim would not discharge two shots of his revolver for, apparently, no other purpose than that of rousing the attention of the nearest passer-by. It was far more likely that it was Mr. Cohen who shot—perhaps wildly into the air, when suddenly attacked from behind. Mr. Ashley's explanation therefore was not only plausible, it was the only possible one.

"You will understand therefore how it was that, after nearly half an hour's examination, the magistrate, the police, and the public were alike pleased to proclaim that the accused left the court without a stain upon his character."

"Yes," interrupted Polly eagerly, since, for once, her acumen had been at least as sharp as his," but suspicion of that horrible crime only shifted its taint from one friend to another, and, of course, I know—"

"But that's just it," he quietly interrupted, "you don't know—Mr. Walter Hatherell, of course, you mean. So did every one else at once. The friend, weak and willing, committing a crime on behalf of his cowardly, yet more assertive friend who had tempted him to evil. It was a good theory; and was held pretty generally, I fancy, even by the police.

"I say 'even' because they worked really hard in order to build up a case against young Hatherell, but the great difficulty was that of time. At the hour when the policeman had seen the two men outside Park Square together, Walter Hatherell was still sitting in the Harewood Club, which he never left until twenty minutes to two. Had he wished to waylay and rob Aaron Cohen he would not have waited surely till the time when presumably the latter would already have reached home.

"Moreover, twenty minutes was an incredibly short time in which to walk from Hanover Square to Regent's Park without the chance of cutting across the squares, to look for a man, whose whereabouts you could not determine to within twenty yards or so, to have an argument with him, murder him, and ransack his pockets. And then there was the total absence of motive."

"But—" said Polly meditatively, for she remembered now that the Regent's Park murder, as it had been popularly called, was one of those which had remained as impenetrable a mystery as any other crime had ever been in the annals of the police.

The man in the corner cocked his funny birdlike head well on one side and looked at her, highly amused evidently at her perplexity.

"You do not see how that murder was committed?" he asked with a grin.

Polly was bound to admit that she did not.

"If you had happened to have been in Mr. John Ashley's predicament," he persisted, "you do not see how you could conveniently have done away with Mr. Aaron Cohen, pocketed his winnings, and then led the police of your country entirely by the nose, by proving an indisputable *alibi?*"

"I could not arrange conveniently," she retorted, "to be in two different places half a mile apart at one and the same time."

"No! I quite admit that you could not do this unless you also had a friend—"

"A friend? But you say—"

"I say that I admired Mr. John Ashley, for his was the head which planned the whole thing, but he could not have accomplished the fascinating and terrible drama without the help of willing and able hands."

"Even then—" she protested.

"Point number one," he began excitedly, fidgeting with his inevitable piece of string. "John Ashley and his friend Walter Hatherell leave the club together, and together decide on the plan of campaign. Hatherell returns to the club, and Ashley goes to fetch the revolver— the revolver which played such an important part in the drama, but not the part assigned to it by the police. Now try to follow Ashley closely, as he dogs Aaron Cohen's footsteps. Do you believe that he entered into conversation with him? That he walked by his side? That he asked for delay? No! He sneaked behind him and caught him by the throat, as the garrotters used to do in the fog. Cohen was apoplectic, and Ashley is young and powerful. Moreover, he meant to kill—"

"But the two men talked together outside the Square gates," protested Polly, "one of whom was Cohen, and the other Ashley."

"Pardon me," he said, jumping up in his seat like a monkey on a stick, "there were not two men talking outside the Square gates. According to the testimony of James Funnell, the constable, two men were leaning arm in arm against the railings and one man was talking."

"Then you think that—"

"At the hour when James Funnell heard Holy Trinity clock striking half-past two Aaron Cohen was already dead. Look how simple the whole thing is," he added eagerly, "and how easy after that— easy, but oh, dear me! how wonderfully, how stupendously clever. As soon as James Funnell has passed on, John Ashley, having opened the gate, lifts the body of Aaron Cohen in his arms and carries him across the Square. The Square is deserted, of course, but the way is easy enough, and we must presume that Ashley had been in it before. Anyway, there was no fear of meeting any one.

"In the meantime Hatherell has left the club: as fast as his athletic legs can carry him he rushes along Oxford Street and Portland Place. It had been arranged between the two miscreants that the Square gate should be left on the latch.

"Close on Ashley's heels now, Hatherell too cuts across the Square, and reaches the further gate in good time to give his confederate a hand in disposing the body against the railings. Then, without another instant's delay, Ashley runs back across the gardens, straight to the Ashton Club, throwing away the keys of the dead man, on the very spot where he had made it a point of being seen and heard by a passer-by.

"Hatherell gives his friend six or seven minutes' start, then he begins the altercation which lasts two or three minutes, and finally rouses the neighbourhood with cries of 'Murder' and report of pistol in order to establish that the crime was committed at the hour when its perpetrator has already made out an indisputable *alibi*.

"I don't know what you think of it all, of course," added the funny creature as he fumbled for his coat and his gloves, "but I call the planning of that murder—on the part of novices, mind you—one of the cleverest pieces of strategy I have ever come across. It is one of those cases where there is no possibility whatever now of bringing the crime home to its perpetrator or his abettor. They have not left a single proof behind them; they foresaw everything, and each acted his part with a coolness and courage which, applied to a great and good cause, would have made fine statesmen of them both.

"As it is, I fear, they are just a pair of young blackguards, who have escaped human justice, and have only deserved the full and ungrudging admiration of yours very sincerely."

He had gone. Polly wanted to call him back, but his meagre person was no longer visible through the glass door. There were many things she would have wished to ask of him—what were his proofs, his facts? His were theories, after all, and yet, somehow, she felt that he had solved once again one of the darkest mysteries of great criminal London.

MYSTERY AND HORROR

MISS BRACEGIRDLE DOES HER DUTY

STACY AUMONIER

"This is the room, madame."

"Ah, thank you . . . thank you."

"Does it appear satisfactory to madame?"

"Oh, yes, thank you . . . quite."

"Does madame require anything further?"

"Er—if not too late, may I have a hot bath?"

"*Parfaitement*, madame. The bathroom is at the end of the passage on the left. I will go and prepare it for madame."

"There is one thing more. . . . I have had a very long journey. I am very tired. Will you please see that I am not disturbed in the morning until I ring?"

"Certainly, madame."

Millicent Bracegirdle was speaking the truth—she was tired. In the sleepy cathedral town of Easingstoke from which she came, it was customary for every one to speak the truth. It was customary, moreover, for every one to lead simple, self-denying lives—to give up their time to good works and elevating thoughts. One had only to glance at little Miss Bracegirdle to see that in her were epitomized all the virtues and ideals of Easingstoke. Indeed, it was the pursuit of duty which had brought her to the Hôtel de l'Ouest at Bordeaux on this summer's night. She had travelled from Easingstoke to London, then without a break to Dover, crossed that horrid stretch of sea to Calais, entrained for Paris, where she of necessity had to spend four hours—a terrifying experience—and then had come on to Bordeaux, arriving at midnight. The reason of this journey being that someone had to come to Bordeaux to meet her young sister-in-law, who was arriving the next day from South America. The sister-in-law was married to a missionary in Paraguay, but the climate not agreeing with her, she was returning to England. Her dear brother, the dean, would have come himself, but the claims on his time were so extensive, the parishioners would miss him so . . . it was clearly Millicent's duty to go.

She had never been out of England before, and she had a horror of travel, and an ingrained distrust of foreigners. She spoke a little French—sufficient for the purposes of travel and for obtaining any modest necessities, but not sufficient for carrying on any kind of conversation. She did not deplore this latter fact, for she was of opinion that French people were not the kind of people that one would naturally want to have conversation with; broadly speaking, they were not quite "nice," in spite of their ingratiating manners. The dear dean had given her endless advice, warning her earnestly not to enter into conversation with strangers, to obtain all information from the police, railway officials—in fact, any one in an official uniform.

He deeply regretted to say that he was afraid that France was not a country for a woman to travel about in alone. There were loose, bad people about, always on the look-out. . . . He really thought perhaps he ought not to let her go. It was only by the utmost persuasion, in which she rather exaggerated her knowledge of the French language and character, her courage, and indifference to discomfort, that she managed to carry the day.

She unpacked her valise, placed her things about the room, tried to thrust back the little stabs of homesickness as she visualized her darling room at the deanery. How strange and hard and unfriendly seemed these foreign hotel bedrooms—heavy and depressing, no chintz and lavender and photographs of . . . all the dear family, the dean, the nephews and nieces, the interior of the cathedral during harvest festival, no samplers and needlework or coloured reproductions of the paintings by Marcus Stone. Oh dear, how foolish she was! What *did* she expect?

She disrobed and donned a dressing-gown; then, armed with a sponge-bag and towel, she crept timidly down the passage to the bathroom, after closing her bedroom door and turning out the light. The gay bathroom cheered her. She wallowed luxuriously in the hot water, regarding her slim legs with quiet satisfaction. And for the first time since leaving home there came to her a pleasant moment— a sense of enjoyment in her adventure. After all, it *was* rather an adventure, and her life had been peculiarly devoid of it. What queer lives some people must live, travelling about, having experiences! How old was she? Not really old—not by any means. Forty-two? Forty-three? She had shut herself up so. She hardly ever regarded the potentialities of age. As the world went, she was a well-preserved woman for her age. A life of self-abnegation, simple living, healthy walking, and fresh air had kept her younger than these hurrying, pampered city people.

Love? yes, once when she was a young girl . . . he was a schoolmaster, a most estimable kind gentleman. They were never engaged—not actually, but it was a kind of understood thing. For three years it went on, this pleasant understanding and friendship. He was so gentle, so distinguished and considerate. She would have been happy to have continued in this strain for ever. But there was something lacking. Stephen had curious restless lapses. From the physical aspect of marriage she shrunk—yes, even with Stephen, who was gentleness and kindness itself. And then one day . . . one day he went away—vanished, and never returned. They told her he had married one of the country girls—a girl who used to work in Mrs. Forbes's dairy—not a very nice girl, she feared, one of these fast, pretty, foolish women. Heigho! well, she had lived that down, destructive as the blow appeared at the time. One lives everything down in time. There is always work, living for others, faith, duty. . . . At the same time she could sympathize with people who found satisfaction in unusual experiences. There would be lots to tell the dear dean when she wrote to him on the morrow: nearly losing her spectacles on the restaurant car; the amusing remarks of an American child on the train to Paris; the curious food everywhere, nothing simple and plain; the two English ladies at the hotel in Paris who told her about the death of their uncle—the poor man being taken ill on Friday and dying on Sunday afternoon, just before tea-time; the kindness of the hotel proprietor who had sat up for her; the prettiness of the chambermaid. Oh, yes, every one was really very kind. The French people, after all, were very nice. She had seen nothing—nothing but was quite nice and decorous. There would be lots to tell the dean to-morrow.

Her body glowed with the friction of the towel. She again donned her night attire and her thick, woollen dressing-gown. She tidied up the bathroom carefully in exactly the same way she was accustomed to do at home, then once more gripping her sponge-bag and towel, and turning out the light, she crept down the passage to her room. Entering the room she switched on the light and shut the door quickly. Then one of those ridiculous things happened—just the kind of thing you would expect to happen in a foreign hotel. The handle of the door came off in her hand. She ejaculated a quiet "Bother!" and sought to replace it with one hand, the other being occupied with the towel and sponge-bag. In doing this she behaved foolishly, for thrusting the knob carelessly against the steel pin—without properly securing it—she only succeeded in pushing the pin farther into the door and the knob was not adjusted. She uttered another little "Bother!" and put her sponge-bag and towel down on the floor. She then tried to recover the pin with her left hand, but it had gone in too far.

"How very foolish!" she thought, "I shall have to ring for the chambermaid—and perhaps the poor girl has gone to bed."

She turned and faced the room, and suddenly the awful horror was upon her.

There was a man asleep in her bed!

The sight of that swarthy face on the pillow, with its black tousled hair and heavy moustache, produced in her the most terrible moment of her life. Her heart nearly stopped. For some seconds she could neither think nor scream, and her first thought was:

"I mustn't scream!"

She stood there like one paralysed, staring at the man's head and the great curved hunch of his body under the clothes. When she began to think she thought very quickly, and all her thoughts worked together. The first vivid realization was that it wasn't the man's fault; it was *her* fault. *She was in the wrong room.* It was the man's room. The rooms were identical, but there were all his things about, his clothes thrown carelessly over chairs, his collar and tie on the wardrobe, his great heavy boots and the strange yellow trunk. She must get out somehow, anyhow. She clutched once more at the door, feverishly driving her finger-nails into the hole where the elusive pin had vanished. She tried to force her fingers in the crack and open the door that way, but it was of no avail. She was to all intents and purposes locked in—locked in a bedroom in a strange hotel alone with a man . . . a foreigner . . . a *Frenchman*!

She must think—she must think! She switched off the light. If the light was off he might not wake up. It might give her time to think how to act. It was surprising that he had not awakened. If he *did* wake up, what would he do? How could she explain herself? He wouldn't believe her. No one would believe her. In an English hotel it would be difficult enough, but here where she wasn't known, where they were all foreigners and consequently antagonistic . . . merciful heavens!

She *must* get out. Should she wake the man? No, she couldn't do that. He might murder her. He might . . . Oh, it was too awful to contemplate! Should she scream? ring for the chambermaid? But no, it would be the same thing. People would come rushing. They would find her there in the strange man's bedroom after midnight—she, Millicent Bracegirdle, sister of the Dean of Easingstoke! Easingstoke! Visions of Easingstoke flashed through her alarmed mind. Visions of the news arriving, women whispering around tea-tables: "Have you heard, my dear? Really no one would have imagined! Her poor brother! He will of course have to resign, you know, my dear. Have a little more cream, my love."

Would they put her in prison? She might be in the room for the purpose of stealing or . . . She might be in the room for the purpose of breaking every one of the ten commandments. There was no explaining it away. She was a ruined woman, suddenly and irretrievably, unless she could open the door. The chimney? Should she climb up the chimney? But where would that lead to? And then she visualized the man pulling her down by her legs when she was already smothered in soot. Any moment he might wake up.... She thought she heard the chambermaid going along the passage. If she had wanted to scream, she ought to have screamed before. The maid would know she had left the bathroom some minutes ago. Was she going to her room? Suddenly she remembered that she had told the chambermaid that she was not to be disturbed until she rang the next morning. That was something. Nobody would be going to her room to find out that she was not there.

An abrupt and desperate plan formed in her mind. It was already getting on for one o'clock. The man was probably a quite harmless commercial traveller or business man. He would probably get up about seven or eight o'clock, dress quickly, and go out. She would hide under his bed until he went. Only a matter of a few hours. Men don't look under their beds, although she made a religious practice of doing so herself. When he went he would be sure to open the door all right. The handle would be lying on the floor as though it had dropped off in the night. He would probably ring for the chamber-maid or open it with a penknife. Men were so clever at those things. When he had gone she would creep out and steal back to her room, and then there would be no necessity to give any explanation to any one. But heavens! What an experience! Once under the white frill of that bed she would be safe till the morning. In daylight nothing seemed so terrifying. With feline precaution she went down on her hands and knees and crept toward the bed. What a lucky thing there was that broad white frill! She lifted it at the foot of the bed and crept under. There was just sufficient depth to take her slim body. The floor was fortunately carpeted all over, but it seemed very close and dusty. Suppose she coughed or sneezed! Anything might happen. Of course ... it would be much more difficult to explain her presence under the bed than to explain her presence just inside the door. She held her breath in suspense. No sound came from above, but under this frill it was difficult to hear anything. It was almost more nerve-racking than hearing everything . . . listening for signs and portents. This temporary escape in any case would give her time to regard the predicament detachedly. Up to the present she had not been able to visualize the full significance of her action. She had in truth lost her head. She had been like a wild animal, consumed with the sole idea of escape . . . a mouse or a cat would do this kind of thing—take cover and lie low. If only it hadn't all happened *abroad!*

She tried to frame sentences of explanation in French, but French escaped her. And then—they talked so rapidly, these people. They didn't listen. The situation was intolerable. Would she be able to endure a night of it? At present she was not altogether uncomfortable, only stuffy and . . . very, very frightened. But she had to face six or seven or eight hours of it—perhaps even then discovery in the end! The minutes flashed by as she turned the matter over and over in her head. There was no solution. She began to wish she had screamed or awakened the man. She saw now that that would have been the wisest and most politic thing to do; but she had allowed ten minutes or a quarter of an hour to elapse from the moment when the chambermaid would know that she had left the bathroom. They would want an explanation of what she had been doing in the man's bedroom all that time. Why hadn't she screamed before?

She lifted the frill an inch or two and listened. She thought she heard the man breathing but she couldn't be sure. In any case it gave her more air. She became a little bolder, and thrust her face partly through the frill so that she could breathe freely. She tried to steady her nerves by concentrating on the fact that—well, there it was. She had done it. She must make the best of it. Perhaps it would be all right after all.

"Of course I shan't sleep," she kept on thinking, "I shan't be able to. In any case it will be safer not to sleep. I must be on the watch."

She set her teeth and waited grimly. Now that she had made up her mind to see the thing through in this manner she felt a little calmer. She almost smiled as she reflected that there would certainly be something to tell the dear dean when she wrote to him to-morrow. How would he take it? Of course he would believe it—he had never doubted a single word that she had uttered in her life—but the story would sound so . . . preposterous. In Easingstoke it would be almost impossible to envisage such an experience. She, Millicent Bracegirdle, spending a night under a strange man's bed in a foreign hotel! What would those women think? Fanny Shields and that garrulous old Mrs. Rusbridger? Perhaps . . . yes, perhaps it would be advisable to tell the dear dean to let the story go no further. One could hardly expect Mrs. Rushbridger to . . . not make implications . . . exaggerate. Oh, dear! What were they all doing now? They would be all asleep, every one in Easingstoke. Her dear brother always retired at ten-fifteen. He would be sleeping calmly and placidly, the sleep of the just . . . breathing the clear sweet air of Sussex, not this—oh, it *was* stuffy! She felt a great desire to cough. She mustn't do that.

Yes, at nine-thirty all the servants summoned to the library—a short service—never more than fifteen minutes, her brother didn't believe in a great deal of ritual—then at ten o'clock cocoa for every one. At ten-fifteen bed for every one. The dear sweet bedroom with the narrow white bed, by the side of which she had knelt every night as long as she could remember—even in her dear mother's day—and said her prayers.

Prayers! Yes, that was a curious thing. This was the first night in her life's experience that she had not said her prayers on retiring. The situation was certainly very peculiar . . . exceptional, one might call it. God would understand and forgive such a lapse. And yet after all, why . . . what was to prevent her saying her prayers? Of course she couldn't kneel in the proper devotional attitude, that would be a physical impossibility; nevertheless, perhaps her prayers might be just as efficacious . . . if they came from the heart.

So little Miss Bracegirdle curved her body and placed her hands in a devout attitude in front of her face and quite inaudibly murmured her prayers under the strange man's bed. "Our Father which art in heaven, Hallowed be Thy name. Thy kingdom come. Thy will be done in earth as it is in heaven; Give us this day our daily bread. And forgive us our trespasses. . . . " Trespasses! Yes, surely she was trespassing on this occasion, but God would understand. She had not wanted to trespass. She was an unwitting sinner. Without uttering a sound she went through her usual prayers in her heart.

At the end she added fervently:

"Please God protect me from the dangers and perils of this night."

Then she lay silent and inert, strangely soothed by the effort of praying. "After all," she thought, "it isn't the attitude which matters—it is that which occurs deep down in us." For the first time she began to meditate—almost to question—church forms and dogma. If an attitude was not indispensable, why a building, a ritual, a church at all? Of course her dear brother couldn't be wrong, the church was so old, so very old, its root deep buried in the story of human life, it was only that . . . well, outward forms could be misleading. Her own present position for instance. In the eyes of the world she had, by one silly careless little action, convicted herself of being the breaker of every single one of the ten commandments. She tried to think of one of which she could not be accused. But no—even to dishonouring her father and mother, bearing false witness, stealing, coveting her neighbour's . . . husband! That was the worst thing of all. Poor man! He might be a very pleasant honourable married gentleman with children and she—she was in a position to compromise him! Why hadn't she screamed? Too late! Too late!

It began to get very uncomfortable, stuffy, but at the same time draughty, and the floor was getting harder every minute. She changed her position stealthily and controlled her desire to cough. Her heart was beating rapidly. Over and over again recurred the vivid impression of every little incident and argument that had occurred to her from the moment she left the bathroom. This must, of course, be the room next to her own. So confusing, with perhaps twenty bedrooms all exactly alike on one side of a passage—how was one to remember whether one's number was 115 or 116? Her mind began to wander idly off into her school-days. She was always very bad at figures. She disliked Euclid and all those subjects about angles and equations—so unimportant, not leading anywhere. History she liked, and botany, and reading about strange foreign lands, although she had always been too timid to visit them. And the lives of great people, *most* fascinating—Oliver Cromwell, Lord Beaconsfield, Lincoln, Grace Darling—*there* was a heroine for you—General Booth, a great, good man, even if a little vulgar. She remembered dear old Miss Trimming talking about him one afternoon at the vicar of St. Bride's garden party. She was so amusing. She—*Good heavens!*

Almost unwittingly, Millicent Bracegirdle had emitted a violent sneeze!

It was finished! For the second time that night she was conscious of her heart nearly stopping. For the second time that night she was so paralysed with fear that her mentality went to pieces. Now she would hear the man get out of bed. He would walk across to the door, switch on the light, and then lift up the frill. She could almost see that fierce moustached face glaring at her and growling something in French. Then he would thrust out an arm and drag her out. And then? O God in heaven! What then?

"I shall scream before he does it. Perhaps I had better scream now. If he drags me out he will clap his hand over my mouth. Perhaps chloroform—"

But somehow she could not scream. She was too frightened even for that. She lifted the frill and listened. Was he moving stealthily across the carpet? She thought—no, she couldn't be sure. Anything might be happening. He might strike her from above—with one of those heavy boots perhaps. Nothing seemed to be happening, but the suspense was intolerable. She realized now that she hadn't the power to endure a night of it. Anything would be better than this—disgrace, imprisonment, even death. She would crawl out, wake the man, and try and explain as best she could.

She would switch on the light, cough, and say: "Monsieur!"

Then he would start up and stare at her.

Then she would say—what should she say?

"*Pardon, monsieur, mais je*—" What on earth was the French for "I have made a mistake."

"*J'ai tort. C'est la chambre*—er—incorrect. *Voulez-vous*—er—"

What was the French for "door-knob," "let me go"?

It didn't matter. She would turn on the light, cough and trust to luck. If he got out of bed, and came toward her, she would scream the hotel down.

The resolution formed, she crawled deliberately out at the foot of the bed. She scrambled hastily toward the door—a perilous journey. In a few seconds the room was flooded with light. She turned toward the bed, coughed, and cried out boldly:

"Monsieur!"

Then, for the third time that night, little Miss Bracegirdle's heart all but stopped. In this case the climax of the horror took longer to develop, but when it was reached, it clouded the other two experiences into insignificance.

The man on the bed was dead!

She had never beheld death before, but one does not mistake death.

She stared at him bewildered, and repeated almost in a whisper: "Monsieur! . . . Monsieur!"

Then she tiptoed toward the bed. The hair and moustache looked extraordinarily black in that grey, wax-like setting. The mouth was slightly open, and the face, which in life might have been vicious and sensual, looked incredibly peaceful and far away. It was as though she were regarding the features of a man across some vast passage of time, a being who had always been completely remote from mundane preoccupations.

When the full truth came home to her, little Miss Bracegirdle buried her face in her hands and murmured:

"Poor fellow—poor fellow!"

For the moment her own position seemed an affair of small consequence. She was in the presence of something greater and more all-pervading. Almost instinctively she knelt by the bed and prayed.

For a few moments she seemed to be possessed by an extraordinary calmness and detachment. The burden of her hotel predicament was a gossamer trouble—a silly, trivial, almost comic episode, something that could be explained away.

But this man—he had lived his life, whatever it was like, and now he was in the presence of his Maker. What kind of man had he been?

Her meditations were broken by an abrupt sound. It was that of a pair of heavy boots being thrown down by the door outside.

She started, thinking at first it was someone knocking or trying to get in. She heard the "boots," however, stumping away down the corridor, and the realization stabbed her with the truth of her own position. She mustn't stop there. The necessity to get out was even more urgent.

To be found in a strange man's bedroom in the night is bad enough, but to be found in a dead man's bedroom was even worse. They could accuse her of murder, perhaps. Yes, that would be it— how could she possibly explain to these foreigners? Good God! they would hang her. No, guillotine her, that's what they do in France. They would chop her head off with a great steel knife. Merciful heavens! She envisaged herself standing blindfold, by a priest and an executioner in a red cap, like that man in the Dickens story—what was his name? . . . Sydney Carton, that was it, and before he went on the scaffold he said:

"It is a far, far better thing that I do than I have ever done." But no, she couldn't say that. It would be a far, far worse thing that she did. What about the dear dean? Her sister-in-law arriving alone from Paraguay to-morrow? All her dear people and friends in Easingstoke? Her darling Tony, the large grey tabby cat? It was her duty not to have her head chopped off if it could possibly be avoided. She could do no good in the room. She could not recall the dead to life. Her only mission was to escape. Any minute people might arrive. The chambermaid, the boots, the manager, the gendarmes. . . . Visions of gendarmes arriving armed with swords and note-books vitalized her almost exhausted energies. She was a desperate woman. Fortunately now she had not to worry about the light. She sprang once more at the door and tried to force it open with her fingers. The result hurt her and gave her pause. If she was to escape she must *think*, and think intensely. She mustn't do anything rash and silly, she must just think and plan calmly.

She examined the lock carefully. There was no keyhole, but there was a slip-bolt, so that the hotel guest could lock the door on the inside, but it couldn't be locked on the outside. Oh, why didn't this poor dear dead man lock his door last night? Then this trouble could not have happened. She could see the end of the steel pin. It was about half an inch down the hole. If any one was passing they must surely notice the handle sticking out foot far the other side! She drew a hairpin out of her hair and tried to coax the pin back, but she only succeeded in pushing it a little farther in. She felt the colour leaving her face, and a strange feeling of faintness come over her.

She was fighting for her life, she mustn't give way. She darted round the room like an animal in a trap, her mind alert for the slightest crevice of escape. The window had no balcony and there was a drop of five stories to the street below. Dawn was breaking. Soon the activities of the hotel and the city would begin. The thing must be accomplished before then.

She went back once more and stared at the lock. She stared at the dead man's property, his razors, and brushes, and writing materials, pens and pencils and rubber and sealing-wax. . . . Sealing-wax!

Necessity is truly the mother of invention. It is in any case quite certain that Millicent Bracegirdle, who had never invented a thing in her life, would never have evolved the ingenious little device she did, had she not believed that her position was utterly desperate. For in the end this is what she did. She got together a box of matches, a candle, a bar of sealing-wax, and a hairpin. She made a little pool of hot sealing-wax, into which she dipped the end of the hairpin. Collecting a small blob on the end of it she thrust it into the hole, and let it adhere to the end of the steel pin. At the seventh attempt she got the thing to move. It took her just an hour and ten minutes to get that steel pin back into the room, and when at length it came far enough through for her to grip it with her finger-nails, she burst into tears through the sheer physical tension of the strain. Very, very carefully she pulled it through, and holding it firmly with her left hand she fixed the knob with her right, then slowly turned it.

The door opened!

The temptation to dash out into the corridor and scream with relief was almost irresistible, but she forbore. She listened; she peeped out. No one was about. With beating heart, she went out, closing the door inaudibly. She crept like a little mouse to the room next door, stole in and flung herself on her bed. Immediately she did so it flashed through her mind that *she had left her sponge-bag and towel in the dead man's room!*

In looking back upon her experience she always considered that that second expedition was the worst of all. She might have left the sponge-bag and towel there, only that the towel—she never used hotel towels—had neatly inscribed in the corner "M. B."

With furtive caution she managed to retrace her steps. She re-entered the dead man's room, reclaimed her property, and returned to her own. When this mission was accomplished she was indeed well-nigh spent. She lay on her bed and groaned feebly. At last she fell into a fevered sleep.

It was eleven o'clock when she awoke and no one had been to disturb her. The sun was shining, and the experiences of the night appeared a dubious nightmare. Surely she had dreamt it all?

With dread still burning in her heart she rang the bell. After a short interval of time the chambermaid appeared. The girl's eyes were bright with some uncontrollable excitement. No, she had not been dreaming. This girl had heard something.

"Will you bring me some tea, please?"

"Certainly, madame." The maid drew back the curtains and fussed about the room. She was under a pledge of secrecy, but she could contain herself no longer. Suddenly she approached the bed and whispered excitedly:

"Oh, madame, I have promised not to tell . . . but a terrible thing has happened. A man, a dead man, has been found in room 117—a guest. Please not to say I tell you. But they have all been there, the gendarmes, the doctors, the inspectors. Oh, it is terrible . . . terrible." The little lady in the bed said nothing. There was indeed nothing to say. But Marie Louise Lancret was too full of emotional excitement to spare her.

"But the terrible thing is—Do you know who he was, madame? They say it is Boldhu, the man wanted for the murder of Jeanne Carreton in the barn at Vincennes. They say he strangled her, and then cut her up in pieces and hid her in two barrels which he threw into the river. . . . Oh, but he was a bad man, madame, a terrible bad man . . . and he died in the room next door . . . suicide, they think; or was it an attack of the heart? . . . Remorse, some shock perhaps. . . . Did you say a *café complet*, madame?"

"No, thank you, my dear . . . just a cup of tea . . . strong tea . . ."

"*Parfaitement*, madame."

The girl retired, and a little later a waiter entered the room with a tray of tea. She could never get over her surprise at this. It seemed so—well, indecorous for a man—although only a waiter— to enter a lady's bedroom. There was no doubt a great deal in what the dear dean said. They were certainly very peculiar, these French people—they had most peculiar notions. It was not the way they behaved at Easingstoke. She got farther under the sheets, but the waiter appeared quite indifferent to the situation. He put the tray down and retired.

When he had gone she sat up and sipped her tea, which gradually warmed her. She was glad the sun was shining. She would have to get up soon. They said that her sister-in-law's boat was due to berth at one o'clock. That would give her time to dress comfortably, write to her brother, and then go down to the docks.

Poor man! So he had been a murderer, a man who cut up the bodies of his victims . . . and she had spent the night in his bedroom! They were certainly a most—how could she describe it?—people. Nevertheless she felt a little glad that at the end she had been there to kneel and pray by his bedside. Probably nobody else had ever done that. It was very difficult to judge people. . . . Something at some time might have gone wrong. He might not have murdered the woman after all. People were often wrongly convicted. She herself . . . If the police had found her in that room at three o'clock that morning . . . It is that which takes place in the heart which counts. One learns and learns. Had she not learnt that one can pray just as effectively lying under a bed as kneeling beside it? Poor man!

She washed and dressed herself and walked calmly down to the writing-room. There was no evidence of excitement among the other hotel guests. Probably none of them knew about the tragedy except herself. She went to a writing-table, and after profound meditation wrote as follows:

"MY DEAR BROTHER,

I arrived late last night after a very pleasant journey. Every one was very kind and attentive, the manager was sitting up for me. I nearly lost my spectacle case in the restaurant car! But a kind old gentleman found it and returned it to me. There was a most amusing American child on the train. I will tell you about her on my return. The people are very pleasant, but the food is peculiar, nothing plain and wholesome. I am going down to meet Annie at one o'clock. How have you been keeping, my dear? I hope you have not had any further return of the bronchial attacks. Please tell Lizzie that I remembered in the train on the way here that that large stone jar of marmalade that Mrs. Hunt made is behind those empty tins in the top shelf of the cupboard next to the coachhouse. I wonder whether Mrs. Butler was able to come to evensong after all? This is a nice hotel, but I think Annie and I will stay at the Grand to-night, as the bedrooms here are rather noisy. Well, my dear, nothing more till I return. Do take care of yourself.

"Your loving sister,

"MILLICENT."

Yes, she couldn't tell Peter about it, neither in the letter nor when she went back to him. It was her duty not to tell him. It would only distress him; she felt convinced of it. In this curious foreign atmosphere the thing appeared possible, but in Easingstoke the mere recounting of the fantastic situations would be positively . . . indelicate. There was no escaping that broad general fact—she had spent a night in a strange man's bedroom. Whether he was a gentleman or a criminal, even whether he was dead or alive, did not seem to mitigate the jar upon her sensibilities, or rather it would not mitigate the jar upon the peculiarly sensitive relationship between her brother and herself. To say that she had been to the bathroom, the knob of the door-handle came off in her hand, she was too frightened to awaken the sleeper or scream, she got under the bed—well, it was all perfectly true. Peter would believe her, but—one simply could not conceive such a situation in Easingstoke deanery. It would create a curious little barrier between them, as though she had been dipped in some mysterious solution which alienated her. It was her duty not to tell.

She put on her hat, and went out to post the letter. She distrusted an hotel letter-box. One never knew who handled these letters. It was not a proper official way of treating them. She walked to the head post office in Bordeaux.

The sun was shining. It was very pleasant walking about amongst these queer excitable people, so foreign and different-looking—and the *cafés* already crowded with chattering men and women, and the flower stalls, and the strange odour of—what was it? Salt? Brine? Charcoal? A military band was playing in the square—very gay and moving. It was all life, and movement, and bustle—thrilling rather.

"I spent a night in a strange man's bedroom."

Little Miss Bracegirdle hunched her shoulders, murmured to herself, and walked faster. She reached the post office and found the large metal plate with the slot for letters and "R.F." stamped above it. Something official at last! Her face was a little flushed—was it the warmth of the day or the contact of movement and life?—as she put her letter into the slot. After posting it she put her hand into the slot and flicked it round to see that there were no foreign contraptions to impede its safe delivery. No, the letter had dropped safely in. She sighed contentedly and walked off in the direction of the docks to meet her sister-in-law from Paraguay.

CUT-THROAT FARM

J. D. BERESFORD

"Ah! Us calls un coot-thro-at farm," said my driver.

"But why?" I asked nervously.

"Yew'll see whoy when yew gets there." And this was all the information I could get from him. So, finding excuse for the driver's ill-temper in the sodden weather, I shielded my strained eyes from the onslaught of the rain and relapsed into silence.

For two miles or thereabouts after leaving Mawdsley we had followed a decent road, but now we were jerking warily down a rutted lane that appeared, so far as I could see through the blur of rain, to creep downwards into a dark, tree-clad valley, the depths of which were obscured in a mass of soaked, depressing verdure. Still the track fell and fell, and on my left I could see a dark slope of trees rising higher and higher above me—a slope that, seen thus dimly, appeared gigantic, overpowering. Then the lane plunged, dipping ever more steeply, into a black wood, and I clung to the side of the swaying cart, expecting catastrophe every moment. I tried desperately to combat the gloom that was overpowering me; I repeated to myself that this was England, that I was within a hundred miles of London, that I was going to spend a delightful summer at the "Valley Farm"; but, despite my efforts, a horror of the place gripped me; I found myself absurdly muttering "The Valley of the Shadow of Death."

The wood ended abruptly, and we came out on the very keel of the valley. "That's un," muttered my driver with a nod; and, shaking the rain from my cap, I discerned a hunched, lop-sided house that crouched in a clearing at the foot of the opposite slope.

I pictured it as having slid down the interminable wave of trees that reared its dim crest into the sky beyond, as having slid till brought to a too sudden standstill in the place where it now remained, dislocated, a confusion.

Such was my coming, my first sight of "Cut-throat Farm." If my subsequent experience seems morbid and unaccountable, my final cowardice indefensible, excuse must be found in that first impression which tinged my mind with a gloom and foreboding I could not afterwards throw off.

It was at starveling place. The stock was meagre: a single cow, whose bones were too prominent even for an Alderney, a scatter of ragged, long-legged fowls, three draggled ducks, an old loose-skinned black sow. This was all, save for "my little pig," as I learned fondly to call him, the one bright, cheerful thing in all the valley; a whimsical creature of quaint moods, full of an odd humour that had in it some quality of sadness. Looking back, I see now that his fun was an attempt, largely successful, to make what he could of his short life, to jest in the face of death. . . . My host and his wife were an awe-inspiring couple. He was short and swarthy, the hairiest man I have ever seen, bearded to the cheek bones, with hair low down over his strip of forehead, and great woolly eyebrows. His wife was tall, predatory, with a high-bridged, bony nose and wistfully hungry eyes; she was thinner, more angular even than the emaciated cow: that hastily covered skeleton who stood mournfully ruminant in the dirty yard.

My first morning at the Valley Farm was marked by an incident, not in itself unduly disconcerting, but typical, an incident surcharged, as I see now, with warning. I had had breakfast. I remember that at the time I considered it scanty (later, it became a memory of plenty) and insufficient even for the standard of thirty shillings a week, a sum that covered the whole cost of my entertainment. I considered this price very reasonable when I answered the advertisement.

After breakfast I stood by the window, which was open at the bottom, the top sash being fixed. Outside were clustered the half-dozen gawky chickens, clamorous and excited, straining their stringy necks to look into the room over the low sill. "The poor brutes are hungry," I muttered with some feeling, and I fetched a fragment of crust and threw it to them. Lord! how they fought for those few crumbs! I turned back into the room to get the remainder of the bread left from my breakfast, and, as I turned, a lanky young cockerel, inflamed by a desperate courage, hopped over the sill and followed me. I heard him come, and, interested to note to what lengths he would go, I retreated further into the room. In an instant he was on the table and had seized the chunk of bread from the platter; then, with a frightened squawk, he was out and off across the yard, sprinting away with impetuous, leaping strides, outstretching his fellows, who had immediately set off after him in hot pursuit. On his way he had to pass my little pig (my first sight of him, and how typical), who was sauntering casually in the direction of the yard gate. An inveterate jester, my little pig; he slewed round suddenly as the straining bird came up to him and made a well-timed snap which startled the rooster, intent only upon the hungry crowd behind, into dropping his booty, a morsel something too large for his gaping beak. I can still see the merry twinkle in my little pig's eyes as he ate that piece of bread. It seemed to me that he was unduly deliberate in the doing of it; maybe he chaffed the resentful but intimidated young cockerel, in some Esperanto of the farmyard, as he ate. . . . Nothing else of any account happened that morning; I remember I saw the farmer sharpening his knife, and wondered what he could find to kill with it. . . .

The next morning the young cockerel was not among the expectant group of five that waited under my window; but I met him again at dinner, and as I essayed to gather nourishment from his ill-covered bones, I smiled again over my recollection of his encounter with my little black pig. He is such a neat, quaint little creature, that pig; we have become friends over a few scraps of food, though he allows no liberties as yet. . . .

Among my notes of that stay at the Valley Farm I have found the following; they seem to me so full of suggestion that I append them just as they stand:

"The stock is disappearing; only one old fowl left—the one that has twice provided me with an egg or so I judge from her ululations. I suppose she will be kept to the last. . . . I was right; there are only two ducks this morning. . . . The ducks are all finished at last (thank Heaven!), but I have a horrible fear upon me. The cow has disappeared! The farmer's wife says they have sold her. Did she buy the suspiciously lean and stringy beef I now live on with the price of her? . . . The sow has gone, and the farmer's wife has bought pork with the money obtained. I may be wrong in thus associating the meat I am given with those vanished animals. Can it be possible that there is some superstition or sentimental affection in buying the flesh of animals similar to those they have just sold? I see points about this theory, but why is the farmer always sharpening his knife? . . . I cannot believe it! He is not there this morning, and yet, surely, no Spanish Conquistadore of the sixteenth century could have had the brutality to kill my little pig, my whimsical, wayward, humorous little companion, the one living thing in all this accursed valley that could smile in the face of doom. . . . More pork! It *must* be the remains of the old sow; but why has she become so suddenly tender? How is it that she has furnished me with the first satisfying meal I have had for weeks? I cannot believe it, and I dare not ask the farmer's wife. I *will* not believe it until the pork is finished. He must have been sold. I am convinced of it. I hope he has found a happier, less hungry home, poor little chap. . . . I had an egg this morning that went off with a pop when I cracked it. I had a curious sensation when it happened. I have not hitherto been a believer in metempsychosis, but an intuition came to me at that moment that the soul of my little pig had entered into that egg. It would have been so like his whimsical, joking way to go off pop. And I was so hungry. . . . I have been writing a story of two men cast away in an open boat, with very striking patches of what one may call local colour. They suffered horribly from hunger. . . . The old hen has gone at last, and the farmer is still sharpening his knife. Why? Is he going to cut vegetables for me? I don't know where he will find them. In my story of the men in the open boat, one of them, driven to desperation. . . . Bread and cheese for dinner. Is this the lull before the storm? I surprised a curious expression in the farmer's eye this afternoon. He was sizing me up with an appraising look. I can't help feeling that he was mentally going through the process I described in my story after the stronger man had. . . . The farmer brought me my breakfast of bread and butter this morning. He says his wife is ill, that she is not getting up, that—I don't know what he said. No! Definitely and finally, I cannot, I will not. . . ." (My notes end here.)

***

After that last breakfast I went for a stroll in the yard, and in an outhouse I saw the farmer sharpening his knife. With an assumed nonchalance worthy of my little pig, I strolled carelessly to the gate; then, with tediously idle steps I sauntered towards the wood. And then—I ran. God, how I ran!

THE DAMNED THING
AMBROSE BIERCE

1: One Does Not Always Eat What is on the Table

By the light of a tallow candle which had been placed on one end of a
rough table a man was reading something written in a book. It was
an old account-book, greatly worn; and the writing was not, apparently,
very legible, for the man sometimes held the page close to the flame of
the candle to get a stronger light on it. The shadow of the book would
then throw into obscurity a half of the room, darkening a number of
faces and figures; for besides the reader, eight other men were present.
Seven of them sat against the rough log walls, silent, motionless, and the
room being small, not very far from the table. By extending an arm anyone of them could have touched the eighth man, who lay on the table,
face upward, partly covered by a sheet, his arms at his sides. He was dead.

The man with the book was not reading aloud, and no one spoke; all seemed to be waiting for something to occur; the dead man only was without expectation. From the blank darkness outside came in, through the aperture that served for a window, all the ever unfamiliar noises of night in the wilderness—the long nameless note of a distant coyote; the stilly pulsing thrill of tireless insects in trees; strange cries of night birds, so different from those of the birds of day; the drone of great blundering beetles, and all that mysterious chorus of small sounds that seem always to have been but half heard when they have suddenly ceased, as if conscious of an indiscretion. But nothing of all this was noted in that company; its members were not overmuch addicted to idle interest in matters of no practical importance; that was obvious in every line of their rugged faces—obvious even in the dim light of the single candle. They were evidently men of the vicinity—farmers and woodsmen.

The person reading was a trifle different; one would have said of him that he was of the world, worldly, albeit there was that in his attire which attested a certain fellowship with the organisms of his environment. His coat would hardly have passed muster in San Francisco; his foot-gear was not of urban origin, and the hat that lay by him on the floor (he was the only one uncovered) was such that if one had considered it as an article of mere personal adornment he would have missed its meaning. In countenance the man was rather prepossessing, with just a hint of sternness; though that he may have assumed or cultivated, as appropriate to one in authority. For he was a coroner. It was by virtue of his office that he had possession of the book in which he was reading; it had been found among the dead man's effects—in his cabin, where the inquest was now taking place.

When the coroner had finished reading he put the book into his breast-pocket. At that moment the door was pushed open and a young man entered. He, clearly, was not of mountain birth and breeding: he was clad as those who dwell in cities. His clothing was dusty, however, as from travel. He had, in fact, been riding hard to attend the inquest.

The coroner nodded; no one else greeted him.

"We have waited for you," said the coroner. "It is necessary to have done with this business to-night."

The young man smiled. "I am sorry to have kept you," he said. "I went away, not to evade your summons, but to post to my newspaper an account of what I suppose I am called back to relate."

The coroner smiled.

"The account that you posted to your newspaper," he said, "differs, probably, from that which you will give here under oath."

"That," replied the other, rather hotly and with a visible flush, "is as you please. I used manifold paper and have a copy of what I sent. It was not written as news, for it is incredible, but as fiction. It may go as a part of my testimony under oath."

"But you say it is incredible."

"That is nothing to you, sir, if I also swear that it is true."

The coroner was silent for a time, his eyes upon the floor. The men about the sides of the cabin talked in whispers, but seldom withdrew their gaze from the face of the corpse. Presently the coroner lifted his eyes and said: "We will resume the inquest."

The men removed their hats. The witness was sworn.

"What is your name?" the coroner asked.

"William Harker."

"Age?"

"Twenty-seven."

"You knew the deceased, Hugh Morgan?"

"Yes."

"You were with him when he died?"

"Near him."

"How did that happen—your presence, I mean?"

"I was visiting him at this place to shoot and fish. A part of my purpose, however, was to study him and his odd, solitary way of life. He seemed a good model for a character in fiction. I sometimes write stories."

"I sometimes read them."

"Thank you."

"Stories in general—not yours."

Some of the jurors laughed. Against a sombre background humour shows high lights. Soldiers in the intervals of battle laugh easily, and a jest in the death-chamber conquers by surprise.

"Relate the circumstances of this man's death," said the coroner. "You may use any notes or memoranda that you please."

The witness understood. Pulling a manuscript from his breast pocket he held it near the candle and turning the leaves until he found the passage that he wanted began to read.

2: What may Happen in a Field of Wild Oats

". . . The sun had hardly risen when we left the house. We were looking for quail, each with a shotgun, but we had only one dog. Morgan said that our best ground was beyond a certain ridge that he pointed out, and we crossed it by a trail through the *chaparral.* On the other side was comparatively level ground, thickly covered with wild oats. As we emerged from the *chaparral* Morgan was but a few yards in advance. Suddenly we heard, at a little distance to our right and partly in front, a noise as of some animal thrashing about in the bushes, which we could see were violently agitated.

"'We've started a deer,' I said, 'I wish we had brought a rifle.'

"Morgan, who had stopped and was intently watching the agitated *chaparral*, said nothing, but had cocked both barrels of his gun and was holding it in readiness to aim. I thought him a trifle excited, which surprised me, for he had a reputation for exceptional coolness, even in moments of sudden and imminent peril.

"'Oh, come,' I said. 'You are not going to fill up a deer with quail-shot, are you?'

"Still he did not reply; but catching a sight of his face as he turned it slightly toward me I was struck by the intensity of his look. Then I understood that we had serious business in hand, and my first conjecture was that we had 'jumped' a grizzly. I advanced to Morgan's side, cocking my piece as I moved.

"The bushes were now quiet and the sounds had ceased, but Morgan was as attentive to the place as before.

"'What is it? What the devil is it?' I asked.

"'That Damned Thing!' he replied, without turning his head. His voice was husky and unnatural. He trembled visibly.

"I was about to speak further, when I observed the wild oats near the place of the disturbance moving in the most inexplicable way. I can hardly describe it. It seemed as if stirred by a streak of wind, which not only bent it, but pressed it down—crushed it so that it did not rise; and this movement was slowly prolonging itself directly toward us.

"Nothing that I had ever seen had affected me so strangely as this unfamiliar and unaccountable phenomenon, yet I am unable to recall any sense of fear. I remember—and tell it here because, singularly enough, I recollected it then—that once in looking carelessly out of an open window I momentarily mistook a small tree close at hand for one of a group of larger trees at a little distance away. It looked the same size as the others, but being more distinctly and sharply defined in mass and detail seemed out of harmony with them. It was a mere falsification of the law of aerial perspective, but it startled, almost terrified me. We so rely upon the orderly operation of familiar natural laws that any seeming suspension of them is noted as a menace to our safety, a warning of unthinkable calamity. So now the apparently causeless movement of the herbiage and the slow, undeviating approach of the line of disturbance were distinctly disquieting. My companion appeared actually frightened, and I could hardly credit my senses when I saw him suddenly throw his gun to his shoulder and fire both barrels at the agitated grain! Before the smoke of the discharge had cleared away I heard a loud savage cry—a scream like that of a wild animal—and flinging his gun upon the ground Morgan sprang away and ran swiftly from the spot. At the same instant I was thrown violently to the ground by the impact of something unseen in the smoke—some soft, heavy substance that seemed thrown against me with great force.

"Before I could get upon my feet and recover my gun, which seemed to have been struck from my hands, I heard Morgan crying out as if in mortal agony, and mingling with his cries were such hoarse, savage sounds as one hears from fighting dogs. Inexpressibly terrified, I struggled to my feet and looked in the direction of Morgan's retreat; and may Heaven in mercy spare me from another sight like that! At a distance of less than thirty yards was my friend, down upon one knee, his head thrown back at a frightful angle, hatless, his long hair in disorder and his whole body in violent movement from side to side, backward and forward. His right arm was lifted and seemed to lack the hand—at least, I could see none. The other arm was invisible. At times, as my memory now reports this extraordinary scene, I could discern but a part of his body; it was as if he had been partly blotted out—I cannot otherwise express it—then a shifting of his position would bring it all into view again.

"All this must have occurred within a few seconds, yet in that time Morgan assumed all the postures of a determined wrestler vanquished by superior weight and strength. I saw nothing but him, and him not always distinctly. During the entire incident his shouts and curses were heard, as if through an enveloping uproar of such sounds of rage and fury as I had never heard from the throat of man or brute!

"For a moment only I stood irresolute, then throwing down my gun I ran forward to my friend's assistance. I had a vague belief that he was suffering from a fit, or some form of convulsion. Before I could reach his side he was down and quiet. All sounds had ceased, but with a feeling of such terror as even these awful events had not inspired I now saw again the mysterious movement of the wild oats, prolonging itself from the trampled area about the prostrate man toward the edge of a wood. It was only when it had reached the wood that I was able to withdraw my eyes and look at my companion. He was dead."

3: A Man though Naked may be in Rags

The coroner rose from his seat and stood beside the dead man. Lifting an edge of the sheet he pulled it away, exposing the entire body, altogether naked and showing in the candlelight a clay-like yellow. It had, however, broad maculations of bluish black, obviously caused by extravasated blood from contusions. The chest and sides looked as if they had been beaten with a bludgeon. There were dreadful lacerations; the skin was torn in strips and shreds.

The coroner moved round to the end of the table and undid a silk handkerchief which had been passed under the chin and knot- ted on the top of the head. When the handkerchief was drawn away it exposed what had been the throat. Some of the jurors who had risen to get a better view repented their curiosity and turned away their faces. Witness Harker went to the open window and leaned out across the sill, faint and sick. Dropping the handkerchief upon the dead man's neck the coroner stepped to an angle of the room and from a pile of clothing produced one garment after another, each of which he held up a moment for inspection. All were torn, and stiff with blood. The jurors did not make a closer inspection. They seemed rather uninterested.

They had, in truth, seen all this before; the only thing that was new to them being Harker's testimony.

"Gentlemen," the coroner said, "we have no more evidence, I think. Your duty has been already explained to you; if there is nothing you wish to ask you may go outside and consider your verdict."

The foreman rose—a tall, bearded man of sixty, coarsely clad.

"I should like to ask one question, Mr. Coroner," he said.

"What asylum did this yer last witness escape from?"

"Mr. Harker," said the coroner gravely and tranquilly, "from what asylum did you last escape?"

Harker flushed crimson again, but said nothing, and the seven jurors rose and solemnly filed out of the cabin.

"If you have done insulting me, sir," said Harker, as soon as he and the officer were left alone with the dead man, "I suppose I am at liberty to go?"

"Yes."

Harker started to leave, but paused, with his hand on the doorlatch. The habit of his profession was strong in him—stronger than his sense of personal dignity. He turned about and said:

"The book that you have there—I recognise it as Morgan's diary. You seemed greatly interested in it; you read in it while I was testifying. May I see it? The public would like—"

"The book will cut no figure in this matter," replied the official, slipping it into his coat pocket; "all the entries in it were made before the writer's death."

As Harker passed out of the house the jury re-entered and stood about the table, on which the now covered corpse showed under the sheet with sharp definition. The foreman seated himself near the candle, produced from his breast-pocket a pencil and scrap of paper and wrote rather laboriously the following verdict, which with various degrees of effort all signed:

"We, the jury, do find that the remains come to their death at the hands of a mountain lion, but some of us thinks, all the same, they had fits."

4: An Explanation from the Tomb

In the diary of the late Hugh Morgan are certain interesting entries having, possibly, a scientific value as suggestions. At the inquest upon his body the book was not put in evidence; possibly the coroner thought it not worth while to confuse the jury. The date of the first of the entries mentioned cannot be ascertained; the upper part of the leaf is torn away; the part of the entry remaining follows:

". . . would run in a half-circle, keeping his head turned always toward the centre, and again he would stand still, barking furiously. At last he ran away into the brush as fast as he could go. I thought at first that he had gone mad, but on returning to the house found no other alteration in his manner than what was obviously due to fear of punishment.

"Can a dog see with his nose? Do odours impress some cerebral centre with images of the thing that emitted them? . . .

"*Sept.* 2.—Looking at the stars last night as they rose above the crest of the ridge east of the house, I observed them successively disappear—from left to right. Each was eclipsed but an instant, and only a few at the same time, but along the entire length of the ridge all that were within a degree or two of the crest were blotted out. It was as if something had passed along between me and them; but I could not see it, and the stars were not thick enough to define its outline. Ugh! don't like this."...

Several weeks' entries are missing, three leaves being torn from the book.

"*Sept*. 27.—It has been about here again—I find evidences of its presence every day. I watched again all last night in the same cover, gun in hand, double-charged with buckshot. In the morning the fresh footprints were there, as before. Yet I would have sworn that I did not sleep—indeed, I hardly sleep at all. It is terrible, insupportable! If these amazing experiences are real I shall go mad; if they are fanciful I am mad already.

"*Oct*. 3.—I shall not go—it shall not drive me away. No, this is *my* house, *my* land. God hates a coward....

"*Oct*. 5.—I can stand it no longer; I have invited Harker to pass a few weeks with me—he has a level head. I can judge from his manner if he thinks me mad.

"*Oct*. 7.—I have the solution of the mystery; it came to me last night—suddenly, as by revelation. How simple—how terribly simple!

"There are sounds that we cannot hear. At either end of the scale are notes that stir no chord of that imperfect instrument, the human ear. They are too high or too grave. I have observed a flock of blackbirds occupying an entire tree-top—the tops of several trees—and all in full song. Suddenly—in a moment—at absolutely the same instant—all spring into the air and fly away. How? They could not all see one another—whole tree-tops intervened. At no point could a leader have been visible to all. There must have been a signal of warning or command, high and shrill above the din, but by me unheard. I have observed, too, the same simultaneous flight when all were silent, among not only blackbirds, but other birds—quail, for example, widely separated by bushes—even on opposite sides of a hill.

"It is known to seamen that a school of whales basking or sporting on the surface of the ocean, miles apart, with the convexity of the earth between, will sometimes dive at the same instant—all gone out of sight in a moment. The signal has been sounded—too grave for the ear of the sailor at the masthead and his comrades on the deck—who nevertheless feel its vibrations in the ship as the stones of a cathedral are stirred by the bass of the organ.

"As with sounds, so with colours. At each end of the solar spectrum the chemist can detect the presence of what are known as 'actinic' rays. They represent colours—integral colours in the composition of light—which we are unable to discern. The human eye is an imperfect instrument; its range is but a few octaves of the real 'chromatic scale.' I am not mad; here are colours that we cannot see.

"And, God help me! the Damned Thing is of such a colour!"

SECRET WORSHIP
ALGERNON BLACKWOOD

Harris, the silk merchant, was in South Germany on his way home from a business trip when the idea came to him suddenly that he would take the mountain railway from Strassbourg and run down to revisit his old school after an interval of something more than thirty years. And it was to this chance impulse of the junior partner in Harris Brothers of St. Paul's Churchyard that John Silence owed one of the most curious cases of his whole experience, for at that very moment he happened to be tramping these same mountains with a holiday knapsack, and from different points of the compass the two men were actually converging towards the same inn.

Now, deep down in the heart that for thirty years had been concerned chiefly with the profitable buying and selling of silk, this school had left the imprint of its peculiar influence, and, though perhaps unknown to Harris, had strongly coloured the whole of his subsequent existence. It belonged to the deeply religious life of a small Protestant community (which it is unnecessary to specify), and his father had sent him there at the age of fifteen, partly because he would learn the German requisite for the conduct of the silk business, and partly because the discipline was strict, and discipline was what his soul and body needed just then more than anything else.

The life, indeed, had proved exceedingly severe, and young Harris benefited accordingly; for though corporal punishment was unknown, there was a system of mental and spiritual correction which somehow made the soul stand proudly erect to receive it, while it struck at the very root of the fault and taught the boy that his character was being cleaned and strengthened, and that he was not merely being tortured in a kind of personal revenge.

That was over thirty years ago, when he was a dreamy and impressionable youth of fifteen; and now, as the train climbed slowly up the winding mountain gorges, his mind travelled back somewhat lovingly over the intervening period, and forgotten details rose vividly again before him out of the shadows. The life there had been very wonderful, it seemed to him, in that remote mountain village, protected from the tumults of the world by the love and worship of the devout Brotherhood that ministered to the needs of some hundred boys from every country in Europe. Sharply the scenes came back to him. He smelt again the long stone corridors, the hot pinewood rooms, where the sultry hours of summer study were passed with bees droning through open windows in the sunshine, and German characters struggling in the mind with dreams of English lawns—and then the sudden awful cry of the master in German—

"Harris, stand up! You sleep!"

And he recalled the dreadful standing motionless for an hour, book in hand, while the knees felt like wax and the head grew heavier than a cannon-ball.

The very smell of the cooking came back to him—the daily *Sauerkraut,* the watery chocolate on Sundays, the flavour of the stringy meat served twice a week at *Mittagessen;* and he smiled to think again of the half-rations that was the punishment for speaking English. The very odour of the milk-bowls—the hot sweet aroma that rose from the soaking peasant-bread at the six-o'clock breakfast—came back to him pungently, and he saw the huge *Speiseaal* with the hundred boys in their school uniform, all eating sleepily in silence, gulping down the coarse bread and scalding milk in terror of the bell that would presently cut them short—and, at the far end where the masters sat, he saw the narrow slit windows with the vistas of enticing field and forest beyond.

And this, in turn, made him think of the great barn-like room on the top floor where all slept together in wooden cots, and he heard in memory the clamour of the cruel bell that woke them on winter mornings at five o'clock and summoned them to the stone-flagged *Waschkammer,* where boys and masters alike, after scanty and icy washing, dressed in complete silence.

From this his mind passed swiftly, with vivid picture-thoughts, to other things, and with a passing shiver he remembered how the loneliness of never being alone had eaten into him, and how everything—work, meals, sleep, walks, leisure—was done with his "division" of twenty other boys and under the eyes of at least two masters. The only solitude possible was by asking for half an hour's practice in the cell-like music rooms, and Harris smiled to himself as he recalled the zeal of his violin studies.

Then, as the train puffed laboriously through the great pine forests that cover these mountains with a giant carpet of velvet, he found the pleasanter layers of memory giving up their dead, and he recalled with admiration the kindness of the masters, whom all addressed as Brother, and marvelled afresh at their devotion in burying themselves for years in such a place, only to leave it, in most cases, for the still rougher life of missionaries in the wild places of the world.

He thought once more of the still, religious atmosphere that hung over the little forest community like a veil, barring the distressful world; of the picturesque ceremonies at Easter, Christmas, and New Year; of the numerous feast-days and charming little festivals. The *Beschehr-Fest*, in particular, came back to him—the feast of gifts at Christmas—when the entire community paired off and gave presents, many of which had taken weeks to make or the savings of many days to purchase. And then he saw the midnight ceremony in the church at New Year, with the shining face of the *Prediger* in the pulpit—the village preacher who, on the last night of the old year, saw in the empty gallery beyond the organ loft the faces of all who were to die in the ensuing twelve months, and who at last recognised himself among them, and, in the very middle of his sermon, passed into a state of rapt ecstasy and burst into a torrent of praise.

Thickly the memories crowded upon him. The picture of the small village dreaming its unselfish life on the mountain-tops, clean, wholesome, simple, searching vigorously for its God, and training hundreds of boys in the grand way, rose up in his mind with all the power of an obsession. He felt once more the old mystical enthusiasm, deeper than the sea and more wonderful than the stars; he heard again the winds sighing from leagues of forest over the red roofs in the moonlight; he heard the Brothers' voices talking of the things beyond this life as though they had actually experienced them in the body; and, as he sat in the jolting train, a spirit of unutterable longing passed over his seared and tired soul, stirring in the depths of him a sea of emotions that he thought had long since frozen into immobility.

And the contrast pained him—the idealistic dreamer then, the man of business now—so that a spirit of unworldly peace and beauty known only to the soul in meditation laid its feathered finger upon his heart, moving strangely the surface of the waters.

Harris shivered a little and looked out of the window of his empty carriage. The train had long passed Hornberg, and far below the streams tumbled in white foam down the limestone rocks. In front of him, dome upon dome of wooded mountains stood against the sky. It was October, and the air was cool and sharp, wood-smoke and damp moss exquisitely mingled in it with the subtle odours of the pines. Overhead, between the tips of the highest firs, he saw the first stars peeping, and the sky was a clean, pale amethyst that seemed exactly the colour all these memories clothed themselves with in his mind.

He leaned back in his corner and sighed. He was a heavy man, and he had not known sentiment for years; he was a big man, and it took much to move him, literally and figuratively; he was a man in whom the dreams of God that haunt the soul in youth, though overlaid by the scum that gathers in the fight for money, had not, as with the majority, utterly died the death. He came back into this little neglected pocket of the years where so much fine gold had collected and lain undisturbed, with all his semi-spiritual emotions aquiver; and, as he watched the mountain-tops come nearer, and smelt the forgotten odours of his boyhood, something melted on the surface of his soul and left him sensitive to a degree he had not known since, thirty years before, he had lived here with his dreams, his conflicts, and his youthful suffering.

A thrill ran through him as the train stopped with a jolt at a tiny station and he saw the name in large black lettering on the grey stone building, and below it, the number of metres it stood above the level of the sea.

"The highest point on the line!" he exclaimed. "How well I remember it—Sommerau—Summer Meadow. The very next station is mine!"

And, as the train ran downhill with brakes on and steam shut off, he put his head out of the window and one by one saw the old familiar landmarks in the dusk. They stared at him like dead faces in a dream. Queer, sharp feelings, half poignant, half sweet, stirred in his heart.

"There's the hot, white road we walked along so often with the two Brüder always at our heels," he thought; "and there, by Jove, is the turn through the forest to '*Die Galgen*,' the stone gallows where they hanged the witches in olden days!"

He smiled a little as the train slid past.

"And there's the copse where the Lilies of the Valley powdered the ground in spring; and, I swear"—he put his head out with a sudden impulse—"if that's not the very clearing where Calame, the French boy, chased the swallow-tail with me, and Brüder Pagel gave us half-rations for leaving the road without permission, and for shouting in our mother tongues!" And he laughed again as the memories came back with a rush, flooding his mind with vivid detail.

The train stopped, and he stood on the grey gravel platform like a man in a dream. It seemed half a century since he last waited there with corded wooden boxes, and got into the train for Strassbourg and home after the two years' exile. Time dropped from him like an old garment and he felt a boy again. Only, things looked so much smaller than his memory of them; shrunk and dwindled they looked, and the distances seemed on a curiously smaller scale.

He made his way across the road to the little Gasthaus, and, as he went, faces and figures of former schoolfellows—German, Swiss, Italian, French, Russian—slipped out of the shadowy woods and silently accompanied him. They flitted by his side, raising their eyes questioningly, sadly, to his. But their names he had forgotten. Some of the Brothers, too, came with them, and most of these he remembered by name—Brüder Rost, Brüder Pagel, Brüder Schliemann, and the bearded face of the old preacher who had seen himself in the haunted gallery of those about to die—Brüder Gysin. The dark forest lay all about him like a sea that any moment might rush with velvet waves upon the scene and sweep all the faces away. The air was cool and wonderfully fragrant, but with every perfumed breath came also a pallid memory. . . .

Yet, in spite of the underlying sadness inseparable from such an experience, it was all very interesting, and held a pleasure peculiarly its own, so that Harris engaged his room and ordered supper feeling well pleased with himself, and intending to walk up to the old school that very evening. It stood in the centre of the community's village, some four miles distant through the forest, and he now recollected for the first time that this little Protestant settlement dwelt isolated in a section of the country that was otherwise Catholic. Crucifixes and shrines surrounded the clearing like the sentries of a beleaguering army. Once beyond the square of the village, with its few acres of field and orchard, the forest crowded up in solid phalanxes, and beyond the rim of trees began the country that was ruled by the priests of another faith. He vaguely remembered, too, that the Catholics had showed sometimes a certain hostility towards the little Protestant oasis that flourished so quietly and benignly in their midst. He had quite forgotten this. How trumpery it all seemed now with his wide experience of life and his knowledge of other countries and the great outside world. It was like stepping back, not thirty years, but three hundred.

There were only two others besides himself at supper. One of them, a bearded, middle-aged man in tweeds, sat by himself at the far end, and Harris kept out of his way because he was English. He feared he might be in business, possibly even in the silk business, and that he would perhaps talk on the subject. The other traveller, however, was a Catholic priest. He was a little man who ate his salad with a knife, yet so gently that it was almost inoffensive, and it was the sight of "the cloth" that recalled his memory of the old antagonism. Harris mentioned by way of conversation the object of his sentimental journey, and the priest looked up sharply at him with raised eyebrows and an expression of surprise and suspicion that somehow piqued him. He ascribed it to his difference of belief.

"Yes," went on the silk merchant, pleased to talk of what his mind was so full, "and it was a curious experience for an English boy to be dropped down into a school of a hundred foreigners. I well remember the loneliness and intolerable Heimweh of it at first." His German was very fluent.

The priest opposite looked up from his cold veal and potato salad and smiled. It was a nice face. He explained quietly that he did not belong here, but was making a tour of the parishes of Württemberg and Baden.

"It was a strict life," added Harris. "We English, I remember, used to call it *Gefängnisleben*—prison life!"

The face of the other, for some unaccountable reason, darkened. After a slight pause, and more by way of politeness than because he wished to continue the subject, he said quietly:

"It was a flourishing school in those days, of course. Afterwards, I have heard—" He shrugged his shoulders slightly, and the odd look—it almost seemed a look of alarm—came back into his eyes. The sentence remained unfinished.

Something in the tone of the man seemed to his listener uncalled for—in a sense reproachful, singular. Harris bridled in spite of himself.

"It has changed?" he asked. "I can hardly believe—"

"You have not heard, then?" observed the priest gently, making a gesture as though to cross himself, yet not actually completing it. "You have not heard what happened there before it was abandoned—?"

It was very childish, of course, and perhaps he was overtired and overwrought in some way, but the words and manner of the little priest seemed to him so offensive—so disproportionately offensive—that he hardly noticed the concluding sentence. He recalled the old bitterness and the old antagonism, and for a moment he almost lost his temper.

"Nonsense," he interrupted with a forced laugh, *"Unsinn!* You must forgive me, sir, for contradicting you. But I was a pupil there myself. I was at school there. There was no place like it. I cannot believe that anything serious could have happened to—to take away its character. The devotion of the Brothers would be difficult to equal anywhere—"

He broke off suddenly, realising that his voice had been raised unduly and that the man at the far end of the table might understand German; and at the same moment he looked up and saw that this individual's eyes were fixed upon his face intently. They were peculiarly bright. Also they were rather wonderful eyes, and the way they met his own served in some way he could not understand to convey both a reproach and a warning. The whole face of the stranger, indeed, made a vivid impression upon him, for it was a face, he now noticed for the first time, in whose presence one would not willingly have said or done anything unworthy. Harris could not explain to himself how it was he had not become conscious sooner of its presence.

But he could have bitten off his tongue for having so far forgotten himself. The little priest lapsed into silence. Only once he said, looking up and speaking in a low voice that was not intended to be overheard, but that evidently *was* overheard, "You will find it different." Presently he rose and left the table with a polite bow that included both the others, and, after him, from the far end rose also the figure in the tweed suit, leaving Harris by himself.

He sat on for a bit in the darkening room, sipping his coffee and smoking his fifteen-pfennig cigar, till the girl came in to light the oil lamps. He felt vexed with himself for his lapse from good manners, yet hardly able to account for it. Most likely, he reflected, he had been annoyed because the priest had unintentionally changed the pleasant character of his dream by introducing a jarring note. Later he must seek an opportunity to make amends. At present, however, he was too impatient for his walk to the school, and he took his suck and hat and passed out into the open air.

And, as he crossed before the Gasthaus, he noticed that the priest and the man in the tweed suit were engaged already in such deep conversation that they hardly noticed him as he passed and raised his hat.

He started off briskly, well remembering the way, and hoping to reach the village in time to have a word with one of the Brüder. They might even ask him in for a cup of coffee. He felt sure of his welcome, and the old memories were in full possession once more. The hour of return was a matter of no consequence whatever.

It was then just after seven o'clock, and the October evening was drawing in with chill airs from the recesses of the forest. The road plunged straight from the railway clearing into its depths, and in a very few minutes the trees engulfed him and the clack of his boots fell dead and echoless against the serried stems of a million firs. It was very black; one trunk was hardly distinguishable from another. He walked smartly, swinging his holly stick. Once or twice he passed a peasant on his way to bed, and the guttural "Gruss Got," unheard for so long, emphasised the passage of time, while yet making it seem as nothing. A fresh group of pictures crowded his mind. Again the figures of former schoolfellows flitted out of the forest and kept pace by his side, whispering of the doings of long ago. One reverie stepped hard upon the heels of another. Every turn in the road, every clearing of the forest, he knew, and each in turn brought forgotten associations to life. He enjoyed himself thoroughly.

He marched on and on. There was powdered gold in the sky till the moon rose, and then a wind of faint silver spread silently between the earth and stars. He saw the tips of the fir trees shimmer, and heard them whisper as the breeze turned their needles towards the light. The mountain air was indescribably sweet. The road shone like the foam of a river through the gloom. White moths flitted here and there like silent thoughts across his path, and a hundred smells greeted him from the forest caverns across the years.

Then, when he least expected it, the trees fell away abruptly on both sides, and he stood on the edge of the village clearing. He walked faster. There lay the familiar outlines of the houses, sheeted with silver; there stood the trees in the little central square with the fountain and small green lawns; there loomed the shape of the church next to the Gasthof der Brüdcrgemeinde; and just beyond, dimly rising into the sky, he saw with a sudden thrill the mass of the huge school building, blocked castle-like with deep shadows in the moonlight, standing square and formidable to face him after the silences of more than a quarter of a century.

He passed quickly down the deserted village street and stopped close beneath its shadow, staring up at the walls that had once held him prisoner for two years—two unbroken years of discipline and homesickness. Memories and emotions surged through his mind; for the most vivid sensations of his youth had focused about this spot, and it was here he had first begun to live and learn values. Not a single footstep broke the silence, though lights glimmered here and there through cottage windows; but when he looked up at the high walls of the school, draped now in shadow, he easily imagined that well-known faces crowded to the windows to greet him—closed windows that really reflected only moonlight and the gleam of stars.

This, then, was the old school building, standing foursquare to the world, with its shuttered windows, its lofty, tiled roof, and the spiked lightning-conductors pointing like black and taloned fingers from the corners. For a long time he stood and stared.

Then, presently, he came to himself again, and realised to his joy that a light still shone in the windows of the *Brüderstube*.

He turned from the road and passed through the iron railings; then climbed the twelve stone steps and stood facing the black wooden door with the heavy bars of iron, a door he had once loathed and dreaded with the hatred and passion of an imprisoned soul, but now looked upon tenderly with a sort of boyish delight.

Almost timorously he pulled the rope and listened with a tremor of excitement to the clanging of the bell deep within the building. And the long-forgotten sound brought the past before him with such a vivid sense of reality that he positively shivered. It was like the magic bell in the fairy-tale that rolls back the curtain of Time and summons the figures from the shadows of the dead. He had never felt so sentimental in his life. It was like being young again. And, at the same time, he began to bulk rather large in his own eyes with a certain spurious importance. He was a big man from the world of strife and action. In this little place of peaceful dreams would he, perhaps, not cut something of a figure?

"I'll try once more," he thought after a long pause, seizing the iron bell-rope, and was just about to pull it when a step sounded on the stone passage within, and the huge door slowly swung open.

A tall man with a rather severe cast of countenance stood facing him in silence.

"I must apologize—it is somewhat late," he began a trifle pompously, "but the fact is I am an old pupil. I have only just arrived and really could not restrain myself." His German seemed not quite so fluent as usual. "My interest is so great. I was here in '70."

The other opened the door wider and at once bowed him in with a smile of genuine welcome.

"I am Brüder Kalkmann," he said quietly in a deep voice. "I myself was a master here about that time. It is a great pleasure always to welcome a former pupil." He looked at him very keenly for a few seconds, and then added, "I think, too, it is splendid of you to come—very splendid."

"It is a very great pleasure," Harris replied, delighted with his reception.

The dimly-lighted corridor with its flooring of grey stone, and the familiar sound of a German voice echoing through it—with the peculiar intonation the Brothers always used in speaking—all combined to lift him bodily, as it were, into the dream-atmosphere of long-forgotten days. He stepped gladly into the building and the door shut with the familiar thunder that completed the reconstruction of the past. He almost felt the old sense of imprisonment, of aching nostalgia, of having lost his liberty.

Harris sighed involuntarily and turned towards his host, who returned his smile faintly and then led the way down the corridor.

"The boys have retired," he explained, "and, as you remember, we keep early hours here. But, at least, you will join us for a little while in the *Brüderstube* and enjoy a cup of coffee." This was precisely what the silk merchant had hoped, and he accepted with an alacrity that he intended to be tempered by graciousness. "And to-morrow," continued the Brüder, "you must come and spend a whole day with us. You may even find acquaintances, for several pupils of your day have come back here as masters."

For one brief second there passed into the man's eyes a look that made the visitor start. But it vanished as quickly as it came. It was impossible to define. Harris convinced himself it was the effect of a shadow cast by the lamp they had just passed on the wall. He dismissed it from his mind.

"You are very kind, I'm sure," he said politely. "It is perhaps a greater pleasure to me than you can imagine to see the place again. Ah"—he stopped short opposite a door with the upper half of glass and peered in—"surely there is one of the music rooms where I used to practise the violin. How it comes back to me after all these years!"

Brüder Kalkmann stopped indulgently, smiling, to allow his guest a moment's inspection.

"You still have the boy's orchestra? I remember I used to play 'zweite Geige' in it. Brüder Schliemann conducted at the piano. Dear me, I can see him now with his long black hair and—and—" He stopped abruptly. Again the odd, dark look passed over the stern face of his companion. For an instant it seemed curiously familiar.

"We still keep up the pupils' orchestra," he said, "but Brüder Schliemann, I am sorry to say—" he hesitated an instant, and then added, "Brüder Schliemann is dead."

"Indeed, indeed," said Harris quickly. "I am sorry to hear it." He was conscious of a faint feeling of distress, but whether it arose from the news of his old music teacher's death, or—from something else—he could not quite determine. He gazed down the corridor that lost itself among shadows. In the street and village everything had seemed so much smaller than he remembered, but here, inside the school building, everything seemed so much bigger. The corridor was loftier and longer, more spacious and vast, than the mental picture he had preserved. His thoughts wandered dreamily for an instant.

He glanced up and saw the face of the Brüder watching him with a smile of patient indulgence.

"Your memories possess you," he observed gently, and the stern look passed into something almost pitying.

"You are right," returned the man of silk, "they do. This was the most wonderful period of my whole life in a sense. At the time I hated it—" He hesitated, not wishing to hurt the Brother's feelings.

"According to English ideas it seemed strict, of course," the other said persuasively, so that he went on.

"—Yes, partly that; and partly the ceaseless nostalgia, and the solitude which came from never being really alone. In English schools the boys enjoy peculiar freedom, you know."

Brüder Kalkmann, he saw, was listening intently.

"But it produced one result that I have never wholly lost," he continued self-consciously, "and am grateful for."

"Ack! Wie so, denn!"

"The constant inner pain threw me headlong into your religious life, so that the whole force of my being seemed to project itself towards the search for a deeper satisfaction—a real resting place for the soul. During my two years here I yearned for God in my boyish way as perhaps I have never yearned for anything since. Moreover, I have never quite lost that sense of peace and inward joy which accompanied the search. I can never quite forget this school and the deep things it taught me."

He paused at the end of his long speech, and a brief silence fell between them. He feared he had said too much, or expressed himself clumsily in the foreign language, and when Brüder Kalkmann laid a hand upon his shoulder, he gave a little involuntary start.

"So that my memories perhaps do possess me rather strongly," he added apologetically; "and this long corridor, these rooms, that barred and gloomy front door, all touch chords that—that—" His German failed him and he glanced at his companion with an explanatory smile and gesture. But the Brother had removed hand from his shoulder and was standing with his back to him, looking down the passage.

"Naturally, naturally so," he said hastily without turning round. *"Es ist doch selbstverständlich.* We shall all understand."

Then he turned suddenly, and Harris saw that his face had turned most oddly and disagreeably sinister. It may only have been the shadows again playing their tricks with the wretched oil lamps on the wall, for the dark expression passed instantly as they retraced their steps down the corridor, but the Englishman somehow got the impression that he had said something to give offence, something that was not quite to the other's taste. Opposite the door of the *Brüderstube* they stopped. Harris realised that it was late and he had possibly steady talking too long. He made a tentative effort to leave, but his companion would not hear of it.

"You must have a cup of coffee with us," he said firmly as though he meant it, "and my colleagues will be delighted to see you. Some of them will remember you, perhaps."

The sound of voices came pleasantly through the door, men's voices talking together. Brüder Kalkmann turned the handle and they entered a room ablaze with light and full of people.

"Ah—but your name?" he whispered, bending down to catch the reply; "you have not told me your name yet."

"Harris," said the Englishman quickly as they went in. He felt nervous as he crossed the threshold, but ascribed the momentary trepidation to the fact that he was breaking the strictest rule of the whole establishment, which forbade a boy under severest penalties to come near this holy of holies where the masters took their brief leisure.

"Ah, yes, of course—Harris," repeated the other as though he remembered it. "Come in, Herr Harris, come in, please. Your visit will be immensely appreciated. It is really very fine, very wonderful of you to have come in this way."

The door closed behind them and, in the sudden light which made his sight swim for a moment, the exaggeration of the language escaped his attention. He heard the voice of Brüder Kalkmann introducing him. He spoke very loud, indeed, unnecessarily—absurdly loud, Harris thought.

"Brothers," he announced, "it is my pleasure and privilege to introduce to you Herr Harris from England. He has just arrived to make us a little visit, and I have already expressed to him on behalf of us all the satisfaction we feel that he is here. He was, as you remember, a pupil in the year '70."

It was a very formal, a very German introduction, but Harris rather liked it. It made him feel important and he appreciated the tact that made it almost seem as though he had been expected.

The black forms rose and bowed; Harris bowed; Kalkmann bowed. Everyone was very polite and very courtly. The room swam with moving figures; the light dazzled him after the gloom of the corridor; there was thick cigar smoke in the atmosphere. He took the chair that was offered to him between two of the Brothers, and sat down, feeling vaguely that his perceptions were not quite as keen and accurate as usual. He felt a trifle dazed perhaps, and the spell of the past came strongly over him, confusing the immediate present and making everything dwindle oddly to the dimensions of long ago. He seemed to pass under the mastery of a great mood that was a composite reproduction of all the moods of his forgotten boyhood.

Then he pulled himself together with a sharp effort and entered into the conversation that had begun again to buzz round him. Moreover, he entered into it with keen pleasure, for the Brothers—there were perhaps a dozen of them in the little room—treated him with a charm of manner that speedily made him feel one of themselves. This, again, was a very subtle delight to him. He felt that he had stepped out of the greedy, vulgar, self-seeking world, the world of silk and markets and profit-making—stepped into the cleaner atmosphere where spiritual ideals were paramount and life was simple and devoted. It all charmed him inexpressibly, so that he realised—yes, in a sense—the degradation of his twenty years' absorption in business. This keen atmosphere under the stars where men thought only of their souls, and of the souls of others, was too rarefied for the world he was now associated with. He found himself making comparisons to his own disadvantage,—comparisons with the mystical little dreamer that had stepped thirty years before from the stern peace of this devout community, and the man of the world that he had since become—and the contrast made him shiver with a keen regret and something like self-contempt.

He glanced round at the other faces floating towards him through tobacco smoke—this acrid cigar smoke he remembered so well: how keen they were, how strong, placid, touched with the nobility of great aims and unselfish purposes. At one or two he looked particularly. He hardly knew why. They rather fascinated him. There was something so very stern and uncompromising about them, and something, too, oddly, subtly, familiar, that yet just eluded him. But whenever their eyes met his own they held undeniable welcome in them; and some held more—a kind of perplexed admiration, he thought, something that was between esteem and deference. This note of respect in all the faces was very flattering to his vanity.

Coffee was served presently, made by a black-haired Brother who sat in the corner by the piano and bore a marked resemblance to Brüder Schliemann, the musical director of thirty years ago. Harris exchanged bows with him when he took the cup from his white hands, which he noticed were like the hands of a woman. He lit a cigar, offered to him by his neighbour, with whom he was chatting delightfully, and who, in the glare of the lighted match, reminded him sharply for a moment of Brüder Pagel, his former room-master.

"Es ist wirlkich merkwürdig," he said, "how many resemblances I see, or imagine. It is really *very* curious!"

"Yes," replied the other, peering at him over his coffee cup, "the spell of the place is wonderfully strong. I can well understand that the old faces rise before your mind's eye—almost to the exclusion of ourselves perhaps."

They both laughed pleasantly. It was soothing to find his mood understood and appreciated. And they passed on to talk of the mountain village, its isolation, its remoteness from worldly life, its peculiar fitness for meditation and worship, and for spiritual development—of a certain kind.

"And your coming back in this way, Herr Harris, has pleased us all so much," joined in the Brüder on his left. "We esteem you for it most highly. We honour you for it."

Harris made a deprecating gesture. "I fear, for my part, it is only a very selfish pleasure," he said a trifle unctuously.

"Not all would have had the courage," added the one who resembled Brüder Pagel.

"You mean," said Harris, a little puzzled, "the disturbing memories—?"

Brüder Pagel looked at him steadily, with unmistakable admiration and respect. "I mean that most men hold so strongly to life, and can give up so little for their beliefs," he said gravely.

The Englishman felt slightly uncomfortable. These worthy men really made too much of his sentimental journey. Besides, the talk was getting a little out of his depth. He hardly followed it.

"The worldly life still has *some* charms for me," he replied smilingly, as though to indicate that sainthood was not yet quite within his grasp.

"All the more, then, must we honour you for so freely coming," said the Brother on his left; "so unconditionally!"

A pause followed, and the silk merchant felt relieved when the conversation took a more general turn, although he noted that it never travelled very far from the subject of his visit and the wonderful situation of the lonely village for men who wished to develop their spiritual powers and practise the rites of a high worship. Others joined in, complimenting him on his knowledge of the language, making him feel utterly at his ease, yet at the same time a little uncomfortable by the excess of their admiration. After all, it was such a very small thing to do, this sentimental journey.

The time passed along quickly; the coffee was excellent, the cigars soft and of the nutty flavour he loved. At length, fearing to outstay his welcome, he rose reluctantly to take his leave. But the others would not hear of it. It *was* not often a former pupil returned to visit them in this simple, unaffected way. The night was young. If necessary they could even find him a corner in the great *Schlafzimmer* upstairs. He was easily persuaded to stay a little longer. Somehow he had become the centre of the little party. He felt pleased, flattered, honoured.

"And perhaps Brüder Schliemann will play something for us—now."

It was Kalkmann speaking, and Harris started visibly as he heard the name, and saw the black-haired man by the piano turn with a smile. For Schliemann was the name of his old music director, who was dead. Could this be his son? They were so exactly alike.

"If Brüder Meyer has not put his Amati to bed, I will accompany him," said the musician suggestively, looking across at a man whom Harris had not yet noticed, and who, he now saw, was the very image of a former master of that name.

Meyer rose and excused himself with a little bow, and the Englishman quickly observed that he had a peculiar gesture as though his neck had a false join on to the body just below the collar and feared it might break. Meyer of old had this trick of movement. He remembered how the boys used to copy it.

He glanced sharply from face to face, feeling as though some silent, unseen process were changing everything about him. All the faces seemed oddly familiar. Pagel, the Brother he had been talking with, was of course the image of Pagel, his former room-master and Kalkmann, he now realised for the first time, was the very twin of another master whose name he had quite forgotten, but whom he used to dislike intensely in the old days. And, through the smoke, peering at him from the corners of the room, he saw that all the Brothers about him had the faces he had known and lived with long ago—Röst, Fluheim, Meinert, Rigel, Gysin.

He stared hard, suddenly grown more alert, and everywhere saw, or fancied he saw, strange likenesses, ghostly resemblances—more, the identical faces of years ago. There was something queer about it all, something not quite right, something that made him feel uneasy. He shook himself, mentally and actually, blowing the smoke from before his eyes with a long breath, and as he did so he noticed to his dismay that every one was fixedly staring. They were watching him.

This brought him to his senses. As an Englishman, and a foreigner, he did not wish to be rude, or to do anything to make himself foolishly conspicuous and spoil the harmony of the evening. He was a guest, and a privileged guest at that. Besides, the music had already begun. Brüder Schliemann's long white fingers were caressing the keys to some purpose.

He subsided into his chair and smoked with half-closed eyes that yet saw everything.

But the shudder had established itself in his being, and, whether he would or not, it kept repeating itself. As a town, far up some inland river, feels the pressure of the distant sea, so he became aware that mighty forces from somewhere beyond his ken were urging themselves up against his soul in this smoky little room. He began to feel exceedingly ill at ease.

And as the music filled the air his mind began to clear. Like a lifted veil there rose up something that had hitherto obscured his vision. The words of the priest at the railway inn flashed across his brain unbidden: "You will find it different." And also, though why he could not tell, he saw mentally the strong, rather wonderful eyes of that other guest at the supper-table, the man who had overheard his conversation, and had later got into earnest talk with the priest. He took out his watch and stole a glance at it. Two hours had slipped by. It was already eleven o'clock.

Schliemann, meanwhile, utterly absorbed in his music, was playing a solemn measure. The piano sang marvellously. The power of a great conviction, the simplicity of great art, the vital spiritual message of a soul that had found itself—all this, and more, were in the chords, and yet somehow the music was what can only be described as impure—atrociously and diabolically impure. And the piece itself, although Harris did not recognize it as anything familiar, was surely the music of a Mass—huge, majestic, sombre? It stalked through the smoky room with slow power, like the passage of something that was mighty, yet profoundly intimate, and as it went there stirred into each and every face about him the signature of the enormous forces of which it was the audible symbol. The countenances round him turned sinister, but not idly, negatively sinister: they grew dark with purpose. He suddenly recalled the face of Brüder Kalkmann in the corridor earlier in the evening. The motives of their secret souls rose to the eyes, and mouths, and foreheads, and hung there for all to see like the black banners of an assembly of ill-starred and fallen creatures. Demons—was the horrible word that flashed through his brain like a sheet of fire.

When this sudden discovery leaped out upon him, for a moment he lost his self-control. Without waiting to think and weigh his extraordinary impression, he did a very foolish but a very natural thing. Feeling himself irresistibly driven by the sudden stress to some kind of action, he sprang to his feet—and screamed! To his own utter amazement he stood up and shrieked aloud!

But no one stirred. No one, apparently, took the slightest notice of his absurdly wild behaviour. It was almost as if no one but himself had heard the scream at all—as though the music had drowned it and swallowed it up—as though after all perhaps he had not really screamed as loudly as he imagined, or had not screamed at all.

Then, as he glanced at the motionless, dark faces before him, something of utter cold passed into his being, touching his very soul. . . . All emotion cooled suddenly, leaving him like a receding tide. He sat down again, ashamed, mortified, angry with himself for behaving like a fool and a boy. And the music, meanwhile, continued to issue from the white and snake-like fingers of Brüder Schliemann, as poisoned wine might issue from the weirdly-fashioned necks of antique phials.

And, with the rest of them, Harris drank it in.

Forcing himself to believe that he had been the victim of some kind of illusory perception, he vigorously restrained his feelings. Then the music presently ceased, and every one applauded and began to talk at once, laughing, changing seats, complimenting the player and behaving naturally and easily as though nothing out of the way had happened. The faces appeared normal once more. The Brothers crowded round their visitor, and he joined in their talk and even heard himself thanking the gifted musician.

But, at the same time, he found himself edging towards the door, nearer and nearer, changing his chair when possible, and joining the groups that stood closest to the way of escape.

"I must thank you all *tausendmal* for my little reception and the great pleasure—the very great honour you have done me," he began in decided tones at length, "but I fear I have trespassed far too long already on your hospitality. Moreover, I have some distance to walk to my inn."

A chorus of voices greeted his words. They would not hear of his going—at least not without first partaking of refreshment. They produced pumpernickel from one cupboard, and rye-bread and sausage from another, and all began to talk again and eat.

More coffee was made, fresh cigars lighted, and Brüder Meyer took out his violin and began to tune it softly.

"There is always a bed upstairs if Herr Harris will accept it," said one.

"And it is difficult to find the way out now, for all the doors are locked," laughed another loudly.

"Let us take our simple pleasures as they come," cried a third. "Brüder Harris will understand how we appreciate the honour of this last visit of his."

They made a dozen excuses. They all laughed, as though the politeness of their words was but formal, and veiled thinly—more and more thinly—a very different meaning.

"And the hour of midnight draws near," added Brüder Kalkmann with a charming smile, but in a voice that sounded to the Englishman like the grating of iron hinges.

Their German seemed to him more and more difficult to understand. He noted that they called him "Brüder" too, classing him as one of themselves.

And then suddenly he had a flash of keener perception, and realised with a creeping of his flesh that he had all along misinterpreted—grossly misinterpreted all they had been saying. They had talked about the beauty of the place, its isolation and remoteness from the world, its peculiar fitness for certain kinds of spiritual development and worship—yet hardly, he now grasped, in the sense in which he had taken the words. They had meant something different. Their spiritual powers, their desire for loneliness, their passion for worship, were not the powers, the solitude, or the worship that *he* meant and understood. He was playing the part in some horrible masquerade; he was among men who cloaked their lives with religion in order to follow their real purposes unseen of men.

What did it all mean? How had he blundered into so equivocal a situation? Had he blundered into it at all? Had he not rather been led into it, deliberately led? His thoughts grew dreadfully confused, and his confidence in himself began to fade. And why, he suddenly thought again, were they so impressed by the mere fact of his coming to revisit his old school? What was it they so admired and wondered at in his simple act? Why did they set such store upon his having the courage to come, to "give himself so freely," "unconditionally" as one of them had expressed it with such a mockery of exaggeration?

Fear stirred in his heart most horribly, and he found no answer to any of his questionings. Only one thing he now understood quite clearly: it was their purpose to keep him here. They did not intend that he should go. And from this moment he realized that they were sinister, formidable and, in some way he had yet to discover, inimical to himself, inimical to his life. And the phrase one of them had used a moment ago—"this *last* visit of his"—rose before his eyes in letters of flame.

Harris was not a man of action, and had never known in all the course of his career what it meant to be in a situation of real danger. He was not necessarily a coward, though, perhaps, a man of untried nerve. He realised at last plainly that he was in a very awkward predicament indeed, and that he had to deal with men who were utterly in earnest. What their intentions were he only vaguely guessed. His mind, indeed, was too confused for definite ratiocination, and he was only able to follow blindly the strongest instincts that moved in him. It never occurred to him that the Brothers might all be mad, or that he himself might have temporarily lost his senses and be suffering under some terrible delusion. In fact, nothing occurred to him—he realised nothing except that he meant to escape—and the quicker the better. A tremendous revulsion of feeling set in and overpowered him.

Accordingly, without further protest for the moment, he ate his pumpernickel and drank his coffee, talking meanwhile as naturally and pleasantly as he could, and when a suitable interval had passed, he rose to his feet and announced once more that he must now take his leave. He spoke very quietly, but very decidedly. No one hearing him could doubt that he meant what he said. He had got very close to the door by this time.

"I regret," he said, using his best German, and speaking to a hushed room, "that our pleasant evening must come to an end, but it is now time for me to wish you all good-night." And then, as no one said anything, he added, though with a trifle less assurance, "And I thank you all most sincerely for your hospitality."

"On the contrary," replied Kalkmann instantly, rising from his chair and ignoring the hand the Englishman had stretched out to him, "it is we who have to thank you; and we do so most gratefully and sincerely."

And at the same moment at least half a dozen of the Brothers took up their position between himself and the door.

"You are very good to say so," Harris replied as firmly as he could manage, noticing this movement out of the corner of his eye, "but really I had no conception that—my little chance visit could have afforded you so much pleasure." He moved another step nearer the door, but Brüder Schliemann came across the room quickly and stood in front of him. His attitude was uncompromising. A dark and terrible expression had come into his face.

"But it was *not* by chance that you came, Brüder Harris," he said so that all the room could hear; "surely we have not misunderstood your presence here?" He raised his black eyebrows.

"No, no," the Englishman hastened to reply. "I was—I am delighted to be here. I told you what pleasure it gave me to find myself among you. Do not misunderstand me, I beg." His voice faltered a little, and he had difficulty in finding the words. More and more, too, he had difficulty in understanding *their* words.

"Of course," interposed Brüder Kalkmann in his iron bass, "*we* have not misunderstood. You have come back in the spirit of true and unselfish devotion. You offer yourself freely, and we all appreciate it. It is your willingness and nobility that have so completely won our veneration and respect." A faint murmur of applause ran around the room. "What we all delight in—what our great Master will especially delight in—is the value of your spontaneous and voluntary—"

He used a word Harris did not understand. He said *"Opfer."* The bewildered Englishman searched his brain for the translation, and searched in vain. For the life of him he could not remember what it meant. But the word, for all his inability to translate it, touched his soul with ice. It was worse, far worse, than anything he had imagined. He felt like a lost, helpless creature, and all power to fight sank out of him from that moment.

"It is magnificent to be such a willing—" added Schliemann, sidling up to him with a dreadful leer on his face. He made use of the same word—"*Opfer.*"

God! What could it all mean? "Offer himself!" "True spirit of devotion!" "Willing," "unselfish," "magnificent!" *Opfer, Opfer, Opfer!* What in the name of heaven did it mean, that strange, mysterious word that struck such terror into his heart?

He made a valiant effort to keep his presence of mind and hold his nerves steady. Turning, he saw that Kalkmann's face was a dead white. Kalkmann! He understood that well enough. *Kalkmann* meant "Man of Chalk"; he knew that. But what did "*Opfer*" mean? That was the real key to the situation. Words poured through his disordered mind in an endless stream—unusual, rare words he had perhaps heard but once in his life—while "*Opfer,*" a word in common use, entirely escaped him. What an extraordinary mockery it all was!

Then Kalkmann, pale as death, but his face hard as iron, spoke a few low words that he did not catch, and the Brothers standing by the walls at once turned the lamps down so that the room became dim. In the half light he could only just discern their faces and movements.

"It is time," he heard Kalkmann's remorseless voice continue just behind him. "The hour of midnight is at hand. Let us prepare. He comes! He comes; Brüder Asmodelius comes!" His voice rose to a chant.

And the sound of that name, for some extraordinary reason, was terrible—utterly terrible; so that Harris shook from head to foot as he heard it. Its utterance filled the air like soft thunder, and a hush came over the whole room. Forces rose all about him, transforming the normal into the horrible, and the spirit of craven fear ran through all his being, bringing him to the verge of collapse.

Asmodelius! Asmodelius! The name was appalling. For he understood at last to whom it referred and the meaning that lay between its great syllables. At the same instant, too, he suddenly understood the meaning of that unremembered word. The import of the word *"Opfer"* flashed upon his soul like a message of death.

He thought of making a wild effort to reach the door, but the weakness of his trembling knees, and the row of black figures that stood between, dissuaded him at once. He would have screamed for help, but remembering the emptiness of the vast building, and the loneliness of the situation, he understood that no help could come that way, and he kept his lips closed. He stood still and did nothing. But he knew now what was coming.

Two of the Brothers approached and took him gently by the arm.

"Brüder Asmodelius accepts you," they whispered; "are you ready?"

Then he found his tongue and tried to speak. "But what have I to do with this Brüder Asm—Asmo—?" he stammered, a desperate rush of words crowding vainly behind the halting tongue.

The name refused to pass his lips. He could not pronounce it as they did. He could not pronounce it at all. His sense of helplessness then entered the acute stage, for this inability to speak the name produced a fresh sense of quite horrible confusion in his mind, and he became extraordinarily agitated.

"I came here for a friendly visit," he tried to say with a great effort, but, to his intense dismay, he heard his voice saying something quite different, and actually making use of that very word they had all used: "I came here as a willing *Opfer*," he heard his own voice say, *"and I am quite ready."*

He was lost beyond all recall now! Not alone his mind, but the very muscles of his body had passed out of control.

He felt that he was hovering on the confines of a phantom or demon-world—a world in which the name they had spoken constituted the Master-name, the word of ultimate power.

What followed he heard and saw as in a nightmare.

"In the half light that veils all truth, let us prepare to worship and adore," chanted Schliemann, who had preceded him to the end of the room.

"In the mists that protect our faces before the Black Throne, let us make ready the willing victim," echoed Kalkmann in his great bass.

They raised their faces, listening expectantly, as a roaring sound, like the passing of mighty projectiles, filled the air, far, far away, very wonderful, very forbidding. The walls of the room trembled.

"He comes! He comes! He comes!" chanted the Brothers in chorus.

The sound of roaring died away, and an atmosphere of still and utter cold established itself over all. Then Kalkmann, dark and unutterably stern, turned in the dim light and faced the rest.

"Asmodelius, our *Haupbrüder*, is about us," he cried in a voice that even while it shook was yet a voice of iron; "Asmodelius is about us. Make ready."

There followed a pause in which no one stirred or spoke. A tall Brother approached the Englishman; but Kalkmann held up his hand.

"Let the eyes remain uncovered," he said, "in honour of so freely giving himself." And to his horror Harris then realised for the first time that his hands were already fastened to his sides.

The Brother retreated again silently, and in the pause that followed all the figures about him dropped to their knees, leaving him standing alone, and as they dropped, in voices hushed with mingled reverence and awe, they cried softly, odiously, appallingly the name of the Being whom they momentarily expected to appear.

Then, at the end of the room, where the windows seemed to have disappeared so that he saw the stars, there rose into view far up against the night sky, grand and terrible, the outline of a man. A kind of grey glory enveloped it so that it resembled a steel-cased statue, immense, imposing, horrific in its distant splendour; while, at the same time, the face was so spiritually mighty, yet so proudly, so austerely sad, that Harris felt as he stared, that the sight was more than his eyes could meet, and that in another moment the power of vision would fail him altogether, and he must sink into utter nothingness.

So remote and inaccessible hung this figure that it was impossible to gauge anything as to its size, yet at the same time so strangely close, that when the grey radiance from its mightily broken visage, august and mournful, beat down upon his soul, pulsing like some dark star with the powers of spiritual evil, he felt almost as though he were looking into a face no farther removed from him in space than the face of any one of the Brothers who stood by his side.

And then the room filled and trembled with sounds that Harris understood full well were the failing voices of others who had preceded him in a long series down the years. There came first a plain, sharp cry, as of a man in the last anguish, choking for his breath, and yet, with the very final expiration of it, breathing the name of the Worship—of the dark Being who rejoiced to hear it. The cries of the strangled; the short, running gasp of the suffocated; and the smothered gurgling of the tightened throat, all these, and more, echoed back and forth between the walls, the very walls in which he now stood a prisoner, a sacrificial victim. The cries, too, not alone of the broken bodies, but—far worse—of beaten, broken souls. And as the ghastly chorus rose and fell, there came also the faces of the lost and unhappy creatures to whom they belonged, and, against that curtain of pale grey light, he saw float past him in the air, an array of white and piteous human countenances that seemed to beckon and gibber at him as though he were already one of themselves.

Slowly, too, as the voices rose, and the pallid crew sailed past, that giant form of grey descended from the sky and approached the room that contained the worshippers and their prisoner. Hands rose and sank about him in the darkness, and he felt that he was being draped in other garments than his own; a circlet of ice seemed to run about his head, while round the waist, enclosing the fastened arms, he felt a girdle tightly drawn. At last, about his very throat, there ran a soft and silken touch which, better than if there had been full light, and a mirror held to his face, he understood to be the cord of sacrifice—and of death.

At this moment the Brothers, still prostrate upon the floor, began again their mournful, yet impassioned chanting, and as they did so a strange thing happened. For, apparently without moving or altering its position, the huge Figure seemed, at once and suddenly, to be inside the room, almost beside him, and to fill the space around him to the exclusion of all else.

He was now beyond all ordinary sensations of fear, only a drab feeling as of death—the death of the soul—stirred in his heart. His thoughts no longer even beat vainly for space. The end was near, and he knew it.

The dreadfully chanting voices rose about him in a wave: "We worship! We adore! We offer!" The sounds filled his ears and hammered, almost meaningless, upon his brain.

Then the majestic grey face turned slowly downwards upon him, and his very soul passed outwards and seemed to become absorbed in the sea of those anguished eyes. At the same moment a dozen hands forced him to his knees, and in the air before him he saw the arm of Kalkmann upraised, and felt the pressure about his throat grow strong.

It was in this awful moment, when he had given up all hope, and the help of gods or men seemed beyond question, that a strange thing happened. For before his fading and terrified vision, there slid, as in a dream of light—yet without apparent rhyme or reason—wholly unbidden and unexplained—the face of that other man at the supper table of the railway inn. And the sight, even mentally, of that strong, wholesome, vigorous English face, inspired him suddenly with a new courage.

It was but a flash of fading vision before he sank into a dark and terrible death, yet, in some inexplicable way, the sight of that face stirred in him unconquerable hope and the certainty of deliverance. It was a face of power, a face, he now realised, of simple goodness such as might have been seen by men of old on the shores of Galilee; a face, by heaven, that could conquer even the devils of outer space.

And, in his despair and abandonment, he called upon it, and called with no uncertain accents. He found his voice in this overwhelming moment to some purpose; though the words he actually used, and whether they were in German or English, he could never remember. Their effect, nevertheless, was instantaneous. The Brothers understood, and that grey Figure of evil understood.

For a second the confusion was terrific. There came a great shattering sound. It seemed that the very earth trembled. But all Harris remembered afterwards was that voices rose about him in the clamour of terrified alarm—

"A man of power is among us! A man of God!"

The vast sound was repeated—the rushing through space as of huge projectiles—and he sank to the floor of the room, unconscious. The entire scene had vanished, vanished like smoke over the roof of a cottage when the wind blows.

And, by his side, sat down a slight un-German figure—the figure of the stranger at the inn—the man who had the "rather wonderful eyes."

When Harris came to himself he felt cold. He was lying under the open sky, and the cool air of field and forest was blowing upon his face. He sat up and looked about him. The memory of the late scene was still horribly in his mind, but no vestige of it remained. No walls or ceiling enclosed him; he was no longer in a room at all. There were no lamps turned low, no cigar smoke, no black forms of sinister worshippers, no tremendous grey Figure hovering beyond the windows.

Open space was about him, and he was lying on a pile of bricks and mortar, his clothes soaked with dew, and the kind stars shining brightly overheard. He was lying, bruised, and shaken, among the heaped-up debris of a ruined building.

He stood up and stared about him. There, in the shadowy distance, lay the surrounding forest, and here, close at hand, stood the outline of the village buildings. But, underfoot, beyond question, lay nothing but the broken heaps of stones that betokened a building long since crumbled to dust. Then he saw that the stones were blackened, and that great wooden beams, half burnt, half rotten, made lines through the general debris.

He stood, then, among the ruins of a burnt and shattered building, the weeds and nettles proving conclusively that it had lain thus for many years.

The moon had already set behind the encircling forest, but the stars that spangled the heavens threw enough light to enable him to make quite sure of what he saw. Harris, the silk merchant, stood among these broken and burnt stones and shivered.

Then he suddenly became aware that out of the gloom a figure had risen and stood beside him. Peering at him, he thought he recognised the face of the stranger at the railway inn.

"Are *you* real?" he asked in a voice he hardly recognised as his own.

"More than real—I'm friendly," replied the stranger; "I followed you up here from the inn."

Harris stood and stared for several minutes without adding anything. His teeth chattered. The least sound made him start; but the simple words in his own language, and the tone in which they were uttered, comforted him inconceivably.

"You're English too, thank God," he said inconsequently. "These German devils—" He broke off and put a hand to his eyes. "But what's become of them all—and the room—and—and—" The hand travelled down to his throat and moved nervously round his neck. He drew a long, long breath of relief. "Did I dream everything—everything?" he said distractedly.

He stared wildly about him, and the stranger moved forward and took his arm. "Come," he said soothingly, yet with a trace of command in the voice, "we will move away from here. The high-road, or even the woods will be more to your taste, for we are standing now on one of the most haunted—and most terribly haunted—spots of the whole world."

He guided his companion's stumbling footsteps over the broken masonry until they reached the path, the nettles stinging their hands, and Harris feeling his way like a man in a dream. Passing through the twisted iron railing they reached the path, and thence made their way to the road, shining white in the night. Once safely out of the ruins, Harris collected himself and turned to look back.

"But, how is it possible?" he exclaimed, his voice still shaking. "How can it be possible? When I came in here I saw the building in the moonlight. They opened the door. I saw the figures and heard the voices and touched, yes touched their very hands, and saw their damned black faces, saw them far more plainly than I see you now." He was deeply bewildered. The glamour was still upon his eyes with a degree of reality stronger than the reality even of normal life. "Was I so utterly deluded?"

Then suddenly the words of the stranger, which he had only half heard or understood, returned to him.

"Haunted?" he asked, looking hard at him; "haunted, did you say?" He paused in the roadway and stared into the darkness where the building of the old school had first appeared to him. But the stranger hurried him forward.

"We shall talk more safely farther on," he said. "I followed you from the inn the moment I realised where you had gone. When I found you it was eleven o'clock—"

"Eleven o'clock," said Harris, remembering with a shudder.

"—I saw you drop. I watched over you till you recovered consciousness of your own accord, and now—now I am here to guide you safely back to the inn. I have broken the spell—the glamour—"

"I owe you a great deal, sir," interrupted Harris again, beginning to understand something of the stranger's kindness, "but I don't understand it all. I feel dazed and shaken." His teeth still chattered, and spells of violent shivering passed over him from head to foot. He found that he was clinging to the other's arm. In this way they passed beyond the deserted and crumbling village and gained the high-road that led homewards through the forest.

"That school building has long been in ruins," said the man at his side presently; "it was burnt down by order of the Elders of the community at least ten years ago. The village has been uninhabited ever since. But the simulacra of certain ghastly events that took place under that roof in past days still continue. And the 'shells' of the chief participants still enact there the dreadful deeds that led to its final destruction, and to the desertion of the whole settlement. They were devil-worshippers!"

Harris listened with beads of perspiration on his forehead that did not come alone from their leisurely pace through the cool night. Although he had seen this man but once before in his life, and had never before exchanged so much as a word with him, he felt a degree of confidence and a subtle sense of safety and wellbeing in his presence that were the most healing influences he could possibly have wished after the experience he had been through. For all that, he still felt as if he were walking in a dream, and though he heard every word that fell from his companion's lips, it was only the next day that the full import of all he said became fully clear to him. The presence of this quiet stranger, the man with the wonderful eyes which he felt now, rather than saw, applied a soothing anodyne to his shattered spirit that healed him through and through. And this healing influence, distilled from the dark figure at his side, satisfied his first imperative need, so that he almost forgot to realise how strange and opportune it was that the man should be there at all.

It somehow never occurred to him to ask his name, or to feel any undue wonder that one passing tourist should take so much trouble on behalf of another. He just walked by his side, listening to his quiet words, and allowing himself to enjoy the very wonderful experience after his recent ordeal, of being helped, strengthened, blessed. Only once, remembering vaguely something of his reading of years ago, he turned to the man beside him, after some more than usually remarkable words, and heard himself, almost involuntarily it seemed, putting the question: "Then are you a Rosicrucian, sir, perhaps?" But the stranger had ignored the words, or possibly not heard them, for he continued with his talk as though unconscious of any interruption, and Harris became aware that another somewhat unusual picture had taken possession of his mind, as they walked there side by side through the cool reaches of the forest, and that he had found his imagination suddenly charged with the childhood memory of Jacob wrestling with an angel—wrestling all night with a being of superior quality whose strength eventually became his own.

"It was your abrupt conversation with the priest at supper that first put me upon the track of this remarkable occurrence," he heard the man's quiet voice beside him in the darkness, "and it was from him I learned after you left the story of the devil-worship that became secretly established in the heart of this simple and devout little community."

"Devil-worship! Here—!" Harris stammered, aghast.

"Yes—here—conducted secretly for years by a group of Brothers before unexplained disappearances in the neighbourhood led to its discovery. For where could they have found a safer place in the whole wide world for their ghastly traffic and perverted powers than here, in the very precincts—under cover of the very shadow of saintliness and holy living?"

"Awful, awful!" whispered the silk merchant, "and when I tell you the words they used to me—"

"I know it all," the stranger said quietly. "I saw and heard everything. My plan first was to wait till the end and then to take steps for their destruction, but in the interest of your personal safety"—he spoke with the utmost gravity and conviction—"in the interest of the safety of your soul, I made my presence known when I did, and before the conclusion had been reached—"

"My safety! The danger, then, was real. They were alive and—" Words failed him. He stopped in the road and turned towards his companion, the shining of whose eyes he could just make out in the gloom.

"It was a concourse of the shells of violent men, spiritually developed but evil men, seeking after death—the death of the body—to prolong their vile and unnatural existence. And had they accomplished their object, you, in turn, at the death of your body, would have passed into their power and helped to swell their dreadful purposes."

Harris made no reply. He was trying hard to concentrate his mind upon the sweet and common things of life. He even thought of silk and St. Paul's Churchyard and the faces of his partners in business.

"For you came all prepared to be caught," he heard the other's voice like some one talking to him from a distance; "your deeply introspective mood had already reconstructed the past so vividly, so intensely, that you were *en rapport* at once with any forces of those days that chanced still to be lingering. And they swept you up all unresistingly."

Harris tightened his hold upon the stranger's arm as he heard. At the moment he had room for one emotion only. It did not seem to him odd that this stranger should have such intimate knowledge of his mind.

"It is, alas, chiefly the evil emotions that are able to leave their photographs upon surrounding scenes and objects," the other added, "and who ever heard of a place haunted by a noble deed, or of beautiful and lovely ghosts revisiting the glimpses of the moon? It is unfortunate. But the wicked passions of men's hearts alone seem strong enough to leave pictures that persist; the good are ever too luke-warm."

The stranger sighed as he spoke. But Harris, exhausted and shaken as he was to the very core, paced by his side, only half listening. He moved as in a dream still. It was very wonderful to him, this walk home under the stars in the early hours of the October morning, the peaceful forest all about them, mist rising here and there over the small clearings, and the sound of water from a hundred little invisible streams filling in the pauses of the talk. In after life he always looked back to it as something magical and impossible, something that had seemed too beautiful, too curiously beautiful, to have been quite true. And, though at the time he heard and understood but a quarter of what the stranger said, it came back to him afterwards, staying with him till the end of his days, and always with a curious, haunting sense of unreality, as though he had enjoyed a wonderful dream of which he could recall only faint and exquisite portions.

But the horror of the earlier experience was effectually dispelled; and when they reached the railway inn, somewhere about three o'clock in the morning, Harris shook the stranger's hand gratefully, effusively, meeting the look of those rather wonderful eyes with a full heart, and went up to his room, thinking in a hazy, dream-like way of the words with which the stranger had brought their conversation to an end as they left the confines of the forest.

"And if thought and emotion can persist in this way so long after the brain that sent them forth has crumbled into dust, how vitally important it must be to control their very birth in the heart, and guard them with the keenest possible restraint."

But Harris, the silk merchant, slept better than might have been expected, and with a soundness that carried him half-way through the day. And when he came downstairs and learned that the stranger had already taken his departure, he realized with keen regret that he had never once thought of asking his name.

"Yes, he signed in the visitors' book," said the girl in reply to his question.

And he turned over the blotted pages and found there, the last entry, in a very delicate and individual handwriting—

"*John Silence*, London."

NO. 17

MRS. E. BLAND

I yawned. I could not help it. But the flat, inexorable voice went on.
"Speaking from the journalistic point of view—I may tell you,
gentlemen, that I once occupied the position of advertisement editor
to the *Bradford Woollen Goods Journal*—and speaking from that point
of view, I hold the opinion that all the best ghost stories have been
written over and over again; and if I were to leave the road and return
to a literary career I should never be led away by ghosts. Realism's
what's wanted nowadays, if you want to be up-to-date."

The large commercial paused for breath.

"You never can tell with the public," said the lean, elderly traveller;
"it's like in the fancy business. You never know how it's going to
be. Whether it's a clockwork ostrich or Sometite silk or a particular
shape of shaded glass novelty or a tobacco-box got up to look like a
raw chop, you never know your luck."

"That depends on who you are," said the dapper man in the corner by the fire. "If you've got the right push about you, you can make a thing go, whether it's a clockwork kitten or imitation meat, and with stories, I take it, it's just the same—realism or ghost stories. But the best ghost story would be the realest one, *I* think."

The large commercial had got his breath.

"I don't believe in ghost stories, myself," he was saying with earnest dullness; "but there was rather a queer thing happened to a second cousin of an aunt of mine by marriage—a very sensible woman with no nonsense about her. And the soul of truth and honour. I shouldn't have believed it if she had been one of your flighty, fanciful sort."

"Don't tell us the story," said the melancholy man who travelled in hardware; "you'll make us afraid to go to bed."

The well-meant effort failed. The large commercial went on, as I had known he would; his words overflowed his mouth, as his person overflowed his chair. I turned my mind to my own affairs, coming back to the commercial room in time to hear the summing up.

"The doors were all locked, and she was quite certain she saw a tall, white figure glide past her and vanish. I wouldn't have believed it if—" And so on *da capo*, from "if she hadn't been the second cousin" to the "soul of truth and honour."

I yawned again.

"Very good story," said the smart little man by the fire. He was a traveller, as the rest of us were; his presence in the room told us that much. He had been rather silent during dinner, and afterwards, while the red curtains were being drawn and the red and black cloth laid between the glasses and the dacanters and the mahogany, he had quietly taken the best chair in the warmest corner. We had got our letters written and the large traveller had been boring for some time before I even noticed that there was a best chair and that this silent, bright-eyed, dapper, fair man had secured it.

"Very good story," he said; "but it's not what I call realism. You don't tell us half enough, sir. You don't say when it happened or where, or the time of year, or what colour your aunt's second cousin's hair was. Nor yet you don't tell us what it was she saw, nor what the room was like where she saw it, nor why she saw it, nor what happened afterwards. And I shouldn't like to breathe a word against anybody's aunt by marriage's cousin, first or second, but I must say I like a story about what a man's seen *himself*."

"So do I," the large commercial snorted, "when I hear it."

He blew his nose like a trumpet of defiance.

"But," said the rabbit-faced man, "we know nowadays, what with the advance of science and all that sort of thing, we know there aren't any such things as ghosts. They're hallucinations; that's what they are—hallucinations."

"Don't seem to matter what you call them," the dapper one urged. "If you see a thing that looks as real as you do yourself, a thing that makes your blood run cold and turns you sick and silly with fear—well, call it ghost, or call it hallucination, or call it Tommy Dodd; it isn't the *name* that matters."

The elderly commercial coughed and said, "You might call it another name. You might call it—"

"No, you mightn't," said the little man, briskly; "not when the man it happened to had been a teetotal Bond of Joy for five years and is to this day."

"Why don't you tell us the story?" I asked.

"I might be willing," he said, "if the rest of the company were agreeable. Only I warn you it's not that sort-of-a-kind-of-a-somebody-fancied-they-saw-a-sort-of-a-kind-of-a-something-sort of a story. No, sir. Everything I'm going to tell you is plain and straightforward and as clear as a time-table—clearer than some. But I don't much like telling it, especially to people who don't believe in ghosts."

Several of us said we did believe in ghosts. The heavy man snorted and looked at his watch. And the man in the best chair began.

"Turn the gas down a bit, will you? Thanks. Did any of you know Herbert Hatteras? He was on this road a good many years. No? Well, never mind. He was a good chap, I believe, with good teeth and a black whisker. But I didn't know him myself. He was before my time. Well, this that I'm going to tell you about happened at a certain commercial hotel. I'm not going to give it a name, because that sort of thing gets about, and, in every other respect it's a good house and reasonable, and we all have our living to get. It was just a good ordinary old-fashioned commercial hotel, as it might be this. And I've often used it since, though they've never put me in that room again. Perhaps they shut it up after what happened.

"Well, the beginning of it was, I came across an old schoolfellow; in Boulter's Lock one Sunday it was, I remember. Jones was his name, Ted Jones. We both had canoes. We had tea at Marlow, and we got talking about this and that and old times and old mates; and do you remember Jim, and what's become of Tom, and so on. Oh, you know. And I happened to ask after his brother, Fred by name. And Ted turned pale and almost dropped his cup, and he said, 'You don't mean to say you haven't heard?' 'No,' says I, mopping up the tea he'd slopped over with my handkerchief. 'No; what?' I said.

"'It was horrible,' he said. 'They wired for me, and I saw him afterwards. Whether he'd done it himself or not, nobody knows; but they'd found him lying on the floor with his throat cut.' No cause could be assigned for the rash act, Ted told me. I asked him where it had happened, and he told me the name of this hotel—I'm not going to name it. And when I'd sympathized with him and drawn him out about old times and poor old Fred being such a good old sort and all that, I asked him what the room was like. I always like to know what the places look like where things happen.

"No, there wasn't anything specially rum about the room, only that it had a French bed with red curtains in a sort of alcove; and a large mahogany wardrobe as big as a hearse, with a glass door; and, instead of a swing-glass, a carved, black-framed glass screwed up against the wall between the windows, and a picture of 'Belshazzar's Feast' over the mantelpiece. I beg your pardon.'" He stopped, for the heavy commercial had opened his mouth and shut it again.

"I thought you were going to say something," the dapper man went on. "Well, we talked about other things and parted, and I thought no more about it till business brought me to—but I'd better not name the town either—and I found my firm had marked this very hotel—where poor Fred had met his death, you know—for me to put up at. And I had to put up there too, because of their addressing everything to me there. And, anyhow, I expect I should have gone there out of curiosity.

"No. I didn't believe in ghosts in those days. I was like you, sir." He nodded amiably to the large commercial.

"The house was very full, and we were quite a large party in the room—very pleasant company, as it might be to-night; and we got talking of ghosts—just as it might be us. And there was a chap in glasses, sitting just over there, I remember—an old man on the road, he was; and he said, just as it might be any of you, 'I don't believe in ghosts, but I wouldn't care to sleep in Number Seventeen, for all that'; and, of course, we asked him why. 'Because,' said he, very short, 'that's why.'

"But when we'd persuaded him a bit, he told us.

"'Because that's the room where chaps cut their throats,' he said. 'There was a chap called Bert Hatteras began it. They found him weltering in his gore. And since that every man that's slept there's been found with his throat cut.'

"I asked him how many had slept there. 'Well, only two beside the first,' he said; 'they shut it up then.' 'Oh, did they?' said I. 'Well, they've opened it again. Number Seventeen's my room!'

"I tell you those chaps looked at me.

"'But you aren't going to *sleep* in it?' one of them said. And I explained that I didn't pay half a dollar for a bedroom to keep awake in.

"'I suppose it's press of business has made them open it up again,' the chap in spectacles said. 'It's a very mysterious affair. There's some secret horror about that room that we don't understand,' he said, 'and I'll tell you another queer thing. Every one of those poor chaps was a commercial gentleman. That's what I don't like about it. There was Bert Hatteras—he was the first, and a chap called Jones—Frederick Jones, and then Donald Overshaw—a Scotchman he was, and travelled in child's underclothing.'

"Well, we sat there and talked a bit, and if I hadn't been a Bond of Joy, I don't know that I mightn't have exceeded, gentlemen—yes, positively exceeded; for the more I thought about it the less I liked the thought of Number Seventeen. I hadn't noticed the room particularly, except to see that the furniture had been changed since poor Fred's time. So I just slipped out, by and by, and I went out to the little glass case under the arch where the booking-clerk sits—just like here, that hotel was—and I said:—

"'Look here, miss; haven't you another room empty except seventeen?'

"'No,' she said; 'I don't think so.'

"'Then what's that?' I said, and pointed to a key hanging on the board, the only one left.

"'Oh,' she said, 'that's sixteen.'

"'Anyone in sixteen?' I said. 'Is it a comfortable room?'

"'No,' said she. 'Yes; quite comfortable. It's next door to yours—much the same class of room.'

"'Then I'll have sixteen, if you've no objection,' I said, and went back to the others, feeling very clever.

"When I went up to bed I locked my door, and, though I didn't believe in ghosts, I wished seventeen wasn't next door to me, and I wished there wasn't a door between the two rooms, though the door was locked right enough and the key on my side. I'd only got the one candle besides the two on the dressing table, which I hadn't lighted; and I got my collar and tie off before I noticed that the furniture in my new room was the furniture out of Number Seventeen; French bed with red curtains, mahogany wardrobe as big as a hearse, and the carved mirror over the dressing-table between the two windows, and 'Belshazzar's Feast' over the mantelpiece. So that, though I'd not got the *room* where the commercial gentlemen had cut their throats, I'd got the *furniture* out of it. And for a moment I thought that was worse than the other. When I thought of what that furniture could tell, if it could speak—

"It was a silly thing to do—but we're all friends here and I don't mind owning up—I looked under the bed and I looked inside the hearse-wardrobe and I looked in a sort of narrow cupboard there was, where a body could have stood upright—"

"A body?" I repeated.

"A man, I mean. You see, it seemed to me that either these poor chaps had been murdered by someone who hid himself in Number Seventeen to do it, or else there was something there that frightened them into cutting their throats; and upon my soul, I can't tell you which idea I liked least!"

He paused, and filled his pipe very deliberately. "Go on," someone said. And he went on.

"Now, you'll observe," he said, "that all I've told you up to the time of my going to bed that night's just hearsay. So I don't ask you to believe it—though the three coroners' inquests would be enough to stagger most chaps, I should say. Still, what I'm going to tell you now's *my* part of the story—what happened to me myself in that room."

He paused again, holding the pipe in his hand, unlighted.

There was a silence, which I broke.

"Well, what *did* happen?" I asked.

"I had a bit of a struggle with myself," he said. "I reminded myself it was not that room, but the next one that it had happened in. I smoked a pipe or two and read the morning paper, advertisements and all. And at last I went to bed. I left the candle burning, though, I own that."

"Did you sleep?" I asked.

"Yes. I slept. Sound as a top. I was awakened by a soft tapping on my door. I sat up. I don't think I've ever been so frightened in my life. But I made myself say, 'Who's there?' in a whisper. Heaven knows I never expected anyone to answer. The candle had gone out and it was pitch-dark. There was a quiet murmur and a shuffling sound outside. And no one answered. I tell you I hadn't expected anyone to. But I cleared my throat and cried out, 'Who's there?' in a real out-loud voice. And 'Me, sir,' said a voice. 'Shaving-water, sir; six o'clock, sir.'

"It was the chambermaid."

A movement of relief ran round our circle.

"I don't think much of your story," said the large commercial.

"You haven't heard it yet," said the story-teller, dryly. "It was six o'clock on a winter's morning, and pitch-dark. My train went at seven. I got up and began to dress. My one candle wasn't much use. I lighted the two on the dressing table to see to shave by. There wasn't any shaving-water outside my door, after all. And the passage was as black as a coal-hole. So I started to shave with cold water; one has to sometimes, you know. I'd gone over my face and I was just going lightly round under my chin, when I saw something move in the looking-glass. I mean something that moved was reflected in the looking-glass. The big door of the wardrobe had swung open, and by a sort of double reflection I could see the French bed with the red curtains. On the edge of it sat a man in his shirt and trousers—a man with black hair and whiskers, with the most awful look of despair and fear on his face that I've ever seen or dreamt of. I stood paralysed, watching him in the mirror. I could not have turned round to save my life. Suddenly he laughed. It was a horrid, silent laugh, and showed all his teeth. They were very white and even. And the next moment he had cut his throat from ear to ear, there before my eyes. Did you ever see a man cut his throat? The bed was all white before."

The story-teller had laid down his pipe, and he passed his hand over his face before he went on.

"When I could look round I did. There was no one in the room. The bed was as white as ever. Well, that's all," he said, abruptly, "except that now, of course, I understood how these poor chaps had come by their deaths. They'd all seen this horror—the ghost of the first poor chap, I suppose—Bert Hatteras, you know; and with the shock their hands must have slipped and their throats got cut before they could stop themselves. Oh! by the way, when I looked at my watch it was two o'clock; there hadn't been any chambermaid at all. I must have dreamed that. But I didn't dream the other. Oh! and one thing more. It was the same room. They hadn't changed the room, they'd only changed the number. *It was the same room!*"

"Look here," said the heavy man; "the room you've been talking about. *My* room's sixteen. And it's got that same furniture in it as what you describe, and the same picture and all."

"Oh, has it?" said the story-teller, a little uncomfortable, it seemed. "I'm sorry. But the cat's out of the bag now, and it can't be helped. Yes, it *was* this house I was speaking of. I suppose they've opened the room again. But you don't believe in ghosts; *you'll* be all right."

"Yes," said the heavy man, and presently got up and left the room.

"He's gone to see if he can get his room changed. You see if he hasn't," said the rabbit-faced man; "and I don't wonder."

The heavy man came back and settled into his chair.

"I could do with a drink," he said, reaching to the bell.

"I'll stand some punch, gentlemen, if you'll allow me," said our dapper story-teller. "I rather pride myself on my punch. I'll step out to the bar and get what I need for it."

"I thought he said he was a teetotaller," said the heavy traveler when he had gone. And then our voices buzzed like a hive of bees. When our story-teller came in again we turned on him—half-a-dozen of us at once—and spoke.

"One at a time," he said, gently. "I didn't quite catch what you said."

"We want to know," I said, "how it was—if seeing that ghost made all those chaps cut their throats by startling them when they were shaving—how was it *you* didn't cut *your* throat when you saw it?"

"I should have," he answered, gravely, "without the slightest doubt—I should have cut my throat, only," he glanced at our heavy friend, "I always shave with a safety razor. I travel in them," he added, slowly, and bisected a lemon.

"But—but," said the large man, when he could speak through our uproar, "I've gone and given up my room."

"Yes," said the dapper man, squeezing the lemon; "I've just had my things moved into it. It's the best room in the house. I always think it worth while to take a little pains to secure it."

THE OPEN BOAT

STEPHEN CRANE

I

N one of them knew the color of the sky. Their eyes glanced level, and were fastened upon the waves that swept toward them. These waves were of the hue of slate, save for the tops, which were of foaming white, and all of the men knew the colors of the sea. The horizon narrowed and widened, and dipped and rose, and at all times its edge was jagged with waves that seemed thrust up in points like rocks. Many a man ought to have a bath-tub larger than the boat which here rode upon the sea. These waves were most wrongfully and barbarously abrupt and tall, and each froth-top was a problem in small-boat navigation.

The cook squatted in the bottom and looked with both eyes at the six inches of gunwale which separated him from the ocean. His sleeves were rolled over his fat forearms, and the two flaps of his unbuttoned vest dangled as he bent to bail out the boat. Often he said: "Gawd! That was a narrow clip." As he remarked it he invariably gazed eastward over the broken sea.

The oiler, steering with one of the two oars in the boat, sometimes raised himself suddenly to keep clear of water that swirled in over the stern. It was a thin little oar and it seemed often ready to snap.

The correspondent, pulling at the other oar, watched the waves and wondered why he was there.

The injured captain, lying in the bow, was at this time buried in that profound dejection and indifference which comes, temporarily at least, to even the bravest and most enduring when, willy nilly, the firm fails, the army loses, the ship goes down. The mind of the master of a vessel is rooted deep in the timbers of her, though he commanded for a day or a decade, and this captain had on him the stern impression of a scene in the greys of dawn of seven turned faces, and later a stump of a top-mast with a white ball on it that slashed to and fro at the waves, went low and lower, and down. Thereafter there was something strange in his voice. Although steady, it was, deep with mourning, and of a quality beyond oration or tears.

"Keep 'er a little more south, Billie," said he.

"'A little more south,' sir," said the oiler in the stern.

A seat in this boat was not unlike a seat upon a bucking bronco, and by the same token, a bronco is not much smaller. The craft pranced and reared, and plunged like an animal. As each wave came, and she rose for it, she seemed like a horse making at a fence outrageously high. The manner of her scramble over these walls of water is a mystic thing, and, moreover, at the top of them were ordinarily these problems in white water, the foam racing down from the summit of each wave, requiring a new leap, and a leap from the air. Then, after scornfully bumping a crest, she would slide, and race, and splash down a long incline, and arrive bobbing and nodding in front of the next menace.

A singular disadvantage of the sea lies in the fact that after successfully surmounting one wave you discover that there is another behind it just as important and just as nervously anxious to do something effective in the way of swamping boats. In a ten-foot dingey one can get an idea of the resources of the sea in the line of waves that is not probable to the average experience which is never at sea in a dingey. As each slatey wall of water approached, it shut all else from the view of the men in the boat, and it was not difficult to imagine that this particular wave was the final outburst of the ocean, the last effort of the grim water. There was a terrible grace in the move of the waves, and they came in silence, save for the snarling of the crests.

In the wan light, the faces of the men must have been grey. Their eyes must have glinted in strange ways as they gazed steadily astern. Viewed from a balcony, the whole thing would doubtless have been weirdly picturesque. But the men in the boat had no time to see it, and if they had had leisure there were other things to occupy their minds. The sun swung steadily up the sky, and they knew it was broad day because the color of the sea changed from slate to emerald-green, streaked with amber lights, and the foam was like tumbling snow. The process of the breaking day was unknown to them. They were aware only of this effect upon the color of the waves that rolled toward them.

In disjointed sentences the cook and the correspondent argued as to the difference between a life-saving station and a house of refuge. The cook had said: "There's a house of refuge just north of the Mosquito Inlet Light, and as soon as they see us, they'll come off in their boat and pick us up."

"As soon as who see us?" said the correspondent.

"The crew," said the cook.

"Houses of refuge don't have crews," said the correspondent. "As I understand them, they are only places where clothes and grub are stored for the benefit of shipwrecked people. They don't carry crews."

"Oh, yes, they do," said the cook.

"No, they don't," said the correspondent.

"Well, we're not there yet, anyhow," said the oiler, in the stern.

"Well," said the cook, "perhaps it's not a house of refuge that I'm thinking of as being near Mosquito Inlet Light. Perhaps it's a life-saving station."

"We're not there yet," said the oiler, in the stern.

II

As the boat bounced from the top of each wave, the wind tore through the hair of the hatless men, and as the craft plopped her stern down again the spray splashed past them. The crest of each of these waves was a hill, from the top of which the men surveyed, for a moment, a broad tumultuous expanse, shining and wind-riven. It was probably splendid. It was probably glorious, this play of the free sea, wild with lights of emerald and white and amber.

"Bully good thing it's an on-shore wind," said the cook; "If not, where would we be? Wouldn't have a show."

"That's right," said the correspondent.

The busy oiler nodded his assent.

Then the captain, in the bow, chuckled in a way that expressed humor, contempt, tragedy, all in one. "Do you think we've got much of a show now, boys?" said he.

Whereupon the three were silent, save for a trifle of hemming and hawing. To express any particular optimism at this time they felt to be childish and stupid, but they all doubtless possessed this sense of the situation in their mind. A young man thinks doggedly at such times. On the other hand, the ethics of their condition was decidedly against any open suggestion of hopelessness. So they were silent.

"Oh, well," said the captain, soothing his children, "We'll get ashore all right."

But there was that in his tone which made them think, so the oiler quoth: "Yes! If this wind holds!"

The cook was bailing: "Yes! If we don't catch hell in the surf."

Canton flannel gulls flew near and far. Sometimes they sat down on the sea, near patches of brown seaweed that rolled on the waves with a movement like carpets on a line in a gale. The birds sat comfortably in groups, and they were envied by some in the dingey, for the wrath of the sea was no more to them than it was to a covey of prairie chickens a thousand miles inland. Often they came very close and stared at the men with black bead-like eyes. At these times they were uncanny and sinister in their unblinking scrutiny, and the men hooted angrily at them, telling them to be gone. One came, and evidently decided to alight on the top of the captain's head. The bird flew parallel to the boat and did not circle, but made short sidelong jumps in the air in chicken-fashion. His black eyes were wistfully fixed upon the captain's head. "Ugly brute," said the oiler to the bird. "You look as if you were made with a jack-knife." The cook and the correspondent swore darkly at the creature. The captain naturally wished to knock it away with the end of the heavy painter; but he did not dare do it, because anything resembling an emphatic gesture would have capsized this freighted boat, and so with his open hand, the captain gently and carefully waved the gull away. After it had been discouraged from the pursuit the captain breathed easier on account of his hair, and others breathed easier because the bird struck their minds at this time as being somehow grewsome and ominous.

In the meantime the oiler and the correspondent rowed. And also they rowed.

They sat together in the same seat, and each rowed an oar. Then the oiler took both oars; then the correspondent took both oars; then the oiler; then the correspondent. They rowed and they rowed. The very ticklish part of the business was when the time came for the reclining one in the stern to take his turn at the oars. By the very last star of truth, it is easier to steal eggs from under a hen than it was to change seats in the dingey. First the man in the stern slid his hand along the thwart and moved with care, as if he were of Sèvres. Then the man in the rowing seat slid his hand along the other thwart. It was all done with most extraordinary care. As the two sidled past each other, the whole party kept watchful eyes on the coming wave, and the captain cried: "Look out now! Steady there!"

The brown mats of seaweed that appeared from time to time were like islands, bits of earth. They were traveling, apparently, neither one way nor the other. They were, to all intents, stationary. They informed the men in the boat that it was making progress slowly toward the land.

The captain, rearing cautiously in the bow, after the dingey soared on a great swell, said that he had seen the light-house at Mosquito Inlet. Presently the cook remarked that he had seen it. The correspondent was at the oars then, and for some reason he too wished to look at the lighthouse, but his back was toward the far shore and the waves were important, and for some time he could not seize an opportunity to turn his head. But at last there came a wave more gentle than the others, and when at the crest of it he swiftly scoured the western horizon.

"See it?" said the captain.

"No," said the correspondent slowly, "I didn't see anything."

"Look again," said the captain. He pointed. "It's exactly in that direction."

At the top of another wave, the correspondent did as he was bid, and this time his eyes chanced on a small still thing on the edge of the swaying horizon. It was precisely like the point of a pin. It took an anxious eye to find a light house so tiny.

"Think we'll make it, captain?"

"If this wind holds and the boat don't swamp, we can't do much else," said the captain.

The little boat, lifted by each towering sea, and splashed viciously by the crests, made progress that in the absence of seaweed was not apparent to those in her. She seemed just a wee thing wallowing, miraculously top-up, at the mercy of five oceans. Occasionally, a great spread of water, like white flames, swarmed into her.

"Bail her, cook," said the captain serenely.

"All right, captain," said the cheerful cook.

III

It would be difficult to describe the subtle brotherhood of men that was here established on the seas. No one said that it was so. No one mentioned it. But it dwelt in the boat, and each man felt it warm him. They were a captain, an oiler, a cook, and a correspondent, and they were friends, friends in a more curiously iron-bound degree than may be common. The hurt captain, lying against the water-jar in the bow, spoke always in a low voice and calmly, but he could never command a more ready and swiftly obedient crew than the motley three of the dingey. It was more than a mere recognition of what was best for the common safety. There was surely in it a quality that was personal and heartfelt. And after this devotion to the commander of the boat there was this comradeship that the correspondent, for instance, who had been taught to be cynical of men, knew even at the time was the best experience of his life. But no one said that it was so. No one mentioned it.

"I wish we had a sail," remarked the captain. "We might try my overcoat on the end of an oar and give you two boys a chance to rest." So the cook and the correspondent held the mast and spread wide the overcoat. The oiler steered, and the little boat made good way with her new rig. Sometimes the oiler had to scull sharply to keep a sea from breaking into the boat, but otherwise sailing was a success.

Meanwhile the lighthouse had been growing slowly larger. It had now almost assumed color, and appeared like a little grey shadow on the sky. The man at the oars could not be prevented from turning his head rather often to try for a glimpse of this little grey shadow.

At last, from the top of each wave the men in the tossing boat could see land. Even as the lighthouse was an upright shadow on the sky, this land seemed but a long black shadow on the sea. It certainly was thinner than paper. "We must be about opposite New Smyrna," said the cook, who had coasted this shore often in schooners. "Captain, by the way, I believe they abandoned that life-saving station there about a year ago."

"Did they?" said the captain.

The wind slowly died away. The cook and the correspondent were not now obliged to slave in order to hold high the oar. But the waves continued their old impetuous swooping at the dingey, and the little craft, no longer under way, struggled woundily over them. The oiler or the correspondent took the oars again.

Shipwrecks are *à propos* of nothing. If men could only train for them and have them occur when the men had reached pink condition, there would be less drowning at sea. Of the four in the dingey none had slept any time worth mentioning for two days and two nights previous to embarking in the dingey, and in the excitement of clambering about the deck of a foundering ship they had also forgotten to eat heartily.

For these reasons, and for others, neither the oiler nor the correspondent was fond of rowing at this time. The correspondent wondered ingenuously how in the name of all that was sane could there be people who thought it amusing to row a boat. It was not an amusement; it was a diabolical punishment, and even a genius of mental aberrations could never conclude that it was anything but a horror to the muscles and a crime against the back. He mentioned to the boat in general how the amusement of rowing struck him, and the weary-faced oiler smiled in full sympathy. Previously to the foundering, by the way, the oiler had worked double-watch in the engine-room of the ship.

"Take her easy, now, boys," said the captain. "Don't spend yourselves. If we have to run a surf you'll need all your strength, because we'll sure have to swim for it. Take your time."

Slowly the land arose from the sea. From a black line it became a line of black and a line of white, trees and sand. Finally, the captain said that he could make out a house on the shore. "That's the house of refuge, sure," said the cook. "They'll see us before long, and come out after us."

The distant lighthouse reared high. "The keeper ought to be able to make us out now, if he's looking through a glass," said the captain. "He'll notify the life-saving people."

"None of those other boats could have got ashore to give word of the wreck," said the oiler, in a low voice. "Else the lifeboat would be out hunting us."

Slowly and beautifully the land loomed out of the sea. The wind came again. It had veered from the north-east to the south-east. Finally, a new sound struck the ears of the men in the boat. It was the low thunder of the surf on the shore. "We'll never be able to make the lighthouse now," said the captain. "Swing her head a little more north, Billie," said he.

"'A little more north,' sir," said the oiler.

Whereupon the little boat turned her nose once more down the wind, and all but the oarsman watched the shore grow. Under the influence of this expansion doubt and direful apprehension was leaving the minds of the men. The management of the boat was still most absorbing, but it could not prevent a quiet cheerfulness. In an hour, perhaps, they would be ashore.

Their backbones had become thoroughly used to balancing in the boat, and they now rode this wild colt of a dingey like circus men. The correspondent thought that he had been drenched to the skin, but happening to feel in the top pocket of his coat, he found therein eight cigars. Four of them were soaked with sea-water; four were perfectly scathless. After a search, somebody produced three dry matches, and thereupon the four waifs rode impudently in their little boat, and with an assurance of an impending rescue shining in their eyes, puffed at the big cigars and judged well and ill of all men. Everybody took a drink of water.

IV

"Cook," remarked the captain, "there don't seem to be any signs of life about your house of refuge."

"No," replied the cook. "Funny they don't see us!"

A broad stretch of lowly coast lay before the eyes of the men. It was of dunes topped with dark vegetation. The roar of the surf was plain, and sometimes they could see the white lip of a wave as it spun up the beach. A tiny house was blocked out black upon the sky. Southward, the slim lighthouse lifted its little grey length.

Tide, wind, and waves were swinging the dingey northward. "Funny they don't see us," said the men.

The surf's roar was here dulled, but its tone was, nevertheless, thunderous and mighty. As the boat swam over the great rollers, the men sat listening to this roar. "We'll swamp sure," said everybody.

It is fair to say here that there was not a life-saving station within twenty miles in either direction, but the men did not know this fact, and in consequence they made dark and opprobrious remarks concerning the eyesight of the nation's life-savers. Four scowling men sat in the dingey and surpassed records in the invention of epithets.

"Funny they don't see us."

The lightheartedness of a former time had completely faded. To their sharpened minds it was easy to conjure pictures of all kinds of incompetency and blindness and, indeed, cowardice. There was the shore of the populous land, and it was bitter and bitter to them that from it came no sign.

"Well," said the captain, ultimately, "I suppose we'll have to make a try for ourselves. If we stay out here too long, we'll none of us have strength left to swim after the boat swamps."

And so the oiler, who was at the oars, turned the boat straight for the shore. There was a sudden tightening of muscle. There was some thinking.

"If we don't all get ashore—" said the captain. "If we don't all get ashore, I suppose you fellows know where to send news of my finish?"

They then briefly exchanged some addresses and admonitions. As for the reflections of the men, there was a great deal of rage in them. Perchance they might be formulated thus: "If I am going to be drowned—if I am going to be drowned—if I am going to be drowned, why, in the name of the seven mad gods who rule the sea, was I allowed to come thus far and contemplate sand and trees? Was I brought here merely to have my nose dragged away as I was about to nibble the sacred cheese of life? It is preposterous. If this old ninny-woman, Fate, cannot do better than this, she should be deprived of the management of men's fortunes. She is an old hen who knows not her intention. If she has decided to drown me, why did she not do it in the beginning and save me all this trouble? The whole affair is absurd. . . . But no, she cannot mean to drown me. She dare not drown me. She cannot drown me. Not after all this work." Afterward the man might have had an impulse to shake his fist at the clouds: "Just you drown me, now, and then hear what I call you!"

The billows that came at this time were more formidable. They seemed always just about to break and roll over the little boat in a turmoil of foam. There was a preparatory and long growl in the speech of them. No mind unused to the sea would have concluded that the dingey could ascend these sheer heights in time. The shore was still afar. The oiler was a wily surfman. "Boys," he said swiftly, "she won't live three minutes more, and we're too far out to swim. Shall I take her to sea again, captain?"

"Yes! Go ahead!" said the captain.

This oiler, by a series of quick miracles, and fast and steady oarsmanship, turned the boat in the middle of the surf and took her safely to sea again.

There was a considerable silence as the boat bumped over the furrowed sea to deeper water. Then somebody in gloom spoke. "Well, anyhow, they must have seen us from the shore by now."

The gulls went in slanting flight up the wind toward the grey desolate east. A squall, marked by dingy clouds, and clouds brick-red, like smoke from a burning building, appeared from the south-east.

"What do you think of those life-saving people? Ain't they peaches?"

"Funny they haven't seen us."

"Maybe they think we're out here for sport! Maybe they think we're fishin'. Maybe they think we're damned fools."

It was a long afternoon. A changed tide tried to force them southward, but the wind and wave said northward. Far ahead, where coast-line, sea, and sky formed their mighty angle, there were little dots which seemed to indicate a city on the shore.

"St. Augustine?"

The captain shook his head. "Too near Mosquito Inlet." And the oiler rowed, and then the correspondent rowed. Then the oiler rowed. It was a weary business. The human back can become the seat of more aches and pains than are registered in books for the composite anatomy of a regiment. It is a limited area, but it can become the theatre of innumerable muscular conflicts, tangles, wrenches, knots, and other comforts.

"Did you ever like to row, Billie?" asked the correspondent.

"No," said the oiler. "Hang it!"

When one exchanged the rowing-seat for a place in the bottom of the boat, he suffered a bodily depression that caused him to be careless of everything save an obligation to wiggle one finger. There was cold sea-water swashing to and fro in the boat, and he lay in it. His head, pillowed on a thwart, was within an inch of the swirl of a wave crest, and sometimes a particularly obstreperous sea came in-board and drenched him once more. But these matters did not annoy him. It is almost certain that if the boat had capsized he would have tumbled comfortably out upon the ocean as if he felt sure that it was a great soft mattress.

"Look! There's a man on the shore!"

"Where?"

"There! See 'im? See 'im?"

"Yes, sure! He's walking along."

"Now he's stopped. Look! He's facing us!"

"He's waving at us!"

"So he is! By thunder!"

"Ah, now we're all right! Now we're all right! There'll be a boat out here for us in half-an-hour."

"He's going on. He's running. He's going up to that house there."

The remote beach seemed lower than the sea, and it required a searching glance to discern the little black figure. The captain saw a floating stick and they rowed to it. A bath-towel was by some weird chance in the boat, and, tying this on the stick, the captain waved it. The oarsman did not dare turn his head, so he was obliged to ask questions.

"What's he doing now?"

"He's standing still again. He's looking, I think. . . . There he goes again. Toward the house. . . . Now he's stopped again."

"Is he waving at us?"

"No, not now! he was, though."

"Look! There comes another man!"

"He's running."

"Look at him go, would you."

"Why, he's on a bicycle. Now he's met the other man. They're both waving at us. Look!"

"There comes something up the beach."

"What the devil is that thing?"

"Why it looks like a boat."

"Why, certainly it's a boat."

"No, it's on wheels."

"Yes, so it is. Well, that must be the life-boat. They drag them along shore on a wagon."

"That's the life-boat, sure."

"No, by ——, it's—it's an omnibus."

"I tell you it's a life-boat."

"It is not! It's an omnibus. I can see it plain. See? One of these big hotel omnibuses."

"By thunder, you're right. It's an omnibus, sure as fate. What do you suppose they are doing with an omnibus? Maybe they are going around collecting the life-crew, hey?"

"That's it, likely. Look! There's a fellow waving a little black flag. He's standing on the steps of the omnibus. There come those other two fellows. Now they're all talking together. Look at the fellow with the flag. Maybe he ain't waving it."

"That ain't a flag, is it? That's his coat. Why, certainly, that's his coat."

"So it is. It's his coat. He's taken it off and is waving it around his head. But would you look at him swing it."

"Oh, say, there isn't any life-saving station there. That's just a winter resort hotel omnibus that has brought over some of the boarders to see us drown."

"What's that idiot with the coat mean? What's he signaling, anyhow?"

"It looks as if he were trying to tell us to go north. There must be a life-saving station up there."

"No! He thinks we're fishing. Just giving us a merry hand. See? Ah, there, Willie!"

"Well, I wish I could make something out of those signals. What do you suppose he means?"

"He don't mean anything. He's just playing."

"Well, if he'd just signal us to try the surf again, or to go to sea and wait, or go north, or go south, or go to hell—there would be some reason in it. But look at him. He just stands there and keeps his coat revolving like a wheel. The ass!"

"There come more people."

"Now there's quite a mob. Look! Isn't that a boat?"

"Where? Oh, I see where you mean. No, that's no boat."

"That fellow is still waving his coat."

"He must think we like to see him do that. Why don't he quit it? It don't mean anything."

"I don't know. I think he is trying to make us go north. It must be that there's a life-saving station there somewhere."

"Say, he ain't tired yet. Look at 'im wave."

"Wonder how long he can keep that up. He's been revolving his coat ever since he caught sight of us. He's an idiot. Why aren't they getting men to bring a boat out? A fishing boat—one of those big yawls—could come out here all right. Why don't he do something?"

"Oh, it's all right, now."

"They'll have a boat out here for us in less than no time, now that they've seen us."

A faint yellow tone came into the sky over the low land. The shadows on the sea slowly deepened. The wind bore coldness with it, and the men began to shiver.

"Holy smoke!" said one, allowing his voice to express his impious mood, "if we keep on monkeying out here! If we've got to flounder out here all night!"

"Oh, we'll never have to stay here all night! Don't you worry. They've seen us now, and it won't be long before they'll come chasing out after us."

The shore grew dusky. The man waving a coat blended gradually into this gloom, and it swallowed in the same manner the omnibus and the group of people. The spray, when it dashed uproariously over the side, made the voyagers shrink and swear like men who were being branded.

"I'd like to catch the chump who waved the coat. I feel like soaking him one, just for luck."

"Why? What did he do?"

"Oh, nothing, but then he seemed so damned cheerful."

In the meantime the oiler rowed, and then the correspondent rowed, and then the oiler rowed. Grey-faced and bowed forward, they mechanically, turn by turn, plied the leaden oars. The form of the lighthouse had vanished from the southern horizon, but finally a pale star appeared, just lifting from the sea. The streaked saffron in the west passed before the all-merging darkness, and the sea to the east was black. The land had vanished, and was expressed only by the low and drear thunder of the surf.

"If I am going to be drowned—if I am going to be drowned—if I am going to be drowned, why, in the name of the seven mad gods who rule the sea, was I allowed to come thus far and contemplate sand and trees? Was I brought here merely to have my nose dragged away as I was about to nibble the sacred cheese of life?"

The patient captain, drooped over the water-jar, was sometimes obliged to speak to the oarsman.

"Keep her head up! Keep her head up!"

"'Keep her head up,' sir." The voices were weary and low.

This was surely a quiet evening. All save the oarsman lay heavily and listlessly in the boat's bottom. As for him, his eyes were just capable of noting the tall black waves that swept forward in a most sinister silence, save for an occasional subdued growl of a crest.

The cook's head was on a thwart, and he looked without interest at the water under his nose. He was deep in other scenes. Finally he spoke. "Billie," he murmured, dreamfully, "what kind of pie do you like best?"

V

"Pie," said the oiler and the correspondent, agitatedly. "Don't talk about those things, blast you!"

"Well," said the cook, "I was just thinking about ham sandwiches, and—"

A night on the sea in an open boat is a long night. As darkness settled finally, the shine of the light, lifting from the sea in the south, changed to full gold. On the northern horizon a new light appeared, a small bluish gleam on the edge of the waters. These two lights were the furniture of the world. Otherwise there was nothing but waves.

Two men huddled in the stern, and distances were so magnificent in the dingey that the rower was enabled to keep his feet partly warmed by thrusting them under his companions. Their legs indeed extended far under the rowing-seat until they touched the feet of the captain forward. Sometimes, despite the efforts of the tired oarsman, a wave came piling into the boat, an icy wave of the night, and the chilling water soaked them anew. They would twist their bodies for a moment and groan, and sleep the dead sleep once more, while the water in the boat gurgled about them as the craft rocked.

The plan of the oiler and the correspondent was for one to row until he lost the ability, and then arouse the other from his sea-water couch in the bottom of the boat.

The oiler plied the oars until his head drooped forward, and the overpowering sleep blinded him. And he rowed yet afterward. Then he touched a man in the bottom of the boat, and called his name. "Will you spell me for a little while?" he said, meekly.

"Sure, Billie," said the correspondent, awakening and dragging himself to a sitting position. They exchanged places carefully, and the oiler, cuddling down in the sea-water at the cook's side, seemed to go to sleep instantly.

The particular violence of the sea had ceased. The waves came without snarling. The obligation of the man at the oars was to keep the boat headed so that the tilt of the rollers would not capsize her, and to preserve her from filling when the crests rushed past. The black waves were silent and hard to be seen in the darkness. Often one was almost upon the boat before the oarsman was aware.

In a low voice the correspondent addressed the captain. He was not sure that the captain was awake, although this iron man seemed to be always awake. "Captain, shall I keep her making for that light north, sir?"

The same steady voice answered him. "Yes. Keep it about two points off the port bow."

The cook had tied a life-belt around himself in order to get even the warmth which this clumsy cork contrivance could donate, and he seemed almost stove-like when a rower, whose teeth invariably chattered wildly as soon as he ceased his labor, dropped down to sleep.

The correspondent, as he rowed, looked down at the two men sleeping under-foot. The cook's arm was around the oiler's shoulders, and, with their fragmentary clothing and haggard faces, they were the babes of the sea, a grotesque rendering of the old babes in the wood.

Later he must have grown stupid at his work, for suddenly there was a growling of water, and a crest came with a roar and a swash into the boat, and it was a wonder that it did not set the cook afloat in his life-belt. The cook continued to sleep, but the oiler sat up, blinking his eyes and shaking with the new cold.

"Oh, I'm awful sorry, Billie," said the correspondent contritely.

"That's all right, old boy," said the oiler, and lay down again and was asleep.

Presently it seemed that even the captain dozed, and the correspondent thought that he was the one man afloat on all the oceans. The wind had a voice as it came over the waves, and it was sadder than the end.

There was a long, loud swishing astern of the boat, and a gleaming trail of phosphorescence, like blue flame, was furrowed on the black waters. It might have been made by a monstrous knife.

Then there came a stillness, while the correspondent breathed with the open mouth and looked at the sea.

Suddenly there was another swish and another long flash of bluish light, and this time it was alongside the boat, and might almost have been reached with an oar. The correspondent saw an enormous fin speed like a shadow through the water, hurling the crystalline spray and leaving the long glowing trail.

The correspondent looked over his shoulder at the captain. His face was hidden, and he seemed to be asleep. He looked at the babes of the sea. They certainly were asleep. So, being bereft of sympathy, he leaned a little way to one side and swore softly into the sea.

But the thing did not then leave the vicinity of the boat. Ahead or astern, on one side or the other, at intervals long or short, fled the long sparkling streak, and there was to be heard the whirroo of the dark fin. The speed and power of the thing was greatly to be admired. It cut the water like a gigantic and keen projectile.

The presence of this biding thing did not affect the man with the same horror that it would if he had been a picnicker. He simply looked at the sea dully and swore in an undertone.

Nevertheless, it is true that he did not wish to be alone. He wished one of his companions to awaken by chance and keep him company with it. But the captain hung motionless over the water-jar, and the oiler and the cook in the bottom of the boat were plunged in slumber.

VI

"If I am going to be drowned—if I am going to be drowned—if I am going to be drowned, why, in the name of the seven mad gods who rule the sea, was I allowed to come thus far and contemplate sand and trees?"

During this dismal night, it may be remarked that a man would conclude that it was really the intention of the seven mad gods to drown him, despite the abominable injustice of it. For it was certainly an abominable injustice to drown a man who had worked so hard, so hard. The man felt it would be a crime most unnatural. Other people had drowned at sea since galleys swarmed with painted sails, but still—

When it occurs to a man that nature does not regard him as important, and that she feels she would not maim the universe by disposing of him, he at first wishes to throw bricks at the temple, and he hates deeply the fact that there are no brick and no temples. Any visible expression of nature would surely be pelleted with his jeers.

Then, if there be no tangible thing to hoot he feels, perhaps, the desire to confront a personification and indulge in pleas, bowed to one knee, and with hands supplicant, saying: "Yes, but I love myself."

A high cold star on a winter's night is the word he feels that she says to him. Thereafter he knows the pathos of his situation.

The men in the dingey had not discussed these matters, but each had, no doubt, reflected upon them in silence and according to his mind. There was seldom any expression upon their faces save the general one of complete weariness. Speech was devoted to the business of the boat.

To chime the notes of his emotion, a verse mysteriously entered the correspondent's head. He had even forgotten that he had forgotten this verse, but it suddenly was in his mind.

"A soldier of the Legion lay dying in Algiers, There was a lack of woman's nursing, there was dearth of woman's tears; But a comrade stood beside him, and he took that comrade's hand, And he said: 'I shall never see my own, my native land.'"

In his childhood, the correspondent had been made acquainted with the fact that a soldier of the Legion lay dying in Algiers, but he had never regarded the fact as important. Myriads of his school-fellows had informed him of the soldier's plight, but the dinning had naturally ended by making him perfectly indifferent. He had never considered it his affair that a soldier of the Legion lay dying in Algiers, nor had it appeared to him as a matter for sorrow. It was less to him than the breaking of a pencil's point.

Now, however, it quaintly came to him as a human, living thing. It was no longer merely a picture of a few throes in the breast of a poet, meanwhile drinking tea and warming his feet at the grate; it was an actuality—stern, mournful, and fine.

The correspondent plainly saw the soldier. He lay on the sand with his feet out straight and still. While his pale left hand was upon his chest in an attempt to thwart the going of his life, the blood came between his fingers. In the far Algerian distance, a city of low square forms was set against a sky that was faint with the last sunset hues. The correspondent, plying the oars and dreaming of the slow and slower movements of the lips of the soldier, was moved by a profound and perfectly impersonal comprehension. He was sorry for the soldier of the Legion who lay dying in Algiers.

The thing which had followed the boat and waited, had evidently grown bored at the delay. There was no longer to be heard the slash of the cut-water, and there was no longer the flame of the long trail. The light in the north still glimmered, but it was apparently no nearer to the boat. Sometimes the boom of the surf rang in the correspondent's ears, and he turned the craft seaward then and rowed harder. Southward, some one had evidently built a watch-fire on the beach. It was too low and too far to be seen, but it made a shimmering, roseate reflection upon the bluff back of it, and this could be discerned from the boat. The wind came stronger, and sometimes a wave suddenly raged out like a mountain-cat, and there was to be seen the sheen and sparkle of a broken crest.

The captain, in the bow, moved on his water-jar and sat erect. "Pretty long night," he observed to the correspondent. He looked at the shore. "Those life-saving people take their time."

"Did you see that shark playing around?"

"Yes, I saw him. He was a big fellow, all right."

"Wish I had known you were awake."

Later the correspondent spoke into the bottom of the boat.

"Billie!" There was a slow and gradual disentanglement. "Billie, will you spell me?"

"Sure," said the oiler.

As soon as the correspondent touched the cold comfortable sea-water in the bottom of the boat, and had huddled close to the cook's life-belt he was deep in sleep, despite the fact that his teeth played all the popular airs. This sleep was so good to him that it was but a moment before he heard a voice call his name in a tone that demonstrated the last stages of exhaustion. "Will you spell me?"

"Sure, Billie."

The light in the north had mysteriously vanished, but the correspondent took his course from the wide-awake captain.

Later in the night they took the boat farther out to sea, and the captain directed the cook to take one oar at the stern and keep the boat facing the seas. He was to call out if he should hear the thunder of the surf. This plan enabled the oiler and the correspondent to get respite together. "We'll give those boys a chance to get into shape again," said the captain. They curled down and, after a few preliminary chattering and trembles, slept once more the dead sleep. Neither knew they had bequeathed to the cook the company of another shark, or perhaps the same shark.

As the boat caroused on the waves, spray occasionally bumped over the side and gave them a fresh soaking, but this had no power to break their repose. The ominous slash of the wind and the water affected them as it would have affected mummies.

"Boys," said the cook, with the notes of every reluctance in his voice, "she's drifted in pretty close. I guess one of you had better take her to sea again." The correspondent, aroused, heard the crash of the toppled crests.

As he was rowing, the captain gave him some whisky-and-water, and this steadied the chills out of him. "If I ever get ashore and anybody shows me even a photograph of an oar—"

At last there was a short conversation.

"Billie.... Billie, will you spell me?"

"Sure," said the oiler.

VII

When the correspondent again opened his eyes, the sea and the sky were each of the grey hue of the dawning. Later, carmine and gold was painted upon the waters. The morning appeared finally, in its splendor, with a sky of pure blue, and the sunlight flamed on the tips of the waves.

On the distant dunes were set many little black cottages, and a tall white windmill reared above them. No man, nor dog, nor bicycle appeared on the beach. The cottages might have formed a deserted village.

The voyagers scanned the shore. A conference was held in the boat. "Well," said the captain, "if no help is coming we might better try a run through the surf right away. If we stay out here much longer we will be too weak to do anything for ourselves at all." The others silently acquiesced in this reasoning. The boat was headed for the beach. The correspondent wondered if none ever ascended the tall wind-tower, and if then they never looked seaward. This tower was a giant, standing with its back to the plight of the ants. It represented in a degree, to the correspondent, the serenity of nature amid the struggles of the individual—nature in the wind, and nature in the vision of men. She did not seem cruel to him then, nor beneficent, nor treacherous, nor wise. But she was indifferent, flatly indifferent. It is, perhaps, plausible that a man in this situation, impressed with the unconcern of the universe, should see the innumerable flaws of his life, and have them taste wickedly in his mind and wish for another chance. A distinction between right and wrong seems absurdly clear to him, then, in this new ignorance of the grave-edge, and he understands that if he were given another opportunity he would mend his conduct and his words, and be better and brighter during an introduction or at a tea.

"Now, boys," said the captain, "she is going to swamp, sure. All we can do is to work her in as far as possible, and then when she swamps, pile out and scramble for the beach. Keep cool now, and don't jump until she swamps sure."

The oiler took the oars. Over his shoulders he scanned the surf. "Captain," he said, "I think I'd better bring her about, and keep her head-on to the seas and back her in."

"All right, Billie," said the captain. "Back her in." The oiler swung the boat then and, seated in the stern, the cook and the correspondent were obliged to look over their shoulders to contemplate the lonely and indifferent shore.

The monstrous in-shore rollers heaved the boat high until the men were again enabled to see the white sheets of water scudding up the slanted beach. "We won't get in very close," said the captain. Each time a man could wrest his attention from the rollers, he turned his glance toward the shore, and in the expression of the eyes during this contemplation there was a singular quality. The correspondent, observing the others, knew that they were not afraid, but the full meaning of their glances was shrouded.

As for himself, he was too tired to grapple fundamentally with the fact. He tried to coerce his mind into thinking of it, but the mind was dominated at this time by the muscles, and the muscles said they did not care. It merely occurred to him that if he should drown it would be a shame.

There were no hurried words, no pallor, no plain agitation. The men simply looked at the shore. "Now, remember to get well clear of the boat when you jump," said the captain.

Seaward the crest of a roller suddenly fell with a thunderous crash, and the long white comber came roaring down upon the boat.

"Steady now," said the captain. The men were silent. They turned their eyes from the shore to the comber and waited. The boat slid up the incline, leaped at the furious top, bounced over it, and swung down the long back of the wave. Some water had been shipped and the cook bailed it out.

But the next crest crashed also. The tumbling, boiling flood of white water caught the boat and whirled it almost perpendicular. Water swarmed in from all sides. The correspondent had his hands on the gunwale at this time, and when the water entered at that place he swiftly withdrew his fingers, as if he objected to wetting them.

The little boat, drunken with this weight of water, reeled and snuggled deeper into the sea.

"Bail her out, cook! Bail her out," said the captain.

"All right, captain," said the cook.

"Now, boys, the next one will do for us, sure," said the oiler. "Mind to jump clear of the boat."

The third wave moved forward, huge, furious, implacable. It fairly swallowed the dingey, and almost simultaneously the men tumbled into the sea. A piece of lifebelt had lain in the bottom of the boat, and as the correspondent went overboard he held this to his chest with his left hand.

The January water was icy, and he reflected immediately that it was colder than he had expected to find it on the coast of Florida. This appeared to his dazed mind as a fact important enough to be noted at the time. The coldness of the water was sad; it was tragic. This fact was somehow so mixed and confused with his opinion of his own situation that it seemed almost a proper reason for tears. The water was cold.

When he came to the surface he was conscious of little but the noisy water. Afterward he saw his companions in the sea. The oiler was ahead in the race. He was swimming strongly and rapidly. Off to the correspondent's left, the cook's great white and corked back bulged out of the water, and in the rear the captain was hanging with his one good hand to the keel of the overturned dingey.

There is a certain immovable quality to a shore, and the correspondent wondered at it amid the confusion of the sea.

It seemed also very attractive, but the correspondent knew that it was a long journey, and he paddled leisurely. The piece of life-preserver lay under him, and sometimes he whirled down the incline of a wave as if he were on a handsled.

But finally he arrived at a place in the sea where travel was beset with difficulty. He did not pause swimming to inquire what manner of current had caught him, but there his progress ceased. The shore was set before him like a bit of scenery on a stage, and he looked at it and understood with his eyes each detail of it.

As the cook passed, much farther to the left, the captain was calling to him, "Turn over on your back, cook! Turn over on your back and use the oar."

"All right, sir." The cook turned on his back, and, paddling with an oar, went ahead as if he were a canoe.

Presently the boat also passed to the left of the correspondent with the captain clinging with one hand to the keel. He would have appeared like a man raising himself to look over a board fence, if it were not for the extraordinary gymnastics of the boat. The correspondent marvelled that the captain could still hold to it.

They passed on, nearer to shore—the oiler, the cook, the captain—and following them went the water-jar, bouncing gaily over the seas.

The correspondent remained in the grip of this strange new enemy—a current. The shore, with its white slope of sand and its green bluff, topped with little silent cottages, was spread like a picture before him. It was very near to him then, but he was impressed as one who in a gallery looks at a scene from Brittany or Holland.

He thought: "I am going to drown? Can it be possible? Can it be possible? Can it be possible?" Perhaps an individual must consider his own death to be the final phenomenon of nature.

But later a wave perhaps whirled him out of this small, deadly current, for he found suddenly that he could again make progress toward the shore. Later still, he was aware that the captain, clinging with one hand to the keel of the dingey, had his face turned away from the shore and toward him, and was calling his name. "Come to the boat! Come to the boat!"

In his struggle to reach the captain and the boat, he reflected that when one gets properly wearied, drowning must really be a comfortable arrangement, a cessation of hostilities accompanied by a large degree of relief, and he was glad of it, for the main thing in his mind for some months had been horror of the temporary agony. He did not wish to be hurt.

Presently he saw a man running along the shore. He was undressing with most remarkable speed. Coat, trousers, shirt, everything flew magically off him.

"Come to the boat," called the captain.

"All right, captain." As the correspondent paddled, he saw the captain let himself down to bottom and leave the boat. Then the correspondent performed his one little marvel of the voyage. A large wave caught him and flung him with ease and supreme speed completely over the boat and far beyond it. It struck him even then as an event in gymnastics, and a true miracle of the sea. An over-turned boat in the surf is not a plaything to a swimming man.

The correspondent arrived in water that reached only to his waist, but his condition did not enable him to stand for more than a moment. Each wave knocked him into a heap, and the under-tow pulled at him.

Then he saw the man who had been running and undressing, and undressing and running, come bounding into the water. He dragged ashore the cook, and then waded towards the captain, but the captain waved him away, and sent him to the correspondent. He was naked, naked as a tree in winter, but a halo was about his head, and he shone like a saint. He gave a strong pull, and a long drag, and a bully heave at the correspondent's hand. The correspondent, schooled in the minor formulae, said: "Thanks, old man." But suddenly the man cried: "What's that?" He pointed a swift finger. The correspondent said: "Go."

In the shallows, face downward, lay the oiler. His forehead touched sand that was periodically, between each wave, clear of the sea.

The correspondent did not know all that transpired afterward. When he achieved safe ground he fell, striking the sand with each particular part of his body. It was as if he had dropped from a roof, but the thud was grateful to him.

It seems that instantly the beach was populated with men with blankets, clothes, and flasks, and women with coffeepots and all the remedies sacred to their minds. The welcome of the land to the men from the sea was warm and generous, but a still and dripping shape was carried slowly up the beach, and the land's welcome for it could only be the different and sinister hospitality of the grave.

When it came night, the white waves paced to and fro in the moonlight, and the wind brought the sound of the great sea's voice to the men on shore, and they felt that they could then be interpreters.

RIESENBERG

FORD MADOX FORD

A feeling of desolation seemed for Philip Hands to overhang the little German bathing-establishment. The rain dripped down among the all enveloping fir trees; the heavy mists hung all above the deep valley. Geheimer Sanitätsrath Dr. von Salzer with his long flaked beard, his bent back, his scurrying gait and his peering, spectacled eyes, that seemed always to be spying out invisible mice or spiders in unseen corners—the incredible nerve-doctor whom Philip Hands did not know whether to venerate or to desire to kick—had just scuttled for all the world like a large goat over the further edge of the little white Platz and had vanished round the corner into the door of the room occupied by Philip Hands' mother. And Dr. von Salzer's visits to his mother always intensely exasperated Philip. It was like giving over that beloved and tortured lady into the hands of an inscrutable spider. It might be a benevolent spider; it might be a wicked and hateful charlatan. There was not any means of knowing. But at any rate, for the moment everything was disgusting.

You could not make anything out of this beastly foreign place, half of whose inmates at least were miserable creatures tottering on the verge of insanity and ministered to by the other half who might be like Philip Hands himself, devoted children, or paid attendants whose business in life it was to look cheerful, to dress well, to dance to the band and to play skittles. And indeed normally they kept it up very well in Drieselheim. It was probably—and even in his black mood Philip had to acknowledge it—made up of about the best people you could find in the whole of Europe. For all you had to allow that it is just the best people of Europe, the oldest of families, who provide the greatest proportion of haunted persons with odd mental skeletons in the shadowy cupboards of their minds. And indeed that autumn, which was the first autumn after the Boxer risings and the attack on the Legations in China, found them nearly all almost a family party—a sort of diplomatic clan in Bad-Drieselheim which was the private property of the Grand Duke of Trevers. For just as the soldiers of the several nations of Europe had fought side by side in the march to Pekin, so the sufferers from mental horrors—a crop of whom always survive the horrors of widespread bloodshed—were gathered together here to be cured of their troubles or to drop out of life in one asylum or another. It was because Philip Hands' mother had seen his father die with an arrow through his throat and had suffered from hallucinations that she knew to be hallucinations, it was because of this that she and her son were there, just as it was because Annette von Droste's father had seen her younger sister sicken and die within the enclosures that Annette von Droste was there waiting hand and foot upon the erect and benevolent old man who would tell you anecdotes of all the kingly personages of Europe and would yet sometimes pass both hands down his face as if he were trying to brush away drops of blood. The von Drostes and the Hands had been in Pekin at that time together. So had the Rodes, the Kesselheims, the Lussacs and three or four of the other families, that were there in the little Bath. And they were all families that had rubbed shoulders together all over the world in Legations and Embassies.

They might meet at Madrid one year, in St. Petersburg the next; one of them might be His Majesty's envoy at Bangkok and be met on the steamer by another family going out to represent His Very Christian Majesty of Portugal at the Court of Tokyo. But Bad-Drieselheim as a rule was so enormously expensive that the mere diplomatic service would not ordinarily have been able to get their pockets to run to it. They wouldn't have been there at all, they would have been scattered over Switzerland from Interlaken to Salso-Maggiore, if it had not been that the Grand Duke of Treves had lost his favourite son in Pekin too. Ordinarily, Bad-Drieselheim was a place where princes of foreign houses retired to get cured of their megrims. Now Philip Hands' mother and the von Drostes and the Rodes and the Kesselheims and the Lussacs were there because the bereaved Grand Duke had extended to them an invitation that made them practically his guests.

And for the life of him, Philip Hands could not see what attractions Drieselheim could offer to royal and Imperial Princes. The Bath itself was an old and abandoned convent, set down on an embankment that was like a dam across a solitary valley, an immense steep valley covered to the very tips of the ranges with melancholy and weeping firs. Up the valley they were never allowed to go. Upon coming there they were made to give their words that they would not. The official reason given by Dr. von Salzer was that the valley contained quarries where blasting was very frequent, and that in consequence his patients might be crushed by falls of rock. For himself, Philip Hands cared very little for this mystery, though he did not in the least believe Dr. von Salzer's explanation. He was inclined to believe with everyone in Bad-Drieselheim that the Grand Duke's Government had there a secret depot for testing new patterns of field guns and high explosives. At any rate, it was none of Philip Hands' business, as a gentleman, who had passed his word, to attempt to interfere with the quarries or the secret, whatever it was.

Annette von Droste, however, took it differently. She was convinced that the mad uncle and predecessor of the Grand Duke of Treves was hidden somewhere in that deep valley, and the thought of this mysterious and eminent person with his romantic career and his absolute disappearance twelve years before, filled Annette with an enthusiastic curiosity, that was the only one of her enthusiasms that Mr. Hands had not been able to share. He had shared almost all her other fancies for as long as he could remember, from the time when he had been fourteen and she eleven in St. Petersburg, or when he had been eighteen and she fifteen in Paris or during the season before last in London—till half-past nine of the night before when she had, with an unaccountable strangeness in her manner, very definitely refused to marry him. That had been the night before.

He had proposed to her about four o'clock. They had been drinking coffee and eating sweet chocolate biscuits made to resemble true-love knots, while all the invalids were taking their afternoon sleeps. She had not said no; she had not said yes; she had been quite gay. She had gone away into the woods as she said, laughing, to talk it over with the mad ex-Duke in the forbidden valley. And Philip Hands had remained to drink more coffee and eat more chocolate biscuits in the autumn sunshine at the little table in the Platz near the bandstand. The band did not play till five o'clock because till that hour all the invalids rested. But upon the stroke, it struck up the solemn Chorale with which it habitually got all the patients out of bed. Philip Hands had gone to his mother's room to fetch her for her slow promenade along the gravel walk, in the sunshine of the lower valley. Here they had been joined by old von Droste who, having heard from Philip that his daughter had gone for a walk in the woods, proceeded to tell them the true story of what the Crown Prince of Wallachia had actually done at Tiplitz. The sun had shone; Philip's mother had seemed much better; the eminent and venerable diplomat had been so more than usually cordial that Philip had thought he was beginning to understand something of what was attractive in a place even as dull as Drieselheim.

They dined, as the custom of the place was, each patient in his own room, accompanied by his attendant. Afterwards, for an hour, the attendant was supposed to read the daily papers to his invalid. There there came the night assembly round the bandstand, which was illuminated with small strings of lamps, whilst those who cared for dancing were provided with a small orchestra of their own in the large and ghostly hall that had formerly served the nuns as a refectory.

Philip Hands had not found Annette among the dancers, so he went to look for her on the terrace which was erected, as it were, on a high rampart before the frowning round archway of the old white convent. The moon was high in the South, the valley opened out wide and far below his feet. The black woodlands, all of stiff pines, came down on each side of the terrace. It was very still; it was a warm autumn evening and Philip Hands felt confident that very soon Annette would come to find him. He leant upon the parapet and gazed into the spaces of the moonlight. He was twenty-seven—he was second attaché at a first class embassy; he knew he could have the governorship of the Leeward Islands for the asking and he hadn't the least doubt that Annette loved him.

It was very still for a time, and then they began blasting again in the forbidden valley. Philip Hands could hear the familiar but mysterious screams, like human voices of enormous power, heard at a great distance. That, of course, he thought, must be the high explosive. That sort of thing gave off the most extraordinary noises. He remembered to have heard that the explosion of Gelsonite gave an overtone thirteen eighths above its first note, very like the sort of screaming sound that fills the air when great bells are played. They must therefore be using some very high explosive indeed in the forbidden valley. That did away with any idea of quarrying, if they quarried with a high explosive in at all the quantity in which they must obviously be using it to-night, they would blow all the mountains from Drieselheim into the Mosel within two or three hours. So that it was pretty obvious what *was* going on there. It could not be anything else but the most intensely secret of military operations.

The noises died away again; it became all of a deathly stillness in the valley; only the thin sound of the violins thrilled through the thick wall from the nuns' refectory where they were dancing, and suddenly Philip Hands heard a crackling in the deep woods—footsteps and the splitting of the small dry lateral twigs of the high firs. In the deep blackness his eyes perceived the bluish and as if phosphorescent gleam of a white dress. It came down in the darkness, it reached the terrace; it was Annette coming to him out of the woods.

"Have you been there all this time?" he asked.

She came towards him silently, her hands were stretched out, not as if it were towards him, but as though she were in the darkness feeling her way towards the light.

***

She had refused him! She had refused him then and there on the terrace in the moonlight. She had not given him any reason, she had said that there was absolutely no reason to give. None at all. She said only that she could not marry; that she was not fit to marry. That had been the night before!

Philip Hands had been possibly rather complacent, sure of an easy conquest. But he had an amount of emotion during the night that was sufficient to denote a very violent passion. He passed the dark hours in pacing up and down his small room, swearing violently. The whole thing was inexplicable and it was insulting. The girl, gay, high spirited, raven-haired and flushed, had listened to his proposals and had gone off into the woods to meditate on them. Philip Hands hadn't had the slightest doubt that she had gone into those deep woods to sing the song whose first line runs, *"Er der herrlichste von allen"*—words which mean "He the most noble of all!" and a song which the correct German maiden is supposed to sing upon being proposed to by a man who is the noblest work of God. Young Mr. Hands was not German enough exactly to put these thoughts into words. Indeed he was too Anglo-Saxon to put any thoughts into words at all. He had just waited, happy in the sunlight. A pleasant young man, with a pleasant career opening before him, the only danger which his parents or friends could have imagined would overhang him would be that he was so obviously going to marry a dark, passionate, romantically unreasonable young girl who might give him the very deuce of a time.

So that Annette's inexplicable refusal struck Mr. Hands as being not only unreasonable but sharply insulting. She had gone into the wood tidy, with a swinging step, her black hair carefully braided round her head, in a flimsy white dress. She had come out beneath the moon tottering, pallid, her dress torn, and green with the green of tree-trunks, whilst her hair was disordered and furry, a pine twig caught in it falling across her temples, and wetted so that it gleamed in the moonlight. And she had refused Mr. Hands!

Mr. Hands could not imagine that during her several hours of reflection she had discovered that he was unworthy of her. She had known him for too long, and he was not unworthy of her. Similarly, she was not unworthy of him. Their families and fortunes were remarkably well matched! Then it must have been some damned thing that had happened in the damned woods of this ridiculous and damned Grand Duchy. That was all Philip Hands could make of it, in his outraged pride.

He supposed Annette must have gone up the forbidden valley and had seen or heard—what the devil had she seen or heard? What the devil had happened to her? Mr. Hands' mind being distinctly concrete, he could think of nothing but the precautions that the Government of the Grand Duchy would take to conceal its secret armaments, its newly invented firearms or its high explosives. But what silly precautions could the rotten Government of an absurd Grand Duchy take? that, supposing she had poked her inquisitive nose into their secrets, could prevent a young lady of good family and excellent prospects from marrying a gentleman of the Diplomatic Corps in every way her equal?

Towards morning, while he paced and fumed, absurd ideas began to get into his mind. Perhaps his Annette, in the forbidden valley, had come upon the mad Grand Duke, that legendary figure of Treves, who had disappeared twenty years before. She must have come upon the mad Grand Duke and have been married to him by force. God knows what! And with his mind fatigued and full of grotesque images, Mr. Philip Hands thought he must be going mad. Annette von Droste must have gone mad. They were in that place, a great old convent building that was full of mad people. For there was no denying that the patients were all mad. They heard voices; they saw shapes; they were troubled by unseen hands, brushed by invisible wings, and in those ghostly cells and corridors, the pressure was too much for the sane people that were with them. This whole place represented a horrible and ghostly manufactory of lunatics, with Dr. von Salzer a spider-like lunatic at the head of them all. And in the darkness the whole ghastly conventual building, of which he occupied an old nun's cell in the far east corner of the inner courtyard, seemed to whisper and gibber with the brushings of the dresses of long dead nuns. Annette must have gone mad. He himself must be going mad....

In the grey of the morning, Philip Hands heard the hoofs of horses strike hard and clattering on the cobbles of that small inner courtyard. He strode to the window and fell back with an oath of horror that seemed to be shaken out of the very pit of his stomach. He grasped at both his eyes with the palms of his hands. In the dim white small courtyard stood two grotesque shapes, two indescribable, ghostly, black simulacra of horses. Black trappings covered them from their heads right down to the ground, so that they resembled the sable ghosts of chargers upon which medieval knights must have ridden, whilst from socketless eyeholes they appeared to shed hollow, forbidding, and unspeakably mournful glances. They seemed to be the apparitions of horses that had been dead five hundred years, and for the moment Philip Hands' whole brain seemed to be turning round inside his head. What was he looking at? There was no knowing what didn't survive, what mightn't survive in this extraordinary, old-fashioned Grand Duchy. It was one half modern quick-firing guns of deadly precision and the other half peasants in three cornered hats, short jackets, knee-breeches and stockings with ribands at the knee, practising the most old-fashioned ceremonials, gifted as they were said to be, all of them, with second sight, and perceiving daily in their thick and fantastic woods all the hob-goblins of Grimm, the spectres of the Brocken and the ghostly charcoal burners of the Harz mountains. There was no knowing what old, forgotten horrors, what dim fragments of the spectral past might not here survive along with the high explosives of the forbidden valley. In Central Africa, as he had read that morning, in a deep lake, they had discovered, still surviving, a monstrous prehistoric lizard that was said to be a survival of the first slime of the world—a monstrous scaled animal like a winged tortoise, as large as a town hall, and with jaws as deep as a cathedral portal. And this absurd forgotten country was as little explored as Central Africa. Why, the peasants still sacrificed mares and buried them beneath the corner posts of their houses, as they had done in the pagan days of Odin, thousands of years before the birth of Christ.

***

Altogether, Mr. Philip Hands passed a very bad night of it—a night of which not even his morning bath could altogether wash out the traces. Of course, upon taking a second view of the horses, he had perceived behind them an elaborate, ebony, gilded and glazed structure, and shortly afterwards four men in their shirtsleeves carrying down a coffin of polished brass, with bright steel handles. And he had realised that they were merely carrying away to an early train, for trans-shipment to Berlin, where the funeral was to take place in the Hedwigskirche, the body of Hofrath von Kellermann who had died, according to the official bulletin, of lesion of the brain the day before. But even that, though it was commonplace, was disagreeable. For, in spite of the discreet official silence and the removal of the body in early hours of the morning, the rumour ran among the assistants and servants of the place that the body of the Hofrath had been horribly mangled and crushed out of all human semblance. He was supposed, in fact, to have escaped from his attendants and, wandering into the forbidden valley, to have been crushed by one of the huge rocks that hurtled through space from the blastings in the forgotten fir woods.

Whilst Philip Hands sat in the large courtyard in the rain beneath the awning of the bandstand, waiting in the drip and depression of it all for the Sanitätsrath to come from his mother's room, a new and equally horrible surmise crossed his mind. Supposing that Annette, wandering too, into the deep woods, had been crushed by such a fall of rock, or had even witnessed the death of that unfortunate man? And the thought of this was so much more than he could bear, that he got up and began to pace up and down amongst the wet tables and chairs beneath the dripping awning. From the distant fir woods to right and to left the mysterious sounds of the quarries in the Driesel called from time to time like immense, rustling, human voices.

And suddenly, Mr. Hands perceived Annette von Droste in her white dress, half covered in a brown mackintosh. She came out of the door of her father's rooms on the opposite side of the courtyard, and made for the small nun's postern that gave on to the deep woods.

Philip followed her over the wet gravel of the Platz. He soon checked himself, but he could not have told you exactly why. Yesterday, perhaps he would have followed her without hesitation; to-day he was a rejected suitor! And yet he could not but feel, he had an irresistible impulse to believe, that in her white dress and brown mackintosh she was going into danger. The idea, indeed, came to him that she was going to meet the mad Grand Duke!

Suddenly, round the corner that led to his mother's room, there came, with an odd air of its being a procession, Dr. von Salzer, with his long, foamlike beard, and Philip Hands' little, old, and much loved, mother. Behind them followed Dr. Salzer's assistant, a short-sighted blond young man with a face like a bun, and large gold spectacles. He was called Schultz, and he was pushing before him a light bath-chair with spider wheels and rubber tyres. It was usual at this hour for Dr. Salzer to approach Philip, and to give him encouraging news of his mother's progress. To-day, therefore, Philip hurried towards them. The rain had ceased, though heavy drops fell from all the gutters, and the noises no longer came from the forbidden valley.

Philip's mother was a little old woman, very bent with age, but with a quaint manner that was half dictatorial and half humourous. Her eyes always twinkled; her cheeks were of the texture of a red and shrivelled apple and she spoke always with a very clear and fluting intonation, turning her head a little on one side, like a bird that surveys you from its perch. But for all her quaint precision and her air of tranquil widowhood, Philip Hands was aware that this most sane of creatures heard voices and saw appalling visions of demons that resembled the images of Buddhist temples. She had heard and seen them ever since his father had been murdered beneath her eyes in China.

"Tell Dr. von Salzer," she cried, before Philip had reached them, "that I am perfectly capable of walking two and a half miles. I do not need this grotesque machine to follow behind me." The Sanitätsrath combed his long beard with three fingers, and holding its ends together, looked with a long glance at Philip Hands. "Ah!" he said. "Yes." He spoke very slowly, but with a sort of lisp. "But this is a very special duty, this is a very special test. This is, if you will be pleased to let me call it so, the great test of the cure that I make."

"Nevertheless," the little old woman piped out, "I am perfectly able to walk two and a half miles."

"Ah, gracious lady," the doctor said, and he surveyed her a long time and enigmatically. "But will you be able to walk back, that is the question?"

"If I am not able to walk back," she replied, "I shan't be worth carrying back upon a velocipede."

The Sanitätsrath slowly shrugged his shoulders up to his ears, and as slowly let them fall. He glanced at her and then quickly at her son.

"But it is I that must take the responsibility," he said, "and I prefer not to take it."

"Then, if I am to faint or do anything unseemly," Mrs. Hands exclaimed in English, "I am not going to have this young man with the spectacles observing me in disorder."

The Sanitätsrath bowed his back so that his beard appeared to be about to sweep the ground.

"Gracious lady," he said, "it was my intention from the first to wheel you back myself, for I do not permit even my excellent colleague Schultz to penetrate into the arcana of my mysteries. Besides," he added, "it is very dangerous."

"If there is any danger for my mother—" Philip Hands exclaimed.

"Very excellent Mr. Second Secretary of Legation," the Sanitätsrath said, very softly, "it is impossible that there should be no danger. In all the things of this life there is danger, and living itself is a dangerous operation. But it is equally impossible that you should accompany us."

Philip's mother's cheek balls were of a flush that indicated very much of inward excitement.

"It's quite impossible that you should come with me," she said to her son. "It's kill or cure, as they used to say with the Kildarragh hounds, and it's not I that am going to cumber the ground."

"Oh, it will be cure, it will be cure," the Sanitätsrath lisped softly, and he appeared to push the little old woman gently by the arm across the Platz. They moved away from Philip very slowly, as if they were a shooting party going to execution with the passive and silent Dr. Schultz pushing the bath-chair in the rear for all the world as if he were carrying the coffin in which to bring back a corpse. They were going towards the main archway of the convent, and Philip Hands suddenly strode off towards the postern gate, through which half an hour before Annette von Droste had disappeared. His mother and the Sanitätsrath refused to allow him to follow them and he was too well disciplined to attempt to disobey their orders. But now he was going to do something.

He was in an extraordinary state of nervous tension. As soon as he was outside the gate, the silence of the deep fir woods closed upon him. The dark branches of the trees brushed against the very walls. From the gate a dark path through the woods led straight to the village of Bortshausen five miles away in an open valley beyond the range. The woods and paths on the right-hand side—those that descended the valley—were all open to the guests of the Bath. But on the left the woods were forbidden ground, for they ascended into the valley behind the convent. On this side every second tree bore a label with the word *Schonung* painted upon it, and the word *Schonung* meant that this was preserved land—as who should say *"Trespassers will be prosecuted."* And it occurred to Mr. Hands at that moment that the ground upon which the convent stood must have been built right across the valley like a dam, a bulwark erected even in the old days when the convent had been first built, to prevent access to the valley itself. This was absurd—for parts of the convent were six hundred years old, and there could not have been at that date any quarries or high explosives. Nevertheless, the thought was oppressive.

It was as if for centuries and centuries the valley with its deep woods had concealed secrets which the nuns and the Church formerly, and now Dr. Salzer and the authorities of the Grand Duchy, desired to keep from the world. Absurd! Yet there the convent was upon its high dam right across the valley, with the fir woods brushing its walls. And at the bottom of the embankment was a tunnel through which the mountain torrents from the valley burst downwards towards the open plains. Thus, upon the one side of the buildings it was all light and openness, for they stood very high; to the rear it was all silence, darkness and deep woods. An ominous and depressing thought—for Philip Hands was certain that it was into these woods that Annette had gone. Placards bearing the words *Schonung* would be sufficient to prevent an army of orderly Germans from penetrating into those woods, but Annette, for all her good old German name, was three parts of a gipsy. She was certainly there. And Philip Hands was so assured of this that he climbed the hill sharply along the path that led to Bortshausen. Half-way up this he knew, there was a pathway leading to the left before which, upon a tree, there was a placard with the words *"Entrance Absolutely Forbidden. Very Dangerous Path."* Here also, there was a sort of shelter of boughs beneath which there stood always a man in the grey-green uniform of a ducal forester, with a blond bearded face, and a dark green hat decorated with a tuft of feathers. This man's name was Hans Jorgenheim, and Philip knew him very well; he stopped almost every day to chat with him a little about the deer, wild boar, and wild cat, with which the forest abounded.

Philip Hands was going to ask him whether he had seen Annette pass that way, or whether he had heard her going through the woods below, for he knew perfectly well that the forester's keen ears let him know from the cries of disturbed birds whatever passed in the woods immediately beneath his care.

But, even whilst he mounted the steep path, he heard the sound of heavy footsteps descending in a sort of clumsy gallop, as if a frightened beast were coming down the hill. And suddenly there burst upon him Hans Jorgenheim, his honest blue eyes dilated, his mouth open, his face all one great panic.

"Das Fraulein!" he exclaimed, and he caught heavily at a tree trunk to stop his downward career. "Das Fraulein! She has gone up the path amongst the horrible beasts that the Sanitätsrath keeps there."

"And what then, idiot! Dog!" Philip Hands exclaimed. "Why did you not stop her?"

"Could I use physical force? Against an Excellency? A highborn lady? It is unthinkable."

"But, where is she? Why did you not follow her?" Philip Hands shouted.

"That is against discipline," the forester answered. "I have to find the Sanitätsrath and tell him."

"Forester, you are a coward," Philip Hands cried out. "You should have followed the lady, but you were afraid."

The forester let go the tree and drew himself up to his six foot of green and grey.

"Well, yes, I was afraid!" he said. "Very afraid. I have my orders from the Grand Duke. From the Grand Duke himself. Excellency, go you yourself, and if I have the Sanitätsrath's orders I will follow you."

Philip thought quickly.

"The Sanitätsrath," he said, "has gone out with my mother and a bath chair." For it came into his mind that without doubt the forester would know which way the doctor had gone and would thus get orders from him the more quickly.

"Ah, then," the forester exclaimed, "he has gone there by the lower path." And suddenly he plunged in amongst the trees, crashing his way down behind the rear of the convent in the deep woods.

Philip Hands ran quickly up the steep path. It was a very steep ascent for a man not much in training, and the blood drummed in his ears. By the placard that bore the words "Entrance Absolutely Forbidden," he paused to listen. There was nothing but the silence of the deep woods. There was no brook; there were no birds, even the heavy drip from the trees had ceased with the ceasing of the rain and a heavy mist clung all around him.

He turned into the narrow lateral path. He shuffled along as fast as he could, for he was very much out of breath still with the ascent. The path was very narrow and winding, and, as he got deeper in, the woods appeared infinitely old. The trees were black and twisted with age; ghostly lichen seemed to drip from their extended branches. They towered immensely high, so that their tops whispered unseen amongst the mists. And even as he hurried, Philip Hands was overwhelmed with the sense that he was being watched. He imagined that in all the shadows there were eyes, and from behind the stiff columnar trunks, unknown and forgotten men appeared to peep out at him. The doctor kept horrible beasts in these woods! The forester had said it. At any moment he might come upon them. . . . What might he not come upon? Two or three times he stopped to listen, but always there was the deep silence. The intolerable silence so absolutely solemn and assured, that it was a folly to imagine for your own comfort a sound that did not exist. Suddenly the path divided into two.

One arm went downwards sharply into the huge pines, and huge pines descended as sharply at his right hand without any path. He must be upon the top of the ridge of the valley divided into two. Before him the other arm of the path wound very steeply upwards, between a desolate underwood of brambles and beneath primeval hornbeams. Amongst flakes of shale and slaty rock, it climbed, almost erect, and zigzagging. There was no doubt about the path. There was a footstep in the black mud of a little rill and some bright scarlet toadstools that had formed a circle were broken, scattered, and gleamed white. Annette's dress had brushed them like that. Annette had gone up that way. He panted up its tortuous steepness.

The bushes gleamed with drops of dew and spiders' webs. In amongst a tangle of brambles he perceived the white skeleton of some beast. From the tusks in the skull it must have been that of a wild boar. Great fragments of rock were crushed all round it. Here and there branches had been ripped from the ancient trees, and white fissures showed down their green-grey trunks. He panted up the very steep and very slippery path. As high as he was, a considerable breeze was blowing and scattered the mist. The trees became thinner like old grey hair. He had glimpses of immense panoramas, of grey mountains, of long marching armies, of black fir woods. He was immensely high—so high up that he could perceive no villages. It was all grey silences and grey heights, and he was highest of them all. He felt himself to be in the highest place in the world, amongst the oldest silences. The path climbed still more steeply and suddenly in a desolate and mournful greyness of sky he came out upon a bare ridge of slate and shale like a hog's back. This ridge descended, with a terrifying, slippery steepness of loose stones, upon each side into an odd, bare valley—each valley like a cup, lined with grey loose slates and thinly clothed with torn and shattered pines. A high ridge; the two desolate valleys—and above all the grey slag!

And forty yards before him, upon a pinnacle of basalt, silent and motionless, like a listening chamois, he perceived Annette von Droste. She gazed down first into one valley and then into another. Then, slowly she put her hands over her eyes. He ran towards her at the end of his breath, hardly keeping his feet upon the slippery and scattering flakes of stone, that seemed hideously set on letting him fall into the cup-like valleys. He would have fallen a hundred feet down into the shattered pines.

He climbed the pinnacle of basalt that went up like a building. Up there the footing was at least firm and flat as if it were a platform. He caught her in his arms. She screamed, a shrill and violent sound like the cry of an eagle, that dissipated itself in the tenuous and desolate air.

"Do not touch me," she cried out. "I am mad. I have gone mad. Do not touch me! Look down! What do you see?"

Philip Hands gazed carelessly upon the mountains that marched in a tremendous procession all round and below them.

"Yes, it is very high here," he said soothingly. "It is much too high here. It is enough to turn anybody's brain. Why did you come here? Let us go back."

"I am never going back," she answered. "I tell you I am gone mad. There must be madness in our family. It is a very old family. I could not stand the strain of waiting in that place. That is why I can never marry you. That is why I am here. That is why I will never go away from here."

Philip Hands said:

"Oh, come!"

For the moment he could find nothing better to say. And then he pleaded the long agony of his ascent, all the terrible thoughts he had thought. He asked her to remember how faithfully he had followed her; he asked her to look how he had torn his clothes, and at the scratches on his hands.

Whilst he talked, his eyes wandered aimlessly down into one of the valleys, sheer down below their feet. It was a valley, but still it might have been the very top of a mountain—so high it was, like the crater of a very old, a very extinct, a hoary, a cold volcano. . . .

"And after I have followed you so faithfully," he pleaded, desolately, "you are going to throw me over? You can't mean to say you are going to throw me over?"

And then, suddenly, he exclaimed, "My God!" and with an irresistible action, impulsive of protection and of sudden flight, he clutched at her, and:

"The whole mountain's moving!" he cried out.

She looked at him and caught the direction of his eyes. A sudden and incredulous joy appeared to fill her face.

"What do you see?" she called out. "What is it you see?"

"No, no," he said. "Let us get away from here!"

She repeated imperiously, "Tell me what it is you see? Tell me, tell me!"

"What does it matter?" he said fiercely. "The mountain is moving. It looks like a man rolling over. An immense man! But it's the mountain moving. We shall be killed."

She caught him by the wrist and dragged him to the other side of the flat platform of their firm rock. A great screaming sound filled all the upper air, dissipating itself thinly in the immense reaches of space. She pointed.

"What is it you see?" she exclaimed imperiously. "What is it you see there?"

"It's the same thing," he said, "the mountain is moving. The whole mountain is moving under our feet. The rocks are flying about."

And it appeared to him that an immense rock, as large as his father's house, was thrown hurtling slowly into space far above them, to descend, passing right over their heads at a great height, crashing amongst the trees below.

"But what is it you see?" Annette insisted, until her tone had become an agony to his ears. "What is that thing there? What is it that moves?"

"Oh, it's absurd," he answered.

"In the name of God," she cried out. "What is it? My whole life—my reason depends on this."

He answered unwillingly and shamefaced.

"It's all this fantastic mist. It's a great, an immense man. It's a mountain! It's two mountains! One of them is throwing great rocks into the air. The other is scratching its side. That's what makes the noise. Each time it scratches you hear that screaming. Do you see? There's a deer running out of the wood; it looks smaller than an ant. Have we both gone mad?"

"No, no," she answered. "We are neither of us mad. I see it. You see it. Oh, thank my God, I'm not mad. If I had seen it alone I should have been mad."

And she threw her arms round him, and hid her face upon his shoulder that was wet with the mist.

"But the danger," he said. "We're in great danger. They've thrown another rock! Look!"

"Oh, what does it matter?" she answered passionately. "What does all the danger in the world matter? Don't you understand? I saw this last night. I thought it was all nonsense about there being danger in this valley, and I was looking for the lost Grand Duke. I wanted to look for the Grand Duke and I saw all this! Don't you understand? I thought I was mad!"

On the lower and easier slope, from the edge of the woods that curled up to the ridge, Philip perceived that there had slowly emerged the goat-like form of Dr. von Salzer. He was pushing before him the bath-chair, the ends of his immense beard brushing his laborious hands. Beside him walked Philip Hands' mother, a little, odd figure, in black.

The Sanitätsrath came along very slowly. He was in his shirt sleeves and with his white arms he pointed energetically first down one slope of the ridge, then down the other, and, with his beard flowing out across his chest, he appeared to address long speeches to Mrs. Hands. Once, when a great rock was passing through the sky he began to run, dragging Mrs. Hands behind him and glancing apprehensively upwards. His motion reminded Philip Hands exactly of the attitudes of people as they ran to take shelter from bomb-fire, he had seen in sieges during the South African war. But the rock, thrown very high, fell far beyond the ridge.

"My God!" Philip Hands exclaimed, "it's hit the other chap on the crown."

The Sanitätsrath and Mrs. Hands were approaching them very slowly so that:

"Gracious lady," his voice came up to them, "if these visions appear as real or seem as unreal as the other visions that you see and if one illusion appears no greater than the other, surely your cure should be completed. For all life is real; or all life is illusions. And who are we to say which are illusions or which are real? When we have such a little bit of life given to us surely it is unworthy of a man or of a woman to trouble about his, or about her illusions! If you hear voices, hear them and there is an end; if you see devils, see them and there is an end of it. Just as if you see and hear these danger zones of mine there is an end of it too. And this is an end of my cure. It is all I can do for you."

He stopped and bowed to the old lady. They were at the very foot of the pinnacle upon which stood Philip Hands and Annette von Droste. And Mrs. Hands walking slowly forward, disappeared right under their feet.

"A bomb-proof shelter," Philip Hands exclaimed, for he recognized that beneath their feet the pinnacle must be hollow towards the west. "A bomb-proof shelter, that's exactly what this place appears to be."

The Sanitätsrath had pushed the bath-chair away in front of him. He stood surveying Philip and Annette looking upwards with an attentive and a bland glance.

"Your two Excellencies," he said mildly, "had better descend. That is not the safest place in the world for tragic explanations."

They found von Salzer and Mrs. Hands in a little alcove that had been carved out of the pinnacle. It was exactly like the summer-houses you find at the top of every German hill. There were wooden seats fitted into the semi-circular wall. In the centre of the horse-shoe was a wooden table painted rusty red, and upon trestles at one side there stood a cask, and on the red table were four glass beer mugs.

The Sanitätsrath was wiping his perspiring brow with his white shirt sleeve and Mrs. Hands was fanning herself slowly with a very white handkerchief.

"Yes, that is all there is to it," the Sanitätsrath lisped amiably. He combed his beard with three fingers. He peeped at them all with a queer smile and, bending down, he picked up from the bath-chair his black alpaca jacket which he slowly put on, and his brown straw hat which he crushed down over his eyes.

"So!" he ejaculated comfortably.

Annette had sunk down upon a seat, her head leaning back against the stone wall and her eyes closed. Mrs. Hands was leaning forward towards the table upon which her fingers drummed slowly. And Philip Hands, lost in an Anglo-Saxon amazement at the inappropriateness of the doctor's actions, asked with a slight touch of irritation, "What the deuce is the meaning of it all?"

The doctor glanced at him quickly and negligently across his shoulder. He reached out and took a large beer mug from the table. He put it beneath the tap of the barrel and when it was filled he held it to his lips and drank with deep satisfaction.

"So!" he exclaimed once more. Then he sat down beside Mrs. Hands and slowly extended his spidery fingers to her wrist.

"It is a very good pulse," he said. He remained for some time gazing at the ground, then he looked at Annette von Droste.

"So, Excellency," he said, with an air of tender malice, "last night we were mad, and to-day we are sane again?"

Annette slowly opened her eyes.

"Oh, we are all quite sane again," the Sanitätsrath said. He pointed a thin, white and curved forefinger exactly at her nose.

"Listen, you," he said. "I will tell you how it was. You were about to promise to marry his young Excellency the Second Secretary of Embassy. You say to yourself: Now you will have your last moment of freedom! You will come and seek for the lost Grand Duke. For when you are married to this gentleman you will lose your liberty and never will he agree to permit you such a breach of the laws. So you creep up through the woods and you are frightened and alarmed, and after a long climb you come last night upon my two large ones. Last night my large ogres were very merry and noisy. I heard them far down below and you saw them, and you thought you have become mad because of your ancestors, and all such nonsense as I am for ever contesting. So you run back and tell our young friend that you are unfit to marry him. And then again once more this morning in your agony of mind you run here again to see if still the shapes of your madness existed. . . . Yes, is that not all true?"

Annette von Droste gazed with all her large eyes at the Sanitätsrath.

"And I was not mad," she whispered.

The Sanitätsrath slowly crossed his arms in their alpaca sleeves. "Then there is an end of it," he said, "and it all ends very well."

"But it isn't an end of it at all," Philip Hands exclaimed. "I must have some explanation of all this foolery!"

The Sanitätsrath looked at him penetratingly for a long time. Suddenly he rose and catching Hands by the wrist in his firm doctor's grasp, he led him swiftly out on to the ridge. He pointed straight down into each of the rocky cups decorated with the torn pines that were below them, one on each hand.

"What do you see?" he said.

Philip answered, "Oh, I know all that."

"They are quite still now," the professor said. "Both large ones. They are asleep. But I will give you a thousand pounds to go down into either of those valleys. I will give two thousand. I will give you ten thousand. I will give you all my fortune if you will bring me the thigh bone of the skeleton that is near the shoulder of the Large One on our left."

"Damn you!" Philip exclaimed. "Don't you know I am just engaged to be married?"

"I do not need the thigh bone," the professor lisped gently. "It is nothing to me. Yet I offer you a quarter of a million marks if you will fetch it for me. And you will not do it. . . . Then you may tell Her Excellency Annette that you are paying a quarter of a million marks in order to prove her sanity. For if you believed my large ones mere illusions, you would go down and fetch me that thigh bone. Yet now! There! You shudder all over your body and start back when I draw your wrist one-fifth of an inch downwards as if I were about to force you towards the slope."

Philip swore beneath his breath. The Sanitätsrath led him back towards the little alcove.

"So then," he said, "there is an end of it."

Annette leant suddenly forward.

"Excellent Wirkicher Geheim Sanitätsrath," she pleaded, "would it not help in the cure both of myself and Mrs. Hands if you would explain a little more?"

Von Salzer caught all the ends of his beard into his right hand.

"It is all explained that I can explain," he said. "I am a child in these matters. . . . Oh, oh!" he checked the expostulations that were rising to her lips. "If you could ask the Hofrath von Kellermann— a biologist now! But a mere nerve-doctor like myself! How can I explain these things? There they are, my two large ogres. They help me to cure my patients of a certain class. My business is to cure patients of a certain class, and that is the end of it, for me."

"But the Hofrath von Kellermann was buried this morning," Philip Hands exclaimed.

"No, no," the doctor answered amiably, "his body was taken to the train. He is to be buried in Berlin in the Hedwigs Kirche in four days' time. There will a great ceremony and many speeches. He was a biologist of world-wide fame."

Over his folded arms the doctor looked reminiscently at the ground.

"For three years," he said, "on and off for every day the Hofrath has sat here observing my Large Ones. He had a little donkey cart. It brought up this barrel of good beer that he will never drink again. He has surveyed them with field glasses; he has measured them with geometric projections, he has watched them in their sleep. For hours and hours he has sat here alone, he has sat here with me and never have I known a man of such unflagging industry and of such enormous skill. I wish I could show you the model of the skeleton of one of my Large Ones that he has made by conjecture. They differ, he says, as much from man as from the larger apes, only in the disproportionately enormous length of the spine from the lower ribs downwards."

"But where is the romance in all this?" Annette von Droste said. "Where is all the wonder?"

The doctor smiled at her—a sunny and friendly smile.

"Child," he said, "you have heard of Woden and Thor. Well, the Hofrath in consultation with Professor Dr. von Gobel the historian of the University of Isclimgen arrived at the conclusion that my Large Ones gave rise to the legend of Woden and Thor, the deities of the high and wonderful past of us Teutons. I know nothing of these things, for I am neither a historian nor a biologist. But this opinion is by no means a new one in the Christian world since the convent of Drieselheim, as you will find in any guide book, was built in the year 969 just after the date of the conversion of this part of Germany to Christianity. In order to enclose for ever within these valleys, two immense devils—*duo imtnanes diaboli*. And from that date until the convent was shelled during the war between Prussia and Austria and the nuns dispersed—from that date until the year 1866 the convent was never without these brave and courageous sisters who were of the opinion that by their prayers alone they kept back from our beloved nation the horrors of pagan worship."

"But hang it all!" Philip Hands said. "You don't mean to say that these things were really pagan gods, or that the prayers of nuns kept them shut up in a valley?"

"I don't mean to tell you anything, my friend," the doctor said. "These are things for specialists. Specialists in the history of religion will tell you one thing; specialists in biology another; historians another; I, I am a humble nerve doctor. And if I report to you the conclusions of the Hofrath von Kellermann and his scientific colleagues which will be published in a lucid and compendious volume, I don't do any more than give you the faintest shadows of their splendid arguments which, according to my humble lights, I have mastered in order to be of service to my patients. For my business is to assure people who are in doubt as to their sanity that they are sane."

"But the Hofrath von Kellermann—" Philip Hands began.

"The Hofrath von Kellermann," the doctor continued, "died here yesterday on his four hundred and twenty-first visit to my Large Ones. How he died is not known. He was found crushed to pieces at the bottom of the mountain. But whether he was killed by a rock falling upon him or whether he himself was taken up and thrown down to this great distance, it is very difficult to say. For my Large Ones are of a placid and amiable disposition. They do not eat nor do they, as a rule, touch any living animal, though, at intervals of about a month, the Hofrath observed that one or the other of them would take a pine tree and grind it between his teeth. But the Hofrath was of opinion that this was not done for the sake of nourishment but more probably in order to while away the time as you might chew the stump of an unlit cigar."

"But—" Mr. Hands began again.

"Excellent Mr. Second Secretary of Embassy," the Sanitätsrath said, "in order to save you the trouble of incessant questions I will try to sum up for you the conclusions arrived at by these eminent professors."

Philip Hands couldn't restrain himself from remarking, "I don't see why you haven't got some American agent to boom these—these giants? It would have been the sensation of the world."

And at the same moment Mrs. Hands exclaimed:

"Don't continue to exhibit yourself as an indomitable ass, Philip!" The Fraulein von Droste, intent upon her more romantic train of mind, asked:

"And the lost Grand Duke?"

The doctor glanced at her quietly and amiably.

"Ah, my never to be sufficiently lamented and glorious lord!" he said. "It was his case that set me on to preach the crusade that I am never tired of preaching—the crusade that there is no such thing as madness. They said he was mad but he was a man of grandiloquent schemes and magnificent achievements. It was simply that he was outside the plan of his circumstances. He desired to be greater than Tiberias so he built splendid palaces that his subjects couldn't pay for. He desired to be greater than Alexander so he was perpetually raising forces to prepare for a struggle against Prussia. He desired to emulate Hercules and so he came here to fight with the Large Ones, the secret of whose existence was the heritage of his illustrious position. He came here, you understand, alone, the sisters of the convent and the officials of his court begging him to desist from the dangerous adventure. And that is all that is known of him! There was never another trace. Where do his bones lie rotting? Who knows? As a young man, being his body physician, I searched every nook of the valley, I climbed in between the legs of the Large Ones as they slept."

"You!" Mr. Philip Hands exclaimed.

"Excellent Mr. Second Secretary," the doctor said ironically, "if you will climb down and examine these beings who appear to be now once more asleep, you will discover that their forms are covered with a grey-black hair, so coarse that it resembles the plants known as mares'-tails, and the grain of their flesh is so huge that with its indentations and the dirt that is upon it, it resembles a rough and uncultivated field, whilst the warmth that they give out is so considerable that each of these little valleys like cups appears like a greenhouse for heat and the stench is intolerable. If you will only climb you will observe all these things."

"Oh, thanks," Mr. Hands explained, "I am not a connoisseur in stinks!"

"Yet all these things I observed thirty-six years ago," the Sanitätsrath said, "when I was a young doctor, and spent six months in this valley, searching for the lost Grand Duke, of whom no vestige was ever discovered."

"Then he may be still alive—still here!" Annette von Droste exclaimed.

"Assuredly he may be still alive and still here," the doctor said, "who knows? The peasants say they see him from time to time riding all glorious upon his *schimmel*."

"But, I say," Philip Hands interrupted again. "If these fellows have been here all this time, how is it that nobody has ever talked of them?"

"My friend," the Sanitätsrath answered, "for centuries the peasants have talked of them. Twenty years ago you might have heard from any of these peasants of the feats of what they call the giants. You would hear now, when they desire to tell each other that it is time to light the stove to cook their bread, they thrown great rocks from one side of the mountain to the other, as you have witnessed. The learned Vonggobel interprets this action of theirs differently. He says these actions are the outcome of a rudimentary desire for play, as you would observe the larger apes take up curiously a fragment of straw, and then cast it from them. And you would have heard from the peasants twenty years ago of how, when my Large

Ones scratch their sides, it gives off a sound like the screaming of a thousand fiends. In this, the learned Von Kellermann agrees, though he says the sounds more rightly resemble that made by the crushing of metals under the stamp of gold-refining machines—a sort of metallic scream. In short, you have heard it. Twenty years ago you might have heard these things from the lips of the peasants, but now, fearing ridicule, they keep silent, though they talk amongst themselves, as they do of the lost Grand Duke, of great fowls resembling cocks, whose footsteps, twenty yards long, are seen in winter mornings in the snow, and of the Witches' Sabbaths called Walpürgis Nights, and of all the other things of which the peasants discourse in winter, when the snow is high over the roofs and the pine-knots burn merrily and the spinning-wheels turn in those lonely valleys."

"Oh, we know all about folk-lore," Mr. Philip Hands said.

"Then here you have the making of the folk-lore for yourself," the Sanitätsrath said, "such folk-lore as you yourself will tell your grandchildren when the snow is thick above your roof and above the limbs of my Large Ones, who do not mind snow upon their mountain-tops. For folk-lore is the interpretation set by common minds to explain facts which they cannot otherwise explain. How you will explain them I do not know."

"Then, why don't *you* explain them?" the indomitable Mr. Hands exclaimed.

"I do not explain them," the doctor said, "because in these matters I have an uninstructed mind. They have been explained as Woden and Thor, but they are not gods. They have been explained as immense devils, but they are not immense devils, since the existence of gods or devils presupposes a will, and my Large Ones have no wills, having reclined for thousands of years in the same valley. They have been explained as the secret warnings of the Grand Ducal House, since it is said that when one of them cries out, every twenty years or so, a

Grand Duke dies. Yet assuredly their purpose cannot have been to warn Grand Dukes of their approaching deaths, since they existed thousands of years before there were any grand dukes. For me, they are the instruments of curing people who imagine themselves mad through the hearing of strange sounds and the seeing of incredible sights. I bring these people up here and I say, 'Listen and behold!' and they hear sounds, and they see sights, stranger than any that they can imagine. Thus by the Grace of God, in Whose hands we all are, 67.3 per cent of my patients find cures. So you have many explanations afforded to you. For the Early Pagans they were Woden and Thor, and some used their fame for their own purposes. For me they are strange things that exist, and I use them for my own purposes; for the peasant women they are the Giant Brothers, and the peasant women use the stories of them in lulling their children to sleep, which is, perhaps, the most sensible purpose of all."

"But what *does* it all amount to?" Mr. Philip Hands asked.

"Oh, my excellent Anglo-Saxon friend!" the doctor ejaculated, with his first sign of exasperation. "What does it amount to? The well-known Professor of General Knowledge, von Imhoff zu Reutershausen, is contributing a general preface to the monumental work of the deceased Hofrath von Kellermann. In this the professor says—but I must warn you that he is regarded by his colleagues as romantic and unsound—the professor utters, if I can remember, these words:

"'Here, therefore, amongst these stupendous and grave vastnesses, there lie these grey survivals of a time which went before the very foundations of our splendid Teutonic race, whose destinies have broadened down to the imperial heritage so well known to our own day. It is to be observed (see page 126 of text) that here are two adult males of an unknown and obviously prehistoric race. That there were giants before our days has been observed by many a classical writer. Thus we have the phrase, *'Vixerunt fortes ante Agamemnon.'* And traces of the existence of such giants are to be observed in the mythology and legends of almost every race—'"

"But hang it all!" Philip Hands exclaimed. "These chaps appear to me immortal?"

"'Immortal these survivors of a heavy antiquity may appear to our limited conceptions, but the flesh of which they are made up is not indestructible. In what cataclysm their fellows perished who shall tell? But traces of many cataclysms are to be observed upon our globe sufficient to have destroyed all that was destructible of these immortal beings. Here, then, these two survivors sit—these two adult males. And if, as Professor von Gagern observes, all life, all will, all emotion, all motion, all passion, all appetite, is brought about by the search of the eternal male for the eternal female, then their listless immobility is sufficiently explained. Here they sit, having exhausted the limits of the globe in the unavailing search for a female of their own species. But all such females are dead—are destroyed. They sit close together in an eternal ennui of immortality, casting into the air from time to time that which comes next to their hands, waiting through the eternal ages! And what shall be the end of them—'"

"But, I say," Mr. Hands exclaimed, "if this blessed book about them is published, there will be an end of your practice?"

Dr. von Salzer looked for a long time at the young man.

"The essence of my practice is," he said, "the principle, and the principle will remain. Still, in the world there will be a thousand inexplicable things. For you will never be able to explain to me or any other man how it is that the Fraulein Annette von Droste should desire to unite herself to yourself."

"Oh, I say!" Philip exclaimed. "You don't mean to say that that is a form of madness?"

"I say merely," the Sanitätsrath answered dryly, "that it is inexplicable."

He pulled out his watch and said, "My consultation hour will have arrived in three-quarters of an hour. We have just time to descend the hill."

Annette von Droste rose briskly:

"So that the Grand Duke William," she said, "may be still in these valleys?"

The Sanitätsrath pushed the rubbed-tyred bath-chair out of the opening of the grotto.

"The Grand Duke may well exist," he said. "But you have done with Grand Dukes. Your business is to darn stockings."

"At any rate," Mrs. Hands piped suddenly, "I shall walk down the hill upon my own feet."

"But I say, you haven't explained . . . ?" Philip Hands was beginning.

"My friend," von Salzer answered, "even for the Second Secretary of a Legation, there must arrive a time when he shall stand naked upon the shores of the world and discover that each of us is alone here and without one single companion. Then he must do all his explaining for himself or leave it to God. It is now a very good moment to cross the ridge and descend the hill. The Large Ones arc now slumbering, who can say when they will wake or what perils we should miss when they did awaken? Let us go now towards the naked beaches of the end of the world."

"Now, what the deuce does that mean?" Philip Hands grumbled in the ear of Annette von Droste.

"Oh, the darling Sanitätsrath is so sentimental," she answered. "I wonder if *he* has ever seen the ghost of the Grand Duke riding splendidly upon his *schimmel?*"

THE PRAYER
VIOLET HUNT

I

"It is but giving over of a game.

That must be lost."—PHILASTER

"Come, Mrs. Arne—come, my dear, you must not give way like this! You can't stand it—you really can't! Let Miss Kate take you away—now do!" urged the nurse, with her most motherly of intonations.

"Yes, Alice, Mrs. Joyce is right. Come away—do come away—you are only making yourself ill. It is all over; you can do nothing! Oh, oh, do come away!" implored Mrs. Arne's sister, shivering with excitement and nervousness.

A few moments ago Dr. Graham had relinquished his hold on the pulse of Edward Arne with the hopeless movement of the eyebrows that meant—the end.

The nurse had made the little gesture of resignation that was possibly a matter of form with her. The young sister-in-law had hidden her face in her hands. The wife had screamed a scream that had turned them all hot and cold—and flung herself on the bed over her dead husband. There she lay; her cries were terrible, her sobs shook her whole body.

The three gazed at her pityingly, not knowing what to do next. The nurse, folding her hands, looked towards the doctor for directions, and the doctor drummed with his fingers on the bed-post. The young girl timidly stroked the shoulder that heaved and writhed under her touch.

"Go away! Go away!" her sister reiterated continually, in a voice hoarse with fatigue and passion.

"Leave her alone, Miss Kate," whispered the nurse at last; "she will work it off best herself, perhaps."

She turned down the lamp as if to draw a veil over the scene. Mrs. Arne raised herself on her elbow, showing a face stained with tears and purple with emotion.

"What! Not gone?" she said harshly. "Go away, Kate, go away! It is my house. I don't want you, I want no one—I want to speak to my husband. Will you go away—all of you. Give me an hour, half-an-hour—five minutes!"

She stretched out her arms imploringly to the doctor.

"Well . . ." said he, almost to himself.

He signed to the two women to withdraw, and followed them out into the passage. "Go and get something to eat," he said peremptorily, "while you can. We shall have trouble with her presently. I'll wait in the dressing-room."

He glanced at the twisting figure on the bed, shrugged his shoulders, and passed into the adjoining room, without, however, closing the door of communication. Sitting down in an arm-chair drawn up to the fire, he stretched himself and closed his eyes. The professional aspects of the case of Edward Arne rose up before him in all its interesting forms of complication . . .

***

It was just this professional attitude that Mrs. Arne unconsciously resented both in the doctor and in the nurse. Through all their kindness she had realised and resented their scientific interest in her husband, for to them he had been no more than a curious and complicated case; and now that the blow had fallen, she regarded them both in the light of executioners. Her one desire, expressed with all the shameless sincerity of blind and thoughtless misery, was to be free of their hateful presence and alone—alone with her dead!

She was weary of the doctor's subdued manly tones—of the nurse's commonplace motherliness, too habitually adapted to the needs of all to be appreciated by the individual—of the childish consolation of the young sister, who had never loved, never been married, did not know what sorrow was! Their expressions of sympathy struck her like blows, the touch of their hands on her body, as they tried to raise her, stung her in every nerve.

With a sigh of relief she buried her head in the pillow, pressed her body more closely against that of her husband, and lay motionless.

Her sobs ceased.

***

The lamp went out with a gurgle. The fire leaped up, and died. She raised her head and stared about her helplessly, then sinking down again she put her lips to the ear of the dead man.

"Edward—dear Edward!" she whispered, "why have you left me? Darling, why have you left me? I can't stay behind—you know I can't. I am too young to be left. It is only a year since you married me. I never thought it was only for a year. 'Till death us do part' Yes, I know that's in it, but nobody ever thinks of that! I never thought of living without you! I meant to die with you . . .

"No—no—I can't die—I must not—till my baby is born. You will never see it. Don't you want to see it? Don't you? Oh, Edward, speak! Say something, darling, one word—one little word! Edward! Edward! are you there? Answer me for God's sake, answer me!

"Darling, I am so tired of waiting. Oh, think, dearest. There is so little time. They only gave me half-an-hour. In half-an-hour they will come and take you away from me—take you where I can't come to you—with all my love I can't come to you! I know the place—I saw it once. A great lonely place full of graves, and little stunted trees dripping with dirty London rain . . . and gas-lamps flaring all round . . . but quite, quite dark where the grave is . . . a long grey stone just like the rest. How could you stay there?—all alone—all alone—without me?

"Do you remember, Edward, what we once said—that whichever of us died first should come back to watch over the other, in the spirit? I promised you, and you promised me. What children we were! Death is not what we thought. It comforted us to say that then.

"Now, it's nothing—nothing—worse than nothing—don't want your spirit—I can't see it—or feel it—I want you, you, your eyes that looked at me, your mouth that kissed me—"

She raised his arms and clasped them round her neck, and lay there very still, murmuring, "Oh, hold me, hold me! Love me if you can. Am I hateful? This is me! These are your arms . . ."

The doctor in the next room moved in his chair. The noise awoke her from her dream of contentment, and she unwound the dead arm from her neck, and, holding it up by the wrist, considered it ruefully.

"Yes, I can put it round me, but I have to hold it there. It is quite cold—it doesn't care. Ah, my dear, you don't care! You are dead. I kiss you, but you don't kiss me. Edward! Edward! Oh, for heaven's sake kiss me once. Just once!

"No, no, that won't do—that's not enough! that's nothing! worse than nothing! I want you back, you, all you . . . What shall I do? . . . I often pray . . . Oh, if there be a God in heaven, and if He ever answered a prayer, let Him answer mine—my only prayer. I'll never ask another—and give you back to me! As you were—as I loved you—as I adored you! He must listen. He must! My God, my God, he's mine—he's my husband, he's my lover—give him back to me!"

***

—"Left alone for half-an-hour or more with the corpse! It's not right!"

The muttered expression of the nurse's revolted sense of professional decency came from the head of the staircase, where she had been waiting for the last few minutes. The doctor joined her.

"Hush, Mrs. Joyce! I'll go to her now."

The door creaked on its hinges as he gently pushed it open and went in.

"What's that? What's that?" screamed Mrs. Arne. "Doctor! Doctor! Don't touch me! Either I am dead or he is alive!"

"Do you want to kill yourself, Mrs. Arne?" said Dr. Graham, with calculated sternness, coming forward; "come away!"

"Not dead! Not dead!" she murmured.

"He is dead, I assure you. Dead and cold an hour ago! Feel!" He took hold of her, as she lay face downwards, and in so doing he touched the dead man's cheek—it was not cold! Instinctively his finger sought a pulse.

"Stop! Wait!" he cried in his intense excitement. "My dear Mrs. Arne, control yourself!"

But Mrs. Arne had fainted, and fallen heavily off the bed on the other side. Her sister, hastily summoned, attended to her, while the man they had all given over for dead was, with faint gasps and sighs and reluctant moans, pulled, as it were, hustled and dragged back over the threshold of life.

II

"Why do you always wear black, Alice?" asked Esther Graham. "You are not in mourning that I know of."

She was Dr. Graham's only daughter and Mrs. Arne's only friend. She sat with Mrs. Arne in the dreary drawing-room of the house in Chelsea. She had come to tea. She was the only person who ever did come to tea there.

She was brusque, kind, and blunt, and had a talent for making inappropriate remarks. Six years ago Mrs. Arne had been a widow for an hour! Her husband had succumbed to an apparently modal illness, and for the space of an hour had lain dead. When suddenly and inexplicably he had revived from his trance, the shock, combined with six weeks' nursing, had nearly killed his wife. All this Esther had heard from her father. She herself had only come to know Mrs. Arne after her child was born, and all the tragic circumstances of her husband's illness put aside, and it was hoped forgotten. And when her idle question received no answer from the pale absent woman who sat opposite, with listless lack-lustre eyes fixed on the green and blue flames dancing in the fire, she hoped it had passed unnoticed. She waited for five minutes for Mrs. Arne to resume the conversation, then her natural impatience got the better of her.

"Do say something, Alice!" she implored.

"Esther, I beg your pardon!" said Mrs. Arne. "I was thinking."

"What were you thinking of?"

"I don't know."

"No, of course you don't. People who sit and stare into the fire never do think, really. They are only brooding and making themselves ill, and that is what you are doing. You mope, you take no interest in anything, you never go out—I am sure you have not been out of doors today?"

"No—yes—I believe not. It is so cold."

"You are sure to feel the cold if you sit in the house all day, and sure to get ill! Just look at yourself!"

Mrs. Arne rose and looked at herself in the Italian mirror over the chimney-piece. It reflected faithfully enough her even pallor, her dark hair and eyes, the sweeping length of her eyelashes, the sharp curves of her nostrils, and the delicate arch of her eyebrows, that formed a thin sharp black line, so clear as to seem almost unnatural.

"Yes, I do look ill," she said with conviction.

"No wonder. You choose to bury yourself alive."

"Sometimes I do feel as if I lived in a grave. I look up at the ceiling and fancy it is my coffin-lid."

"Don't please talk like that!" expostulated Miss Graham, pointing to Mrs. Arne's little girl. "If only for Dolly's sake, I think you should not give way to such morbid fancies. It isn't good for her to see you like this always."

"Oh, Esther," the other exclaimed, stung into something like vivacity, "don't reproach me! I hope I am a good mother to my child!"

"Yes, dear, you are a model mother—and model wife too. Father says the way you look after your husband is something wonderful, but don't you think for your own sake you might try to be a little gayer? You encourage these moods, don't you? What is it? Is it the house?"

She glanced around her—at the high ceiling, at the heavy damask portières, the tall cabinets of china, the dim oak panelling—it reminded her of a neglected museum. Her eye travelled into the farthest corners, where the faint filmy dusk was already gathering, lit only by the bewildering cross-lights of the glass panels of cabinet doors—to the tall narrow windows—then back again to the woman in her mourning dress, cowering by the fire. She said sharply—

"You should go out more."

"I do not like to—leave my husband."

"Oh, I know that he is delicate and all that, but still, does he never permit you to leave him? Does he never go out by himself?"

"Not often!"

"And you have no pets! It is very odd of you. I simply can't imagine a house without animals."

"We did have a dog once," answered Mrs. Arne plaintively, "but it howled so we had to give it away. It would not go near Edward.... But please don't imagine that I am dull! I have my child." She laid her hand on the flaxen head at her knee.

Miss Graham rose, frowning.

"Ah, you are too bad!" she exclaimed. "You are like a widow exactly, with one child, stroking its orphan head and saying, 'Poor fatherless darling.'"

Voices were heard outside. Miss Graham stopped talking quite suddenly, and sought her veil and gloves on the mantelpiece.

"You need not go, Esther," said Mrs. Arne. "It is only my husband."

"Oh, but it is getting late," said the other, crumpling up her gloves in her muff, and shuffling her feet nervously.

"Come!" said her hostess, with a bitter smile, "put your gloves on properly—if you must go—but it is quite early still."

"Please don't go, Miss Graham," put in the child.

"I must. Go and meet your papa, like a good girl."

"I don't want to."

"You mustn't talk like that, Dolly," said the doctor's daughter absently, still looking towards the door. Mrs. Arne rose and fastened the clasps of the big fur-cloak for her friend. The wife's white, sad, oppressed face came very close to the girl's cheerful one, as she murmured in a low voice—

"You don't like my husband, Esther? I can't help noticing it. Why don't you?"

"Nonsense!" retorted the other, with the emphasis of one who is repelling an over-true accusation. "I do, only—"

"Only what?"

"Well, dear, it is foolish of me, of course, but I am—a little afraid of him."

"Afraid of Edward!" said his wife slowly. "Why should you be?"

"Well, dear—you see—I—I suppose women can't help being a little afraid of their friends' husbands—they can spoil their friendships with their wives in a moment, if they choose to disapprove of them. I really must go! Good-bye, child; give me a kiss! Don't ring, Alice. Please don't! I can open the door for myself—"

"Why should you?" said Mrs. Arne. "Edward is in the hall; I heard him speaking to Foster."

"No; he has gone into his study. Good-bye, you apathetic creature!" She gave Mrs. Arne a brief kiss and dashed out of the room. The voices outside had ceased, and she had reasonable hopes of reaching the door without being intercepted by Mrs. Arne's husband. But he met her on the stairs. Mrs. Arne, listening intently from her seat by the fire, heard her exchange a few shy sentences with him, the sound of which died away as they went downstairs together. A few moments after, Edward Arne came into the room and dropped into the chair just vacated by his wife's visitor.

He crossed his legs and said nothing. Neither did she.

His nearness had the effect of making the woman look at once several years older. Where she was pale he was well-coloured; the net-work of little filmy wrinkles that, on a close inspection, covered her face, had no parallel on his smooth skin. He was handsome; soft, well-groomed flakes of auburn hair lay over his forehead, and his steely blue eyes shone equably, a contrast to the sombre fire of hers, and the masses of dark crinkly hair that shaded her brow. The deep lines of permanent discontent furrowed that brow as she sat with her chin propped on her hands, and her elbows resting on her knees. Neither spoke. When the hands of the clock over Mrs. Arne's head pointed to seven, the white-aproned figure of the nurse appeared in the doorway, and the little girl rose and kissed her mother very tenderly.

Mrs. Arne's forehead contracted. Looking uneasily at her husband, she said to the child tentatively, yet boldly, as one grasps the nettle, "Say good night to your father!"

The child obeyed, saying "Good night" indifferently in her father's direction.

"Kiss him!"

"No, please—please not."

Her mother looked down on her curiously, sadly.

"You are a naughty, spoilt child!" she said, but without conviction. "Excuse her, Edward."

He did not seem to have heard.

"Well, if you don't care—" said his wife bitterly. "Come, child." She caught the little girl by the hand and left the room.

At the door she half turned and looked fixedly at her husband. It was a strange ambiguous gaze; in it passion and dislike were strangely combined. Then she shivered and closed the door softly after her.

The man in the arm-chair sat with no perceptible change of attitude, his unspeculative eyes fixed on the fire, his hands clasped idly in front of him. The pose was obviously habitual. The servant brought lights and closed the shutters, drew the curtains, and made up the fire noisily, without, however, eliciting any reproof from his master.

Edward Arne was an ideal master, as far as Foster was concerned. He kept cases of cigars, but never smoked them, although the supply had often to be renewed. He did not care what he ate or drank, although he kept as good a cellar as most gentlemen— Foster knew that. He never interfered, he counted for nothing, he gave no trouble. Foster had no intention of ever leaving such an easy place. True, his master was not cordial; he very seldom addressed him or seemed to know whether he was there, but then neither did he grumble if the fire in the study was allowed to go out, or interfere with Foster's liberty in any way. He had a better place of it than Annette, Mrs. Arne's maid, who would be called up in the middle of the night to bathe her mistress's forehead with eau-de-Cologne, or made to brush her long hair for hours together to soothe her.

Naturally enough Foster and Annette compared notes as to their respective situations, and drew unflattering parallels between this capricious wife and model husband.

III

Miss Graham was not a demonstrative woman. On her return home she somewhat startled her father, as he sat by his study table, deeply interested in his diagnosis book, by the sudden violence of her embrace.

"Why this excitement?" he asked, smiling and turning round. He was a young-looking man for his age; his thin wiry figure and clear colour belied the evidence of his hair, tinged with grey, and the tired wrinkles that gave value to the acuteness and brilliancy of the eyes they surrounded.

"I don't know!" she replied, "only you are so nice and alive somehow. I always feel like this when I come back from seeing the Arnes."

"Then don't go to see the Arnes."

"I'm so fond of her, father, and she will never come here to me, as you know. Or else nothing would induce me to enter her tomb of a house, and talk to that walking funeral of a husband of hers. I managed to get away today without having to shake hands with him. I always try to avoid it. But, father, I do wish you would go and see Alice."

"Is she ill?"

"Well, not exactly ill, I suppose, but her eyes make me quite uncomfortable, and she says such odd things! I don't know if it is you or the clergyman she wants, but she is all wrong somehow! She never goes out except to church; she never pays a call, or has any one to call on her! Nobody ever asks the Arnes to dinner, and I'm sure I don't blame them—the sight of that man at one's table would spoil any party—and they never entertain. She is always alone. Day after day I go in and find her sitting over the fire, with that same brooding expression. I shouldn't be surprised in the least if she were to go mad some day. Father, what is it? What is the tragedy of the house? There is one, I am convinced. And yet, though I have been the intimate friend of that woman for years, I know no more about her than the man in the street."

"She keeps her skeleton safe in the cupboard," said Dr. Graham. "I respect her for that. And please don't talk nonsense about tragedies. Alice Arne is only morbid—the malady of the age. And she is a very religious woman."

"I wonder if she complains of her odious husband to Mr. Bligh. She is always going to his services."

"Odious?"

"Yes, odious." Miss Graham shuddered. "I cannot stand him! I cannot bear the touch of his cold froggy hands, and the sight of his fishy eyes! That inane smile of his simply makes me shrivel up. Father, honestly, do you like him yourself?"

"My dear, I hardly know him! It is his wife I have known ever since she was a child, and I a boy at college. Her father was my tutor. I never knew her husband till six years ago, when she called me in to attend him in a very serious illness. I suppose she never speaks of it? No? A very odd affair. For the life of me I cannot tell how he managed to recover. You needn't tell people, for it affects my reputation, but I didn't save him! Indeed I have never been able to account for it. The man was given over for dead!"

"He might as well be dead for all the good he is," said Esther scornfully. "I have never heard him say more than a couple of sentences in my life."

"Yet he was an exceedingly brilliant young man; one of the best men of his year at Oxford—a good deal run after—poor Alice was wild to marry him!"

"In love with that spiritless creature? He is like a house with someone dead in it, and all the blinds down!"

"Come, Esther, don't be morbid—not to say silly! You are very hard on the poor man! What's wrong with him? He is the ordinary, common-place, cold-blooded specimen of humanity, a little stupid, a little selfish—people who have gone through a serious illness like that are apt to be—but on the whole, a good husband, a good father, a good citizen—"

"Yes, and his wife is afraid of him, and his child hates him!" exclaimed Esther.

"Nonsense!" said Dr. Graham sharply. "The child is spoilt. Only children are apt to be—and the mother wants a change or a tonic of some kind. I'll go and talk to her when I have time. Go along and dress. Have you forgotten that George Graham is coming to dinner?"

After she had gone the doctor made a note on the corner of his blotting-pad, "Mem.: to go and see Mrs. Arne," and dismissed the subject of the memorandum entirely from his mind.

***

George Graham was the doctor's nephew, a tall, weedy, cumbrous young man, full of fads and fallacies, with a gentle manner that somehow inspired confidence. He was several years younger than Esther, who loved to listen to his semi-scientific, semi-romantic stories of things met with in the course of his profession. "Oh, I come across very queer things!" he would say mysteriously. "There's a queer little widow—!"

"Tell me about your little widow?" asked Esther that day after dinner, when, her father having gone back to his study, she and her cousin sat together as usual.

He laughed.

"You like to hear of my professional experiences? Well, she certainly interested me," he said thoughtfully. "She is an odd psychological study in her way. I wish I could come across her again."

"Where did you come across her, and what is her name?"

"I don't know her name, I don't want to; she is not a personage to me, only a case. I hardly know her face even. I have never seen it except in the twilight. But I gathered that she lived somewhere in Chelsea, for she came out on to the Embankment with only a kind of lacy thing over her head; she can't live far off, I fancy."

Esther became instantly attentive. "Go on," she said.

"It was three weeks ago," said George Graham. "I was coming along the Embankment about ten o'clock. I walked through that little grove, you know, just between Cheyne Walk and the river, and I heard in there someone sobbing very bitterly. I looked and saw a woman sitting on a seat, with her head in her hands, crying. I was most awfully sorry, of course, and I thought I could perhaps do something for her, get her a glass of water, or salts, or something. I took her for a woman of the people—it was quite dark, you know. So I asked her very politely if I could do anything for her, and then I noticed her hands—they were quite white and covered with diamonds."

"You were sorry you spoke, I suppose," said Esther.

"She raised her head and said—I believe she laughed—'Are you going to tell me to move on?'"

"She thought you were a policeman?"

"Probably—if she thought at all—but she was in a semi-dazed condition. I told her to wait till I came back, and dashed round the corner to the chemist's and bought a bottle of salts. She thanked me, and made a little effort to rise and go away. She seemed very weak. I told her I was a medical man, I started in and talked to her."

"And she to you?"

"Yes, quite straight. Don't you know that women always treat a doctor as if he were one step removed from their father confessor—not human—not in the same category as themselves? It is not complimentary to one as a man, but one hears a good deal one would not otherwise hear. She ended by telling me all about herself—in a veiled way, of course. It soothed her—relieved her—she seemed not to have had an outlet for years!"

"To a mere stranger!"

"To a doctor. And she did not know what she was saying half the time. She was hysterical, of course. Heavens! what nonsense she talked! She spoke of herself as a person somehow haunted, cursed by some malign fate, a victim of some fearful spiritual catastrophe, don't you know? I let her run on. She was convinced of the reality of a sort of 'doom' that she had fancied had befallen her. It was quite pathetic. Then it got rather chilly—she shivered—I suggested her going in. She shrank back; she said, 'If you only knew what a relief it is, how much less miserable I am out here! I can breathe; I can live—it is my only glimpse of the world that is alive—I live in a grave—oh, let me stay!' She seemed positively afraid to go home."

"Perhaps someone bullied her at home."

"I suppose so, but then—she had no husband. He died, she told me, years ago. She had adored him, she said—"

"Is she pretty?"

"Pretty! Well, I hardly noticed. Let me see! Oh, yes, I suppose she was pretty—no, now I think of it, she would be too worn and faded to be what you call pretty."

Esther smiled.

"Well, we sat there together for quite an hour, then the clock of Chelsea church struck eleven, and she got up and said 'Good-bye,' holding out her hand quite naturally, as if our meeting and conversation had been nothing out of the common. There was a sound like a dead leaf trailing across the walk and she was gone."

"Didn't you ask if you should see her again?"

"That would have been a mean advantage to take."

"You might have offered to see her home."

"I saw she did not mean me to."

"She was a lady, you say," pondered Esther. "How was she dressed?"

"Oh, all right, like a lady—in black—mourning, I suppose. She has dark crinkly hair, and her eyebrows are very thin and arched—I noticed that in the dusk."

"Does this photograph remind you of her?" asked Esther suddenly, taking him to the mantelpiece.

"Rather!"

"Alice! Oh, it couldn't be—she is not a widow, her husband is alive—has your friend any children?"

"Yes, one, she mentioned it."

"How old?"

"Six years old, I think she said. She talks of the 'responsibility of bringing up an orphan.'"

"George, what time is it?" Esther asked suddenly.

"About nine o'clock."

"Would you mind coming out with me?"

"I should like it. Where shall we go?"

"To St. Adhelm's! It is close by here. There is a special late service tonight, and Mrs. Arne is sure to be there."

"Oh, Esther—curiosity!"

"No, not mere curiosity. Don't you see if it is my Mrs. Arne who talked to you like this, it is very serious? I have thought her ill for a long time; but as ill as that—"

At St. Adhelm's Church, Esther Graham pointed out a woman who was kneeling beside a pillar in an attitude of intense devotion and abandonment. She rose from her knees, and turned her rapt face up towards the pulpit whence the Reverend Ralph Bligh was holding his impassioned discourse. George Graham touched his cousin on the shoulder, and motioned to her to leave her place on the outermost rank of worshippers.

"That is the woman!" said he.

IV

"Mem.: to go and see Mrs. Arne." The doctor came across this note in his blotting-pad one day six weeks later. His daughter was out of town. He had heard nothing of the Arnes since her departure. He had promised to go and see her. He was a little conscience-stricken. Yet another week elapsed before he found time to call upon the daughter of his old tutor.

At the corner of Tite Street he met Mrs. Arne's husband, and stopped. A doctor's professional kindliness of manner is, or ought to be, independent of his personal likings and dislikings, and there was a pleasant cordiality about his greeting which should have provoked a corresponding fervour on the part of Edward Arne.

"How are you, Arne?" Graham said. "I was on my way to call on your wife."

"Ah—yes!" said Edward Arne, with the ascending inflection of polite acquiescence. A ray of blue from his eyes rested transitorily on the doctor's face, and in that short moment the latter noted its intolerable vacuity, and for the first time in his life he felt a sharp pang of sympathy for the wife of such a husband.

"I suppose you are off to your club?—er—good bye!" he wound up abruptly. With the best will in the world he somehow found it almost impossible to carry on a conversation with Edward Arne, who raised his hand to his hat-brim in token of salutation, smiled sweetly, and walked on.

"He really is extraordinarily good-looking," reflected the doctor, as he watched him down the street and safely over the crossing with a certain degree of solicitude for which he could not exactly account. "And yet one feels one's vitality ebbing out at the finger-ends as one talks to him. I shall begin to believe in Esther's absurd fancies bout him soon. Ah, there's the little girl!" he exclaimed, as he turned into Cheyne Walk and caught sight of her with her nurse, making violent demonstrations to attract his attention. "She is alive, at any rate. How is your mother, Dolly?" he asked.

"Quite well, thank you," was the child's reply. She added, "She's crying. She sent me away because I looked at her. So I did. Her cheeks are quite red."

"Run away—run away and play!" said the doctor nervously. He ascended the steps of the house, and rang the bell very gently and neatly.

"Not at—" began Foster, with the intonation of polite falsehood, but stopped on seeing the doctor, who, with his daughter, was a privileged person. "Mrs. Arne will see you, Sir."

"Mrs. Arne is not alone?" he said interrogatively.

"Yes, Sir, quite alone. I have just taken tea in."

Dr. Graham's doubts were prompted by the low murmur as of a voice, or voices, which came to him through the open door of the room at the head of the stairs. He paused and listened while Foster stood by, merely remarking, "Mrs. Arne do talk to herself sometimes, Sir."

It was Mrs. Arne's voice—the doctor recognised it now. It was not the voice of a sane or healthy woman. He at once mentally removed his visit from the category of a morning call, and prepared for a semi-professional inquiry.

"Don't announce me," he said to Foster, and quietly entered the back drawing-room, which was separated by a heavy tapestry portière from the room where Mrs. Arne sat, with an open book on the table before her, from which she had been apparently reading aloud. Her hands were now clasped tightly over her face, and when, presently, she removed them and began feverishly to turn page after page of her book, the crimson of her cheeks was seamed with white where her fingers had impressed themselves.

The doctor wondered if she saw him, for though her eyes were fixed in his direction, there was no apprehension in them. She went on reading, and it was the text, mingled with passionate interjection and fragmentary utterances, of the Burial Service that met his ears.

"'For as in Adam all die!' All die! It says all! For he must reign . . . The last enemy that shall be destroyed is Death. What shall they do if the dead rise not at all! . . . I die daily! . . . Daily! No, no, better get it over . . . dead and buried . . . out of sight, out of mind . . . under a stone. Dead men don't come back . . . Go on! Get it over. I want to hear the earth rattle on the coffin, and then I shall know it is done. "Flesh and blood cannot inherit!" Oh, what did I do? What have I done? Why did I wish it so fervently? Why did I pray for it so earnestly? God gave me my wish—"

"Alice! Alice!" groaned the doctor.

She looked up. "'When this corruptible shall have put on incorruption—' 'Dust to dust, ashes to ashes, earth to earth—' Yes, that is it. 'After death, though worms destroy this body—'"

She flung the book aside and sobbed.

"That is what I was afraid of. My God! My God! Down there—in the dark—for ever and ever and ever! I could not bear to think of it! My Edward! And so I interfered . . . and prayed . . . and prayed till . . . Oh! I am punished. Flesh and blood could not inherit! I kept him there—I would not let him go . . . I kept him . . . I prayed . . . I denied him Christian burial. . . . Oh, how could I know. . . ."

"Good heavens, Alice!" said Graham, coming sensibly forward, "what does this mean? I have heard of schoolgirls going through the marriage service by themselves, but the burial service—"

He laid down his hat and went on severely, "What have you to do with such things? Your child is flourishing—your husband alive and here—"

"And who kept him here?" interrupted Alice Arne fiercely, accepting the fact of his appearance without comment.

"You did," he answered quickly, "with your care and tenderness. I believe the warmth of your body, as you lay beside him for that half-hour, maintained the vital heat during that extraordinary suspension of the heart's action, which made us all give him up for dead. You were his best doctor, and brought him back to us."

"Yes, it was I—it was I—you need not tell me it was I!"

"Come, be thankful!" he said cheerfully. "Put that book away, and give me some tea, I'm very cold."

"Oh, Dr. Graham, how thoughtless of me!" said Mrs. Arne, rallying at the slight imputation on her politeness he had purposely made. She tottered to the bell and rang it before he could anticipate her.

"Another cup," she said quite calmly to Foster, who answered it. Then she sat down quivering all over with the suddenness of the constraint put upon her.

"Yes, sit down and tell me all about it," said Dr. Graham good-humouredly, at the same time observing her with the closeness he gave to difficult cases.

"There is nothing to tell," she said simply, shaking her head, and futilely altering the position of the tea-cups on the tray. "It all happened years ago. Nothing can be done now. Will you have sugar?"

He drank his tea and made conversation. He talked to her of some Dante lectures she was attending; of some details connected with her child's Kindergarten classes. These subjects did not interest her. There was a subject she wished to discuss, he could see that a question trembled on her tongue, and tried to lead up to it.

She introduced it herself, quite quietly, over a second cup. "Sugar, Dr. Graham? I forget. Dr. Graham, tell me, do you believe that prayers—wicked unreasonable prayers—are granted?"

He helped himself to another slice of bread and butter before answering.

"Well," he said slowly, "it seems hard to believe that every fool who has a voice to pray with, and a brain where to conceive idiotic requests with, should be permitted to interfere with the economy of the universe. As a rule, if people were long-sighted enough to see the result of their petitions, I fancy very few of us would venture to interfere."

Mrs. Arne groaned.

She was a good Churchwoman, Graham knew, and he did not wish to sap her faith in any way, so he said no more, but inwardly wondered if a too rigid interpretation of some of the religious dogmas of the Vicar of St. Adhelm's, her spiritual adviser, was not the clue to her distress. Then she put another question—"Eh! What?" he said.

"Do I believe in ghosts? I will believe you if you will tell me you have seen one."

"You know, Doctor," she went on, "I was always afraid of ghosts—of spirits—things unseen. I couldn't ever read about them. I could not bear the idea of some one in the room with me that I could not see. There was a text that always frightened me that hung up in my room: 'Thou, God, seest me!' It frightened me when I was a child, whether I had been doing wrong or not. But now," shuddering, "I think there are worse things than ghosts."

"Well, now, what sort of things?" he asked good-humouredly. "Astral bodies—?"

She leaned forward and laid her hot hand on his.

"Oh, Doctor, tell me, if a spirit—without the body we know it by—is terrible, what of a body"—her voice sank to a whisper, "a body—senseless—lonely—stranded on this earth—without a spirit?"

She was watching his face anxiously. He was divided between a morbid inclination to laugh and the feeling of intense discomfort provoked by this wretched scene. He longed to give the conversation a more cheerful turn, yet did not wish to offend her by changing it too abruptly.

"I have heard of people not being able to keep body and soul together," he replied at last, "but I am not aware that practically such a division of forces has ever been achieved. And if we could only accept the theory of the de-spiritualised body, what a number of antipathetic people now wandering about in the world it would account for!"

The piteous gaze of her eyes seemed to seek to ward off the blow of his misplaced jocularity.

He left his seat and sat down on the couch beside her.

"Poor child! poor girl! you are ill, you are over-excited. What is it? Tell me," he asked her as tenderly as the father she had lost in early life might have done. Her head sank on his shoulder.

"Are you unhappy?" he asked her gently.

"Yes!"

"You are too much alone. Get your mother or your sister to come and stay with you."

"They won't come," she wailed. "They say the house is like a grave. Edward has made himself a study in the basement. It's an impossible room—but he has moved all his things in, and I can't—I won't go to him there. . . ."

"You're wrong. For it's only a fad," said Graham, "he'll tire of it. And you must see more people somehow. It's a pity my daughter is away. Had you any visitors today?"

"Not a soul has crossed the threshold for eighteen days."

"We must change all that," said the doctor vaguely. "Meantime you must cheer up. Why, you have no need to think of ghosts and graves— no need to be melancholy—you have your husband and your child—"

"I have my child—yes."

The doctor took hold of Mrs. Arne by the shoulder and held her a little away from him. He thought he had found the cause of her trouble—a more commonplace one than he had supposed.

"I have known you, Alice, since you were a child," he said gravely. "Answer me! You love your husband, don't you?"

"Yes." It was as if she were answering futile prefatory questions in the witness-box. Yet he saw by the intense excitement in her eyes that he had come to the point she feared, and yet desired to bring forward.

"And he loves you?"

She was silent.

"Well, then, if you love each other, what more can you want? Why do you say you have only your child in that absurd way?"

She was still silent, and he gave her a little shake.

"Tell me, have you and he had any difference lately? Is there any—coldness—any—temporary estrangement between you?"

He was hardly prepared for the burst of foolish laughter that proceeded from the demure Mrs. Arne as she rose and confronted him, all the blood in her body seeming for the moment to rush to her usually pale cheeks.

"Coldness! Temporary estrangement! If that were all! Oh, is every one blind but me? There is all the world between us!—all the difference between this world and the next!"

She sat down again beside the doctor and whispered in his ear, and her words were like a breath of hot wind from some Gehenna of the soul.

"Oh, Doctor, I have borne it for six years, and I must speak. No other woman could bear what I have borne, and yet be alive! And I loved him so; you don't know how I loved him! That was it—that was my crime—"

"Crime?" repeated the doctor.

"Yes, crime! It was impious, don't you see? But I have been punished. Oh, Doctor, you don't know what my life is! Listen! Listen! I must tell you. To live with a—At first before I guessed when I used to put my arms round him, and he merely submitted—and then it dawned on me what I was kissing! It is enough to turn a living woman into stone—for I am living, though sometimes I forget it. Yes, I am a live woman, though I live in a grave. Think what it is!—to wonder every night if you will be alive in the morning, to lie down every night in an open grave—to smell death in every corner—every room—to breathe death—to touch it. . . ."

The portière in front of the door shook, a hoopstick parted it, a round white clad bundle supported on a pair of mottled red legs peeped in, pushing a hoop in front of her. The child made no noise. Mrs. Arne seemed to have heard her, however. She slewed round violently as she sat on the sofa beside Dr. Graham, leaving her hot hands clasped in his.

"You ask Dolly," she exclaimed. "She knows it, too—she feels it."

"No, no, Alice, this won't do!" the doctor adjured her very low. Then he raised his voice and ordered the child from the room. He had managed to lift Mrs. Arne's feet and laid her full length on the sofa by the time the maid reappeared. She had fainted.

He pulled down her eyelids and satisfied himself as to certain facts he had up till now dimly apprehended. When Mrs. Arne's maid returned, he gave her mistress over to her care and proceeded to Edward Arne's new study in the basement.

"Morphia!" he muttered to himself, as he stumbled and faltered through gaslit passages, where furtive servants eyed him and scuttled to their burrows.

"What is he burying himself down here for?" he thought. "Is it to get out of her way? They are a nervous pair of them!"

***

Arne was sunk in a large arm-chair drawn up before the fire. There was no other light, except a faint reflection from the gas-lamp in the road, striking down past the iron bars of the window that was sunk below the level of the street. The room was comfortless and empty, there was little furniture in it except a large bookcase at Arne's right hand and a table with a Tantalus on it standing some way off. There was a faded portrait in pastel of Alice Arne over the mantelpiece, and beside it, a poor pendant, a pen and ink sketch of the master of the house. They were quite discrepant, in size and medium, but they appeared to look at each other with the stolid attentiveness of newly married people.

"Seedy, Arne?" Graham said.

"Rather, today. Poke the fire for me, will you?"

"I've known you quite seven years," said the doctor cheerfully, "so I presume I can do that . . . There, now! . . . And I'll presume further— What have we got here?"

He took a small bottle smartly out of Edward Arne's fingers and raised his eyebrows. Edward Arne had rendered it up agreeably; he did not seem upset or annoyed.

"Morphia. It isn't a habit. I only got hold of the stuff yesterday—found it about the house. Alice was very jumpy all day, and communicated her nerves to me, I suppose. I've none as a rule, but do you know, Graham, I seem to be getting them—feel things a good deal more than I did, and want to talk about them."

"What, are you growing a soul?" said the doctor carelessly, lighting a cigarette.

"Heaven forbid!" Arne answered equably. "I've done very well without it all these years. But I'm fond of old Alice, you know, in my own way. When I was a young man, I was quite different. I took things hardly and got excited about them. Yes, excited. I was wild about Alice, wild! Yes, by Jove! though she has forgotten all about it."

"Not that, but still it's natural she should long for some little demonstration of affection now and then . . . and she'd be awfully distressed if she saw you fooling with a bottle of morphia! You know, Arne, after that narrow squeak you had of it six years ago, Alice and I have a good right to consider that your life belongs to us!"

Edward Arne settled in his chair and replied, rather fretfully—

"All very well, but you didn't manage to do the job thoroughly. You didn't turn me out lively enough to please Alice. She's annoyed because when I take her in my arms, I don't hold her tight enough. I'm too quiet, too languid! . . . Hang it all, Graham, I believe she'd like me to stand for Parliament! . . . Why can't she let me just go along my own way? Surely a man who's come through an illness like mine can be let off parlour tricks? All this worry—it culminated the other day when I said I wanted to colonise a room down here, and did, with a spurt that took it out of me horribly,—all this worry, I say, seeing her upset and so on, keeps me low, and so I feel as if I wanted to take drugs to soothe me."

"Soothe!" said Graham. "This stuff is more than soothing if you take enough of it. I'll send you something more like what you want, and I'll take this away, by your leave."

"I really can't argue!" replied Arne. "If you see Alice, tell her you find me fairly comfortable and don't put her off this room. I really like it best. She can come and see me here, I keep a good fire, tell her. . . . I feel as if I wanted to sleep. . . ." he added brusquely.

"You have been indulging already," said Graham softly. Arne had begun to doze off. His cushion had sagged down, the doctor stooped to rearrange it, carelessly laying the little phial for the moment in a crease of the rug covering the man's knees.

***

Mrs. Arne in her mourning dress was crossing the hall as he came to the top of the basement steps and pushed open the swing door. She was giving some orders to Foster, the butler, who disappeared as the doctor advanced.

"You're about again," he said, "good girl!"

"Too silly of me," she said, "to be hysterical! After all these years! One should be able to keep one's own counsel. But it is over now, I promise I will never speak of it again."

"We frightened poor Dolly dreadfully. I had to order her out like a regiment of soldiers."

"Yes, I know. I'm going to her now."

On his suggestion that she should look in on her husband first she looked askance.

"Down there!"

"Yes, that's his fancy. Let him be. He is a good deal depressed about himself and you. He notices a great deal more than you think.

He isn't quite as apathetic as you describe him to be. . . . Come here!" He led her into the unlit dining-room a little way. "You expect too much, my dear. You do really! You make too many demands on the vitality you saved."

"What did one save him for?" she asked fiercely. She continued more quietly, "I know. I am going to be different."

"Not you," said Graham fondly. He was very partial to Alice Arne in spite of her silliness. "You'll worry about Edward till the end of the chapter. I know you. And"—he turned her round by the shoulder so that she fronted the light in the hall—"you elusive thing, let me have a good look at you. . . . Hum! Your eyes, they're a bit starey. . . ."

He let her go again with a sigh of impotence. Something must be done . . . soon . . . he must think. . . . He got hold of his coat and began to get into it. . . .

Mrs. Arne smiled, buttoned a button for him and then opened the front door, like a good hostess, a very little way. With a quick flirt of his hat he was gone, and she heard the clap of his brougham door and the order "Home."

***

"Been saying good-bye to that thief Graham?" said her husband gently, when she entered his room, her pale eyes staring a little, her thin hand busy at the front of her dress.

"Thief? Why? One moment! Where's your switch?"

She found it and turned on a blaze of light from which her husband seemed to shrink.

"Well, he carried off my drops. Afraid of my poisoning myself, I suppose?"

"Or acquiring the morphia habit," said his wife in a dull level voice, "as I have."

She paused. He made no comment. Then, picking up the little phial Dr. Graham had left in the crease of the rug, she spoke—

"You are the thief, Edward, as it happens, this is mine."

"Is it? I found it knocking about; I didn't know it was yours. Well, will you give me some?"

"I will, if you like."

"Well, dear, decide. You know I am in your hands and Graham's. He was rubbing that into me today."

"Poor lamb!" she said derisively; "I'd not allow my doctor, or my wife either, to dictate to me whether I should put an end to myself, or not."

"Ah, but you've got a spirit, you see!" Arne yawned. "However, let me have a go at the stuff and then you put it on top of the wardrobe or a shelf, where I shall know it is, but never reach out to get it, I promise you."

"No, you wouldn't reach out a hand to keep yourself alive, let alone kill yourself," said she. "That is you all over, Edward."

"And don't you see that is why I did die," he said, with earnestness unexpected by her. "And then, unfortunately, you and Graham bustled up and wouldn't let Nature take its course. . . . I rather wish you hadn't been so officious."

"And let you stay dead," said she carelessly. "But at the time I cared for you so much that I should have had to kill myself, or commit suttee like a Bengali widow. Ah, well!"

She reached out for a glass half-full of water that stood on the low ledge of a bookcase close by the arm of his chair. . . . "Will this glass do? What's in it? Only water? How much morphia shall I give you? An overdose?"

"I don't care if you do, and that's a fact."

"It was a joke, Edward," she said piteously.

"No joke to me. This fag end of life I've clawed hold of, doesn't interest me. And I'm bound to be interested in what I'm doing or I'm no good. I'm no earthly good now. I don't enjoy life, I've nothing to enjoy it with—in here—" he struck his breast. "It's like a dull party one goes to by accident. All I want to do is to get into a cab and go home."

His wife stood over him with the half-full glass in one hand and the little bottle in the other.

Her eyes dilated . . . her chest heaved.

"Edward!" she breathed. "Was it all so useless?"

"Was what useless? Yes, as I was telling you, I go as one in a dream—a bad, bad dream, like the dreams I used to have when I overworked at college. I was brilliant, Alice, brilliant, do you hear? At some cost, I expect! Now I hate people—my fellow creatures. I've left them. They come and go, jostling me, and pushing me, on the pavements as I go along, avoiding them. Do you know where they should be, really, in relation to me?"

He rose a little in his seat—she stepped nervously aside, made as if to put down the bottle and the glass she was holding, then thought better of it and continued to extend them mechanically.

"They should be over my head. I've already left them and their petty nonsense of living. They mean nothing to me, no more than if they were ghosts walking. Or perhaps, it's I who am a ghost to them? . . . You don't understand it. It's because I suppose you have no imagination. You just know what you want and do your best to get it. You blurt out your blessed petition to your Deity and the idea that you're irrelevant never enters your head, soft, persistent, High Church thing that you are! . . ."

Alice Arne smiled, and balanced the objects she was holding. He motioned her to pour out the liquid from one to the other, but she took no heed; she was listening with all her ears. It was the nearest approach to the language of compliment, to anything in the way of loverlike personalities that she had heard fall from his lips since his illness. He went on, becoming as it were lukewarm to his subject—

"But the worst of it is that once break the cord that links you to humanity—it can't be mended. Man doesn't live by bread alone . . . or lives to disappoint you. What am I to you, without my own poor personality? . . . Don't stare so, Alice! I haven't talked so much or so intimately for ages, have I? Let me try and have it out. . . . Are you in any sort of hurry?"

"No, Edward."

"Pour that stuff out and have done. . . . Well, Alice, it's a queer feeling, I tell you. One goes about with one's looks on the ground, like a man who eyes the bed he is going to lie down in, and longs for. Alice, the crust of the earth seems a barrier between me and my own place. I want to scratch the boardings with my nails and shriek something like this: 'Let me get down to you all, there where I belong!' It's a horrible sensation, like a vampire reversed! . . ."

"Is that why you insisted on having this room in the basement?" she asked breathlessly.

"Yes, I can't bear being upstairs, somehow. Here, with these barred windows and stone-cold floors . . . I can see the people's feet walking above there in the street . . . one has some sort of illusion . . ."

"Oh!" She shivered and her eyes travelled like those of a caged creature round the bare room and fluttered when they rested on the sombre windows imperiously barred. She dropped her gaze to the stone flags that showed beyond the oasis of Turkey carpet on which Arne's chair stood. . . .

Then to the door, the door that she had closed on entering. It had heavy bolts, but they were not drawn against her, though by the look of her eyes it seemed she half imagined they were. . . .

She made a step forward and moved her hands slightly. She looked down on them and what they held . . . then changed the relative positions of the two objects and held the bottle over the glass. . . .

"Yes, come along!" her husband said. "Are you going to be all day giving it me?"

With a jerk, she poured the liquid out into a glass and handed it to him. She looked away—towards the door. . . .

"Ah, your way of escape!" said he, following her eyes. Then he drank, painstakingly.

The empty bottle fell out of her hands. She wrung them, murmuring—

"Oh, if I had only known!"

"Known what? That I should go near to cursing you for bringing me back?"

He fixed his cold eyes on her, as the liquid passed slowly over his tongue.

"—Or that you would end by taking back the gift you gave?"

THE WELL
W. W. JACOBS

I

Two men stood in the billiard-room of an old country house, talking. Play, which had been of a half-hearted nature, was over, and they sat at the open window, looking out over the park stretching away beneath them, conversing idly.

"Your time's nearly up, Jem," said one at length, "this time six weeks you'll be yawning out the honeymoon and cursing the man—woman I mean—who invented them."

Jem Benson stretched his long limbs in the chair and grunted in dissent.

"I've never understood it," continued Wilfred Carr, yawning. "It's not in my line at all; I never had enough money for my own wants, let alone for two. Perhaps if I were as rich as you or Croesus I might regard it differently."

There was just sufficient meaning in the latter part of the remark for his cousin to forbear to reply to it. He continued to gaze out of the window and to smoke slowly.

"Not being as rich as Croesus—or you," resumed Carr, regarding him from beneath lowered lids, "I paddle my own canoe down the stream of Time, and, tying it to my friends' door-posts, go in to eat their dinners."

"Quite Venetian," said Jem Benson, still looking out of the window. "It's not a bad thing for you, Wilfred, that you have the doorposts and dinners—and friends."

Mr. Carr grunted in his turn. "Seriously though, Jem," he said, slowly, "you're a lucky fellow, a very lucky fellow. If there is a better girl above ground than Olive, I should like to see her."

"Yes," said the other, quietly.

"She's such an exceptional girl," continued Carr, staring out of the window. "She's so good and gentle. She thinks you are a bundle of all the virtues."

He laughed frankly and joyously, but the other man did not join him.

"Strong sense—of right and wrong, though," continued Carr, musingly. "Do you know, I believe that if she found out that you were not—"

"Not what?" demanded Benson, turning upon him fiercely. "Not what?"

"Everything that you are," returned his cousin, with a grin that belied his words. "I believe she'd drop you."

"Talk about something else," said Benson, slowly; "your pleasantries are not always in the best taste."

Wilfred Carr rose and taking a cue from the rack, bent over the board and practiced one or two favourite shots. "The only other

subject I can talk about just at present is my own financial affairs,"
he said slowly, as he walked round the table.

"Talk about something else," said Benson again, bluntly.

"And the two things are connected," said Carr, and dropping his
cue he half sat on the table and eyed his cousin.

There was a long silence. Benson pitched the end of his cigar out
of the window, and leaning back closed his eyes.

"Do you follow me?" inquired Carr at length.

Benson opened his eyes and nodded at the window.

"Do you want to follow my cigar?" he demanded.

"I should prefer to depart by the usual way for your sake," returned
the other, unabashed. "If I left by the window all sorts of questions
would be asked, and you know what a talkative chap I am."

"So long as you don't talk about my affairs," returned the other,
restraining himself by an obvious effort, "you can talk yourself hoarse."

"I'm in a mess," said Carr, slowly, "a devil of a mess. If I don't raise
fifteen hundred by this day fortnight, I may be getting my board and
lodging free."

"Would that be any change?" questioned Benson.

"The quality would," retorted the other. "The address also would
not be good. Seriously, Jem, will you let me have the fifteen hundred?"

"No," said the other, simply.

Carr went white. "It's to save me from ruin," he said, thickly.

"I've helped you till I'm tired," said Benson, turning and regarding
him, "and it is all to no good. If you've got into a mess, get out of it.
You should not be so fond of giving autographs away."

"It's foolish, I admit," said Carr, deliberately. "I won't do so any
more. By the way, I've got some to sell. You needn't sneer. They're not
my own."

"Whose are they?" inquired the other.

"Yours."

Benson got up from his chair and crossed over to him. "What is this?" he asked, quietly. "Blackmail?"

"Call it what you like," said Carr. "I've got some letters for sale, price fifteen hundred. And I know a man who would buy them at that price for the mere chance of getting Olive from you. I'll give you first offer."

"If you have got any letters bearing my signature, you will be good enough to give them to me," said Benson, very slowly.

"They're mine," said Carr, lightly; "given to me by the lady you wrote them to. I must say that they are not all in the best possible taste."

His cousin reached forward suddenly, and catching him by the collar of his coat pinned him down on the table.

"Give me those letters," he breathed, sticking his face close to Carr's.

"They're not here," said Carr, struggling. "I'm not a fool. Let me go, or I'll raise the price."

The other man raised him from the table in his powerful hands, apparently with the intention of dashing his head against it. Then suddenly his hold relaxed as an astonished-looking maid-servant entered the room with letters. Carr sat up hastily.

"That's how it was done," said Benson, for the girl's benefit as he took the letters.

"I don't wonder at the other man making him pay for it, then," said Carr, blandly.

"You will give me those letters?" said Benson, suggestively, as the girl left the room.

"At the price I mentioned, yes," said Carr; "but so sure as I am a living man, if you lay your clumsy hands on me again, I'll double it. Now, I'll leave you for a time while you think it over."

He took a cigar from the box and lighting it carefully quitted the room. His cousin waited until the door had closed behind him, and then turning to the window sat there in a fit of fury as silent as it was terrible.

The air was fresh and sweet from the park, heavy with the scent of new-mown grass. The fragrance of a cigar was now added to it, and glancing out he saw his cousin pacing slowly by. He rose and went to the door, and then, apparently altering his mind, he returned to the window and watched the figure of his cousin as it moved slowly away into the moonlight. Then he rose again, and, for a long time, the room was empty.

***

It was empty when Mrs. Benson came in some time later to say good-night to her son on her way to bed. She walked slowly round the table, and pausing at the window gazed from it in idle thought, until she saw the figure of her son advancing with rapid strides toward the house. He looked up at the window.

"Good-night," said she.

"Good-night," said Benson, in a deep voice.

"Where is Wilfred?"

"Oh, he has gone," said Benson.

"Gone?"

"We had a few words; he was wanting money again, and I gave him a piece of my mind. I don't think we shall see him again."

"Poor Wilfred!" sighed Mrs. Benson. "He is always in trouble of some sort. I hope that you were not too hard upon him."

"No more than he deserved," said her son, sternly. "Good night."

II

The well, which had long ago fallen into disuse, was almost hidden by the thick tangle of undergrowth which ran riot at that corner of the old park. It was partly covered by the shrunken half of a lid, above which a rusty windlass creaked in company with the music of the pines when the wind blew strongly. The full light of the sun never reached it, and the ground surrounding it was moist and green when other parts of the park were gaping with the heat.

Two people walking slowly round the park in the fragrant stillness of a summer evening strayed in the direction of the well.

"No use going through this wilderness, Olive," said Benson, pausing on the outskirts of the pines and eyeing with some disfavour the gloom beyond.

"Best part of the park," said the girl briskly; "you know it's my favourite spot."

"I know you're very fond of sitting on the coping," said the man slowly, "and I wish you wouldn't. One day you will lean back too far and fall in."

"And make the acquaintance of Truth," said Olive lightly. "Come along."

She ran from him and was lost in the shadow of the pines, the bracken crackling beneath her feet as she ran. Her companion followed slowly, and emerging from the gloom saw her poised daintily on the edge of the well with her feet hidden in the rank grass and nettles which surrounded it. She motioned her companion to take a seat by her side, and smiled softly as she felt a strong arm passed about her waist.

"I like this place," said she, breaking a long silence, "it is so dismal —so uncanny. Do you know I wouldn't dare to sit here alone, Jem. I should imagine that all sorts of dreadful things were hidden behind the bushes and trees, waiting to spring out on me. Ugh!"

"You'd better let me take you in," said her companion tenderly; "the well isn't always wholesome, especially in the hot weather.

"Let's make a move."

The girl gave an obstinate little shake, and settled herself more securely on her seat.

"Smoke your cigar in peace," she said quietly. "I am settled here for a quiet talk. Has anything been heard of Wilfred yet?"

"Nothing."

"Quite a dramatic disappearance, isn't it?" she continued. "Another scrape, I suppose, and another letter for you in the same old strain: 'Dear Jem, help me out.'"

Jem Benson blew a cloud of fragrant smoke into the air, and holding his cigar between his teeth brushed away the ash from his coat sleeves.

"I wonder what he would have done without you," said the girl, pressing his arm affectionately. "Gone under long ago, I suppose. When we are married, Jem, I shall presume upon the relationship to lecture him. He is very wild, but he has his good points, poor fellow."

"I never saw them," said Benson, with startling bitterness. "God knows I never saw them."

"He is nobody's enemy but his own," said the girl, startled by this outburst.

"You don't know much about him," said the other, sharply. "He was not above blackmail; not above ruining the life of a friend to do himself a benefit. A loafer, a cur, and a liar!"

The girl looked up at him soberly but timidly and took his arm without a word, and they both sat silent while evening deepened into night and the beams of the moon, filtering through the branches, surrounded them with a silver network. Her head sank upon his shoulder, till suddenly with a sharp cry she sprang to her feet.

"What was that?" she cried breathlessly.

"What was what?" demanded Benson, springing up and clutching her fast by the arm.

She caught her breath and tried to laugh.

"You're hurting me, Jem."

His hold relaxed.

"What is the matter?" he asked gently.

"What was it startled you?"

"I was startled," she said, slowly, putting her hands on his shoulder. "I suppose the words I used just now are ringing in my ears, but I fancied that somebody behind us whispered 'Jem, help me out.'"

"Fancy," repeated Benson, and his voice shook; "but these fancies are not good for you. You—are frightened—at the dark and the gloom of these trees. Let me take you back to the house."

"No, I'm not frightened," said the girl, reseating herself. "I should never be really frightened of anything when you were with me, Jem. I'm surprised at myself for being so silly."

The man made no reply but stood, a strong, dark figure, a yard or two from the well, as though waiting for her to join him.

"Come and sit down, sir," cried Olive, patting the brickwork with her small, white hand, "one would think that you did not like your company."

He obeyed slowly and took a seat by her side, drawing so hard at his cigar that the light of it shone upon his fare at every breath. He passed his arm, firm and rigid as steel, behind her, with his hand resting on the brickwork beyond.

"Are you warm enough?" he asked tenderly, as she made a little movement.

"Pretty fair," she shivered; "one oughtn't to be cold at this time of the year, but there's a cold, damp air comes up from the well."

As she spoke a faint splash sounded from the depths below, and for the second time that evening, she sprang from the well with a little cry of dismay.

"What is it now?" he asked in a fearful voice. He stood by her side and gazed at the well, as though half expecting to see the cause of her alarm emerge from it.

"Oh, my bracelet," she cried in distress, "my poor mother's bracelet. I've dropped it down the well."

"Your bracelet!" repeated Benson, dully. "Your bracelet? The diamond one?"

"The one that was my mother's," said Olive. "Oh, we can get it back surely. We must have the water drained off."

"Your bracelet!" repeated Benson, stupidly.

"Jem," said the girl in terrified tones, "dear Jem, what is the matter?"

For the man she loved was standing regarding her with horror. The moon which touched it was not responsible for all the whiteness of the distorted face, and she shrank back in fear to the edge of the well. He saw her fear and by a mighty effort regained his composure and took her hand.

"Poor little girl," he murmured, "you frightened me. I was not looking when you cried, and I thought that you were slipping from my arms, down—down—"

His voice broke, and the girl throwing herself into his arms clung to him convulsively.

"There, there," said Benson, fondly, "don't cry, don't cry."

"To-morrow," said Olive, half-laughing, half-crying, "we will all come round the well with hook and line and fish for it. It will be quite a new sport."

"No, we must try some other way," said Benson. "You shall have it back."

"How?" asked the girl.

"You shall see," said Benson. "To-morrow morning at latest you shall have it back. Till then promise me that you will not mention your loss to anyone. Promise."

"I promise," said Olive, wonderingly. "But why not?"

"It is of great value, for one thing, and—but there—there are many reasons. For one thing it is my duty to get it for you."

"Wouldn't you like to jump down for it?" she asked mischievously. "Listen."

She stooped for a stone and dropped it down.

"Fancy being where that is now," she said, peering into the blackness; "fancy going round and round like a mouse in a pail, clutching at the slimy sides, with the water filling your mouth, and looking up to the little patch of sky above."

"You had better come in," said Benson, very quietly. "You are developing a taste for the morbid and horrible."

The girl turned, and taking his arm walked slowly in the direction of the house; Mrs. Benson, who was sitting in the porch, rose to receive them.

"You shouldn't have kept her out so long," she said chidingly. "Where have you been?"

"Sitting on the well," said Olive, smiling, "discussing our future."

"I don't believe that place is healthy," said Mrs. Benson, emphatically. "I really think it might be filled in, Jem."

"All right," said her son, slowly. "Pity it wasn't filled in long ago."

He took the chair vacated by his mother as she entered the house with Olive, and with his hands hanging limply over the sides sat in deep thought. After a time he rose, and going upstairs to a room which was set apart for sporting requisites selected a sea fishing line and some hooks and stole softly downstairs again. He walked swiftly across the park in the direction of the well, turning before he entered the shadow of the trees to look back at the lighted windows of the house. Then having arranged his line he sat on the edge of the well and cautiously lowered it.

He sat with his lips compressed, occasionally looking about him in a startled fashion, as though he half expected to see something peering at him from the belt of trees. Time after time he lowered his line until at length in pulling it up he heard a little metallic tinkle against the side of the well.

He held his breath then, and forgetting his fears drew the line in inch by inch, so as not to lose its precious burden. His pulse beat rapidly, and his eyes were bright. As the line came slowly in he saw the catch hanging to the hook, and with a steady hand drew the last few feet in. Then he saw that instead of the bracelet he had hooked a bunch of keys.

With a faint cry he shook them from the hook into the water below, and stood breathing heavily. Not a sound broke the stillness of the night. He walked up and down a bit and stretched his great muscles; then he came back to the well and resumed his task.

For an hour or more the line was lowered without result. In his eagerness he forgot his fears, and with eyes bent down the well fished slowly and carefully. Twice the hook became entangled in something, and was with difficulty released. It caught a third time, and all his efforts failed' to free it. Then he dropped the line down the well, and with head bent walked toward the house.

He went first to the stables at the rear, and then retiring to his room for some time paced restlessly up and down. Then without removing his clothes he flung himself upon the bed and fell into a troubled sleep.

III

Long before anybody else was astir he arose and stole softly downstairs. The sunlight was stealing in at every crevice, and flashing in long streaks across the darkened rooms. The dining-room into which he looked struck chill and cheerless in the dark yellow light which came through the lowered blinds. He remembered that it had the same appearance when his father lay dead in the house; now, as then, everything seemed ghastly and unreal; the very chairs standing as their occupants had left them the night before seemed to be indulging in some dark communication of ideas.

Slowly and noiselessly he opened the hall door and passed into the fragrant air beyond. The sun was shining on the drenched grass and trees, and a slowly vanishing white mist rolled like smoke about the grounds. For a moment he stood, breathing deeply the sweet air of the morning, and then walked slowly in the direction of the stables.

The rusty creaking of a pump-handle and a spatter of water upon the red-tiled courtyard showed that somebody else was astir, and a few steps farther he beheld a brawny, sandy-haired man gasping wildly under severe self-infliction at the pump.

"Everything ready, George?" he asked quietly.

"Yes, sir," said the man, straightening up suddenly and touching his forehead. "Bob's just finishing the arrangements inside. It's a lovely morning for a dip. The water in that well must be just icy."

"Be as quick as you can," said Benson, impatiently.

"Very good, sir," said George, burnishing his face harshly with a very small towel which had been hanging over the top of the pump. "Hurry up, Bob."

In answer to his summons a man appeared at the door of the stable with a coil of stout rope over his arm and a large metal candlestick in his hand.

"Just to try the air, sir," said George, following his master's glance, "a well gets rather foul sometimes, but if a candle can live down it, a man can."

His master nodded, and the man, hastily pulling up the neck of his shirt and thrusting his arms into his coat, followed him as he led the way slowly to the well.

"Beg pardon, sir," said George, drawing up to his side, "but you are not looking over and above well this morning. If you'll let me go down I'd enjoy the bath."

"No, no," said Benson, peremptorily.

"You ain't fit to go down, sir," persisted his follower. "I've never seen you look so before. Now if—"

"Mind your business," said his master curtly.

George became silent and the three walked with swinging strides through the long wet grass to the well. Bob flung the rope on the ground and at a sign from his master handed him the candlestick.

"Here's the line for it, sir," said Bob, fumbling in his pockets.

Benson took it from him and slowly tied it to the candlestick. Then he placed it on the edge of the well, and striking a match, lit the candle and began slowly to lower it.

"Hold hard, sir," said George, quickly, laying his hand on his arm, "you must tilt it or the string'll burn through."

Even as he spoke the string parted and the candlestick fell into the water below.

Benson swore quietly.

"I'll soon get another," said George, starting up.

"Never mind, the well's all right," said Benson.

"It won't take a moment, sir," said the other over his shoulder.

"Are you master here, or am I?" said Benson hoarsely.

George came back slowly, a glance at his master's face stopping the protest upon his tongue, and he stood by watching him sulkily as he sat on the well and removed his outer garments. Both men watched him curiously, as having completed his preparations he stood grim and silent with his hands by his sides.

"I wish you'd let me go, sir," said George, plucking up courage to address him. "You ain't fit to go, you've got a chill or something. I shouldn't wonder it's the typhoid. They've got it in the village bad."

For a moment Benson looked at him angrily, then his gaze softened. "Not this time, George," he said, quietly. He took the looped end of the rope and placed it under his arms, and sitting down threw one leg over the side of the well.

"How are you going about it, sir?" queried George, laying hold of the rope and signing to Bob to do the same.

"I'll call out when I reach the water," said Benson; "then pay out three yards more quickly so that I can get to the bottom."

"Very good, sir," answered both.

Their master threw the other leg over the coping and sat motionless. His back was turned toward the men as he sat with head bent, looking down the shaft. He sat for so long that George became uneasy.

"All right, sir?" he inquired.

"Yes," said Benson, slowly. "If I tug at the rope, George, pull up at once. Lower away."

The rope passed steadily through their hands until a hollow cry from the darkness below and a faint splashing warned them that he had reached the water. They gave him three yards more and stood with relaxed grasp and strained ears, waiting.

"He's gone under," said Bob in a low voice.

The other nodded, and moistening his huge palms took a firmer grip of the rope.

Fully a minute passed, and the men began to exchange uneasy glances. Then a sudden tremendous jerk followed by a series of feebler ones nearly tore the rope from their grasp.

"Pull!" shouted George, placing one foot on the side and hauling desperately. "Pull! pull! He's stuck fast; he's not coming; P—U—LL!"

In response to their terrific exertions the rope came slowly in, inch by inch, until at length a violent splashing was heard, and at the same moment a scream of unutterable horror came echoing up the shaft.

"What a weight he is!" panted Bob. "He's stuck fast or something. Keep still, sir; for heaven's sake, keep still."

For the taut rope was being jerked violently by the struggles of the weight at the end of it. Both men with grunts and sighs hauled it in foot by foot.

"All right, sir," cried George, cheerfully.

He had one foot against the well, and was pulling manfully; the burden was nearing the top. A long pull and a strong pull, and the face of a dead man with mud in the eyes and nostrils came peering over the edge. Behind it was the ghastly face of his master; but this he saw too late, for with a great cry he let go his hold of the rope and stepped back. The suddenness overthrew his assistant, and the rope tore through his hands. There was a frightful splash.

"You fool!" stammered Bob, and ran to the well helplessly.

"Run!" cried George. "Run for another line."

He bent over the coping and called eagerly down as his assistant sped back to the stables shouting wildly. His voice re-echoed down the shaft, but all else was silence.

MR. JUSTICE HARBOTTLE

J. S. LE FANU

Prologue

On this case Doctor Hesselius has inscribed nothing more than the words, "Harman's Report," and a simple reference to his own extraordinary Essay on "The Interior Sense, and the Conditions of the Opening thereof."

The reference is to Vol. I, Section 317, Note Z^a. The note to which reference is thus made, simply says: "There are two accounts of the remarkable case of the Honourable Mr. Justice Harbottle, one furnished to me by Mrs. Trimmer, of Tunbridge Wells (June, 1805); the other at a much later date, by Anthony Harman, Esq. I much prefer the former; in the first place, because it is minute and detailed, and written, it seems to me, with more caution and knowledge; and in the next, because the letters from Dr. Hedstone, which are embodied in it, furnish matter of the highest value to a right apprehension of the nature of the case. It was one of the best declared cases of an opening of the interior sense which I have met with. It was affected too by the phenomenon which occurs so frequently as to indicate a law of these eccentric conditions; that is to say, it exhibited what I may term the contagious character of this sort of intrusion of the spirit-world upon the proper domain of matter. So soon as the spirit-action has established itself in the case of one patient, its developed energy begins to radiate, more or less effectually, upon others. The interior vision of the child was opened; as was, also, that of its mother, Mrs. Pyneweck; and both the interior vision and hearing of the scullery-maid were opened on the same occasion. After-appearances are the result of the law explained in Vol. II, Sections 17 to 49. The common centre of association, simultaneously recalled, unites, or reunites, as the case may be, for a period measured, as we see, in Section 37. The *maximum* will extend to days, the *minimum* is little more than a second. We see the operation of this principle perfectly displayed, in certain cases of lunacy, of epilepsy, of catalepsy, and of mania, of a peculiar and painful character, though unattended by incapacity of business."

The memorandum of the case of Judge Harbottle, which was written by Mrs. Trimmer, of Tunbridge Wells, which Doctor Hesselius thought the better of the two, I have been unable to discover among his papers. I found in his escritoire a note to the effect that he had lent the Report of Judge Harbottle's case, written by Mrs. Trimmer, to Dr. F. Heyne. To that learned and able gentleman accordingly I wrote, and received from him, in his reply, which was full of alarms and regrets, on account of the uncertain safety of that "valuable MS.," a line written long since by Dr. Hesselius, which completely exonerated him, inasmuch as it acknowledged the safe return of the papers. The narrative of Mr. Harman is, therefore, the only one available for this collection. The late Dr. Hesselius, in another passage of the note that I have cited, says, "As to the facts (non-medical) of the case, the narrative of Mr. Harman exactly tallies with that furnished by Mrs. Trimmer." The strictly scientific view of the case would scarcely interest the popular reader; and, possibly, for the purposes of this selection, I should, even had I both papers to choose between, have referred that of Mr. Harman, which is given in full in the following pages.

Chapter I

The Judge's House

Thirty years ago an elderly man, to whom I paid quarterly a small annuity charged on some property of mine, came on the quarter-day to receive it. He was a dry, sad, quiet man, who had known better days, and had always maintained an unexceptionable character. No better authority could be imagined for a ghost story.

He told me one, though with a manifest reluctance; he was drawn into the narration by his choosing to explain what I should not have remarked, that he had called two days earlier than that week after the strict day of payment, which he had usually allowed to elapse. His reason was a sudden determination to change his lodgings, and the consequent necessity of paying his rent a little before it was due.

He lodged in a dark street in Westminster, in a spacious old house, very warm, being wainscoted from top to bottom, and furnished with no undue abundance of windows, and those fitted with thick sashes and small panes.

This house was, as the bills upon the windows testified, offered to be sold or let. But no one seemed to care to look at it.

A thin matron, in rusty black silk, very taciturn, with large, steady, alarmed eyes, that seemed to look in your face, to read what you might have seen in the dark rooms and passages through which you had passed, was in charge of it, with a solitary "maid-of-all-work" under her command. My poor friend had taken lodgings in this house, on account of their extraordinary cheapness. He had occupied them for nearly a year without the slightest disturbance, and was the only tenant, under rent, in the house. He had two rooms; a sitting-room and a bed-room with a closet opening from it, in which he kept his books and papers locked up. He had gone to his bed, having also locked the outer door. Unable to sleep, he had lighted a candle, and after having read for a time, had laid the book beside him. He heard the old clock at the stair-head strike one; and very shortly after, to his alarm, he saw the closet-door, which he thought he had locked, open stealthily, and a slight dark man, particularly sinister, and somewhere about fifty, dressed in mourning of a very antique fashion, such a suit as we see in Hogarth, entered the room on tip-toe. He was followed by an elder man, stout, and blotched with scurvy, and whose features, fixed as a corpse's, were stamped with dreadful force with a character of sensuality and villainy.

This old man wore a flowered silk dressing-gown and ruffles, and he remarked a gold ring on his finger, and on his head a cap of velvet, such as, in the days of perukes, gentlemen wore in undress.

This direful old man carried in his ringed and ruffled hand a coil of rope; and these two figures crossed the floor diagonally, passing the foot of his bed, from the closet door at the farther end of the room, at the left, near the window, to the door opening upon the lobby, close to the bed's head, at his right.

He did not attempt to describe his sensations as these figures passed so near him. He merely said, that so far from sleeping in that room again, no consideration the world could offer would induce him so much as to enter it again alone, even in the daylight. He found both doors, that of the closet and that of the room opening upon the lobby, in the morning fast locked as he had left them before going to bed.

In answer to a question of mine, he said that neither appeared the least conscious of his presence. They did not seem to glide, but walked as living men do, but without any sound, and he felt a vibration on the floor as they crossed it. He so obviously suffered from speaking about the apparitions, that I asked him no more questions.

There were in his description, however, certain coincidences so very singular, as to induce me, by that very post, to write to a friend much my senior, then living in a remote part of England, for the information which I knew he could give me. He had himself more than once pointed out that old house to my attention, and told me, though very briefly, the strange story which I now asked him to give me in greater detail.

His answer satisfied me; and the following pages convey its substance.

Your letter (he wrote) tells me you desire some particulars about the closing years of the life of Mr. Justice Harbottle, one of the judges of the Court of Common Pleas. You refer, of course, to the extraordinary occurrences that made that period of his life long after a theme for "winter tales" and metaphysical speculation. I happen to know perhaps more than any other man living of those mysterious particulars.

The old family mansion, when I revisited London, more than thirty years ago, I examined for the last time. During the years that have passed since then, I hear that improvement, with its preliminary demolitions, has been doing wonders for the quarter of Westminster in which it stood. If I were quite certain that the house had been taken down, I should have no difficulty about naming the street in which it stood. As what I have to tell, however, is not likely to improve its letting value, and as I should not care to get into trouble, I prefer being silent on that particular point.

How old the house was, I can't tell. People said it was built by Roger Harbottle, a Turkey merchant, in the reign of King James I. I am not a good opinion upon such questions; but having been in it, though in its forlorn and deserted state, I can tell you in a general way what it was like. It was built of dark-red brick, and the door and windows were faced with stone that had turned yellow by time. It receded some feet from the line of the other houses in the street, and it had a florid and fanciful rail of iron about the broad steps that invited your ascent to the hall-door, in which were fixed, under a file of lamps among scrolls and twisted leaves, two immense "extinguishers," like the conical caps of fairies, into which, in old times, the footmen used to thrust their flambeaux when their chairs or coaches had set down their great people, in the hall or at the steps, as the case might be. That hall is panelled up to the ceiling, and has a large fireplace. Two or three stately old rooms open from it at each side. The windows of these are tall, with many small panes. Passing through the arch at the back of the hall, you come upon the wide and heavy well-staircase. There is a back staircase also. The mansion is large, and has not as much light, by any means, in proportion to its extent, as modern houses enjoy. When I saw it, it had long been untenanted, and had the gloomy reputation beside of a haunted house. Cobwebs floated from the ceilings or spanned the corners of the cornices, and dust lay thick over everything. The windows were stained with the dust and rain of fifty years, and darkness had thus grown darker.

When I made it my first visit, it was in company with my father, when I was still a boy, in the year 1808. I was about twelve years old, and my imagination impressible, as it always is at that age. I looked about me with great awe. I was here in the very centre and scene of those occurrences which I had heard recounted at the fireside at home, with so delightful a horror.

My father was an old bachelor of nearly sixty when he married. He had, when a child, seen Judge Harbottle on the bench in his robes and wig a dozen times at least before his death, which took place in 1748, and his appearance made a powerful and unpleasant impression, not only on his imagination, but upon his nerves.

The Judge was at that time a man of some sixty-seven years. He had a great mulberry-coloured face, a big, carbuncled nose, fierce eyes, and a grim and brutal mouth. My father, who was young at the time, thought it the most formidable face he had ever seen; for there were evidences of intellectual power in the formation and lines of the forehead. His voice was loud and harsh, and gave effect to the sarcasm which was his habitual weapon on the bench.

This old gentleman had the reputation of being about the wickedest man in England. Even on the bench he now and then showed his scorn of opinion. He had carried cases his own way, it was said, in spite of counsel, authorities, and even of juries, by a sort of cajolery, violence, and bamboozling, that somehow confused and overpowered resistance. He had never actually committed himself; he was too cunning to do that. He had the character of being, however, a dangerous and unscrupulous judge; but his character did not trouble him. The associates he chose for his hours of relaxation cared as little as he did about it.

Chapter II

Mr. Peters

One night during the session of 1746 this old Judge went down in his chair to wait in one of the rooms of the House of Lords for the result of a division in which he and his order were interested.

This over, he was about to return to his house close by, in his chair; but the night had become so soft and fine that he changed his mind, sent it home empty, and with two footmen, each with a flambeau, set out on foot in preference. Gout had made him rather a slow pedestrian. It took him some time to get through the two or three streets he had to pass before reaching his house.

In one of those narrow streets of tall houses, perfectly silent at that hour, he overtook, slowly as he was walking, a very singular-looking old gentleman.

He had a bottle-green coat on, with a cape to it, and large stone buttons, a broad-leafed low-crowned hat, from under which a big powdered wig escaped; he stooped very much, and supported his bending knees with the aid of a crutch-handled cane, and so shuffled and tottered along painfully.

"I ask your pardon, sir," said this old man, in a very quavering voice, as the burly Judge came up with him, and he extended his hand feebly towards his arm.

Mr. Justice Harbottle saw that the man was by no means poorly dressed, and his manner that of a gentleman.

The Judge stopped short, and said, in his harsh peremptory tones, "Well, sir, how can I serve you?"

"Can you direct me to Judge Harbottle's house? I have some intelligence of the very last importance to communicate to him."

"Can you tell it before witnesses?" asked the Judge.

"By no means; it must reach *his* ear only," quavered the old man earnestly.

"If that be so, sir, you have only to accompany me a few steps farther to reach my house, and obtain a private audience; for I am Judge Harbottle."

With this invitation the infirm gentleman in the white wig complied very readily; and in another minute the stranger stood in what was then termed the front parlour of the Judge's house, tête-à-tête with that shrewd and dangerous functionary.

He had to sit down, being very much exhausted, and unable for a little time to speak; and then he had a fit of coughing, and after that a fit of gasping; and thus two or three minutes passed, during which the Judge dropped his roquelaure on an arm-chair, and threw his cocked-hat over that.

The venerable pedestrian in the white wig quickly recovered his voice. With closed doors they remained together for some time.

There were guests waiting in the drawing-rooms, and the sound of men's voices laughing, and then of a female voice singing to a harpsichord, were heard distinctly in the hall over the stairs; for old Judge Harbottle had arranged one of his dubious jollifications, such as might well make the hair of godly men's heads stand upright for that night.

This old gentleman in the powdered white wig, that rested on his stooped shoulders, must have had something to say that interested the Judge very much; for he would not have parted on easy terms with the ten minutes and upwards which that conference filched from the sort of revelry in which he most delighted, and in which he was the roaring king, and in some sort the tyrant also, of his company.

The footman who showed the aged man out observed that the Judge's mulberry-coloured face, pimples and all, were bleached to a dingy yellow, and there was the abstraction of agitated thought in his manner, as he bid the stranger good-night. The servant saw that the conversation had been of serious import, and that the Judge was frightened.

Instead of stumping upstairs forthwith to his scandalous hilarities, his profane company, and his great china bowl of punch—the identical bowl from which a bygone Bishop of London, good easy man, had baptised this Judge's grandfather, now clinking round the rim with silver ladles, and hung with scrolls of lemon-peel—instead, I say, of stumping and clambering up the great staircase to the cavern of his Circean enchantment, he stood with his big nose flattened against the window-pane, watching the progress of the feeble old man, who clung stiffly to the iron rail as he got down, step by step, to the pavement.

The hall-door had hardly closed, when the old Judge was in the hall bawling hasty orders, with such stimulating expletives as old colonels under excitement sometimes indulge in now-a-days, with a stamp or two of his big foot, and a waving of his clenched fist in the air. He commanded the footman to overtake the old gentleman in the white wig, to offer him his protection on his way home, and in no case to show his face again without having ascertained where he lodged, and who he was, and all about him.

"By ——, sirrah! if you fail me in this, you doff my livery to-night!"

Forth bounced the stalwart footman, with his heavy cane under his arm, and skipped down the steps, and looked up and down the street after the singular figure, so easy to recognize.

What were his adventures I shall not tell you just now.

The old man, in the conference to which he had been admitted in that stately panelled room, had just told the Judge a very strange story. He might be himself a conspirator; he might possibly be crazed; or possibly his whole story was straight and true.

The aged gentleman in the bottle-green coat, on finding himself alone with Mr. Justice Harbottle, had become agitated. He said:

"There is, perhaps you are not aware, my lord, a prisoner in Shrewsbury jail, charged with having forged a bill of exchange for a hundred and twenty pounds, and his name is Lewis Pyneweck, a grocer of that town."

"Is there?" says the Judge, who knew well that there was.

"Yes, my lord," says the old man.

"Then you had better say nothing to affect this case. If you do, by —— I'll commit you! for I'm to try it," says the Judge, with his terrible look and tone.

"I am not going to do anything of the kind, my lord; of him or his case I know nothing, and care nothing. But a fact has come to my knowledge which it behoves you to well consider."

"And what may that fact be?" inquired the Judge; "I'm in haste, sir, and beg you will use dispatch."

"It has come to my knowledge, my lord, that a secret tribunal is in process of formation, the object of which is to take cognizance of the conduct of the judges; and first, of *your* conduct, my lord: it is a wicked conspiracy."

"Who are of it?" demands the Judge.

"I know not a single name as yet. I know but the fact, my lord; it is most certainly true."

"I'll have you before the Privy Council, sir," says the Judge.

"That is what I most desire; but not for a day or two, my lord."

"And why so?"

"I have not as yet a single name, as I told your lordship; but I expect to have a list of the most forward men in it, and some other papers connected with the plot, in two or three days."

"You said one or two just now."

"About that time, my lord."

"Is this a Jacobite plot?"

"In the main I think it is, my lord."

"Why, then, it is political. I have tried no State prisoners, nor am like to try any such. How, then, doth it concern me?"

"From what I can gather, my lord, there are those in it who desire private revenges upon certain judges."

"What do they call their cabal?"

"The High Court of Appeal, my lord."

"Who are you, sir? What is your name?"

"Hugh Peters, my lord."

"That should be a Whig name?"

"It is, my lord."

"Where do you lodge, Mr. Peters?"

"In Thames Street, my lord, over against the sign of the 'Three Kings.'"

"'Three Kings?' Take care one be not too many for you, Mr. Peters! How come you, an honest Whig, as you say, to be privy to a Jacobite plot? Answer me that."

"My lord, a person in whom I take an interest has been seduced to take a part in it; and being frightened at the unexpected wickedness of their plans, he is resolved to become an informer for the Crown."

"He resolves like a wise man, sir. What does he say of the persons? Who are in the plot? Doth he know them?"

"Only two, my lord; but he will be introduced to the club in a few days, and he will then have a list, and more exact information of their plans, and above all of their oaths, and their hours and places of meeting, with which he wishes to be acquainted before they can have any suspicions of his intentions. And being so informed, to whom, think you, my lord, had he best go then?"

"To the king's attorney-general straight. But you say this concerns me, sir, in particular? How about this prisoner, Lewis Pyneweck? Is he one of them?"

"I can't tell, my lord; but for some reason, it is thought your lordship will be well advised if you try him not. For if you do, it is feared 'twill shorten your days."

"So far as I can learn, Mr. Peters, this business smells pretty strong of blood and treason. The king's attorney-general will know how to deal with it. When shall I see you again, sir?"

"If you give me leave, my lord, either before your lordship's court sits, or after it rises, to-morrow. I should like to come and tell your lordship what has passed."

"Do so, Mr. Peters, at nine o'clock to-morrow morning. And see you play me no trick, sir, in this matter; if you do, by —— sir, I'll lay you by the heels!"

"You need fear no trick from me, my lord; had I not wished to serve you, and acquit my own conscience, I never would have come all this way to talk with your lordship."

"I'm willing to believe you, Mr. Peters; I'm willing to believe you, sir."

And upon this they parted.

"He has either painted his face, or he is consumedly sick," thought the old Judge.

The light had shone more effectually upon his features as he turned to leave the room with a low bow, and they looked, he fancied, unnaturally chalky.

"D—— him!" said the Judge ungraciously, as he began to scale the stairs: "he has half-spoiled my supper."

But if he had, no one but the Judge himself perceived it, and the evidence was all, as anyone might perceive, the other way.

Chapter III

Lewis Pyneweck

In the meantime the footman dispatched in pursuit of Mr. Peters speedily overtook that feeble gentleman. The old man stopped when he heard the sound of pursuing steps, but any alarms that may have crossed his mind seemed to disappear on his recognizing the livery. He very gratefully accepted the proffered assistance, and placed his tremulous arm within the servant's for support. They had not gone far, however, when the old man stopped suddenly, saying:

"Dear me! as I live, I have dropped it. You heard it fall. My eyes, I fear, won't serve me, and I'm unable to stoop low enough; but if *you* will look, you shall have half the find. It is a guinea; I carried it in my glove."

The street was silent and deserted. The footman had hardly descended to what he termed his "hunkers," and begun to search the pavement about the spot which the old man indicated, when Mr. Peters, who seemed very much exhausted, and breathed with difficulty, struck him a violent blow, from above, over the back of the head with a heavy instrument, and then another; and leaving him bleeding and senseless in the gutter, ran like a lamp-lighter down a lane to the right, and was gone.

When, an hour later, the watchman brought the man in livery home, still stupid and covered with blood, Judge Harbottle cursed his servant roundly, swore he was drunk, threatened him with an indictment for taking bribes to betray his master, and cheered him with a perspective of the broad street leading from the Old Bailey to Tyburn, the cart's tail, and the hangman's lash.

Notwithstanding this demonstration, the Judge was pleased. It was a disguised "affidavit man," or footpad, no doubt, who had been employed to frighten him. The trick had fallen through.

A "court of appeal," such as the false Hugh Peters had indicated, with assassination for its sanction, would be an uncomfortable institution for a "hanging judge" like the Honourable Justice Harbottle. That sarcastic and ferocious administrator of the criminal code of England, at that time a rather pharisaical, bloody and heinous system of justice, had reasons of his own for choosing to try that very Lewis Pyneweck, on whose behalf this audacious trick was devised. Try him he would. No man living should take that morsel out of his mouth.

Of Lewis Pyneweck, of course, so far as the outer world could see, he knew nothing. He would try him after his fashion, without fear, favour, or affection.

But did he not remember a certain thin man, dressed in mourning, in whose house, in Shrewsbury, the Judge's lodgings used to be, until a scandal of his ill-treating his wife came suddenly to light? A grocer with a demure look, a soft step, and a lean face as dark as mahogany, with a nose sharp and long, standing ever so little awry, and a pair of dark steady brown eyes under thinly-traced black brows—a man whose thin lips wore always a faint unpleasant smile.

Had not that scoundrel an account to settle with the Judge? had he not been troublesome lately? and was not his name Lewis Pyneweck, some time grocer in Shrewsbury, and now prisoner in the jail of that town?

The reader may take it, if he pleases, as a sign that Judge Harbottle was a good Christian, that he suffered nothing ever from remorse. That was undoubtedly true. He had, nevertheless, done this grocer, forger, what you will, some five or six years before, a grievous wrong; but it was not that, but a possible scandal, and possible complications, that troubled the learned Judge now.

Did he not, as a lawyer, know, that to bring a man from his shop to the dock, the chances must be at least ninety-nine out of a hundred that he is guilty?

A weak man like his learned brother Withershins was not a judge to keep the high-roads safe, and make crime tremble. Old Judge Harbottle was the man to make the evil-disposed quiver, and to refresh the world with showers of wicked blood, and thus save the innocent, to the refrain of the ancient saw he loved to quote:

Foolish pity
Ruins a city.

In hanging that fellow he could not be wrong. The eye of a man accustomed to look upon the dock could not fail to read "villain" written sharp and clear in his plotting face. Of course he would try him, and no one else should.

A saucy-looking woman, still handsome, in a mob-cap gay with blue ribbons, in a saque of flowered silk, with lace and rings on, much too fine for the Judge's housekeeper, which nevertheless she was, peeped into his study next morning, and, seeing the Judge alone, stepped in.

"Here's another letter from him, come by the post this morning. Can't you do nothing for him?" she said wheedlingly, with her arm over his neck, and her delicate finger and thumb fiddling with the lobe of his purple ear.

"I'll try," said Judge Harbottle, not raising his eyes from the paper he was reading.

"I knew you'd do what I asked you," she said.

The Judge clapt his gouty claw over his heart, and made her an ironical bow.

"What," she asked, "will you do?"

"Hang him," said the Judge with a chuckle.

"You don't mean to; no, you don't, my little man," said she, surveying herself in a mirror on the wall.

"I'm d——d but I think you're falling in love with your husband at last!" said Judge Harbottle.

"I'm blest but I think you're growing jealous of him," replied the lady with a laugh. "But no; he was always a bad one to me; I've done with him long ago."

"And he with you, by George! When he took your fortune, and your spoons, and your ear-rings, he had all he wanted of you. He drove you from his house; and when he discovered you had made yourself comfortable, and found a good situation, he'd have taken your guineas, and your silver, and your ear-rings over again, and then allowed you half-a-dozen years more to make a new harvest for his mill. You don't wish him good; if you say you do, you lie."

She laughed a wicked, saucy laugh, and gave the terrible Rhadamanthus a playful tap on the chops.

"He wants me to send him money to fee a counsellor," she said, while her eyes wandered over the pictures on the wall, and back again to the looking-glass; and certainly she did not look as if his jeopardy troubled her very much.

"Confound his impudence, the *scoundrel*!" thundered the old Judge, throwing himself back in his chair, as he used to do *in furore* on the bench, and the lines of his mouth looked brutal, and his eyes ready to leap from his sockets. "If you answer his letter from my house to please yourself, you'll write your next from somebody else's to please me. You understand, my pretty witch, I'll not be pestered. Come, no pouting; whimpering won't do. You don't care a brass farthing for the villain, body or soul. You came here but to make a row. You are one of Mother Carey's chickens; and where you come, the storm is up. Get you *gone*, baggage! get you gone!" he repeated, with a stamp; for a knock at the hall door made her instantaneous disappearance indispensable.

I need hardly say that the venerable Hugh Peters did not appear again. The Judge never mentioned him. But oddly enough, considering how he laughed to scorn the weak invention which he had blown into dust at the very first puff, his white-wigged visitor and the conference in the dark front parlour was often in his memory.

His shrewd eye told him that allowing for change of tints and such disguises as the playhouse affords every night, the features of this false old man, who had turned out too hard for his tall footman, were identical with those of Lewis Pyneweck.

Judge Harbottle made his registrar call upon the crown solicitor and tell him that there was a man in town who bore a wonderful resemblance to a prisoner in Shrewsbury jail named Lewis Pyneweck, and to make inquiry through the post forthwith whether anyone was personating Pyneweck in prison, and whether he had thus or otherwise made his escape.

The prisoner was safe, however, and no question as to his identity.

Chapter IV

Interruption in Court

In due time Judge Harbottle went circuit; and in due time the judges were in Shrewsbury. News travelled slowly in those days, and newspapers, like the wagons and stage-coaches, took matters easily. Mrs. Pyneweck, in the Judge's house, with a diminished household—the greater part of the Judge's servants having gone with him, for he had given up riding circuit, and travelled in his coach in state—kept house rather solitarily at home.

In spite of quarrels, in spite of mutual injuries—some of them inflicted by herself, enormous—in spite of a married life of spited bickerings—a life in which there seemed no love or liking or forbearance, for years—now that Pyneweck stood in near danger of death, something like remorse came suddenly upon her. She knew that in Shrewsbury were transacting the scenes which were to determine his fate. She knew she did not love him; but she could not have supposed, even a fortnight before, that the hour of suspense could have affected her so powerfully.

She knew the day on which the trial was expected to take place. She could not get it out of her head for a minute; she felt faint as it drew towards evening.

Two or three days passed; and then she knew that the trial must be over by this time. There were floods between London and Shrewsbury, and news was long delayed. She wished the floods would last for ever. It was dreadful waiting to hear; dreadful to know that the event was over, and that she could not hear till self-willed rivers subsided; dreadful to know that they must subside and the news come at last.

She had some vague trust in the Judge's good-nature, and much in the resources of chance and accident. She had contrived to send the money he wanted. He would not be without legal advice and energetic and skilled support.

At last the news did come—a long arrear all in a gush: a letter from a female friend in Shrewsbury; a return of the sentences, sent up for the Judge; and most important, because most easily got at, being told with great aplomb and brevity, the long-deferred intelligence of the Shrewsbury Assizes in the *Morning Advertiser*. Like an impatient reader of a novel, who reads the last page first, she read with dizzy eyes the list of the executions.

Two were respited, seven were hanged; and in that capital catalogue was this line:

"Lewis Pyneweck—forgery."

She had to read it half-a-dozen times over before she was sure she understood it. Here was the paragraph:

"Sentence, Death—7.

"Executed accordingly, on Friday the 13th instant,
to wit:

"Thomas Primer, alias Duck—highway robbery.

"Flora Guy—stealing to the value of 11s. 6d.

"Arthur Pounden—burglary.

"Matilda Mummery—riot.

"Lewis Pyneweck—forgery, bill of exchange."

And when she reached this, she read it over and over, feeling very cold and sick.

This buxom housekeeper was known in the house as Mrs. Carwell—Carwell being her maiden name, which she had resumed.

No one in the house except its master knew her history. Her introduction had been managed craftily. No one suspected that it had been concerted between her and the old reprobate in scarlet and ermine.

Flora Carwell ran up the stairs now and snatched her little girl, hardly seven years of age, whom she met on the lobby, hurriedly up in her arms, and carried her into her bedroom, without well knowing what she was doing, and sat down, placing the child before her. She was not able to speak. She held the child before her, and looked in the little girl's wondering face, and burst into tears of horror.

She thought the Judge could have saved him. I daresay he could. For a time she was furious with him, and hugged and kissed her bewildered little girl, who returned her gaze with large round eyes.

That little girl had lost her father, and knew nothing of the matter. She had been always told that her father was dead long ago.

A woman, coarse, uneducated, vain, and violent, does not reason, or even feel, very distinctly; but in these tears of consternation were mingling a self-upbraiding. She felt afraid of that little child.

But Mrs. Carwell was a person who lived not upon sentiment, but upon beef and pudding; she consoled herself with punch; she did not trouble herself long even with resentments; she was a gross and material person, and could not mourn over the irrevocable for more than a limited number of hours, even if she would.

Judge Harbottle was soon in London again. Except the gout, this savage old epicurean never knew a day's sickness. He laughed, and coaxed, and bullied away the young woman's faint upbraidings, and in a little time Lewis Pyneweck troubled her no more; and the Judge secretly chuckled over the perfectly fair removal of a bore, who might have grown little by little into something very like a tyrant.

It was the lot of the Judge whose adventures I am now recounting to try criminal cases at the Old Bailey shortly after his return. He had commenced his charge to the jury in a case of forgery, and was, after his wont, thundering dead against the prisoner, with many a hard aggravation and cynical gibe, when suddenly all died away in silence, and, instead of looking at the jury, the eloquent Judge was gaping at some person in the body of the court.

Among the persons of small importance who stand and listen at the sides was one tall enough to show with a little I prominence; a slight mean figure, dressed in seedy black, lean and dark of visage. He had just handed a letter to the crier, before he caught the Judge's eye.

That Judge descried, to his amazement, the features of Lewis Pyneweck. He had the usual faint thin-lipped smile; and with his blue chin raised in air, and as it seemed quite unconscious of the distinguished notice he had attracted, he was stretching his low cravat with his crooked fingers, while he slowly turned his head from side to side—a process which enabled the Judge to see distinctly a stripe of swollen blue round his neck, which indicated, he thought, the grip of the rope.

This man, with a few others, had got a footing on a step, from which he could better see the court. He now stepped down, and the Judge lost sight of him.

His lordship signed energetically with his hand in the direction in which this man had vanished. He turned to the tipstaff. His first effort to speak ended in a gasp. He cleared his throat, and told the astounded official to arrest that man who had interrupted the court.

"He's but this moment gone down there. Bring him in custody before me, within ten minutes' time, or I'll strip your gown from your shoulders and fine the sheriff!" he thundered, while his eyes flashed round the court in search of the functionary.

Attorneys, counsellors, idle spectators, gazed in the direction in which Mr. Justice Harbottle had shaken his gnarled old hand. They compared notes. Not one had seen anyone making a disturbance. They asked one another if the Judge was losing his head.

Nothing came of the search. His lordship concluded his charge a great deal more tamely; and when the jury retired, he stared round the court with a wandering mind, and looked as if he would not have given sixpence to see the prisoner hanged.

Chapter V

Caleb Searcher

The Judge had received the letter; had he known from whom it came, he would no doubt have read it instantaneously. As it was he simply read the direction:

To the Honourable

The Lord Justice

Elijah Harbottle,

One of his Majesty's Justices of

the Honourable Court of Common Pleas.

It remained forgotten in his pocket till he reached home.

When he pulled out that and others from the capacious pocket of his coat, it had its turn, as he sat in his library in his thick silk dressing-gown; and then he found its contents to be a closely-written letter, in a clerk's hand, and an enclosure in "secretary hand," as I believe the angular scrivenary of law-writings in those days was termed, engrossed on a bit of parchment about the size of this page. The letter said:

"*Mr. Justice Harbottle,*—My Lord,

"*I am ordered by the High Court of Appeal to ac-quaint your lordship, in order to your better preparing yourself for your trial, that a true bill hath been sent down, and the indictment lieth against your lordship for the murder of one Lewis Pyneweck of Shrews-bury, citizen, wrongfully executed for the forgery of a bill of exchange, on the —th day of —— last, by reason of the wilful perversion of the evidence, and the undue pressure put upon the jury, together with the illegal admission of evidence by your lordship, well knowing the same to be illegal, by all which the promoter of the prosecution of the said indictment, before the High Court of Appeal, hath lost his life.*

"*And the trial of the said indictment, I am farther ordered to acquaint your lordship, is fixed for the 10th day of —— next ensuing, by the right honourable the Lord Chief Justice Twofold, of the court aforesaid, to wit, the High Court of Appeal, on which day it will most certainly take place. And I am farther to acquaint your lordship, to prevent any surprise or miscarriage, that your case stands first for the said day, and that the said High Court of Appeal sits day and night, and never rises; and herewith, by order of the said court, I furnish your lordship with a copy (extract) of the record in this case, except of the indictment, whereof, notwithstanding, the substance and effect is supplied to your lordship in this Notice. And farther I am to inform you, that in case the jury then to try your lordship should find you guilty, the right honourable the Lord Chief Justice will, in passing sentence of death upon you, fix the day of execution for the 10th day of ——, being one calendar month from the day of your trial.*"

It was signed by

"*Caleb Searcher, "Officer of the Crown Solicitor in the Kingdom of Life and Death.*"

The Judge glanced through the parchment.

"'Sblood! Do they think a man like me is to be bamboozled by their buffoonery?"

The Judge's coarse features were wrung into one of his sneers; but he was pale. Possibly, after all, there was a conspiracy on foot. It was queer. Did they mean to pistol him in his carriage? or did they only aim at frightening him?

Judge Harbottle had more than enough of animal courage. He was not afraid of highwaymen, and he had fought more than his share of duels, being a foul-mouthed advocate while he held briefs at the bar. No one questioned his fighting qualities. But with respect to this particular case of Pyneweck, he lived in a house of glass. Was there not his pretty, dark-eyed, over-dressed housekeeper, Mrs. Flora Carwell? Very easy for people who knew Shrewsbury to identify Mrs. Pyneweck, if once put upon the scent; and had he not stormed and worked hard in that case? Had he not made it hard sailing for the prisoner? Did he not know very well what the bar thought of it? It would be the worst scandal that ever blasted Judge.

So much there was intimidating in the matter, but nothing more. The Judge was a little bit gloomy for a day or two after, and more testy with everyone than usual.

He locked up the papers; and about a week after he asked his housekeeper, one day, in the library:

"Had your husband never a brother?"

Mrs. Carwell squalled on this sudden introduction of the funereal topic, and cried exemplary "piggins full," as the Judge used pleasantly to say. But he was in no mood for trifling now, and he said sternly:

"Come, madam! this wearies me. Do it another time; and give me an answer to my question." So she did.

Pyneweck had no brother living. He once had one; but he died in Jamaica.

"How do you know he is dead? " asked the Judge.

"Because he told me so."

"Not the dead man."

"Pyneweck told me so."

"Is that all?" sneered the Judge.

He pondered this matter; and time went on. The Judge was growing a little morose, and less enjoying. The subject struck nearer to his thoughts than he fancied it could have done. But so it is with most undivulged vexations, and there was no one to whom he could tell this one.

It was now the ninth; and Mr. Justice Harbottle was glad. He knew nothing would come of it. Still it bothered him; and to-morrow would see it well over.

[What of the paper I have cited? No one saw it during his life; no one, after his death. He spoke of it to Dr. Hedstone; and what purported to be "a copy," in the old Judge's handwriting, was found. The original was nowhere. Was it a copy of an illusion, incident to brain disease? Such is my belief.]

Chapter VI

Arrested

Judge Harbottle went this night to the play at Drury Lane. He was one of those old fellows who care nothing for late hours, and occasional knocking about in pursuit of pleasure. He had appointed with two cronies of Lincoln's Inn to come home in his coach with him to sup after the play.

They were not in his box, but were to meet him near the entrance, and get into his carriage there; and Mr. Justice Harbottle, who hated waiting, was looking a little impatiently from the window.

The Judge yawned.

He told the footman to watch for Counsellor Thavies and Counsellor Beller, who were coming; and, with another yawn, he laid his cocked hat on his knees, closed his eyes, leaned back in his corner, wrapped his mantle closer about him, and began to think of pretty Mrs. Abington.

And being a man who could sleep like a sailor, at a moment's notice, he was thinking of taking a nap. Those fellows had no business to keep a judge waiting.

He heard their voices now. Those rake-hell counsellors were laughing, and bantering, and sparring after their wont. The carriage swayed and jerked, as one got in, and then again as the other followed. The door clapped, and the coach was now jogging and rumbling over the pavement. The Judge was a little bit sulky. He did not care to sit up and open his eyes. Let them suppose he was asleep. He heard them laugh with more malice than good-humour, he thought, as they observed it. He would give them a d——d hard knock or two when they got to his door, and till then he would counterfeit his nap.

The clocks were chiming twelve. Beller and Thavies were silent as tombstones. They were generally loquacious and merry rascals.

The Judge suddenly felt himself roughly seized and thrust from his corner into the middle of the seat, and opening his eyes, instantly he found himself between his two companions.

Before he could blurt out the oath that was at his lips, he saw that they were two strangers—evil-looking fellows, each with a pistol in his hand, and dressed like Bow Street officers.

The Judge clutched at the check-string. The coach pulled up. He stared about him. They were not among houses; but through the windows, under a broad moonlight, he saw a black moor stretching lifelessly from right to left, with rotting trees, pointing fantastic branches in the air, standing here and there in groups, as if they held up their arms and twigs like fingers, in horrible glee at the Judge's coming.

A footman came to the window. He knew his long face and sunken eyes. He knew it was Dingly Chuff, fifteen years ago a footman in his service, whom he had turned off at a moment's notice, in a burst of jealousy, and indicted for a missing spoon. The man had died in prison of the jail-fever.

The Judge drew back in utter amazement. His armed companions signed mutely; and they were again gliding over this unknown moor.

The bloated and gouty old man, in his horror, considered the question of resistance. But his athletic days were long over. This moor was a desert. There was no help to be had. He was in the hands of strange servants, even if his recognition turned out to be delusion, and they were under the command of his captors. There was nothing for it but submission, for the present.

Suddenly the coach was brought nearly to a standstill, so that the prisoner saw an ominous sight from the window.

It was a gigantic gallows beside the road; it stood three-sided, and from each of its three broad beams at top depended in chains some eight or ten bodies, from several of which the cere-clothes had dropped away, leaving the skeletons swinging lightly by their chains. A tall ladder reached to the summit of the structure, and on the peat beneath lay bones.

On the top of the dark transverse beam facing the road, from which, as from the other two completing the triangle of death, dangled a row of these unfortunates in chains, a hangman, with a pipe in his mouth, much as we see him in the famous print of the "Idle Apprentice," though here his perch was ever so much higher, was reclining at his ease and listlessly shying bones, from a little heap at his elbow, at the skeletons that hung round, bringing down now a rib or two, now a hand, now half a leg. A long-sighted man could have discerned that he was a dark fellow, lean; and from continually looking down on the earth from the elevation over which, in another sense, he always hung, his nose, his lips, his chin were pendulous and loose, and drawn down into a monstrous grotesque.

This fellow took his pipe from his mouth on seeing the coach, stood up, and cut some solemn capers high on his beam, and shook a new rope in the air, crying with a voice high and distant as the caw of a raven hovering over a gibbet, "A rope for Judge Harbottle!"

The coach was now driving on at its old swift pace.

So high a gallows as that, the Judge had never, even in his most hilarious moments, dreamed of. He thought he must be raving. And the dead footman! He shook his ears and strained his eyelids; but if he was dreaming, he was unable to awake himself.

There was no good in threatening these scoundrels. A *brutum fulmen* might bring a real one on his head.

Any submission to get out of their hands, and then heaven and earth he would move to unearth and hunt them down.

Suddenly they drove round a corner of a vast white building, and under a *porte-cochère*.

Chapter VII

Chief-Justice Twofold

The Judge found himself in a corridor lighted with dingy oil lamps, the walls of bare stone; it looked like a passage in a prison. His guards placed him in the hands of other people. Here and there he saw bony and gigantic soldiers passing to and fro, with muskets over their shoulders. They looked straight before them, grinding their teeth, in bleak fury, with no noise but the clank of their shoes. He saw these by glimpses, round corners, and at the ends of passages, but he did not actually pass them by.

And now, passing under a narrow doorway, he found himself in the dock, confronting a judge in his scarlet robes, in a large court-house. There was nothing to elevate this Temple of Themis above its vulgar kind elsewhere. Dingy enough it looked, in spite of candles lighted in decent abundance. A case had just closed, and the last juror's back was seen escaping through the door in the wall of the jury-box. There were some dozen barristers, some fiddling with pen and ink, others buried in briefs, some beckoning with the plumes of their pens, to their attorneys, of whom there were no lack; there were clerks to-ing and fro-ing, and the officers of the court, and the registrar, who was handing up a paper to the judge; and the tipstaff, who was presenting a note at the end of his wand to a king's counsel over the heads of the crowd between. If this was the High Court of Appeal, which never rose day or night, it might account for the pale and jaded aspect of everybody in it. An air of indescribable gloom hung upon the pallid features of all the people here; no one ever smiled; all looked more or less secretly suffering.

"The King against Elijah Harbottle!" shouted the officer.

"Is the appellant Lewis Pyneweck in court?" asked Chief-Justice Twofold, in a voice of thunder, that shook the woodwork of the court, and boomed down the corridors.

Up stood Pyneweck from his place at the table.

"Arraign the prisoner!" roared the Chief: and Judge Harbottle felt the panels of the dock round him, and the floor and the rails quiver in the vibrations of that tremendous voice.

The prisoner, *in limine*, objected to this pretended court, as being a sham, and non-existent in point of law; and then, that, even if it were a court constituted by law (the Judge was growing dazed), it had not and could not have any jurisdiction to try him for his conduct on the bench.

Whereupon the chief-justice laughed suddenly, and everyone in court, turning round upon the prisoner, laughed also, till the laugh grew and roared all round like a deafening acclamation; he saw nothing but glittering eyes and teeth, a universal stare and grin;

but though all the voices laughed, not a single face of all those that concentrated their gaze upon him looked like a laughing face. The mirth subsided as suddenly as it began.

The indictment was read. Judge Harbottle actually pleaded! He pleaded "Not Guilty." A jury were sworn. The trial proceeded. Judge Harbottle was bewildered. This could not be real. He must be either mad, or *going* mad, he thought.

One thing could not fail to strike even him. This Chief-Justice Twofold, who was knocking him about at every turn with sneer and gibe, and roaring him down with his tremendous voice, was a dilated effigy of himself; an image of Mr. Justice Harbottle, at least double his size, and with all his fierce colouring, and his ferocity of eye and visage, enhanced awfully.

Nothing the prisoner could argue, cite, or state, was permitted to retard for a moment the march of the case towards its catastrophe.

The chief-justice seemed to feel his power over the jury, and to exult and riot in the display of it. He glared at them, he nodded to them; he seemed to have established an understanding with them. The lights were faint in that part of the court. The jurors were mere shadows, sitting in rows; the prisoner could see a dozen pair of white eyes shining, coldly, out of the darkness; and whenever the judge in his charge, which was contemptuously brief, nodded and grinned and gibed, the prisoner could see, in the obscurity, by the dip of all these rows of eyes together, that the jury nodded in acquiescence.

And now the charge was over, the huge chief-justice leaned back panting and gloating on the prisoner. Everyone in the court turned about, and gazed with steadfast hatred on the man in the dock. From the jury-box where the twelve sworn brethren were whispering together, a sound in the general stillness, like a pro-longed "hiss-s-s!" was heard; and then, in answer to the challenge of the officer, "How say you, gentlemen of the jury, guilty or not guilty?" came in a melancholy voice the finding, " Guilty."

The place seemed to the eyes of the prisoner to grow gradually darker and darker, till he could discern nothing distinctly but the lumen of the eyes that were turned upon him from every bench and side and corner and gallery of the building. The prisoner doubtless thought that he had quite enough to say, and conclusive, why sentence of death should not be pronounced upon him; but the lord chief-justice puffed it contemptuously away, like so much smoke, and proceeded to pass sentence of death upon the prisoner, having named the tenth of the ensuing month for his execution.

Before he had recovered the stun of this ominous farce, in obedience to the mandate, "Remove the prisoner," he was led from the dock. The lamps seemed all to have gone out, and there were stoves and charcoal-fires here and there, that threw a faint crimson light on the walls of the corridors through which he passed. The stones that composed them looked now enormous, cracked and unhewn.

He came into a vaulted smithy, where two men, naked to the waist, with heads like bulls, round shoulders, and the arms of giants, were welding red-hot chains together with hammers that pelted like thunderbolts.

They looked on the prisoner with fierce red eyes, and rested on their hammers for a minute; and said the elder to his companion, "Take out Elijah Harbottle's gyves"; and with a pincers he plucked the end which lay dazzling in the fire from the furnace.

"One end locks," said he, taking the cool end of the iron in one hand, while with the grip of a vice he seized the leg of the Judge and locked the ring round his ankle. "The other," he said with a grin, "is welded."

The iron band that was to form the ring for the other leg lay still red hot upon the stone floor, with brilliant sparks sporting up and down its surface.

His companion, in his gigantic hands, seized the old Judge's other leg, and pressed his foot immovably to the stone floor; while his senior, in a twinkling, with a masterly application of pincers and hammer, sped the glowing bar round his ankle so tight that the skin and sinews smoked and bubbled again, and old Judge Harbottle uttered a yell that seemed to chill the very stones and make the iron chains quiver on the wall.

Chains, vaults, smiths, and smithy all vanished in a moment; but the pain continued. Mr. Justice Harbottle was suffering torture all round the ankle on which the infernal smiths had just been operating.

His friends, Thavies and Beller, were startled by the Judge's roar in the midst of their elegant trifling about a marriage *à-la-mode* case which was going on. The Judge was in panic as well as pain. The street lamps and the light of his own hall door restored him.

"I'm very bad," growled he between his set teeth; "my foot's blazing. Who was he that hurt my foot? 'Tis the gout—'tis the gout!" he said, awaking completely. "How many hours have we been coming from the playhouse? 'Sblood, what has happened on the way? I've slept half the night!"

There had been no hitch or delay, and they had driven home at a good pace.

The Judge, however, was in gout; he was feverish too; and the attack, though very short, was sharp; and when, in about a fortnight, it subsided, his ferocious joviality did not return. He could not get this dream, as he chose to call it, out of his head.

Chapter VIII

Somebody Has Got into the House

People remarked that the Judge was in the vapours. His doctor said he should go for a fortnight to Buxton.

Whenever the Judge fell into a brown study he was always conning over the terms of the sentence pronounced upon him in his vision—"in one calendar month from the date of this day"; and then the usual form, "and you shall be hanged by the neck till you are dead," etc. "That will be the 10th—I'm not much in the way of being hanged. I know what stuff dreams are, and I laugh at them; but this is continually in my thoughts, as if it forecast misfortune of some sort. I wish the day my dream gave me were passed and over. I wish I were well purged of my gout. I wish I were as I used to be. 'Tis nothing but vapours, nothing but a maggot." The copy of the parchment and letter which had announced his trial with many a snort and sneer he would read over and over again, and the scenery and people of his dream would rise about him in places the most unlikely, and steal him in a moment from all that surrounded him into a world of shadows.

The Judge had lost his iron energy and banter. He was growing taciturn and morose. The Bar remarked the change, as well they might. His friends thought him ill. The doctor said he was troubled with hypochondria, and that his gout was still lurking in his system, and ordered him to that ancient haunt of crutches and chalk-stones, Buxton.

The Judge's spirits were very low; he was frightened about himself; and he described to his housekeeper, having sent for her to his study to drink a dish of tea, his strange dream in his drive home from Drury Lane Playhouse. He was sinking into the state of nervous dejection in which men lose their faith in orthodox advice, and in despair consult quacks, astrologers, and nursery story-tellers. Could such a dream mean that he was to have a fit, and so die on the 10th? She did not think so. On the contrary, it was certain some good luck must happen on that day.

The Judge kindled; and for the first time for many days he looked for a minute or two like himself, and he tapped her on the cheek with the hand that was not in flannel.

"Odsbud! odsheart! you dear rogue! I had forgot. There is young Tom—yellow Tom, my nephew, you know, lies sick at Harrogate; why shouldn't he go that day as well as another, and if he does, I get an estate by it? Why, lookee, I asked Doctor Hedstone yesterday if I was like to take a fit any time, and he laughed, and swore I was the last man in town to go off that way."

The Judge sent most of his servants down to Buxton to make his lodgings and all things comfortable for him. He was to follow in a day or two.

It was now the 9th; and the next day well over, he might laugh at his visions and auguries.

On the evening of the 9th, Dr. Hedstone's footman knocked at the Judge's door. The Doctor ran up the dusky stairs to the drawing-room. It was a March evening, near the hour of sunset, with an east wind whistling sharply through the chimney-stacks. A wood fire blazed cheerily on the hearth. And Judge Harbottle, in what was then called a brigadier-wig, with his red roquelaure on, helped the glowing effect of the darkened chamber, which looked red all over like a room on fire.

The Judge had his feet on a stool, and his huge grim purple face confronted the fire and seemed to pant and swell, as the blaze alternately spread upward and collapsed. He had fallen again among his blue devils, and was thinking of retiring from the Bench, and of fifty other gloomy things.

But the Doctor, who was an energetic son of Æsculapius, would listen to no croaking, told the Judge he was full of gout, and in his present condition no judge even of his own case, but promised him leave to pronounce on all those melancholy questions a fortnight later.

In the meantime the Judge must be very careful. He was over-charged with gout, and he must not provoke an attack till the waters of Buxton should do that office for him in their own salutary way.

The Doctor did not think him perhaps quite so well as he pretended, for he told him he wanted rest, and would be better if he went forthwith to his bed.

Mr. Gerningham, his valet, assisted him, and gave him his drops; and the Judge told him to wait in his bedroom till he should go to sleep.

Three persons that night had specially odd stories to tell.

The housekeeper had got rid of the trouble of amusing her little girl at this anxious time, by giving her leave to run about the sitting-rooms and look at the pictures and china, on the usual condition of touching nothing. It was not until the last gleam of sunset had for some time faded, and the twilight had so deepened that she could no longer discern the colours on the china figures on the chimneypiece or in the cabinets, that the child returned to the housekeeper's room to find her mother.

To her she related, after some prattle about the china, and the pictures, and the Judge's two grand wigs in the dressing-room off the library, an adventure of an extraordinary kind.

In the hall was placed, as was customary in those times, the sedan-chair which the master of the house occasionally used, covered with stamped leather and studded with gilt nails, and with its red silk blinds down. In this case, the doors of this old-fashioned conveyance were locked, the windows up, and, as I said, the blinds down, but not so closely that the curious child could not peep underneath one of them, and see into the interior.

A parting beam from the setting sun, admitted through the window of a back room, shot obliquely through the open door and, lighting on the chair, shone with a dull transparency through the crimson blind.

To her surprise, the child saw in the shadow a thin man, dressed in black, seated in it; he had sharp dark features; his nose, she fancied, a little awry, and his brown eyes were looking straight before him; his hand was on his thigh, and he stirred no more than the waxen figure she had seen at Southwark fair.

A child is so often lectured for asking questions, and on the propriety of silence, and the superior wisdom of its elders, that it accepts most things at last in good faith; and the little girl acquiesced respectfully in the occupation of the chair by this mahogany-faced person as being all right and proper.

It was not until she asked her mother who this man was, and observed her scared face as she questioned her more minutely upon the appearance of the stranger, that she began to understand that she had seen something unaccountable.

Mrs. Carwell took the key of the chair from its nail over the footman's shelf, and led the child by the hand up to the hall, having a lighted candle in her other hand. She stopped at a distance from the chair, and placed the candlestick in the child's hand.

"Peep in, Margery, again, and try if there's anything there," she whispered; "hold the candle near the blind so as to throw its light through the curtain."

The child peeped, this time with a very solemn face, and intimated at once that he was gone.

"Look again, and be sure," urged her mother.

The little girl was quite certain; and Mrs. Carwell, with her mob-cap of lace and cherry-coloured ribbons, and her dark brown hair, not yet powdered, over a very pale face, unlocked the door, looked in, and beheld emptiness.

"All a mistake, child, you see."

"*There*! ma'am! see there! He's gone round the corner," said the child.

"Where?" said Mrs. Carwell, stepping backward a step.

"Into that room."

"Tut, child! 'twas the shadow," cried Mrs. Carwell, angrily, because she was frightened. "I moved the candle." But she clutched one of the poles of the chair, which leant against the wall in the corner, and pounded the floor furiously with one end of it, being afraid to pass the open door the child had pointed to.

The cook and two kitchen-maids came running upstairs, not knowing what to make of this unwonted alarm.

They all searched the room; but it was still and empty, and no sign of anyone's having been there.

Some people may suppose that the direction given to her thoughts by this odd little incident will account for a very strange illusion which Mrs. Carwell herself experienced about two hours later.

Chapter IX

The Judge Leaves His House

Mrs. Flora Carwell was going up the great staircase with a posset for the Judge in a china bowl, on a little silver tray.

Across the top of the well-staircase there runs a massive oak rail; and, raising her eyes accidentally, she saw an extremely odd-looking stranger, slim and long, leaning carelessly over with a pipe between his finger and thumb. Nose, lips, and chin seemed all to droop downward into extraordinary length, as he leant his odd peering face over the banister. In his other hand he held a coil of rope, one end of which escaped from under his elbow and hung over the rail.

Mrs. Carwell, who had no suspicion at the moment that he was not a real person, and fancied that he was someone employed in cording the Judge's luggage, called to know what he was doing there.

Instead of answering he turned about and walked across the lobby, at about the same leisurely pace at which she was ascending, and entered a room, into which she followed him. It was an uncarpeted and unfurnished chamber. An open trunk lay upon the floor empty, and beside it the coil of rope; but except herself there was no one in the room.

Mrs. Carwell was very much frightened, and now concluded that the child must have seen the same ghost that had just appeared to her. Perhaps, when she was able to think it over, it was a relief to believe so; for the face, figure, and dress described by the child were awfully like Pyneweck; and this certainly was not he.

Very much scared and very hysterical, Mrs. Carwell ran down to her room, afraid to look over her shoulder, and got some companions about her, and wept, and talked, and drank more than one cordial, and talked and wept again, and so on, until, in those early days, it was ten o'clock, and time to go to bed.

A scullery-maid remained up finishing some of her scouring and "scalding" for some time after the other servants—who, as I said, were few in number—that night had got to their beds. This was a low-browed, broad-faced, intrepid wench with black hair, who did not "vally a ghost not a button," and treated the housekeeper's hysterics with measureless scorn.

The old house was quiet now. It was near twelve o'clock, no sounds were audible except the muffled wailing of the wintry winds, piping high among the roofs and chimneys, or rumbling at intervals, in under gusts, through the narrow channels of the street.

The spacious solitudes of the kitchen level were awfully dark, and this sceptical kitchen-wench was the only person now up and about in the house. She hummed tunes to herself, for a time; and then stopped and listened; and then resumed her work again. At last, she was destined to be more terrified than even was the housekeeper.

There was a back kitchen in this house, and from this she heard, as if coming from below its foundations, a sound like heavy strokes, that seemed to shake the earth beneath her feet. Sometimes a dozen in sequence, at regular intervals; sometimes fewer. She walked out softly into the passage, and was surprised to see a dusky glow issuing from this room, as if from a charcoal fire.

The room seemed thick with smoke.

Looking in, she very dimly beheld a monstrous figure, over a furnace, beating with a mighty hammer the rings and rivets of a chain.

The strokes, swift and heavy as they looked, sounded hollow and distant. The man stopped, and pointed to something on the floor, that, through the smoky haze, looked, she thought, like a dead body. She remarked no more; but the servants in the room close by, startled from their sleep by a hideous scream, found her in a swoon on the flags, close to the door, where she had just witnessed this ghastly vision.

Startled by the girl's incoherent asseverations that she had seen the Judge's corpse on the floor, two servants having first searched the lower part of the house, went rather frightened upstairs to inquire whether their master was well. They found him, not in his bed, but in his room. He had a table with candles burning at his bedside, and was getting on his clothes again; and he swore and cursed at them roundly in his old style, telling them that he had business, and that he would discharge on the spot any scoundrel who should dare to disturb him again.

So the invalid was left to his quietude.

In the morning it was rumoured here and there in the street that the Judge was dead. A servant was sent from the house three doors away, by Counsellor Traverse, to inquire at Judge Harbottle's hall door.

The servant who opened it was pale and reserved, and would only say that the Judge was ill. He had had a dangerous accident; Doctor Hedstone had been with him at seven o'clock in the morning.

There were averted looks, short answers, pale and frowning faces, and all the usual signs that there was a secret that sat heavily upon their minds, and the time for disclosing which had not yet come. That time would arrive when the coroner had arrived, and the mortal scandal that had befallen the house could be no longer hidden. For that morning Mr. Justice Harbottle had been found hanging by the neck from the banister at the top of the great staircase, and quite dead.

There was not the smallest sign of any struggle or resistance. There had not been heard a cry or any other noise in the slightest degree indicative of violence. There was medical evidence to show that, in his atrabilious state, it was quite on the cards that he might have made away with himself. The jury found accordingly that it was a case of suicide. But to those who were acquainted with the strange story which Judge Harbottle had related to at least two persons, the fact that the catastrophe occurred on the morning of March 10th seemed a startling coincidence.

A few days after, the pomp of a great funeral attended him to the grave; and so, in the language of Scripture, "the rich man died, and was buried."

THE HAUNTED AND THE HAUNTERS

SIR EDWARD BULWER-LYTTON, LORD LYTTON

A friend of mine, who is a man of letters and a philosopher, said to me one day, as if between jest and earnest—"Fancy! since we last met I have discovered a haunted house in the midst of London."

"Really haunted?—and by what?—ghosts?"

"Well, I can't answer that question—all I know is this—six weeks ago my wife and I were in search of a furnished apartment. Passing a quiet street, we saw on the window of one of the houses a bill, 'Apartments, Furnished.' The situation suited us: we entered the house—liked the rooms—engaged them by the week—and left them the third day. No power on earth could have reconciled my wife to stay longer; and I don't wonder at it."

"What did you see?"

"Excuse me—I have no desire to be ridiculed as a superstitious dreamer—nor, on the other hand, could I ask you to accept on my affirmation what you would hold to be incredible without the evidence of your own senses. Let me only say this, it was not so much what we saw or heard (in which you might fairly suppose that we were the dupes of our own excited fancy, or the victims of imposture in others) that drove us away, as it was an undefinable terror which seized both of us whenever we passed by the door of a certain unfurnished room, in which we neither saw nor heard anything. And the strangest marvel of all was, that for once in my life I agreed with my wife—silly woman though she be—and allowed, after the third night, that it was impossible to stay a fourth in that house. Accordingly, on the fourth morning I summoned the woman who kept the house and attended on us, and told her that the rooms did not quite suit us, and we would not stay out our week. She said dryly: 'I know why; you have stayed longer than any other lodger; few ever stayed a second night; none before you a third. But I take it they have been very kind to you.'

"'They—who?' I asked, affecting to smile.

"'Why, they who haunt the house, whoever they are. I don't mind them; I remember them many years ago, when I lived in this house, not as a servant; but I know they will be the death of me some day. I don't care—I'm old, and must die soon, anyhow; and then I shall be with them, and in this house still.' The woman spoke with so dreary a calmness that really it was a sort of awe that prevented my conversing with her further. I paid for my week, and too happy were my wife and I to get off so cheaply."

"You excite my curiosity," said I; "nothing I should like better than to sleep in a haunted house. Pray give me the address of the one which you left so ignominiously."

My friend gave me the address; and when we parted, I walked straight towards the house thus indicated.

It is situated on the north side of Oxford Street, in a dull but respectable thoroughfare. I found the house shut up—no bill at the window, and no response to my knock. As I was turning away, a beer-boy, collecting pewter pots at the neighboring areas, said to me, "Do you want any one at that house, sir?"

"Yes, I heard it was to be let."

"Let!—why, the woman who kept it is dead—has been dead these three weeks, and no one can be found to stay there, though Mr. J—— offered ever so much. He offered mother, who chars for him, £1 a week just to open and shut the windows, and she would not."

"Would not!—and why?"

"The house is haunted; and the old woman who kept it was found dead in her bed, with her eyes wide open. They say the devil strangled her."

"Pooh!—you speak of Mr. J——. Is he the owner of the house?"

"Yes."

"Where does he live?"

"In G—— Street, No. ——."

"What is he?—in any business?"

"No, sir—nothing particular; a single gentleman."

I gave the pot-boy the gratuity earned by his liberal information, and proceeded to Mr. J——, in G—— Street, which was close by the street that boasted the haunted house. I was lucky enough to find Mr. J—— at home—an elderly man with intelligent countenance and prepossessing manners.

I communicated my name and my business frankly. I said I heard the house was considered to be haunted—that I had a strong desire to examine a house with so equivocal a reputation—that I should be greatly obliged if he would allow me to hire it, though only for a night. I was willing to pay for that privilege whatever he might be inclined to ask. "Sir," said Mr. J——, with great courtesy, "the house is at your service, for as short or as long a time as you please. Rent is out of the question—the obligation will be on my side should you be able to discover the cause of the strange phenomena which at present deprive it of all value. I cannot let it, for I cannot even get a servant to keep it in order or answer the door. Unluckily the house is haunted, if I may use that expression, not only by night, but by day; though at night the disturbances are of a more unpleasant and sometimes of a more alarming character.

The poor old woman who died in it three weeks ago was a pauper whom I took out of a workhouse, for in her childhood she had been known to some of my family, and had once been in such good circumstances that she had rented that house of my uncle. She was a woman of superior education and strong mind, and was the only person I could ever induce to remain in the house. Indeed, since her death, which was sudden, and the coroner's inquest, which gave it a notoriety in the neighbourhood, I have so despaired of finding any person to take charge of it, much more a tenant, that I would willingly let it rent-free for a year to any one who would pay its rates and taxes."

"How long is it since the house acquired this sinister character?"

"That I can scarcely tell you, but very many years since. The old woman I spoke of said it was haunted when she rented it between thirty and forty years ago. The fact is that my life has been spent in the East Indies, and in the civil service of the Company. I returned to England last year on inheriting the fortune of an uncle, among whose possessions was the house in question. I found it shut up and unin-habited. I was told that it was haunted, that no one would inhabit it. I smiled at what seemed to me so idle a story. I spent some money in repairing and roofing—added to its old-fashioned furniture a few modern articles—advertised it, and obtained a lodger for a year. He was a colonel retired on half-pay. He came in with his family, a son and a daughter, and four or five servants: they all left the house the next day, and, although they deponed that they had all seen something different, that something was equally terrible to all. I really could not in conscience sue, nor even blame, the colonel for breach of agreement.

"Then I put in the old woman I have spoken of, and she was empowered to let the house in apartments. I never had one lodger who stayed more than three days. I do not tell you their stories—to no two lodgers have there been exactly the same phenomena repeated. It is better that you should judge for yourself, than enter the house with an imagination influenced by previous narratives; only be prepared to see and to hear something or other, and take whatever precautions you yourself please."

"Have you never had a curiosity yourself to pass a night in that house?"

"Yes. I passed not a night, but three hours in broad daylight alone in that house. My curiosity is not satisfied, but it is quenched. I have no desire to renew the experiment. You cannot complain, you see, sir, that I am not sufficiently candid; and unless your interest be exceedingly eager and your nerves unusually strong, I honestly add that I advise you *not* to pass a night in that house."

"My interest *is* exceedingly keen," said I, "and though only a coward will boast of his nerves in situations wholly unfamiliar to him, yet my nerves have been seasoned in such variety of danger that I have the right to rely on them—even in a haunted house."

Mr. J—— said very little more; he took the keys of the house out of his bureau, gave them to me,—and thanking him cordially for his frankness, and his urbane concession to my wish, I carried off my prize.

Impatient for the experiment, as soon as I reached home I summoned my confidential servant,—a young man of gay spirits, fearless temper, and as free from superstitious prejudice as any one I could think of.

"F——," said I, "you remember in Germany how disappointed we were at not finding a ghost in that old castle, which was said to be haunted by a headless apparition? Well, I have heard of a house in London which, I have reason to hope, is decidedly haunted. I mean to sleep there to-night. From what I hear, there is no doubt that something will allow itself to be seen or to be heard—something, perhaps, excessively horrible. Do you think, if I take you with me, I may rely on your presence of mind, what ever may happen?"

"Oh, sir! pray trust me," answered F——, grinning with delight.

"Very well—then here are the keys of the house—this is the address. Go now—select for me any bedroom you please; and since the house has not been inhabited for weeks, make up a good fire, air the bed well—see, of course, that there are candles as well as fuel. Take with you my revolver and my dagger—so much for my weapons—arm yourself equally well; and if we are not a match for a dozen ghosts, we shall be but a sorry couple of Englishmen."

I was engaged for the rest of the day on business so urgent that I had not leisure to think much on the nocturnal adventure to which I had plighted my honor. I dined alone, and very late, and while dining, read, as is my habit. I selected one of the volumes of Macaulay's Essays. I thought to myself that I would take the book with me; there was so much of healthfulness in the style, and practical life in the subjects, that it would serve as an antidote against the influences of superstitious fancy.

Accordingly, about half-past nine, I put the book into my pocket, and strolled leisurely towards the haunted house. I took with me a favorite dog—an exceedingly sharp, bold, and vigilant bull-terrier—a dog fond of prowling about strange ghostly corners and passages at night in search of rats—a dog of dogs for a ghost.

It was a summer night, but chilly, the sky somewhat gloomy and overcast. Still there was a moon—faint and sickly, but still a moon—and if the clouds permitted, after midnight it would be brighter.

I reached the house, knocked, and my servant opened with a cheerful smile.

"All right, sir, and very comfortable."

"Oh!" said I, rather disappointed; "have you not seen nor heard anything remarkable?"

"Well, sir, I must own I have heard something queer."

"What?—what?"

"The sound of feet pattering behind me; and once or twice small noises like whispers close at my ear—nothing more."

"You are not at all frightened?"

"I! not a bit of it, sir"; and the man's bold look reassured me on one point—viz. that, happen what might, he would not desert me.

We were in the hall, the street-door closed, and my attention was now drawn to my dog. He had at first run in eagerly enough, but had sneaked back to the door, and was scratching and whining to get out. After patting him on the head, and encouraging him gently, the dog seemed to reconcile himself to the situation, and followed me and F—— through the house, but keeping close at my heels instead of hurrying inquisitively in advance, which was his usual and normal habit in all strange places. We first visited the subterranean apartments, the kitchen and other offices, and especially the cellars, in which last there were two or three bottles of wine still left in a bin, covered with cobwebs, and evidently, by their appearance, undisturbed for many years. It was clear that the ghosts were not winebibbers.

For the rest we discovered nothing of interest. There was a gloomy little backyard, with very high walls. The stones of this yard were very damp—and what with the damp, and what with the dust and smoke-grime on the pavement, our feet left a slight impression where we passed. And now appeared the first strange phenomenon witnessed by myself in this strange abode. I saw, just before me, the print of a foot suddenly form itself, as it were. I stopped, caught hold of my servant, and pointed to it. In advance of that footprint as suddenly dropped another. We both saw it. I advanced quickly to the place; the footprint kept advancing before me, a small footprint—the foot of a child: the impression was too faint thoroughly to distinguish the shape, but it seemed to us both that it was the print of a naked foot. This phenomenon ceased when we arrived at the opposite wall, nor did it repeat itself on returning.

We remounted the stairs, and entered the rooms on the ground-floor, a dining parlor, a small back-parlor, and a still smaller third room that had been probably appropriated to a footman—all still as death. We then visited the drawing-rooms, which seemed fresh and new. In the front room I seated myself in an arm-chair. F—— placed on the table the candlestick with which he had lighted us. I told him to shut the door. As he turned to do so, a chair opposite to me moved from the wall quickly and noiselessly, and dropped itself about a yard from my own chair, immediately fronting it.

"Why, this is better than the turning-tables," said I, with a half-laugh—and as I laughed, my dog put back his head and howled.

F——, coming back, had not observed the movement of the chair. He employed himself now in stilling the dog. I continued to gaze on the chair, and fancied I saw on it a pale blue, misty outline of a human figure, but an outline so indistinct that I could only distrust my own vision. The dog now was quiet. "Put back that chair opposite to me," said I to F—; "put it back to the wall."

F—— obeyed. "Was that you, sir?" said he, turning abruptly.

"I—what?"

"Why, something struck me. I felt it sharply on the shoulder—just here."

"No," said I. "But we have jugglers present, and though we may not discover their tricks, we shall catch *them* before they frighten *us*."

We did not stay long in the drawing-rooms—in fact, they felt so damp and so chilly that I was glad to get to the fire upstairs. We locked the doors of the drawing-rooms—a precaution which, I should observe, we had taken with all the rooms we had searched below. The bedroom my servant had selected for me was the best on the floor—a large one, with two windows fronting the street. The four-posted bed, which took up no inconsiderable space, was opposite to the fire, which burned clear and bright; a door in the wall to the left, between the bed and the window, communicated with the room which my servant appropriated to himself.

This last was a small room with a sofa-bed, and had no communication with the landing-place—no other door but that which conducted to the bedroom I was to occupy. On either side of my fireplace was a cupboard, without locks, flushed with the wall, and covered with the same dull-brown paper. We examined these cupboards—only hooks to suspend female dresses—nothing else; we sounded the walls—evidently solid—the outer walls of the building. Having finished the survey of these apartments, warmed myself a few moments, and lighted my cigar, I then, still accompanied by F——, went forth to complete my reconnoitre. In the landing-place there was another door; it was closed firmly. "Sir," said my servant, in surprise, "I unlocked this door with all the others when I first came; it cannot have got locked from the inside, for it is a—"

Before he had finished his sentence, the door, which neither of us then was touching, opened quietly of itself. We looked at each other a single instant. The same thought seized both—some human agency might be detected here. I rushed in first, my servant followed. A small, blank, dreary room without furniture—a few empty boxes and hampers in a corner—a small window—the shutters closed—

not even a fireplace—no other door but that by which we had entered—no carpet on the floor, and the floor seemed very old, uneven, worm-eaten, mended here and there, as was shown by the whiter patches on the wood; but no living being, and no visible place in which a living being could have hidden. As we stood gazing round, the door by which we had entered closed as quietly as it had before opened: we were imprisoned.

For the first time I felt a creep of undefinable horror. Not so my servant. "Why, they don't think to trap us, sir; I could break that trumpery door with a kick of my boot."

"Try first if it will open to your hand," said I, shaking off the vague apprehension that had seized me, "while I unclosed the shutters and see what is without."

I unbarred the shutters—the window looked on the little backyard I have before described; there was no ledge without—nothing but sheer descent. No man getting out of that window would have found any footing till he had fallen on the stones below.

F——, meanwhile, was vainly attempting to open the door. He now turned round to me and asked my permission to use force. And I should here state, in justice to the servant, that, far from evincing any superstitious terrors, his nerve, composure, and even gaiety amidst circumstances so extraordinary compelled my admiration, and made me congratulate myself on having secured a companion in every way fitted to the occasion. I willingly gave him the permission he required. But though he was a remarkably strong man, his force was as idle as his milder efforts; the door did not even shake to his stoutest kick. Breathless and panting, he desisted. I then tried the door myself, equally in vain.

As I ceased from the effort, again that creep of horror came over me; but this time it was more cold and stubborn. I felt as if some strange and ghastly exhalation were rising up from the chinks of that rugged floor, and filling the atmosphere with a venomous influence hostile to human life. The door now very slowly and quietly opened as of its own accord. We precipitated ourselves into the landing-place. We both saw a large, pale light—as large as the human figure, but shapeless and unsubstantial—move before us, and ascend the stairs that led from the landing into the attics. I followed the light, and my servant followed me. It entered, to the right of the landing, a small garret, of which the door stood open. I entered in the same instant. The light then collapsed into a small globule, exceedingly brilliant and vivid; rested a moment on a bed in the corner, quivered, and vanished. We approached the bed and examined it—a half-tester, such as is commonly found in attics devoted to servants. On the drawers that stood near it we perceived an old faded silk kerchief, with the needle still left in a rent half repaired. The kerchief was covered with dust; probably it had belonged to the old woman who had last died in that house, and this might have been her sleeping-room.

I had sufficient curiosity to open the drawers; there were a few odds and ends of female dress, and two letters tied round with a narrow ribbon of faded yellow. I took the liberty to possess myself of the letters. We found nothing else in the room worth noticing—nor did the light reappear; but we distinctly heard, as we turned to go, a pattering footfall on the floor—just before us. We went through the other attics (in all four), the footfall still preceding us. Nothing to be seen—nothing but the footfall heard. I had the letters in my hand; just as I was descending the stairs I distinctly felt my wrist seized, and a faint, soft effort made to draw the letters from my clasp. I only held them the more tightly, and the effort ceased.

We regained the bedchamber appropriated to myself, and I then remarked that my dog had not followed us when we had left it. He was thrusting himself close to the fire, and trembling.

I was impatient to examine the letters; and while I read them, my servant opened a little box in which he had deposited the weapons I had ordered him to bring, took them out, placed them on a table close at my bed-head, and then occupied himself in soothing the dog, who, however, seemed to heed him very little.

The letters were short—they were dated; the dates exactly thirty-five years ago. They were evidently from a lover to his mistress, or a husband to some young wife. Not only the terms of expression, but a distinct reference to a former voyage, indicated the writer to have been a seafarer. The spelling and handwriting were those of a man imperfectly educated, but still the language itself was forcible. In the expressions of endearment there was a kind of rough, wild love; but here and there were dark unintelligible hints at some secret not of love—some secret that seemed of crime. "We ought to love each other," was one of the sentences I remember, "for how every one else would execrate us if all was known." Again: "Don't let anyone be in the same room with you at night—you talk in your sleep." And again: "What's done can't be undone; and I tell you there's nothing against us unless the dead could come to life." Here there was underlined in a better handwriting (a female's), "They do!" At the end of the letter latest in date the same female hand had written these words: "Lost at sea the 4th of June, the same day as—"

I put down the letters, and began to muse over their contents.

Fearing, however, that the train of thought into which I fell might unsteady my nerves, I fully determined to keep my mind in a fit state to cope with whatever of marvellous the advancing night might bring forth. I roused myself—laid the letters on the table—stirred up the fire, which was still bright and cheering—and opened my volume of Macaulay. I read quietly enough till about half-past eleven. I then threw myself dressed upon the bed, and told my servant he might retire to his own room, but must keep himself awake. I bade him leave open the door between the two rooms. Thus alone, I kept two candles burning on the table by my bed-head. I placed my watch beside the weapons, and calmly resumed my Macaulay.

Opposite to me the fire burned clear; and on the hearthrug, seemingly asleep, lay the dog. In about twenty minutes I felt an exceedingly cold air pass by my cheek, like a sudden draught. I fancied the door to my right, communicating with the landing-place, must have got open; but no—it was closed. I then turned my glance to my left, and saw the flame of the candles violently swayed as by a wind. At the same moment the watch beside the revolver softly slid from the table—softly, softly—no visible hand—it was gone. I sprang up, seizing the revolver with the one hand, the dagger with the other; I was not willing that my weapons should share the fate of the watch. Thus armed, I looked round the floor—no sign of the watch. Three slow, loud, distinct knocks were now heard at the bed-head; my servant called out, "Is that you, sir?"

"No; be on your guard."

The dog now roused himself and sat on his haunches, his ears moving quickly backwards and forwards. He kept his eyes fixed on me with a look so strange that he concentred all my attention on himself. Slowly he rose up, all his hair bristling, and stood perfectly rigid, and with the same wild stare. I had no time, however, to examine the dog. Presently my servant emerged from his room; and if ever I saw horror in the human face, it was then. I should not have recognized him had we met in the street, so altered was every lineament. He passed by me quickly, saying, in a whisper that seemed scarcely to come from his lips, "Run—run! it is after me!" He gained the door to the landing, pulled it open, and rushed forth. I followed him into the landing involuntarily, calling him to stop; but, without heeding me, he bounded down the stairs, clinging to the balusters, and tak-ing several steps at a time. I heard, where I stood, the street-door open—heard it again clap to. I was left alone in the haunted house.

It was but for a moment that I remained undecided whether or not to follow my servant; pride and curiosity alike forbade so dastardly a flight. I re-entered my room, closing the door after me, and proceeded cautiously into the interior chamber. I encountered nothing to justify my servant's terror. I again carefully examined the walls, to see if there were any concealed door. I could find no trace of one—not even a seam in the dull-brown paper with which the room was hung. How, then, had the Thing, whatever it was, which had so scared him, obtained ingress except through my own chamber?

I returned to my room, shut and locked the door that opened upon the interior one, and stood on the hearth, expectant and prepared. I now perceived that the dog had slunk into an angle of the wall, and was pressing himself close against it, as if literally striving to force his way into it. I approached the animal and spoke to it; the poor brute was evidently beside itself with terror. It showed all its teeth, the slaver dropping from its jaws, and would certainly have bitten me if I had touched it. It did not seem to rec-ognize me. Whoever has seen at the Zoological Gardens a rabbit, fascinated by a serpent, cowering in a corner, may form some idea of the anguish which the dog exhibited. Finding all efforts to soothe the animal in vain, and fearing that his bite might be as venomous in that state as in the madness of hydrophobia, I left him alone, placed my weapons on the table beside the fire, seated myself, and recommenced my Macaulay.

Perhaps, in order not to appear seeking credit for a courage, or rather a coolness, which the reader may conceive I exaggerate, I may be pardoned if I pause to indulge in one or two egotistical remarks.

As I hold presence of mind, or what is called courage, to be precisely proportioned to familiarity with the circumstances that lead to it, so I should say that I had been long sufficiently familiar with all experiments that appertain to the marvellous. I had witnessed many very extraordinary phenomena in various parts of the world—phenomena that would be either totally disbelieved if I stated them, or ascribed to supernatural agencies. Now, my theory is that the Supernatural is the Impossible, and that what is called supernatural is only a something in the laws of nature of which we have been hitherto ignorant. Therefore, if a ghost rise before me, I have not the right to say, "So, then, the supernatural is possible," but rather, "So, then, the apparition of a ghost, is, contrary to received opinion, within the laws of nature—i.e., not supernatural."

Now, in all that I had hitherto witnessed, and indeed in all the wonders which the amateurs of mystery in our age record as facts, a material living agency is always required. On the Continent you will find still magicians who assert that they can raise spirits. Assume for the moment that they assert truly, still the living material form of the magician is present; and he is the material agency by which from some constitutional peculiarities, certain strange phenomena are represented to your natural senses.

Accept, again, as truthful, the tales of Spirit-Manifestation in America—musical or other sounds—writings on paper, produced by no discernible hand—articles of furniture moved without apparent human agency—or the actual sight and touch of hands, to which no bodies seem to belong—still there must be found the *medium* or living being, with constitutional peculiarities capable of obtaining these signs. In fine, in all such marvels, supposing even that there is no imposture, there must be a human being like ourselves by whom, or through whom, the effects presented to human beings are produced. It is so with the now familiar phenomena of mesmerism or electro-biology; the mind of the person operated on is affected through a material living agent. Nor, supposing it true that a mesmerized patient can respond to the will or passes of a mesmerizer a hundred miles distant, is the response less occasioned by a material being; it may be through a material fluid—call it Electric, call it Odic, call it what you will—which has the power of traversing space and passing obstacles, that the material effect is communicated from one to the other.

Hence all that I had hitherto witnessed, or expected to witness, in this strange house, I believed to be occasioned through some agency or medium as mortal as myself; and this idea necessarily prevented the awe with which those who regard as supernatural things that are not within the ordinary operations of nature, might have been impressed by the adventures of that memorable night.

As, then, it was my conjecture that all that was presented, or would be presented, to my senses, must originate in some human being gifted by constitution with the power so to present them, and having some motives so to do, I felt an interest in my theory which, in its way, was rather philosophical than superstitious. And I can sincerely say that I was in as tranquil a temper for observation as any practical experimentalist could be in awaiting the effects of some rare though perhaps perilous chemical combination. Of course, the more I kept my mind detached from fancy, the more the temper fitted for observation would be obtained; and I therefore riveted eye and thought on the strong daylight sense in the page of my Macaulay.

I now became aware that something interposed between the page and the light—the page was over-shadowed; I looked up, and I saw what I shall find it very difficult, perhaps impossible, to describe.

It was a Darkness shaping itself forth from the air in very undefined outline. I cannot say it was of a human form, and yet it had more resemblance to a human form, or rather shadow, than anything else. As it stood, wholly apart and distinct from the air and the light around it, its dimensions seemed gigantic, the summit nearly touching the ceiling. While I gazed, a feeling of intense cold seized me. An iceberg before me could not more have chilled me; nor could the cold of an iceberg have been more purely physical. I feel convinced that it was not the cold caused by fear. As I continued to gaze, I thought—but this I cannot say with precision—that I distinguished two eyes looking down on me from the height. One moment I fancied that I distinguished them clearly, the next they seemed gone; but still two rays of a pale-blue light frequently shot through the darkness, as from the height on which I half-believed, half-doubted, that I had encountered the eyes.

I strove to speak—my voice utterly failed me; I could only think to myself, "Is this fear? it is *not* fear!" I strove to rise—in vain; I felt as if weighed down by an irresistible force. Indeed, my impression was that of an immense and overwhelming Power opposed to my volition; that sense of utter inadequacy to cope with a force beyond men's, which one may feel *physically* in a storm at sea, in a conflagration, or when confronting some terrible wild beast, or rather, perhaps, the shark of the ocean, I felt *morally*. Opposed to my will was another will, as far superior to its strength as storm, fire, and shark are superior in material force to the force of men.

And now, as this impression grew on me, now came, at last, horror—horror to a degree that no words can convey. Still I retained pride, if not courage; and in my own mind I said, "This is horror, but it is not fear; unless I fear I cannot be harmed; my reason rejects this thing; it is an illusion—I do not fear." With a violent effort I succeeded at last in stretching out my hand towards the weapon on the table; as I did so, on the arm and shoulder I received a strange shock, and my arm fell to my side powerless. And now, to add to my horror, the light began slowly to wane from the candles—they were not, as it were, extinguished, but their flame seemed very gradually withdrawn; it was the same with the fire— the light was extracted from the fuel; in a few minutes the room was in utter darkness.

The dread that came over me, to be thus in the dark with that dark Thing, whose power was so intensely felt, brought a reaction of nerve. In fact, terror had reached that climax, that either my senses must have deserted me, or I must have burst through the spell. I did burst through it. I found voice, though the voice was a shriek. I remember that I broke forth with words like these—"I do not fear, my soul does not fear;" and at the same time I found strength to rise. Still in that profound gloom I rushed to one of the windows—tore aside the curtain—flung open the shutters; my first thought was—LIGHT. And when I saw the moon high, clear, and calm, I felt a joy that almost compensated for the previous terror. There was the moon, there was also the light from the gas-lamps in the deserted slumberous street. I turned to look back into the room; the moon penetrated its shadow very palely and partially—but still there was light. The dark Thing, whatever it might be, was gone—except that I could yet see a dim shadow, which seemed the shadow of that shade, against the opposite wall.

My eye now rested on the table, and from under the table (which was without cloth or cover—an old mahogany round-table) there rose a hand, visible as far as the wrist. It was a hand, seemingly, as much of flesh and blood as my own, but the hand of an aged person, lean, wrinkled, small too—a woman's hand.

That hand very softly closed on the two letters that lay on the table: hand and letters both vanished. There then came the same three loud, measured knocks I had heard at the bed-head before this extraordinary drama had commenced.

As those sounds slowly ceased, I felt the whole room vibrate sensibly; and at the far end there rose, as from the floor, sparks or globules like bubbles of light, many coloured—green, yellow, fire-red, azure. Up and down, to and fro, hither, thither, as tiny will-o'-the-wisps, the sparks moved, slow or swift, each at its own caprice. A chair (as in the drawing-room below) was now advanced from the wall without apparent agency, and placed at the opposite side of the table. Suddenly, as forth from the chair, there grew a shape—a woman's shape. It was distinct as a shape of life—ghastly as a shape of death. The face was that of youth, with a strange, mournful beauty; the throat and shoulders were bare, the rest of the form in a loose robe of cloudy white. It began sleeking its long, yellow hair, which fell over its shoulders; its eyes were not turned towards me, but to the door; it seemed listening, watching, waiting. The shadow of the shade in the background grew darker; and again I thought I beheld the eyes gleaming out from the summit of the shadow—eyes fixed upon that shape.

As if from the door, though it did not open, there grew out another shape, equally distinct, equally ghastly—a man's shape—a young man's. It was in the dress of the last century, or rather in a likeness of such dress; for both the male shape and the female, though defined, were evidently unsubstantial, impalpable—simulacra—phantasms; and there was something incongruous, grotesque, yet fearful, in the contrast between the elaborate finery, the courtly precision of that old-fashioned garb, with its ruffles and lace and buckles, and the corpse-like aspect and ghost-like stillness of the flitting wearer. Just as the male shape approached the female, the dark Shadow started from the wall, all three for a moment wrapped in darkness. When the pale light returned, the two phantoms were as if in the grasp of the Shadow that towered between them; and there was a bloodstain on the breast of the female; and the phantom-male was leaning on its phantom-sword, and blood seemed trickling fast from the ruffles, from the lace; and the darkness of the intermediate Shadow swallowed them up—they were gone. And again the bubbles of light shot, and sailed, and undulated, growing thicker and thicker and more wildly confused in their movements.

The closet-door to the right of the fireplace now opened, and from the aperture there came the form of an aged woman. In her hand she held letters—the very letters over which I had seen *the* Hand close; behind her I heard a footstep. She turned round as if to listen, then she opened the letters and seemed to read; and over her shoulder I saw a livid face, the face as of a man long drowned— bloated, bleached—seaweed tangled in its dripping hair; and at her feet lay a form as of a corpse and beside the corpse there cowered a child, a miserable, squalid child, with famine in its cheeks and fear in its eyes. And as I looked in the old woman's face, the wrinkles and lines vanished, and it became a face of youth—hard-eyed, stony, but still youth; and the Shadow darted forth, and darkened over these phantoms as it had darkened over the last.

Nothing now was left but the Shadow, and on that my eyes were intently fixed, till again eyes grew out of the Shadow— malignant, serpent eyes. And the bubbles of light again rose and fell, and in their disordered, irregular, turbulent maze, mingled with the wan moonlight. And now from these globules them- selves, as from the shell of an egg, monstrous things burst out; the air grew filled with them: larvae so bloodless and so hideous that I can in no way describe them except to remind the reader of the swarming life which the solar microscope brings before his eyes in a drop of water—things transparent, supple, agile, chasing each other, devouring each, other—forms like nought ever beheld by the naked eye. As the shapes were without symmetry, so their movements were without order. In their very vagrancies there was no sport; they came round me and round, thicker and faster and swifter, swarming over my head, crawling over my right arm, which was outstretched in involuntary command against all evil beings.

Sometimes I felt myself touched, but not by them; invisible hands touched me. Once I felt the clutch as of cold soft fingers at my throat. I was still equally conscious that if I gave way to fear I should be in bodily peril; and I concentrated all my faculties in the single focus of resisting, stubborn will. And I turned my sight from the Shadow—above all, from those strange serpent eyes— eyes that had now become distinctly visible. For there, though in nought else around me, I was aware that there was a *will*, and a will of intense, creative, working evil, which might crush down my own.

The pale atmosphere in the room began now to redden as if in the air of some near conflagration. The larvæ grew lurid as things that live in fire. Again the room vibrated; again were heard the three measured knocks; and again all things were swallowed up in the darkness of the dark Shadow, as if out of that darkness all had come, into that darkness all returned.

As the gloom receded, the Shadow was wholly gone. Slowly, as it had been withdrawn, the flame grew again into the candles on the table, again into the fuel in the grate. The whole room came once more calmly, healthfully into sight.

The two doors were still closed, the door communicating with the servant's room still locked. In the corner of the wall, into which he had so convulsively niched himself, lay the dog. I called to him— no movement; I approached—the animal was dead; his eyes protruded; his tongue out of his mouth; the froth gathered round his jaws. I took him in my arms; I brought him to the fire. I felt acute grief for the loss of my poor favorite—acute self-reproach; I accused myself of his death; I imagined he had died of fright. But what was my surprise on finding that his neck was actually broken—actually twisted out of the vertebrae. Had this been done in the dark?—must it not have been by a hand human as mine?—must there not have been a human agency all the while in that room? Good cause to suspect it. I cannot tell. I cannot do more than state the fact fairly; the reader may draw his own inference.

Another surprising circumstance—my watch was restored to the table from which it had been so mysteriously withdrawn; but it had stopped at the very moment it was so withdrawn; nor, despite all the skill of the watchmaker, has it ever gone since—that is, it will go in a strange, erratic way for a few hours, and then come to a dead stop—it is worthless.

Nothing more chanced for the rest of the night. Nor, indeed, had I long to wait before the dawn broke. Not till it was broad daylight did I quit the haunted house. Before I did so, I revisited the little blind room in which my servant and myself had been for a time imprisoned. I had a strong impression—for which I could not account—that from that room had originated the mechanism of the phenomena—if I may use the term—which had been experienced in my chamber. And though I entered it now in the clear day, with the sun peering through the filmy window, I still felt, as I stood on its floors, the creep of the horror which I had first there experienced the night before, and which had been so aggravated by what had passed in my own chamber. I could not, indeed, bear to stay more than half a minute within those walls. I descended the stairs, and again I heard the footfall before me; and when I opened the street door, I thought I could distinguish a very low laugh. I gained my own home, expecting to find my runaway servant there; but he had not presented himself; nor did I hear more of him for three days, when I received a letter from him, dated from Liverpool to this effect:—

"HONORED SIR,—I humbly entreat your pardon, though I can scarcely hope that you will think that I deserve it, unless—which Heaven forbid!—you saw what I did. I feel that it will be years before I can recover myself; and as to being fit for service, it is out of the question. I am therefore going to my brother-in-law at Melbourne. The ship sails to-morrow. Perhaps the long voyage may set me up. I do nothing now but start and tremble, and fancy It is behind me. I humbly beg you, honoured sir, to order my clothes, and whatever wages are due to me, to be sent to my mother's, at Walworth—John knows her address."

The letter ended with additional apologies, somewhat incoherent, and explanatory details as to effects that had been under the writer's charge.

This flight may perhaps warrant a suspicion that the man wished to go to Australia, and had been somehow or other fraudulently mixed up with the events of the night. I say nothing in refutation of that conjecture; rather, I suggest it as one that would seem to many persons the most probable solution of improbable occurrences. My own theory remained unshaken. I returned in the evening to the house, to bring away in a hack cab the things I had left there, with my poor dog's body. In this task I was not disturbed, nor did any incident worth note befall me, except that still, on ascending and descending the stairs I heard the same footfall in advance. On leaving the house, I went to Mr. J——'s. He was at home. I returned him the keys, told him that my curiosity was sufficiently gratified, and was about to relate quickly what had passed, when he stopped me, and said, though with much politeness, that he had no longer any interest in a mystery which none had ever solved.

I determined at least to tell him of the two letters I had read, as well as of the extraordinary manner in which they had disappeared; and I then inquired if he thought they had been addressed to the woman who had died in the house, and if there were anything in her early history which could possibly confirm the dark suspicions to which the letters gave rise. Mr. J—— seemed startled, and, after musing a few moments, answered, "I know but little of the woman's earlier history, except as I before told you, that her family were known to mine. But you revive some vague reminiscences to her prejudice. I will make inquiries, and inform you of their result. Still, even if we could admit the popular superstition that a person who had been either the perpetrator or the victim of dark crimes in life could revisit, as a restless spirit, the scene in which those crimes had been committed, I should observe that the house was infested by strange sights and sounds before the old woman died—you smile—what would you say?"

"I would say this, that I am convinced, if we could get to the bottom of these mysteries, we should find a living human agency."

"What! you believe it is all an imposture? For what object?"

"Not an imposture in the ordinary sense of the word. If suddenly I were to sink into a deep sleep, from which you could not awake me, but in that sleep could answer questions with an accuracy which I could not pretend to when awake—tell you what money you had in your pocket, nay, describe your very thoughts—it is not necessarily an imposture, any more than it is necessarily supernatural. I should be, unconsciously to myself, under a mesmeric influence, conveyed to me from a distance by a human being who had acquired power over me by previous *rapport*."

"Granting mesmerism, so far carried, to be a fact, you are right. And you would infer from this that a mesmeriser might produce the extraordinary effects you and others have witnessed over inanimate objects—fill the air with sights and sounds?"

"Or impress our senses with the belief in such effects—we never having been *en rapport* with the person acting on us? No. What is commonly called mesmerism could not do this; but there may be a power akin to mesmerism, and superior to it—the power that in the old days was called Magic. That such a power may extend to all inanimate objects of matter, I do not say; but if so, it would not be against nature, only a rare power in nature which might be given to constitutions with certain peculiarities, and cultivated by practice to an extraordinary degree. That such a power might extend over the dead—that is, over certain thoughts and memories that the dead may still retain—and compel, not that which ought properly to be called the *soul*, and which is far beyond human reach, but rather a phantom of what has been most earth-stained on earth, to make itself apparent to our senses—is a very ancient though obsolete theory upon which I will hazard no opinion. But I do not conceive the power would be supernatural.

"Let me illustrate what I mean from an experiment which Paracelsus describes as not difficult, and which the author of the *Curiosities of Literature* cites as credible: A flower perishes; you burn it. Whatever were the elements of that flower while it lived are gone, dispersed, you know not whither; you can never discover nor re-collect them. But you can, by chemistry, out of the burned dust of that flower, raise a spectrum of the flower, just as it seemed in life. It may be the same with the human being. The soul has as much escaped you as the essence or elements of the flower. Still you may make a spectrum of it. And this phantom, though in the popular superstition it is held to be the soul of the departed, must not be confounded with the true soul; it is but the eidolon of the dead form.

"Hence, like the best attested stories of ghosts or spirits, the thing that most strikes us is the absence of what we hold to be soul—that is, of superior emancipated intelligence. They come for little or no object—they seldom speak, if they do come; they utter no ideas above those of an ordinary person on earth. These American spirit-seers have published volumes of communications in prose and verse, which they assert to be given in the names of the most illustrious dead—Shakespeare, Bacon—heaven knows whom. Those communications, taking the best, are certainly not a whit of higher order than would be communications from living persons of fair talent and education; they are wondrously inferior to what Bacon, Shakespeare, and Plato said and wrote when on earth.

Nor, what is more noticeable, do they ever contain an idea that was not on the earth before. Wonderful, therefore, as such phenomena may be (granting them to be truthful), I see much that philosophy may question, nothing that it is incumbent on philosophy to deny—viz., nothing supernatural. They are but ideas conveyed somehow or other (we have not yet discovered the means) from one mortal brain to another. Whether, in so doing, tables walk of their own accord, or fiendlike shapes appear in a magic circle, or bodiless hands rise and remove material objects, or a Thing of Darkness, such as presented itself to me, freeze our blood—still am I persuaded that these are but agencies conveyed, as by electric wires, to my own brain from the brain of another. In some constitutions there is a natural chemistry, and those may produce chemic wonders—in others a natural fluid, call it electricity, and these may produce electric wonders. But they differ in this from Normal Science—they are alike objectless, purposeless, puerile, frivolous. They lead on to no grand results; and therefore the world does not heed, and true sages have not cultivated them. But sure I am, that of all I saw or heard, a man, human as myself, was the remote originator; and I believe unconsciously to himself as to the exact effects produced, for this reason: no two persons, you say, have ever told you that they experienced exactly the same thing. Well, observe, no two persons ever experience exactly the same dream. If this were an ordinary imposture, the machinery would be arranged for results that would but little vary; if it were a supernatural agency permitted by the Almighty, it would surely be for some definite end.

These phenomena belong to neither class; my persuasion is, that they originate in some brain now far distant; that that brain had no distinct volition in anything that occurred; that what does occur reflects but its devious, motley, ever-shifting, half-formed thoughts; in short, that it has been but the dreams of such a brain put into action and invested with a semi-substance. That this brain is of immense power, that it can set matter into movement, that it is malignant and destructive, I believe; some material force must have killed my dog; it might, for aught I know, have sufficed to kill myself, had I been as subjugated by terror as the dog—had my intellect or my spirit given me no countervailing resistance in my will."

"It killed your dog! that is fearful! indeed it is strange that no animal can be induced to stay in that house; not even a cat. Bats and mice are never found in it."

"The instincts of the brute creation detect influences deadly to their existence. Man's reason has a sense less subtle, because it has a resisting power more supreme. But enough; do you comprehend my theory?"

"Yes, though imperfectly—and I accept any crotchet (pardon the word), however odd, rather than embrace at once the notion of ghosts and hobgoblins we imbibed in our nurseries. Still, to my unfortunate house, the evil is the same. What on earth can I do with the house?"

"I will tell you what I would do. I am convinced from my own internal feelings that the small, unfurnished room at right angles to the door of the bed-room which I occupied, forms a starting-point or receptacle for the influences which haunt the house; and I strongly advise you to have the walls opened, the floor removed—nay, the whole room pulled down. I observe that it is detached from the body of the house, built over the small backyard, and could be removed without injury to the rest of the building."

"And you think, if I did that—"

"You would cut off the telegraph wires. Try it. I am so persuaded that I am right, that I will pay half the expense if you will allow me to direct the operations."

"Nay, I am well able to afford the cost; for the rest allow me to write to you."

About ten days after I received a letter from Mr. J——, telling me that he had visited the house since I had seen him; that he had found the two letters I had described, replaced in the drawer from which I had taken them; that he had read them with misgivings like my own; that he had instituted a cautious inquiry about the woman to whom I rightly conjectured they had been written. It seemed that thirty-six years ago (a year before the date of the letters) she had married, against the wish of her relations, an American of very suspicious character; in fact, he was generally believed to have been a pirate. She herself was the daughter of very respectable trades-people, and had served in the capacity of a nursery governess before her marriage. She had a brother, a widower, who was considered wealthy, and who had one child of about six years old. A month after the marriage the body of this brother was found in the Thames, near London Bridge; there seemed some marks of violence about his throat, but they were not deemed sufficient to warrant the inquest in any other verdict than that of "found drowned."

The American and his wife took charge of the little boy, the de-ceased brother having by his will left his sister the guardian of his only child—and in event of the child's death the sister inherited. The child died about six months afterwards—it was supposed to have been neglected and ill-treated. The neighbors deposed to have heard it shriek at night. The surgeon who had examined it after death said that it was emaciated as if from want of nourishment, and the body was covered with livid bruises. It seemed that one winter night the child had sought to escape—crept out into the backyard—tried to scale the wall—fallen back exhausted, and been found at morning on the stones in a dying state. But though there was some evidence of cruelty, there was none of murder; and the aunt and her husband had sought to palliate cruelty by alleging the exceeding stubbornness and perversity of the child, who was declared to be half-witted. Be that as it may, at the orphan's death the aunt inherited her brother's fortune.

Before the first wedded year was out, the American quitted England abruptly, and never returned to it. He obtained a cruising vessel, which was lost in the Atlantic two years afterwards. The widow was left in affluence, but reverses of various kinds had befallen her: a bank broke—an investment failed—she went into a small business and became insolvent—then she entered into service, sinking lower and lower, from housekeeper down to maid-of-all-work—never long retaining a place, though nothing peculiar against her character was ever alleged. She was considered sober, honest, and peculiarly quiet in her ways; still nothing prospered with her. And so she had dropped into the workhouse, from which Mr. J—— had taken her, to be placed in charge of the very house which she had rented as mistress in the first year of her wedded life.

Mr. J—— added that he had passed an hour alone in the unfurnished room which I had urged him to destroy, and that his impressions of dread while there were so great, though he had neither heard nor seen anything, that he was eager to have the walls bared and the floors removed as I had suggested. He had engaged persons for the work, and would commence any day I would name.

The day was accordingly fixed. I repaired to the haunted house—we went into the blind, dreary room, took up the skirting, and then the floors. Under the rafters, covered with rubbish, was found a trap-door, quite large enough to admit a man. It was closely nailed down, with clamps and rivets of iron. On removing these we descended into a room below, the existence of which had never been suspected. In this room there had been a window and a flue, but they had been bricked over, evidently for many years. By the help of candles we examined this place; it still retained some mouldering furniture—three chairs, an oak settle, a table—all of the fashion of about eighty years ago. There was a chest of drawers against the wall, in which we found, half-rotted away, old-fashioned articles of a man's dress, such as might have been worn eighty or a hundred years ago by a gentleman of some rank—costly steel buckles and buttons, like those yet worn in court-dresses—a handsome court sword—in a waistcoat which had once been rich with gold-lace, but which was now blackened and foul with damp, we found five guineas, a few silver coins, and an ivory ticket, probably for some place of entertainment long since passed away. But our main discovery was in a kind of iron safe fixed to the wall, the lock of which it cost us much trouble to get picked.

In this safe were three shelves and two small drawers. Ranged on the shelves were several small bottles of crystal, hermetically stopped. They contained colourless volatile essences, of what nature of which I shall only say that they were not poisons—phosphor and ammonia entered into some of them. There were also some very curious glass tubes, and a small pointed rod of iron, with a large lump of rock-crystal, and another of amber—also a loadstone of great power.

In one of the drawers we found a miniature portrait set in gold, and retaining the freshness of its colors most remarkably, considering the length of time it had probably been there. The portrait was that of a man who might be somewhat advanced in middle life, perhaps forty-seven or forty-eight.

It was a most peculiar face—a most impressive face. If you could fancy some mighty serpent transformed into man, preserving in the human lineaments the old serpent type, you would have a better idea of that countenance than long descriptions can convey: the width and flatness of frontal—the tapering elegance of contour disguising the strength of the deadly jaw—the long, large, terrible eye, glittering and green as the emerald—and withal a certain ruthless calm, as if from the consciousness of an immense power. The strange thing was this—the instant I saw the miniature I recognised a startling likeness to one of the rarest portraits in the world—the portrait of a man of a rank only below that of royalty, who in his own day had made a considerable noise. History says little or nothing of him; but search the correspondence of his contemporaries, and you find reference to his wild daring, his bold profligacy, his restless spirit, his taste for the occult sciences. While still in the meridian of life he died and was buried, so say the chronicles, in a foreign land. He died in time to escape the grasp of the law, for he was accused of crimes which would have given him to the headsman.

After his death, the portraits of him, which had been numerous, for he had been a munificent encourager of art, were brought up and destroyed—it was supposed by his heirs, who might have been glad could they have razed his very name from their splendid line. He had enjoyed a vast wealth; a large portion of this was believed to have been embezzled by a favourite astrologer or soothsayer—at all events, it had unaccountably vanished at the time of his death. One portrait alone of him was supposed to have escaped the general destruction; I had seen it in the house of a collector some months before. It had made on me a wonderful impression, as it does on all who behold it—a face never to be forgotten; and there was that face in the miniature that lay within my hand. True, that in the miniature the man was a few years older than in the portrait I had seen, or than the original was even at the time of his death. But a few years!— why, between the date in which flourished that direful noble, and the date in which the miniature was evidently painted, there was an interval of more than two centuries. While I was thus gazing, silent and wondering, Mr. J—— said:

"But is it possible? I have known this man."

"How—where?" I cried.

"In India. He was high in the confidence of the Rajah of ——, and wellnigh drew him into a revolt which would have lost the Rajah his dominions. The man was a Frenchman—his name de V——, clever, bold, lawless. We insisted on his dismissal and banishment: it must be the same man—no two faces like his—yet this miniature seems nearly a hundred years old."

Mechanically I turned round the miniature to examine the back of it, and on the back was engraved a pentacle; in the middle of the pentacle a ladder, and the third step of the ladder was formed by the date 1765. Examining still more minutely, I detected a spring; this, on being pressed, opened the back of the miniature as a lid. Within-side the lid were engraved, "Marianna to thee. Be faithful in life and in death to ——." Here follows a name that I will not mention, but it was not unfamiliar to me. I had heard it spoken of by old men in my childhood as the name borne by a dazzling charlatan who had made a great sensation in London for a year or so, and had fled the country on the charge of a double murder within his own house—that of his mistress and his rival. I said nothing of this to Mr. J——, to whom reluctantly I resigned the miniature.

We had found no difficulty in opening the first drawer within the iron safe; we found great difficulty in opening the second: it was not locked, but it resisted all efforts till we inserted in the chinks the edge of a chisel. When we had thus drawn it forth, we found a very singular apparatus in the nicest order. Upon a small, thin book, or rather tablet, was placed a saucer of crystal; this saucer was filled with a clear liquid—on that liquid floated a kind of compass, with a needle shifting rapidly round; but instead of the usual points of a compass were seven strange characters, not very unlike those used by astrologers to denote the planets. A very peculiar, but not strong nor displeasing odour came from this drawer, which was lined with a wood that we afterwards discovered to be hazel. Whatever the cause of this odour, it produced a material effect on the nerves. We all felt it, even the two workmen who were in the room—a creeping, tingling sensation from the tips of the fingers to the roots of the hair. Impatient to examine the tablet, I removed the saucer. As I did so the needle of the compass went round and round with exceeding swiftness, and I felt a shock that ran through my whole frame, so that I dropped the saucer on the floor. The liquid was spilt—the saucer was broken—the compass rolled to the end of the room—and at that instant the walls shook to and fro, as if a giant had swayed and rocked them.

The two workmen were so frightened that they ran up the ladder by which we had descended from the trap-door; but seeing that nothing more happened, they were easily induced to return.

Meanwhile I had opened the tablet: it was bound in plain red leather, with a silver clasp; it contained but one sheet of thick vellum, and on that sheet were inscribed, within a double pentacle, words in old monkish Latin, which are literally to be translated thus—"On all that it can reach within these walls—sentient or inanimate, living or dead—as moves the needle, so work my will! Accursed be the house, and restless be the dwellers therein."

We found no more. Mr. J—— burned the tablet and its anathema. He razed to the foundations the part of the building containing the secret room with the chamber over it. He had then the courage to inhabit the house himself for a month, and a quieter, better-conditioned house could not be found in all London. Subsequently he let it to advantage, and his tenant has made no complaints.

But my story is not yet done. A few days after Mr. J—— had removed into the house, I paid him a visit. We were standing by the open window and conversing. A van containing some articles of furniture which he was moving from his former house was at the door. I had just urged on him my theory that all those phenomena regarded as supermundane had emanated from a human brain; adducing the charm, or rather curse, we had found and destroyed in support of my philosophy. Mr. J—— was observing in reply, "That even if mesmerism, or whatever analogous power it might be called, could really thus work in the absence of the operator, and produce effects so extraordinary, still could those effects continue when the operator himself was dead? and if the spell had been wrought, and, indeed, the room walled up, more than seventy years ago, the probability was, that the operator had long since departed this life"; Mr. J——, I say, was thus answering, when I caught hold of his arm and pointed to the street below.

A well-dressed man had crossed from the opposite side, and was accosting the carrier in charge of the van. His face, as he stood, was exactly fronting our window. It was the face of the miniature we had discovered; it was the face of the portrait of the noble three centuries ago.

"Good heavens!" cried Mr. J——, "that is the face of de V——, and scarcely a day older than when I saw it in the Rajah's court in my youth!"

Seized by the same thought, we both hastened downstairs. I was first in the street; but the man had already gone. I caught sight of him, however, not many yards in advance, and in another moment I was by his side.

I had resolved to speak to him, but when I looked into his face I felt as if it were impossible to do so. That eye—the eye of the serpent—fixed and held me spellbound. And withal, about the man's whole person there was a dignity, an air of pride and station and superiority, that would have made any one, habituated to the usages of the world, hesitate long before venturing upon a liberty or impertinence. And what could I say? what was it I would ask? Thus ashamed of my first impulse, I fell a few paces back, still, however, following the stranger, undecided what else to do. Meanwhile he turned the corner of the street; a plain carriage was in waiting, with a servant out of livery, dressed like a *valet-de-place*, at the carriage door. In another moment he had stepped into the carriage, and it drove off. I returned to the house. Mr. J—— was still at the street door. He had asked the carrier what the stranger had said to him.

"Merely asked whom that house now belonged to."

The same evening I happened to go with a friend to a place in town called the Cosmopolitan Club, a place open to men of all countries, all opinions, all degrees. One orders one's coffee, smokes one's cigars. One is always sure to meet agreeable, sometimes remarkable persons.

I had not been two minutes in the room before I beheld at a table, conversing with an acquaintance of mine, whom I will designate by the initial G——, the man—the Original of the Miniature. He was now without his hat, and the likeness was yet more startling, only I observed that while he was conversing there was less severity in the countenance; there was even a smile, though a very quiet and very cold one. The dignity of mien I had acknowledged in the street was also more striking; a dignity akin to that which invests some prince of the East—conveying the idea of supreme indifference and habitual, indisputable, indolent, but resistless power.

G—— soon after left the stranger, who then took up a scientific journal, which seemed to absorb his attention.

I drew G—— aside. "Who and what is that gentleman?"

"That? Oh, a very remarkable man indeed. I met him last year amidst the caves of Petra—the scriptural Edom. He is the best Oriental scholar I know. We joined company, had an adventure with robbers, in which he showed a coolness that saved our lives; afterwards he invited me to spend a day with him in a house he had bought at Damascus—a house buried amongst almond blossoms and roses— the most beautiful thing! He had lived there for some years, quite as an Oriental, in grand style. I half suspect he is a renegade, immensely rich, very odd; by the by, a great mesmeriser. I have seen him with my own eyes produce an effect on inanimate things. If you take a letter from your pocket and throw it to the other end of the room, he will order it to come to his feet, and you will see the letter wriggle itself along the floor till it has obeyed his command. 'Pon my honour, 'tis true: I have seen him affect even the weather, disperse or collect clouds, by means of a glass tube or wand. But he does not like talking of these matters to strangers. He has only just arrived in England; says he has not been for a great many years; let me introduce him to you."

"Certainly! He is English, then? What is his name?"

"Oh!—a very homely one—Richards."

"And what is his birth—his family?"

"How do I know? What does it signify!—no doubt some parvenu, but rich—so infernally rich!"

G—— drew me up to the stranger, and the introduction was effected. The manners of Mr. Richards were not those of an adventurous traveller. Travellers are in general constitutionally gifted with high animal spirits: they are talkative, eager, imperious. Mr. Richards was calm and subdued in tone, with manners which were made distant by the loftiness of punctilious courtesy—the manners of a former age. I observed that the English he spoke was not exactly of our day. I should even have said that the accent was slightly foreign. But then Mr. Richards remarked that he had been little in the habit for many years of speaking in his native tongue. The conversation fell upon the changes in the aspect of London since he had last visited our metropolis. G—— then glanced off to the moral changes—literary, social, political—the great men who were removed from the stage within the last twenty years—the new great men who were coming on. In all this Mr. Richards evinced no interest. He had evidently read none of our living authors, and seemed scarcely acquainted by name with our younger statesmen. Once and only once he laughed; it was when G—— asked him whether he had any thought of getting into Parliament. And the laugh was inward—sarcastic—sinister—a sneer raised into a laugh. After a few minutes G—— left us to talk to some other acquaintances who had just lounged into the room, and I then said quietly:

"I have seen a miniature of you, Mr. Richards, in the house you once inhabited, and perhaps built, if not wholly, at least in part, in —— Street. You passed by that house this morning."

Not till I had finished did I raise my eyes to his, and then his fixed my gaze so steadfastly that I could not withdraw it—those fascinating serpent eyes. But involuntarily, and as if the words that translated my thought were dragged from me, I added in a low whisper, "I have been a student in the mysteries of life and nature; of those mysteries I have known the occult professors. I have the right to speak to you thus." And I uttered a certain pass-word.

"Well," said he, dryly, "I concede the right—what would you ask?"

"To what extent human will in certain temperaments can extend?"

"To what extent can thought extend? Think, and before you draw breath you are in China."

"True. But my thought has no power in China."

"Give it expression, and it may have: you may write down a thought which, sooner or later, may alter the whole condition of China. What is a law but a thought? Therefore thought is infinite— therefore thought has power; not in proportion to its value—a bad thought may make a bad law as potent as a good thought can make a good one."

"Yes; what you say confirms my own theory. Through invisible currents one human brain may transmit its ideas to other human brains with the same rapidity as a thought promulgated by visible means. And as thought is imperishable—as it leaves its stamp behind it in the natural world even when the thinker has passed out of this world—so the thought of the living may have power to rouse up and revive the thoughts of the dead—such as those thoughts *were in life*—though the thought of the living cannot reach the thoughts which the dead *now* may entertain. Is it not so?"

"I decline to answer, if, in my judgment, thought has the limit you would fix to it; but proceed. You have a special question you wish to put."

"Intense malignity in an intense will, engendered in a peculiar temperament, and aided by natural means within the reach of science, may produce effects like those ascribed of old to evil magic. It might thus haunt the walls of a human habitation with spectral revivals of all guilty thoughts and guilty deeds once conceived and done within those walls; all, in short, with which the evil will claims *rapport* and affinity—imperfect, incoherent, fragmentary snatches at the old dramas acted therein years ago. Thoughts thus crossing each other haphazard, as in the nightmare of a vision, growing up into phantom sights and sounds, and all serving to create horror, not because those sights and sounds are really visitations from a world without, but that they are ghastly monstrous renewals of what have been in this world itself, set into malignant play by a malignant mortal.

"And it is through the material agency of that human brain that these things would acquire even a human power—would strike as with the shock of electricity, and might kill, if the thought of the person assailed did not rise superior to the dignity of the original assailer—might kill the most powerful animal if unnerved by fear, but not injure the feeblest man, if, while his flesh crept, his mind stood out fearless. Thus, when in old stories we read of a magician rent to pieces by the fiends he had evoked—or still more, in Eastern legends, that one magician succeeds by arts in destroying another—there may be so far truth, that a material being has clothed, from its own evil propensities, certain elements and fluids, usually quiescent or harmless, with awful shape and terrific force—just as the lightning that had lain hidden and innocent in the cloud becomes by natural law suddenly visible, takes a distinct shape to the eye, and can strike destruction on the object to which it is attracted."

"You are not without glimpses of a very mighty secret," said Mr. Richards, composedly. "According to your view, could a mortal obtain the power you speak of, he would necessarily be a malignant and evil being."

"If the power were exercised as I have said, most malignant and most evil—though I believe in the ancient traditions that he could not injure the good. His will could only injure those with whom it has established an affinity, or over whom it forces unresisted sway. I will now imagine an example that may be within the laws of nature, yet seem wild as the fables of a bewildered monk.

"You will remember that Albertus Magnus, after describing minutely the process by which spirits may be invoked and commanded, adds emphatically that the process will instruct and avail only to the few—that *a man must be born a magician!*—that is, born with a peculiar physical temperament, as a man is born a poet. Rarely are men in whose constitution lurks this occult power of the highest order of intellect;—usually in the intellect there is some twist, perversity, or disease. But, on the other hand, they must possess, to an astonishing degree, the faculty to concentrate thought on a single object—the energic faculty that we call *will*. Therefore, though their intellect be not sound, it is exceedingly forcible for the attainment of what it desires. I will imagine such a person, pre-eminently gifted with this constitution and its concomitant forces. I will place him in the loftier grades of society. I will suppose his desires emphatically those of the sensualist—he has, therefore, a strong love of life. He is an absolute egotist—his will is concentrated in himself—he has fierce passions—he knows no enduring, no holy affections, but he can covet eagerly what for the moment he desires—he can hate implacably what opposes itself to his objects—he can commit fearful crimes, yet feel small remorse—he resorts rather to curses upon others, than to penitence for his misdeeds. Circumstances, to which his constitution guides him, lead him to a rare knowledge of the natural secrets which may serve his egotism. He is a close observer where his passions encourage observation, he is a minute calculator, not from love of truth, but where love of self sharpens his faculties—therefore he can be a man of science.

"I suppose such a being, having by experience learned the power of his arts over others, trying what may be the power of will over his own frame, and studying all that in natural philosophy may increase that power. He loves life, he dreads death; he *wills to live on*. He cannot restore himself to youth, he cannot entirely stay the progress of death, he cannot make himself immortal in the flesh and blood; but he may arrest for a time so prolonged as to appear incredible, if I said it—that hardening of the parts which constitutes old age. A year may age him no more than an hour ages another. His intense will, scientifically trained into system, operates, in short, over the wear and tear of his own frame. He lives on. That he may not seem a portent and a miracle, he dies from time to time, seemingly, to certain persons.

Having schemed the transfer of a wealth that suffices to his wants, he disappears from one corner of the world, and contrives that his obsequies shall be celebrated. He reappears at another corner of the world, where he resides undetected, and does not revisit the scenes of his former career till all who could remember his features are no more. He would be profoundly miserable if he had affections—he has none but for himself. No good man would accept his longevity, and to no men, good or bad, would he or could he communicate its true secret. Such a man might exist; such a man as I have described I see now before me!—Duke of ——, in the court of ——, dividing time between lust and brawl, alchemists and wizards;—again, in the last century, charlatan and criminal, with name less noble, domiciled in the house at which you gazed to-day, and flying from the law you had outraged, none knew whither; traveller once more revisiting London, with the same earthly passion which filled your heart when races now no more walked through yonder streets; outlaw from the school of all the nobler and diviner mystics; execrable Image of Life in Death and Death in Life, I warn you back from the cities and homes of healthful men; back to the ruins of departed empires; back to the deserts of nature unredeemed!"

There answered me a whisper so musical, so potently musical, that it seemed to enter into my whole being, and subdue me despite myself. Thus it said:

"I have sought one like you for the last hundred years. Now I have found you, we part not till I know what I desire. The vision that sees through the Past, and cleaves through the veil of the Future, is in you at this hour; never before, never to come again. The vision of no puling fantastic girl, of no sick-bed somnambule, but of a strong man, with a vigorous brain. Soar and look forth!"

As he spoke I felt as if I rose out of myself upon eagle wings. All the weight seemed gone from air—roofless the room, roofless the dome of space. I was not in the body—where I knew not—but aloft over time, over earth.

Again I heard the melodious whisper,—"You say right. I have mastered great secrets by the power of Will; true, by Will and by Science I can retard the process of years: but death comes not by age alone. Can I frustrate the accidents which bring death upon the young?"

"No; every accident is a providence. Before a providence snaps every human will."

"Shall I die at last, ages and ages hence, by the slow, though inevitable, growth of time, or by the cause that I call accident?"

"By a cause you call accident."

"Is not the end still remote?" asked the whisper with a slight tremor.

"Regarded as my life regards time, it is still remote."

"And shall I, before then, mix with the world of men as I did ere I learned these secrets, resume eager interest in their strife and their trouble—battle with ambition, and use the power of the sage to win the power that belongs to kings?"

"You will yet play a part on the earth that will fill earth with commotion and amaze. For wondrous designs have you, a wonder yourself, been permitted to live on through the centuries. All the secrets you have stored will then have their uses—all that now makes you a stranger amidst the generations will contribute then to make you their lord. As the trees and the straws are drawn into a whirlpool—as they spin round, are sucked to the deep, and again tossed aloft by the eddies, so shall races and thrones be plucked into the charm of your vortex. Awful Destroyer—but in destroying, made, against your own will, a Constructor!"

"And that date, too, is far off?"

"Far off; when it comes, think your end in this world is at hand!"

"How and what is the end? Look east, west, south, and north."

"In the north, where you never yet trod, towards the point whence your instincts have warned you, there a spectre will seize you. 'Tis Death! I see a ship—it is haunted—'tis chased—it sails on. Baffled navies sail after that ship. It enters the regions of ice. It passes a sky red with meteors. Two moons stand on high, over ice-reefs. I see the ship locked between white defiles—they are icerocks. I see the dead strew the decks—stark and livid, green mould on their limbs. All are dead, but one man—it is you! But years, though so slowly they come, have then scathed you. There is the coming of age on your brow, and the will is relaxed in the cells of the brain. Still that will, though enfeebled, exceeds all that man knew before you, through the will you live on, gnawed with famine; and nature no longer obeys you in that death-spreading region; the sky is a sky of iron, and the air has iron clamps, and the ice-rocks wedge in the ship. Hark how it cracks and groans. Ice will imbed it as amber imbeds a straw. And a man has gone forth, living yet, from the ship and its dead; and he has clambered up the spikes of an iceberg, and the two moons gaze down on his form. That man is yourself; and terror is on you—terror; and terror has swallowed your will. And I see swarming up the steep ice-rock, grey grisly things. The bears of the north have scented their quarry—they come near you and nearer, shambling and rolling their bulk. And in that day every moment shall seem to you longer than the centuries through which you have passed. And heed this—after life, moments continued make the bliss or the hell of eternity."

"Hush," said the whisper; "but the day, you assure me, is far off—very far! I go back to the almond and rose of Damascus!—sleep!"

The room swam before my eyes. I became insensible. When I recovered, I found G—— holding my hand and smiling. He said, "You who have always declared yourself proof against mesmerism have succumbed at last to my friend Richards."

"Where is Mr. Richards?"

"Gone, when you passed into a trance—saying quietly to me. 'Your friend will not wake for an hour.'"

I asked, as collectedly as I could, where Mr. Richards lodged.

"At the Trafalgar Hotel."

"Give me your arm," said I to G——; "let us call on him; I have something to say."

When we arrived at the hotel, we were told that Mr. Richards had returned twenty minutes before, paid his bill, left directions with his servant (a Greek) to pack his effects and proceed to Malta by the steamer that should leave Southampton the next day. Mr. Richards had merely said of his own movements that he had visits to pay in the neighbourhood of London, and it was uncertain whether he should be able to reach Southampton in time for that steamer; if not, he should follow in the next one.

The waiter asked me my name. On my informing him, he gave me a note that Mr. Richards had left for me, in case I called.

The note was as follows: "I wished you to utter what was in your mind. You obeyed. I have therefore established power over you. For three months from this day you can communicate to no living man what has passed between us—you cannot even show this note to the friend by your side. During three months, silence complete as to me and mine. Do you doubt my power to lay on you this command?—try to disobey me. At the end of the third month, the spell is raised. For the rest I spare you. I shall visit your grave a year and a day after it has received you."

So ends this strange story, which I ask no one to believe. I write it down exactly three months after I received the above note. I could not write it before, nor could I show to G——, in spite of his urgent request, the note which I read under the gas-lamp by his side.

THE GREAT RETURN

ARTHUR MACHEN

Chapter I

The Rumor of the Marvelous

There are strange things lost and forgotten in obscure corners of the newspaper. I often think that the most extraordinary item of intelligence that I have read in print appeared a few years ago in the London Press. It came from a well known and most respected news agency; I imagine it was in all the papers. It was astounding.

The circumstances necessary—not to the understanding of this paragraph, for that is out of the question—but, we will say, to the understanding of the events which made it possible, are these. We had invaded Thibet, and there had been trouble in the hierarchy of that country, and a personage known as the Tashai Lama had taken refuge with us in India. He went on pilgrimage from one Buddhist shrine to another, and came at last to a holy mountain of Buddhism, the name of which I have forgotten. And thus the morning paper:

> *His Holiness the Tashai Lama then ascended the Mountain and was transfigured.—Reuter.*

That was all. And from that day to this I have never heard a word of explanation or comment on this amazing statement.

***

There was no more, it seemed, to be said. "Reuter," apparently, thought he had made his simple statement of the facts of the case, had thereby done his duty, and so it all ended. Nobody, so far as I know, ever wrote to any paper asking what Reuter meant by it, or what the Tashai Lama meant by it. I suppose the fact was that nobody cared two-pence about the matter; and so this strange event—if there were any such event—was exhibited to us for a moment, and the lantern show revolved to other spectacles.

This is an extreme instance of the manner in which the marvellous is flashed out to us and then withdrawn behind its black veils and concealments; but I have known of other cases. Now and again, at intervals of a few years, there appear in the newspapers strange stories of the strange doings of what are technically called *poltergeists*. Some house, often a lonely farm, is suddenly subjected to an infernal bombardment. Great stones crash through the windows, thunder down the chimneys, impelled by no visible hand. The plates and cups and saucers are whirled from the dresser into the middle of the kitchen, no one can say how or by what agency. Upstairs the big bedstead and an old chest or two are heard bounding on the floor as if in a mad ballet. Now and then such doings as these excite a whole neighbourhood; sometimes a London paper sends a man down to make an investigation. He writes half a column of description on the Monday, a couple of paragraphs on the Tuesday, and then returns to town. Nothing has been explained, the matter vanishes away; and nobody cares. The tale trickles for a day or two through the Press, and then instantly disappears, like an Australian stream, into the bowels of darkness. It is possible, I suppose, that this singular incuriousness as to marvellous events and reports is not wholly unaccountable. It may be that the events in question are, as it were, psychic accidents and misadventures. They are not meant to happen, or, rather, to be manifested. They belong to the world on the other side of the dark curtain; and it is only by some queer mischance that a corner of that curtain is twitched aside for an instant. Then—for an instant—we see; but the personages whom Mr. Kipling calls the Lords of Life and Death take care that we do not see too much. Our business is with things higher and things lower, with things different, anyhow; and on the whole we are not suffered to distract ourselves with that which does not really concern us. The Transfiguration of the Lama and the tricks of the *poltergeist* are evidently no affairs of ours; we raise an uninterested eyebrow and pass on—to poetry or to statistics.

***

Be it noted; I am not professing any fervent personal belief in the reports to which I have alluded. For all I know, the Lama, in spite of Reuter, was not transfigured, and the *poltergeist*, in spite of the late Mr. Andrew Lang, may in reality be only mischievous Polly, the servant girl at the farm. And to go farther: I do not know that I should be justified in putting either of these cases of the marvellous in line with a chance paragraph that caught my eye last summer; for this had not, on the face of it at all events, anything wildly out of the common. Indeed, I dare say that I should not have read it, should not have seen it, if it had not contained the name of a place which I had once visited, which had then moved me in an odd manner that I could not understand. Indeed, I am sure that this particular paragraph deserves to stand alone, for even if the *poltergeist* be a real *poltergeist*, it merely reveals the psychic whimsicality of some region that is not our region. There were better things and more relevant things behind the few lines dealing with Llantrisant, the little town by the sea in Arfonshire.

Not on the surface, I must say, for the cutting I have preserved it—reads as follows:—

LLANTRISANT.—The season promises very favourably: temperature of the sea yesterday at noon, 65 deg. Remarkable occurrences are supposed to have taken place during the recent Revival. The lights have not been observed lately. "The Crown." "The Fisherman's Rest."

The style was odd certainly; knowing a little of newspapers. I could see that the figure called, I think, *tmesis*, or cutting, had been generously employed; the exuberances of the local correspondent had been pruned by a Fleet Street expert. And these poor men are often hurried; but what did those "lights" mean? What strange matters had the vehement blue pencil blotted out and brought to naught?

That was my first thought, and then, thinking still of Llantrisant and how I had first discovered it and found it strange, I read the paragraph again, and was saddened almost to see, as I thought, the obvious explanation. I had forgotten for the moment that it was war-time, that scares and rumours and terrors about traitorous signals and flashing lights were current everywhere by land and sea; someone, no doubt, had been watching innocent farmhouse windows and thoughtless fanlights of lodging houses; these were the "lights" that had not been observed lately.

I found out afterwards that the Llantrisant correspondent had no such treasonous lights in his mind, but something very different. Still; what do we know? He may have been mistaken, "the great rose of fire" that came over the deep may have been the port light of a coasting-ship. Did it shine at last from the old chapel on the headland? Possibly; or possibly it was the doctor's lamp at Sarnau, some miles away. I have had wonderful opportunities lately of analysing the marvels of lying, conscious and unconscious; and indeed almost incredible feats in this way can be performed. If I incline to the less likely explanation of the "lights" at Llantrisant, it is merely because this explanation seems to me to be altogether congruous with the "remarkable occurrences" of the newspaper paragraph.

After all, if rumour and gossip and hearsay are crazy things to be utterly neglected and laid aside: on the other hand, evidence is evidence, and when a couple of reputable surgeons assert, as they do assert in the case of Olwen Phillips, Croeswen, Llantrisant, that there has been a "kind of resurrection of the body," it is merely foolish to say that these things don't happen. The girl was a mass of tuberculosis, she was within a few hours of death; she is now full of life. And so, I do not believe that the rose of fire was merely a ship's light, magnified and transformed by dreaming Welsh sailors.

***

But now I am going forward too fast. I have not dated the paragraph, so I cannot give the exact day of its appearance, but I think it was somewhere between the second and third week of June. I cut it out partly because it was about Llantrisant, partly because of the "remarkable occurrences." I have an appetite for these matters, though I also have this misfortune, that I require evidence before I am ready to credit them, and I have a sort of lingering hope that some day I shall be able to elaborate some scheme or theory of such things.

But in the meantime, as a temporary measure, I hold what I call the doctrine of the jig-saw puzzle. That is: this remarkable occurrence, and that, and the other may be, and usually are, of no significance. Coincidence and chance and unsearchable causes will now and again make clouds that are undeniable fiery dragons, and potatoes that resemble Eminent Statesmen exactly and minutely in every feature, and rocks that are like eagles and lions. All this is nothing; it is when you get your set of odd shapes and find that they fit into one another, and at last that they are but parts of a large design; it is then that research grows interesting and indeed amazing, it is then that one queer form confirms the other, that the whole plan displayed justifies, corroborates, explains each separate piece.

So, it was within a week or ten days after I had read the paragraph about Llantrisant and had cut it out that I got a letter from a friend who was taking an early holiday in those regions.

"You will be interested," he wrote, "to hear that they have taken to ritualistic practices at Llantrisant. I went into the church the other day, and instead of smelling like a damp vault as usual, it was positively reeking with incense."

I knew better than that. The old parson was a firm Evangelical; he would rather have burnt sulphur in his church than incense any day. So I could not make out this report at all; and went down to Arfon a few weeks later determined to investigate this and any other remarkable occurrence at Llantrisant.

Chapter II

Odors of Paradise

I went down to Arfon in the very heat and bloom and fragrance of the wonderful summer that they were enjoying there. In London there was no such weather; it rather seemed as if the horror and fury of the war had mounted to the very skies and were there reigning. In the mornings the sun burnt down upon the city with a heat that scorched and consumed; but then clouds heavy and horrible would roll together from all quarters of the heavens, and early in the afternoon the air would darken, and a storm of thunder and lightning, and furious, hissing rain would fall upon the streets. Indeed, the torment of the world was in the London weather. The city wore a terrible vesture; within our hearts was dread; without we were clothed in black clouds and angry fire.

It is certain that I cannot show in any words the utter peace of that Welsh coast to which I came; one sees, I think, in such a change a figure of the passage from the disquiets and the fears of earth to the peace of paradise. A land that seemed to be in a holy, happy dream, a sea that changed all the while from olivine to emerald, from emerald to sapphire, from sapphire to amethyst, that washed in white foam at the bases of the firm, grey rocks, and about the huge crimson bastions that hid the western bays and inlets of the waters; to this land I came, and to hollows that were purple and odorous with wild thyme, wonderful with many tiny, exquisite flowers. There was benediction in centaury, pardon in eye-bright, joy in lady's slipper; and so the weary eyes were refreshed, looking now at the little flowers and the happy bees about them, now on the magic mirror of the deep, changing from marvel to marvel with the passing of the great white clouds, with the brightening of the sun. And the ears, torn with jangle and racket and idle, empty noise, were soothed and comforted by the ineffable, unutterable, unceasing murmur, as the tides swam to and fro, uttering mighty, hollow voices in the caverns of the rocks.

***

For three or four days I rested in the sun and smelt the savour of the blossoms and of the salt water, and then, refreshed, I remembered that there was something queer about Llantrisant that I might as well investigate. It was no great thing that I thought to find, for, it will be remembered, I had ruled out the apparent oddity of the reporter's or commissioner's?—reference to lights, on the ground that he must have been referring to some local panic about signalling to the enemy; who had certainly torpedoed a ship or two off Lundy in the Bristol Channel. All that I had to go upon was the reference to the "remarkable occurrences" at some revival, and then that letter of Jackson's, which spoke of Llantrisant church as "reeking" with incense, a wholly incredible and impossible state of things. Why, old Mr. Evans, the rector, looked upon coloured stoles as the very robe of Satan and his angels, as things dear to the heart of the Pope of Rome. But as to incense! As I have already familiarly observed, I knew better.

But as a hard matter of fact, this may be worth noting: when I went over to Llantrisant on Monday, August 9th, I visited the church, and it was still fragrant and exquisite with the odour of rare gums that had fumed there.

***

Now I happened to have a slight acquaintance with the rector. He was a most courteous and delightful old man, and on my last visit he had come across me in the churchyard, as I was admiring the very fine Celtic cross that stands there. Besides the beauty of the interlaced ornament there is an inscription in Ogham on one of the edges, concerning which the learned dispute; it is altogether one of the more famous crosses of Celtdom. Mr. Evans, I say, seeing me looking at the cross, came up and began to give me, the stranger, a resume—somewhat of a shaky and uncertain resume, I found afterwards—of the various debates and questions that had arisen as to the exact meaning of the inscription, and I was amused to detect an evident but underlying belief of his own: that the supposed Ogham characters were, in fact, due to boys' mischief and weather and the passing of the ages. But then I happened to put a question as to the sort of stone of which the cross was made, and the rector brightened amazingly. He began to talk geology, and, I think, demonstrated that the cross or the material for it must have been brought to Llantrisant from the south-west coast of Ireland. This struck me as interesting, because it was curious evidence of the migrations of the

Celtic saints, whom the rector, I was delighted to find, looked upon as good Protestants, though shaky on the subject of crosses; and so, with concessions on my part, we got on very well. Thus, with all this to the good, I was emboldened to call upon him.

I found him altered. Not that he was aged; indeed, he was rather made young, with a singular brightening upon his face, and something of joy upon it that I had not seen before, that I have seen on very few faces of men. We talked of the war, of course, since that is not to be avoided; of the farming prospects of the county; of general things, till I ventured to remark that I had been in the church, and had been surprised, to find it perfumed with incense.

"You have made some alterations in the service since I was here last? You use incense now?"

The old man looked at me strangely, and hesitated.

"No," he said, "there has been no change. I use no incense in the church. I should not venture to do so."

"But," I was beginning, "the whole church is as if High Mass had just been sung there, and—"

He cut me short, and there was a certain grave solemnity in his manner that struck me almost with awe.

"I know you are a railer," he said, and the phrase coming from this mild old gentleman astonished, me unutterably. "You are a railer and a bitter railer; I have read articles that you have written, and I know your contempt and your hatred for those you call Protestants in your derision; though your grandfather, the vicar of Caerleon-on-Usk, called himself Protestant and was proud of it, and your great-grand-uncle Hezekiah, *ffeiriad coch yr Castletown*—the Red Priest of Castletown—was a great man with the Methodists in his day, and the people flocked by their thousands when he administered the Sacrament. I was born and brought up in Glamorganshire, and old men have wept as they told me of the weeping and contrition that there was when the Red Priest broke the Bread and raised the Cup. But you are a railer, and see nothing but the outside and the show. You are not worthy of this mystery that has been done here."

I went out from his presence rebuked indeed, and justly rebuked; but rather amazed. It is curiously true that the Welsh are still one people, one family almost, in a manner that the English cannot understand, but I had never thought that this old clergyman would have known anything of my ancestry or their doings. And as for my articles and such-like, I knew that the country clergy sometimes read, but I had fancied my pronouncements sufficiently obscure, even in London, much more in Arfon.

But so it happened, and so I had no explanation from the rector of Llantrisant of the strange circumstance, that his church was full of incense and odours of paradise.

***

I went up and down the ways of Llantrisant wondering, and came to the harbour, which is a little place, with little quays where some small coasting trade still lingers. A brigantine was at anchor here, and very lazily in the sunshine they were loading it with anthracite; for it is one of the oddities of Llantrisant that there is a small colliery in the heart of the wood on the hillside. I crossed a causeway which parts the outer harbour from the inner harbour, and settled down on a rocky beach hidden under a leafy hill. The tide was going out, and some children were playing on the wet sand, while two ladies—their mothers, I suppose—talked together as they sat comfortably on their rugs at a little distance from me.

At first they talked of the war, and I made myself deaf, for of that talk one gets enough, and more than enough, in London. Then there was a period of silence, and the conversation had passed to quite a different topic when I caught the thread of it again. I was sitting on the further side of a big rock, and I do not think that the two ladies had noticed my approach. However, though they spoke of strange things, they spoke of nothing which made it necessary for me to announce my presence.

"And, after all," one of them was saying, "what is it all about? I can't make out what is come to the people."

This speaker was a Welshwoman; I recognised the clear, over-emphasised consonants, and a faint suggestion of an accent. Her friend came from the Midlands, and it turned out that they had only known each other for a few days. Theirs was a friendship of the beach and of bathing; such friendships are common, at small seaside places.

"There is certainly something odd about the people here. I have never been to Llantrisant before, you know; indeed, this is the first time we've been in Wales for our holidays, and knowing nothing about the ways of the people and not being accustomed to hear Welsh spoken, I thought, perhaps, it must be my imagination. But you think there really is something a little queer?"

"I can tell you this: that I have been in two minds whether I should not write to my husband and ask him to take me and the children away. You know where I am at Mrs. Morgan's, and the Morgans' sitting-room is just the other side of the passage, and sometimes they leave the door open, so that I can hear what they say quite plainly. And you see I understand the Welsh, though they don't know it. And I hear them saying the most alarming things!"

"What sort of things?"

"Well, indeed, it sounds like some kind of a religious service, but it's not Church of England, I know that. Old Morgan begins it, and the wife and children answer. Something like; 'Blessed be God for the messengers of Paradise.' 'Blessed be His Name for Paradise in the meat and in the drink.' 'Thanksgiving for the old offering.' 'Thanksgiving for the appearance of the old altar,' 'Praise for the joy of the ancient garden.' 'Praise for the return of those that have been long absent.' And all that sort of thing. It is nothing but madness."

"Depend upon it," said the lady from the Midlands, "there's no real harm in it. They're Dissenters; some new sect, I dare say. You know some Dissenters are very queer in their ways."

"All that is like no Dissenters that I have ever known in all my life whatever," replied the Welsh lady somewhat vehemently, with a very distinct intonation of the land. "And have you heard them speak of the bright light that shone at midnight from the church?"

Chapter III

A Secret in a Secret Place

Now here was I altogether at a loss and quite bewildered. The children broke into the conversation of the two ladies and cut it all short, just as the midnight lights from the church came on the field, and when the little girls and boys went back again to the sands whooping, the tide of talk had turned, and Mrs. Harland and Mrs. Williams were quite safe and at home with Janey's measles, and a wonderful treatment for infantile earache, as exemplified in the case of Trevor. There was no more to be got out of them, evidently, so I left the beach, crossed the harbour causeway, and drank beer at the "Fishermen's Rest" till it was time to climb up two miles of deep lane and catch the train for Penvro, where I was staying. And I went up the lane, as I say, in a kind of amazement; and not so much, I think, because of evidences and hints of things strange to the senses, such as the savour of incense where no incense had smoked for three hundred and fifty years and more, or the story of bright light shining from the dark, closed church at dead of night, as because of that sentence of thanksgiving "for paradise in meat and in drink."

For the sun went down and the evening fell as I climbed the long hill through the deep woods and the high meadows, and the scent of all the green things rose from the earth and from the heart of the wood, and at a turn of the lane far below was the misty glimmer of the still sea, and from far below its deep murmur sounded as it washed on the little hidden, enclosed bay where Llantrisant stands. And I thought, if there be paradise in meat and in drink, so much the more is there paradise in the scent of the green leaves at evening and in the appearance of the sea and in the redness of the sky; and there came to me a certain vision of a real world about us all the while, of a language that was only secret because we would not take the trouble to listen to it and discern it.

It was almost dark when I got to the station, and here were the few feeble oil lamps lit, glimmering in that lonely land, where the way is long from farm to farm. The train came on its way, and I got into it; and just as we moved from the station I noticed a group under one of those dim lamps. A woman and her child had got out, and they were being welcomed by a man who had been waiting for them. I had not noticed his face as I stood on the platform, but now I saw it as he pointed down the hill towards Llantrisant, and I think I was almost frightened.

He was a young man, a farmer's son, I would say, dressed in rough brown clothes, and as different from old Mr. Evans, the rector, as one man might be from another. But on his face, as I saw it in the lamplight, there was the like brightening that I had seen on the face of the rector. It was an illuminated face, glowing with an ineffable joy, and I thought it rather gave light to the platform lamp than received light from it. The woman and her child, I inferred, were strangers to the place, and had come to pay a visit to the young man's family. They had looked about them in bewilderment, half alarmed, before they saw him; and then his face was radiant in their sight, and it was easy to see that all their troubles were ended and over. A wayside station and a darkening country, and it was as if they were welcomed by shining, immortal gladness—even into paradise.

***

But though there seemed in a sense light all about my ways, I was myself still quite bewildered. I could see, indeed, that something strange had happened or was happening in the little town hidden under the hill, but there was so far no clue to the mystery, or rather, the clue had been offered to me, and I had not taken it, I had not even known that it was there; since we do not so much as see what we have determined, without judging, to be incredible, even though it be held up before our eyes. The dialogue that the Welsh Mrs. Williams had reported to her English friend might have set me on the right way; but the right way was outside all my limits of possibility, outside the circle of my thought. The palæontologist might see monstrous, significant marks in the slime of a river bank, but he would never draw the conclusions that his own peculiar science would seem to suggest to him; he would choose any explanation rather than the obvious, since the obvious would also be the outrageous—according to our established habit of thought, which we deem final.

***

The next day I took all these strange things with me for consideration to a certain place that I knew of not far from Penvro. I was now in the early stages of the jig-saw process, or rather I had only a few pieces before me, and—to continue the figure my difficulty was this: that though the markings on each piece seemed to have design and significance, yet I could not make the wildest guess as to the nature of the whole picture, of which these were the parts. I had clearly seen that there was a great secret; I had seen that on the face of the young farmer on the platform of Llantrisant station; and in my mind there was all the while the picture of him going down the dark, steep, winding lane that led to the town and the sea, going down through the heart of the wood, with light about him.

But there was bewilderment in the thought of this, and in the endeavour to match it with the perfumed church and the scraps of talk that I had heard and the rumour of midnight brightness; and though Penvro is by no means populous, I thought I would go to a certain solitary place called the Old Camp Head, which looks towards Cornwall and to the great deeps that roll beyond Cornwall to the far ends of the world; a place where fragments of dreams—they seemed such then—might, perhaps, be gathered into the clearness of vision.

It was some years since I had been to the Head, and I had gone on that last time and on a former visit by the cliffs, a rough and difficult path. Now I chose a landward way, which the county map seemed to justify, though doubtfully, as regarded the last part of the journey. So I went inland and climbed the hot summer by-roads, till I came at last to a lane which gradually turned turfy and grass-grown, and then on high ground, ceased to be. It left me at a gate in a hedge of old thorns; and across the field beyond there seemed to be some faint indications of a track. One would judge that sometimes men did pass by that way, but not often.

It was high ground but not within sight of the sea. But the breath of the sea blew about the hedge of thorns, and came with a keen savour to the nostrils. The ground sloped gently from the gate and then rose again to a ridge, where a white farmhouse stood all alone. I passed by this farmhouse, threading an uncertain way, followed a hedgerow doubtfully; and saw suddenly before me the Old Camp, and beyond it the sapphire plain of waters and the mist where sea and sky met. Steep from my feet the hill fell away, a land of gorse-blossom, red-gold and mellow, of glorious purple heather. It fell into a hollow that went down, shining with rich green bracken, to the glimmering sea; and before me and beyond the hollow rose a height of turf, bastioned at the summit with the awful, age-old walls of the Old Camp; green, rounded circumvallations, wall within wall, tremendous, with their myriad years upon them.

***

Within these smoothed, green mounds, looking across the shining and changing of the waters in the happy sunlight, I took out the bread and cheese and beer that I had carried in a bag, and ate and drank, and lit my pipe, and set myself to think over the enigmas of Llantrisant. And I had scarcely done so when, a good deal to my annoyance, a man came climbing up over the green ridges, and took up his stand close by, and stared out to sea. He nodded to me, and began with "Fine weather for the harvest" in the approved manner, and so sat down and engaged me in a net of talk. He was of Wales, it seemed, but from a different part of the country, and was staying for a few days with relations—at the white farmhouse which I had passed on my way. His tale of nothing flowed on to his pleasure and my pain, till he fell suddenly on Llantrisant and its doings. I listened then with wonder, and here is his tale condensed. Though it must be clearly understood that the man's evidence was only second-hand; he had heard it from his cousin, the farmer.

So, to be brief, it appeared that there had been a long feud at Llantrisant between a local solicitor, Lewis Prothero (we will say), and a farmer named James. There had been a quarrel about some trifle, which had grown more and more bitter as the two parties forgot the merits of the original dispute, and by some means or other, which I could not well understand, the lawyer had got the small freeholder "under his thumb." James, I think, had given a bill of sale in a bad season, and Prothero had bought it up; and the end was that the farmer was turned out of the old house, and was lodging in a cottage. People said he would have to take a place on his own farm as a labourer; he went about in dreadful misery, piteous to see. It was thought by some that he might very well murder the lawyer, if he met him.

They did meet, in the middle of the market-place at Llantrisant one Saturday in June. The farmer was a little black man, and he gave a shout of rage, and the people were rushing at him to keep him off Prothero.

"And then," said my informant, "I will tell you what happened. This lawyer, as they tell me, he is a great big brawny fellow, with a big jaw and a wide mouth, and a red face and red whiskers. And there he was in his black coat and his high hard hat, and all his money at his back, as you may say. And, indeed, he did fall down on his knees in the dust there in the street in front of Philip James, and every one could see that terror was upon him. And he did beg Philip James's pardon, and beg of him to have mercy, and he did implore him by God and man and the saints of paradise. And my cousin, John Jenkins, Penmawr, he do tell me that the tears were falling from Lewis Prothero's eyes like the rain. And he put his hand into his pocket and drew out the deed of Pantyreos, Philip James's old farm that was, and did give him the farm back and a hundred pounds for the stock that was on it, and two hundred pounds, all in notes of the bank, for amendment and consolation.

"And then, from what they do tell me, all the people did go mad, crying and weeping and calling out all manner of things at the top of their voices. And at last nothing would do but they must all go up to the churchyard, and there Philip James and Lewis Prothero they swear friendship to one another for a long age before the old cross, and everyone sings praises. And my cousin he do declare to me that there were men standing in that crowd that he did never see before in Llantrisant in all his life, and his heart was shaken within him as if it had been in a whirl-wind."

I had listened to all this in silence. I said then:

"What does your cousin mean by that? Men that he had never seen in Llantrisant? What men?"

"The people," he said very slowly, "call them the Fishermen."

And suddenly there came into my mind the "Rich Fisherman" who in the old legend guards the holy mystery of the Graal.

Chapter IV

The Ringing of the Bell

So far I have not told the story of the things of Llantrisant, but rather the story of how I stumbled upon them and among them, perplexed and wholly astray, seeking, but yet not knowing at all what I sought; bewildered now and again by circumstances which seemed to me wholly inexplicable; devoid, not so much of the key to the enigma, but of the key to the nature of the enigma. You cannot begin to solve a puzzle till you know what the puzzle is about. "Yards divided by minutes," said the mathematical master to me long ago, "will give neither pigs, sheep, nor oxen." He was right; though his manner on this and on all other occasions was highly offensive. This is enough of the personal process, as I may call it; and here follows the story of what happened at Llantrisant last summer, the story as I pieced it together at last.

It all began, it appears, on a hot day, early in last June; so far as I can make out, on the first Saturday in the month. There was a deaf old woman, a Mrs. Parry, who lived by herself in a lonely cottage a mile or so from the town. She came into the market-place early on the Saturday morning in a state of some excitement, and as soon as she had taken up her usual place on the pavement by the churchyard, with her ducks and eggs and a few very early potatoes, she began to tell her neighbours about her having heard the sound of a great bell. The good women on each side smiled at one another behind Mrs. Parry's back, for one had to bawl into her ear before she could make out what one meant; and Mrs. Williams, Penycoed, bent over and yelled: "What bell should that be, Mrs. Parry? There's no church near you up at Penrhiw. Do you hear what nonsense she talks?" said Mrs. Williams in a low voice to Mrs. Morgan. "As if she could hear any bell, whatever."

"What makes you talk nonsense your self?" said Mrs. Parry, to the amazement of the two women. "I can hear a bell as well as you, Mrs. Williams, and as well as your whispers either."

And there is the fact, which is not to be disputed; though the deductions from it may be open to endless disputations; this old woman who had been all but stone deaf for twenty years—the defect had always been in her family—could suddenly hear on this June morning as well as anybody else. And her two old friends stared at her, and it was some time before they had appeased her indignation, and induced her to talk about the bell.

It had happened in the early morning, which was very misty. She had been gathering sage in her garden, high on a round hill looking over the sea. And there came in her ears a sort of throbbing and singing and trembling, "as if there were music coming out of the earth," and then something seemed to break in her head, and all the birds began to sing and make melody together, and the leaves of the poplars round the garden fluttered in the breeze that rose from the sea, and the cock crowed far off at Twyn, and the dog barked down in Kemeys Valley. But above all these sounds, unheard for so many years, there thrilled the deep and chanting note of the bell, "like a bell and a man's voice singing at once."

They stared again at her and at one another. "Where did it sound from?" asked one. "It came sailing across the sea," answered Mrs. Parry quite composedly, "and I did hear it coming nearer and nearer to the land."

"Well, indeed," said Mrs. Morgan, "it was a ship's bell then, though I can't make out why they would be ringing like that."

"It was not ringing on any ship, Mrs. Morgan," said Mrs. Parry.

"Then where do you think it was ringing?"

"Ym Mharadwys," replied Mrs. Parry. Now that means "in Paradise," and the two others changed the conversation quickly.

They thought that Mrs. Parry had got back her hearing suddenly—such things did happen now and then—and that the shock had made her "a bit queer." And this explanation would no doubt have stood its ground, if it had not been for other experiences. Indeed, the local doctor who had treated Mrs. Parry for a dozen years, not for her deafness, which he took to be hopeless and beyond cure, but for a tiresome and recurrent winter cough, sent an account of the case to a colleague at Bristol, suppressing, naturally enough, the reference to Paradise. The Bristol physician gave it as his opinion that the symptoms were absolutely what might have been expected. "You have here, in all probability," he wrote, "the sudden breaking down of an old obstruction in the aural passage, and I should quite expect this process to be accompanied by tinnitus of a pronounced and even violent character."

***

But for the other experiences? As the morning wore on and drew to noon, high market, and to the utmost brightness of that summer day, all the stalls and the streets were full of rumours and of awed faces. Now from one lonely farm, now from another, men and women came and told the story of how they had listened in the early morning with thrilling hearts to the thrilling music of a bell that was like no bell ever heard before. And it seemed that many people in the town had been roused, they knew not how, from sleep; waking up, as one of them said, as if bells were ringing and the organ playing, and a choir of sweet voices singing all together: "There were such melodies and songs that my heart was full of joy."

And a little past noon some fishermen who had been out all night returned, and brought a wonderful story into the town of what they had heard in the mist and one of them said he had seen something go by at a little distance from his boat. "It was all golden and bright," he said, "and there was glory about it." Another fisherman declared "there was a song upon the water that was like heaven."

And here I would say in parenthesis that on returning to town I sought out a very old friend of mine, a man who has devoted a lifetime to strange and esoteric studies. I thought that I had a tale that would interest him profoundly, but I found that he heard me with a good deal of indifference. And at this very point of the sailors' stories I remember saying: "Now what do you make of that? Don't you think it's extremely curious?" He replied: "I hardly think so. Possibly the sailors were lying; possibly it happened as they say. Well; that sort of thing has always been happening." I give my friend's opinion; I make no comment on it.

Let it be noted that there was something remarkable as to the manner in which the sound of the bell was heard—or supposed to be heard. There are, no doubt, mysteries in sound as in all else; indeed, I am informed that during one of the horrible outrages that have been perpetrated on London during this autumn there was an instance of a great block of workmen's dwellings in which the only person who heard the crash of a particular bomb falling was an old deaf woman, who had been fast asleep till the moment of the explosion. This is strange enough of a sound that was entirely in the natural (and horrible) order; and so it was at Llantrisant, where the sound was either a collective auditory hallucination or a manifestation of what is conveniently, if inaccurately, called the supernatural order.

For the thrill of the bell did not reach to all ears—or hearts. Deaf Mrs. Parry heard it in her lonely cottage garden, high above the misty sea; but then, in a farm on the other or western side of Llantrisant, a little child, scarcely three years old, was the only one out of a household of ten people who heard anything. He called out in stammering baby Welsh something that sounded like "Clychau fawr, clychau fawr"—the great bells, the great bells—and his mother wondered what he was talking about. Of the crews of half a dozen trawlers that were swinging from side to side in the mist, not more than four men had any tale to tell. And so it was that for an hour or two the man who had heard nothing suspected his neighbour who had heard marvels of lying; and it was some time before the mass of evidence coming from all manner of diverse and remote quarters convinced the people that there was a true story here. A might suspect B, his neighbour, of making up a tale; but when C, from some place on the hills five miles away, and D, the fisherman on the waters, each had a like report, then it was clear that something had happened.

***

And even then, as they told me, the signs to be seen upon the people were stranger than the tales told by them and among them. It has struck me that many people in reading some of the phrases that I have reported, will dismiss them with laughter as very poor and fantastic inventions; fishermen, they will say, do not speak of "a song like heaven" or of "a glory about it." And I dare say this would be a just enough criticism if I were reporting English fishermen; but, odd though it may be, Wales has not yet lost the last shreds of the grand manner. And let it be remembered also that in most cases such phrases are translated from another language, that is, from the Welsh.

So, they come trailing, let us say, fragments of the cloud of glory in their common speech; and so, on this Saturday, they began to display, uneasily enough in many cases, their consciousness that the things that were reported were of their ancient right and former custom. The comparison is not quite fair; but conceive Hardy's old Durbeyfield suddenly waking from long slumber to find himself in a noble thirteenth-century hall, waited on by kneeling pages, smiled on by sweet ladies in silken côtehardies.

So by evening time there had come to the old people the recollection of stories that their fathers had told them as they sat round the hearth of winter nights, fifty, sixty, seventy years; ago; stories of the wonderful bell of Teilo Sant, that had sailed across the glassy seas from Syon, that was called a portion of Paradise, "and the sound of its ringing was like the perpetual choir of the angels."

Such things were remembered by the old and told to the young that evening, in the streets of the town and in the deep lanes that climbed far hills. The sun went down to the mountain red with fire like a burnt offering, the sky turned violet, the sea was purple, as one told another of the wonder that had returned to the land after long ages.

Chapter V

The Rose of Fire

It was during the next nine days, counting from that Saturday early in June the first Saturday in June, as I believe—that Llantrisant and all the regions about became possessed either by an extraordinary set of hallucinations or by a visitation of great marvels.

This is not the place to strike the balance between the two possibilities. The evidence is, no doubt, readily available; the matter is open to systematic investigation.

But this may be said: The ordinary man, in the ordinary passages of his life, accepts in the main the evidence of his senses, and is entirely right in doing so. He says that he sees a cow, that he sees a stone wall, and that the cow and the stone wall are "there."

This is very well for all the practical purposes of life, but I believe that the metaphysicians are by no means so easily satisfied as to the reality of the stone wall and the cow. Perhaps they might allow that both objects are "there" in the sense that one's reflection is in a glass; there is an actuality, but is there a reality external to oneself? In any event, it is solidly agreed that, supposing a real existence, this much is certain—it is not in the least like our conception of it. The ant and the microscope will quickly convince us that we do not see things as they really are, even supposing that we see them at all. If we could "see" the real cow she would appear utterly incredible, as incredible as the things I am to relate.

Now, there is nothing that I know much more unconvincing than the stories of the red light on the sea. Several sailors, men on small coasting ships, who were working up or down the Channel on that Saturday night, spoke of "seeing" the red light, and it must be said that there is a very tolerable agreement in their tales. All make the time as between midnight of the Saturday and one o'clock on the Sunday morning. Two of those sailormen are precise as to the time of the apparition; they fix it by elaborate calculations of their own as occurring at 12:20 a.m. And the story?

A red light, a burning spark seen far away in the darkness, taken at the first moment of seeing for a signal, and probably an enemy signal. Then it approached at a tremendous speed, and one man said he took it to be the port light of some new kind of navy motor-boat which was developing a rate hitherto unheard of, a hundred or a hundred and fifty knots an hour. And then, in the third instant of the sight, it was clear that this was no earthly speed. At first a red spark in the farthest distance; then a rushing lamp; and then, as if in an incredible point of time, it swelled into a vast rose of fire that filled all the sea and all the sky and hid the stars and possessed the land. "I thought the end of the world had come," one of the sailors said.

And then, an instant more, and it was gone from them, and four of them say that there was a red spark on Chapel Head, where the old grey chapel of St. Teilo stands, high above the water, in a cleft of the limestone rocks.

And thus the sailors; and thus their tales are incredible; but they are not incredible. I believe that men of the highest eminence in physical science have testified to the occurrence of phenomena every whit as marvellous, to things as absolutely opposed to all natural order, as we conceive it; and it may be said that nobody minds them. "That sort of thing has always been happening," as my friend remarked to me. But the men, whether or no the fire had ever been without them, there was no doubt that it was now within them, for it burned in their eyes. They were purged as if they had passed through the Furnace of the Sages, governed with Wisdom that the alchemists know. They spoke without much difficulty of what they had seen, or had seemed to see, with their eyes, but hardly at all of what their hearts had known when for a moment the glory of the fiery rose had been about them.

For some weeks afterwards they were still, as it were, amazed; almost, I would say, incredulous. If there had been nothing more than the splendid and fiery appearance, showing and vanishing, I do believe that they themselves would have discredited their own senses and denied the truth of their own tales. And one does not dare to say whether they would not have been right. Men like Sir William Crookes and Sir Oliver Lodge are certainly to be heard with respect, and they bear witness to all manner of apparent eversions of laws which we, or most of us, consider far more deeply founded than the ancient hills. They may be justified; but in our hearts we doubt. We cannot wholly believe in inner sincerity that the solid table did rise, without mechanical reason or cause, into the air, and so defy that which we name the "law of gravitation." I know what may be said on the other side; I know that there is no true question of "law" in the case; that the law of gravitation really means just this: that I have never seen a table rising without mechanical aid, or an apple, detached from the bough, soaring to the skies instead of falling to the ground. The so-called law is just the sum of common observation and nothing more; yet I say, in our hearts we do not believe that the tables rise; much less do we believe in the rose of fire that for a moment swallowed up the skies and seas and shores of the Welsh coast last June.

And the men who saw it would have invented fairy tales to account for it, I say again, if it had not been for that which was within them.

They said, all of them, and it was certain now that they spoke the truth, that in the moment of the vision, every pain and ache and malady in their bodies had passed away. One man had been vilely drunk on venomous spirit, procured at "Jobson's Hole" down by the Cardiff Docks. He was horribly ill; he had crawled up from his bunk for a little fresh air; and in an instant his horrors and his deadly nausea had left him. Another man was almost desperate with the raging hammering pain of an abscess on a tooth; he says that when the red flame came near he felt as if a dull, heavy blow had fallen on his jaw, and then the pain was quite gone; he could scarcely believe that there had been any pain there.

And they all bear witness to an extraordinary exaltation of the senses. It is indescribable, this; for they cannot describe it. They are amazed, again; they do not in the least profess to know what happened; but there is no more possibility of shaking their evidence than there is a possibility of shaking the evidence of a man who says that water is wet and fire hot.

"I felt a bit queer afterwards," said one of them, "and I steadied myself by the mast, and I can't tell how I felt as I touched it. I didn't know that touching a thing like a mast could be better than a big drink when you're thirsty, or a soft pillow when you're sleepy."

I heard other instances of this state of things, as I must vaguely call it, since I do not know what else to call it. But I suppose we can all agree that to the man in average health, the average impact of the external world on his senses is a matter of indifference. The average impact; a harsh scream, the bursting of a motor tyre, any violent assault on the aural nerves will annoy him, and he may say "damn." Then, on the other hand, the man who is not "fit" will easily be annoyed and irritated by someone pushing past him in a crowd, by the ringing of a bell, by the sharp closing of a book.

But so far as I could judge from the talk of these sailors, the average impact of the external world had become to them a fountain of pleasure. Their nerves were on edge, but an edge to receive exquisite sensuous impressions. The touch of the rough mast, for example; that was a joy far greater than is the joy of fine silk to some luxurious skins; they drank water and stared as if they had been *fins gourmets* tasting an amazing wine; the creak and whine of their ship on its slow way were as exquisite as the rhythm and song of a Bach fugue to an amateur of music.

And then, within; these rough fellows have their quarrels and strifes and variances and envyings like the rest of us; but that was all over between them that had seen the rosy light; old enemies shook hands heartily, and roared with laughter as they confessed one to another what fools they had been.

"I can't exactly say how it has happened or what has happened at all," said one, "but if you have all the world and the glory of it, how can you fight for fivepence?"

***

The church of Llantrisant is a typical example of a Welsh parish church, before the evil and horrible period of "restoration."

This lower world is a palace of lies, and of all foolish lies there is none more insane than a certain vague fable about the mediæval freemasons, a fable which somehow imposed itself upon the cold intellect of Hallam the historian. The story is, in brief, that throughout the Gothic period, at any rate, the art and craft of church building were executed by wandering guilds of "freemasons," possessed of various secrets of building and adornment, which they employed wherever they went. If this nonsense were true, the Gothic of Cologne would be as the Gothic of Colne, and the Gothic of Arles like to the Gothic of Abingdon. It is so grotesquely untrue that almost every county, let alone every country, has its distinctive style in Gothic architecture. Arfon is in the west of Wales; its churches have marks and features which distinguish them from the churches in the east of Wales.

The Llantrisant church has that primitive division between nave and chancel which only very foolish people decline to recognise as equivalent to the Oriental iconostasis and as the origin of the Western rood-screen. A solid wall divided the church into two portions; in the centre was a narrow opening with a rounded arch, through which those who sat towards the middle of the church could see the small, red-carpeted altar and the three roughly shaped lancet windows above it.

The "reading pew" was on the outer side of this wall of partition, and here the rector did his service, the choir being grouped in seats about him. On the inner side were the pews of certain privileged houses of the town and district.

On the Sunday morning the people were all in their accustomed places, not without a certain exultation in their eyes, not without a certain expectation of they knew not what. The bells stopped ringing, the rector, in his old-fashioned, ample surplice, entered the reading-desk, and gave out the hymn: "My God, and is Thy Table spread."

And, as the singing began, all the people who were in the pews within the wall came out of them and streamed through the archway into the nave. They took what places they could find up and down the church, and the rest of the congregation looked at them in amazement.

Nobody knew what had happened. Those whose seats were next to the aisle tried to peer into the chancel, to see what had happened or what was going on there. But somehow the light flamed so brightly from the windows above the altar, those being the only windows in the chancel, one small lancet in the south wall excepted, that no one could see anything at all.

"It was as if a veil of gold adorned with jewels was hanging there," one man said; and indeed there are a few odds and scraps of old painted glass left in the eastern lancets.

But there were few in the church who did not hear now and again voices speaking beyond the veil.

Chapter VI

Olwen's Dream

The well-to-do and dignified personages who left their pews in the chancel of Llantrisant Church and came hurrying into the nave could give no explanation of what they had done. They felt, they said, that they had to go, and to go quickly; they were driven out, as it were, by a secret, irresistible command. But all who were present in the church that morning were amazed, though all exulted in their hearts; for they, like the sailors who saw the rose of fire on the waters, were filled with a joy that was literally ineffable, since they could not utter it or interpret it to themselves.

And they too, like the sailors, were transmuted, or the world was transmuted for them. They experienced what the doctors call a sense of *bien être* but a *bien être* raised, to the highest power. Old men felt young again, eyes that had been growing dim now saw clearly, and saw a world that was like Paradise, the same world, it is true, but a world rectified and glowing, as if an inner flame shone in all things, and behind all things.

And the difficulty in recording this state is this, that it is so rare an experience that no set language to express it is in existence. A shadow of its raptures and ecstasies is found in the highest poetry; there are phrases in ancient books telling of the Celtic saints that dimly hint at it; some of the old Italian masters of painting had known it, for the light of it shines in their skies and about the battlements of their cities that are founded on magic hills. But these are but broken hints.

It is not poetic to go to Apothecaries' Hall for similes. But for many years I kept by me an article from the *Lancet* or the *British Medical Journal*—I forget which—in which a doctor gave an account of certain experiments he had conducted with a drug called the Mescal Button, or Anhelonium Lewinii. He said that while under the influence of the drug he had but to shut his eyes, and immediately before him there would rise incredible Gothic cathedrals, of such majesty and splendour and glory that no heart had ever conceived. They seemed to surge from the depths to the very heights of heaven, their spires swayed amongst the clouds and the stars, they were fretted with admirable imagery. And as he gazed, he would presently become aware that all the stones were living stones, that they were quickening and palpitating, and then that they were glowing jewels, say, emeralds, sapphires, rubies, opals, but of hues that the mortal eye had never seen.

That description gives, I think, some faint notion of the nature of the transmuted world into which these people by the sea had entered, a world quickened and glorified and full of pleasures. Joy and wonder were on all faces; but the deepest joy and the greatest wonder were on the face of the rector. For he had heard through the veil the Greek word for "holy," three times repeated. And he, who had once been a horrified assistant at High Mass in a foreign church, recognised the perfume of incense that filled the place from end to end.

***

It was on that Sunday night that Olwen Phillips of Croeswen dreamed her wonderful dream. She was a girl of sixteen, the daughter of small farming people, and for many months she had been doomed to certain death. Consumption, which flourishes in that damp, warm climate, had laid hold of her; not only her lungs but her whole system was a mass of tuberculosis. As is common enough, she had enjoyed many fallacious brief recoveries in the early stages of the disease, but all hope had long been over, and now for the last few weeks she had seemed to rush vehemently to death. The doctor had come on the Saturday morning, bringing with him a colleague. They had both agreed that the girl's case was in its last stages. "She cannot possibly last more than a day or two," said the local doctor to her mother. He came again on the Sunday morning and found his patient perceptibly worse, and soon afterwards she sank into a heavy sleep, and her mother thought that she would never wake from it.

The girl slept in an inner room communicating with the room occupied by her father and mother. The door between was kept open, so that Mrs. Phillips could hear her daughter if she called to her in the night. And Olwen called to her mother that night, just as the dawn was breaking. It was no faint summons from a dying bed that came to the mother's ears, but a loud cry that rang through the house, a cry of great gladness. Mrs. Phillips started up from sleep in wild amazement, wondering what could have happened. And then she saw Olwen, who had not been able to rise from her bed for many weeks past, standing in the doorway in the faint light of the growing day. The girl called to her mother: "Mam! mam! It is all over. I am quite well again."

Mrs. Phillips roused her husband, and they sat up in bed staring, not knowing on earth, as they said afterwards, what had been done with the world. Here was their poor girl wasted to a shadow, lying on her death-bed, and the life sighing from her with every breath, and her voice, when she last uttered it, so weak that one had to put one's ear to her mouth. And here in a few hours she stood up before them; and even in that faint light they could see that she was changed almost beyond knowing. And, indeed, Mrs. Phillips said that for a moment or two she fancied that the Germans must have come and killed them in their sleep, and so they were all dead together. But Olwen called, out again, so the mother lit a candle and got up and went tottering across the room, and there was Olwen all gay and plump again, smiling with shining eyes. Her mother led her into her own room, and set down the candle there, and felt her daughter's flesh, and burst into prayers and tears of wonder and delight, and thanksgivings, and held the girl again to be sure that she was not deceived. And then Olwen told her dream, though she thought it was not a dream.

She said she woke up in the deep darkness, and she knew the life was fast going from her. She could not move so much as a finger, she tried to cry out, but no sound came from her lips. She felt that in another instant the whole world would fall from her—her heart was full of agony. And as the last breath was passing her lips, she heard a very faint, sweet sound, like the tinkling of a silver bell. It came from far away, from over by Ty-newydd. She forgot her agony and listened, and even then, she says, she felt the swirl of the world as it came back to her. And the sound of the bell swelled and grew louder, and it thrilled all through her body, and the life was in it. And as the bell rang and trembled in her ears, a faint light touched the wall of her room and reddened, till the whole room was full of rosy fire. And then she saw standing before her bed three men in blood-coloured robes with shining faces. And one man held a golden bell in his hand. And the second man held up something shaped like the top of a table. It was like a great jewel, and it was of a blue colour, and there were rivers of silver and of gold running through it and flowing as quick streams flow, and there were pools in it as if violets had been poured out into water, and then it was green as the sea near the shore, and then it was the sky at night with all the stars shining, and then the sun and the moon came down and washed in it. And the third man held up high above this a cup that was like a rose on fire; "there was a great burning in it, and a dropping of blood in it, and a red cloud above it, and I saw a great secret. And I heard a voice that sang nine times, 'Glory and praise to the Conqueror of Death, to the Fountain of Life immortal.' Then the red light went from the wall, and it was all darkness, and the bell rang faint again by Capel Teilo, and then I got up and called to you."

The doctor came on the Monday morning with the death certificate in his pocket-book, and Olwen ran out to meet him. I have quoted his phrase in the first chapter of this record: "A kind of resurrection of the body." He made a most careful examination of the girl; he has stated that he found that every trace of disease had disappeared. He left on the Sunday morning a patient entering into the coma that precedes death, a body condemned utterly and ready for the grave. He met at the garden gate on the Monday morning a young woman in whom life sprang up like a fountain, in whose body life laughed and rejoiced as if it had been a river flowing from an unending well.

***

Now this is the place to ask one of those questions—there are many such—which cannot be answered. The question is as to the continuance of tradition; more especially as to the continuance of tradition among the Welsh Celts of today. On the one hand, such waves and storms have gone over them. The wave of the heathen Saxons went over them, then the wave of Latin mediævalism, then the waters of Anglicanism; last of all the flood of their queer Calvinistic Methodism, half Puritan, half pagan. It may well be asked whether any memory can possibly have survived such a series of deluges. I have said that the old people of Llantrisant had their tales of the Bell of Teilo Sant; but these were but vague and broken recollections. And then there is the name by which the "strangers" who were seen in the market-place were known; that is more precise. Students of the Graal legend know that the keeper of the Graal in the romances is the "King Fisherman," or the "Rich Fisherman"; students of Celtic hagiology know that it was prophesied before the birth of Dewi (or David) that he should be "a man of aquatic life," that another legend tells how a little child, destined to be a saint, was discovered on a stone in the river, how through his childhood a fish for his nourishment was found on that stone every day, while another saint, Ilar, if I remember, was expressly known as "The Fisherman." But has the memory of all this persisted in the church-going and chapel-going people of Wales at the present day? It is difficult to say. There is the affair of the Healing Cup of Nant Eos, or Tregaron Healing Cup, as it is also called. It is only a few years ago since it was shown to a wandering harper, who treated it lightly, and then spent a wretched night, as he said, and came back penitently and was left alone with the sacred vessel to pray over it, till "his mind was at rest." That was in 1887.

Then for my part—I only know modern Wales on the surface, I am sorry to say—I remember three or four years ago speaking to my temporary landlord of certain relics of Saint Teilo, which are supposed to be in the keeping of a particular family in that country. The landlord is a very jovial, merry fellow, and I observed with some astonishment that his ordinary, easy manner was completely altered as he said, gravely, "That will be over there, up by the mountain," pointing vaguely to the north. And he changed the subject, as a Freemason changes the subject.

There the matter lies, and its appositeness to the story of Llantrisant is this: that the dream of Olwen Phillips was, in fact, the Vision of the Holy Graal.

Chapter VII

The Mass of the Sangraal

"*Ffeiriadwyr Melcisidec! Ffeiriadwyr Melcisidec!*" shouted the old Calvinistic Methodist deacon with the grey beard. "Priesthood of Melchizedek! Priesthood of Melchizedek!"

And he went on:

"The Bell that is like *y glwys yr angel ym mharadwys*—the joy of the angels in Paradise—is returned; the Altar that is of a colour that no men can discern is returned, the Cup that came from Syon is returned, the ancient Offering is restored, the Three Saints have come back to the church of the *tri sant*, the Three Holy Fishermen are amongst us, and their net is full. *Gogoniant, gogoniant*—glory, glory!"

Then another Methodist began to recite in Welsh a verse from Wesley's hymn.

> God still respects Thy sacrifice,
> Its savour sweet doth always please;
> The Offering smokes through earth and skies,
> Diffusing life and joy and peace;
> To these Thy lower courts it comes
> And fills them with Divine perfumes.

The whole church was full, as the old books tell, of the odour of the rarest spiceries. There were lights shining within the sanctuary, through the narrow archway.

This was the beginning of the end of what befell at Llantrisant. For it was the Sunday after that night on which Olwen Phillips had been restored from death to life. There was not a single chapel of the Dissenters open in the town that day. The Methodists with their minister and their deacons and all the Nonconformists had returned on this Sunday morning to "the old hive." One would have said, a church of the Middle Ages, a church in Ireland today. Every seat—save those in the chancel —was full, all the aisles were full, the churchyard was full; everyone on his knees, and the old rector kneeling before the door into the holy place.

Yet they can say but very little of what was done beyond the veil. There was no attempt to perform the usual service; when the bells had stopped the old deacon raised his cry, and priest and people fell down on their knees as they thought they heard a choir within singing "Alleluya, alleluya, alleluya." And as the bells in the tower ceased ringing, there sounded the thrill of the bell from Syon, and the golden veil of sunlight fell across the door into the altar, and the heavenly voices began their melodies.

A voice like a trumpet cried from within the brightness.

Agyos, Agyos, Agyos.

And the people, as if an age-old memory stirred in them, replied:

Agyos yr Tâd, agyos yr Mab, agyos yr Yspryd Glan. Sant, sant, sant, Drindod sant vendigeid. Sanctus Arglwydd Dduw Sabaoth, Dominus Deus.

There was a voice that cried and sang from within the altar; most of the people had heard some faint echo of it in the chapels; a voice rising and falling and soaring in awful modulations that rang like the trumpet of the Last Angel. The people beat upon their breasts, the tears were like rain of the mountains on their cheeks; those that were able fell down flat on their faces before the glory of the veil. They said afterwards that men of the hills, twenty miles away, heard that cry and that singing, roaring upon them on the wind, and they fell down on their faces, and cried, "The offering is accomplished," knowing nothing of what they said.

There were a few who saw three come out of the door of the sanctuary, and stand for a moment on the pace before the door. These three were in dyed vesture, red as blood. One stood before two, looking to the west, and he rang the bell. And they say that all the birds of the wood, and all the waters of the sea, and all the leaves of the trees, and all the winds of the high rocks uttered their voices with the ringing of the bell. And the second and the third; they turned their faces one to another. The second held up the lost altar that they once called Sapphirus, which was like the changing of the sea and of the sky, and like the immixture of gold and silver. And the third heaved up high over the altar a cup that was red with burning and the blood of the offering.

And the old rector cried aloud then before the entrance:

Bendigeid yr Offeren yn oes oesoedd—blessed be the Offering unto the age of ages.

And then the Mass of the Sangraal was ended, and then began the passing out of that land of the holy persons and holy things that had returned to it after the long years. It seemed, indeed, to many that the thrilling sound of the bell was in their ears for days, even for weeks after that Sunday morning. But thenceforth neither bell nor altar nor cup was seen by anyone; not openly, that is, but only in dreams by day and by night. Nor did the people see Strangers again in the market of Llantrisant, nor in the lonely places where certain persons oppressed by great affliction and sorrow had once or twice encountered them.

***

But that time of visitation will never be forgotten by the people. Many things happened in the nine days that have not been set down in this record—or legend. Some of them were trifling matters, though strange enough in other times. Thus a man in the town who had a fierce dog that was always kept chained up found one day that the beast had become mild and gentle.

And this is odder: Edward Davies, of Lanafon, a farmer, was roused from sleep one night by a queer yelping and barking in his yard. He looked out of the window and saw his sheep-dog playing with a big fox; they were chasing each other by turns, rolling over and over one another, "cutting such capers as I did never see the like," as the astonished farmer put it. And some of the people said that during this season of wonder the corn shot up, and the grass thickened, and the fruit was multiplied on the trees in a very marvellous manner.

More important, it seemed, was the case of Williams, the grocer; though this may have been a purely natural deliverance. Mr. Williams was to marry his daughter Mary to a smart young fellow from Carmarthen, and he was in great distress over it. Not over the marriage itself, but because things had been going very badly with him for some time, and he could not see his way to giving anything like the wedding entertainment that would be expected of him. The wedding was to be on the Saturday—that was the day on which the lawyer, Lewis Prothero, and the farmer, Philip James, were reconciled—and this John Williams, without money or credit, could not think how shame would not be on him for the meagreness and poverty of the wedding feast. And then on the Tuesday came a letter from his brother, David Williams, Australia, from whom he had not heard for fifteen years. And David, it seemed, had been making a great deal of money, and was a bachelor, and here was with his letter a paper good for a thousand pounds: "You may as well enjoy it now as wait till I am dead." This was enough, indeed, one might say; but hardly an hour after the letter had come the lady from the big house (Plas Mawr) drove up in all her grandeur, and went into the shop and said, "Mr. Williams, your daughter Mary has always been a very good girl, and my husband and I feel that we must give her some little thing on her wedding, and we hope she'll be very happy." It was a gold watch worth fifteen pounds. And after Lady Watcyn, advances the old doctor with a dozen of port, forty years upon it, and a long sermon on how to decant it. And the old rector's old wife brings to the beautiful dark girl two yards of creamy lace, like an enchantment, for her wedding veil, and tells Mary how she wore it for her own wedding fifty years ago; and the squire, Sir Watcyn, as if his wife had not been already with a fine gift, calls from his horse, and brings out Williams and barks like a dog at him, "Goin' to have a weddin', eh, Williams? Can't have a weddin' without champagne, y' know; wouldn't be legal, don't y' know. So look out for a couple of cases." So Williams tells the story of the gifts; and certainly there was never so famous a wedding in Llantrisant before.

All this, of course, may have been altogether in the natural order; the "glow," as they call it, seems more difficult to explain. For they say that all through the nine days, and indeed after the time had ended, there never was a man weary or sick at heart in Llantrisant, or in the country round it. For if a man felt that his work of the body or the mind was going to be too much for his strength, then there would come to him of a sudden a warm glow and a thrilling all over him and he felt as strong as a giant, and happier than he had ever been in his life before, so that lawyer and hedger each rejoiced in the task that was before him, as if it were sport and play.

And much more wonderful than this or any other wonders was forgiveness, with love to follow it. There were meetings of old enemies in the market-place and in the street that made the people lift up their hands and declare that it was as if one walked the miraculous streets of Syon.

***

But as to the "phenomena," the occurrences for which, in ordinary talk, we should reserve the word "miraculous"? Well, what do we know? The question that I have already stated comes up again, as to the possible survival of old tradition in a kind of dormant, or torpid, semi-conscious state. In other words, did the people "see" and "hear" what they expected to see and hear? This point, or one similar to it, occurred in a debate between Andrew Lang and Anatole France as to the visions of Joan of Arc. M. France stated that when Joan saw St. Michael, she saw the traditional archangel of the religious art of her day, but to the best of my belief Andrew Lang proved that the visionary figure Joan described was not in the least like the fifteenth-century conception of St. Michael. So, in the case of

Llantrisant, I have stated that there was a sort of tradition about the Holy Bell of Teilo Sant; and it is, of course, barely possible that some vague notion of the Graal Cup may have reached even Welsh country folks through Tennyson's Idylls. But so far I see no reason to suppose that these people had ever heard of the portable altar (called Sapphirus in William of Malmesbury) or of its changing colours "that no man could discern."

And then there are the other questions of the distinction between hallucination and vision, of the average duration of one and the other, and of the possibility of collective hallucination. If a number of people all see (or think they see) the same appearances, can this be merely hallucination? I believe there is a leading case on the matter, which concerns a number of people seeing the same appearance on a church wall in Ireland; but there is, of course, this difficulty, that one may be hallucinated and communicate his impression to the others, telepathically.

But at the last, what do we know?

THE STORY OF THE GREEK SLAVE

FREDERICK MARRYAT

I am a Greek by birth, my parents were poor people residing at Smyrna. I was an only son, and brought up to my father's profession—that of a cooper. When I was twenty years old, I had buried both my parents, and was left to shift for myself. I had been for some time in the employ of a Jewish wine-merchant, and I continued there for three years after my father's death, when a circumstance occurred which led to my subsequent prosperity and present degradation.

At the time that I am speaking of, I had, by strict diligence and sobriety, so pleased my employer, that I had risen to be his foreman; and although I still superintended and occasionally worked at the cooperage, I was entrusted with the drawing off and fining of the wines, to prepare them for market. There was an Ethiopian slave, who worked under my orders, a powerful, broad-shouldered, and most malignant wretch whom my master found it almost impossible to manage; the bastinado, or any other punishment, he derided, and after the application only became more sullen and discontented than before. The fire that flashed from his eyes, upon any fault being found by me on account of his negligence, was so threatening, that I every day expected I should be murdered. I repeatedly requested my master to part with him; but the Ethiopian being a very powerful man, and able, when he chose, to move a pipe of wine without assistance, the avarice of the Jew would not permit him to accede to my repeated solicitations.

One morning I entered the cooperage, and found the Ethiopian fast asleep by the side of a cask which I had been wanting for some time, and expected to have found ready. Afraid to punish him myself, I brought my master to witness his conduct. The Jew, enraged at his idleness, struck him on the head with one of the staves. The Ethiopian sprung up in a rage, but on seeing his master with the stave in his hand, contented himself with muttering, "That he would not remain to be beaten in that manner," and re-applied himself to his labour. As soon as my master had left the cooperage, the Ethiopian vented his anger upon me for having informed against him, and seizing the stave, flew at me with the intention of beating out my brains. I stepped behind the cask; he followed me, and just as I had seized an adze to defend myself, he fell over the stool which lay in his way; he was springing up to renew the attack, when I struck him a blow with the adze which entered his skull, and laid him dead at my feet.

I was very much alarmed at what had occurred; for although I felt justified in self-defence, I was aware that my master would be very much annoyed at the loss of the slave, and as there were no witnesses, it would go hard with me when brought before the cadi. After some reflection I determined, as the slave had said "He would not remain to be beaten," that I would leave my master to suppose he had run away, and in the meantime conceal the body. But to effect this was difficult, as I could not take it out of the cooperage without being perceived. After some cogitation, I decided upon putting it into the cask, and heading it up. It required all my strength to lift the body in, but at last I succeeded. Having put in the lead of the pipe, I hammered down the hoops and rolled it into the store, where I had been waiting to fill it with wine for the next year's demand. As soon as it was in its place, I pumped off the wine from the vat, and having filled up the cask and put in the bung, I felt as if a heavy load had been removed from my mind, as there was no chance of immediate discovery.

I had but just completed my task, and was sitting down on one of the settles, when my master came in, and inquired for the slave. I replied that he had left the cooperage, swearing that he would work no more. Afraid of losing him, the Jew hastened to give notice to the authorities, that he might be apprehended; but after some time, as nothing could be heard of the supposed runaway, it was imagined that he had drowned himself in a fit of sullenness, and no more was thought about him. In the meanwhile I continued to work there as before, and as I had the charge of everything I had no doubt that, some day or another, I should find means of quietly disposing of my incumbrance.

The next spring, I was busy pumping off from one cask into the other, according to our custom, when the aga of the janissaries came in. He was a great wine-bibber, and one of our best customers. As his dependants were all well known, it was not his custom to send them for wine, but to come himself to the store and select a pipe. This was carried away in a litter by eight strong slaves, with the curtains drawn close, as if it had been a new purchase which he had added to his harem. My master showed him the pipes of wine prepared for that year's market, which were arranged in two rows; and I hardly need observe that the one containing the Ethiopian was not in the foremost. After tasting one or two which did not seem to please him, the aga observed, "Friend Issachar, thy tribe will always put off the worst goods first, if possible. Now I have an idea that there is better wine in the second tier, than in the one thou hast recommended. Let thy Greek put a spile into that cask," continued he, pointing to the very one in which I had headed-up the black slave. As I made sure that as soon as he had tasted the contents he would spit them out, I did not hesitate to bore the cask and draw off the wine, which I handed to him. He tasted it, and held it to the light—tasted it again and smacked his lips—then turning to my master, exclaimed, "Thou dog of a Jew! wouldst thou have palmed off upon me vile trash, when thou hadst in thy possession wine which might be sipped with the houris in Paradise?"

The Jew appealed to me if the pipes of wine were not all of the same quality; and I confirmed his assertion.

"Taste it then," replied the aga, "and then taste the first which you recommended to me."

My master did so, and was evidently astonished. "It certainly has more body," replied he; "yet how can that be, I know not. Taste it, Charis." I held the glass to my lips, but nothing could induce me to taste the contents. I contented myself with agreeing with my master, (as I conscientiously could), "that it certainly had more *body* in it than the rest."

The aga was so pleased with the wine, that he tasted two or three more pipes of the back tier, hoping to find others of the same quality, probably intending to have laid in a large stock; but finding no other of the same flavour, he ordered his slaves to roll the one containing the body of the slave into the litter, and carried it to his own house.

"Stop a moment, thou lying kafir!" said the pacha, "dost thou really mean to say that the wine was better than the rest?"

"Why should I tell a lie to your sublime highness—am I not a worm that you may crush? As I informed you, I did not taste it, your highness; but after the aga had departed, my master expressed his surprise at the excellence of the wine, which he affirmed to be superior to any thing that he had ever tasted—and his sorrow that the aga had taken away the cask, which prevented him from ascertaining the cause. But one day I was narrating the circumstance to a Frank in this country, who expressed no surprise at the wine being improved. He had been a wine-merchant in England, and he informed me that it was the custom there to throw large pieces of raw beef into the wine to feed it; and that some particular wines were very much improved thereby."

"Allah kebur! God is great!" cried the pacha—"Then it must be so—I have heard that the English are very fond of beef. Now go on with thy story."

Your highness cannot imagine the alarm which I felt when the cask was taken away by the aga's slaves. I gave myself up for a lost man, and resolved upon immediate flight from Smyrna. I calculated the time that it would take for the aga to drink the wine, and made my arrangements accordingly. I told my master that it was my intention to leave him, as I had an offer to go into business with a relation at Zante. My master, who could not well do without me, entreated me to stay; but I was positive. He then offered me a share of the business if I would remain, but I was not to be persuaded. Every rap at the door, I thought that the aga and his janissaries were coming for me; and I hastened my departure, which was fixed for the following day—when in the evening my master came into the store with a paper in his hand.

"Charis," said he, "perhaps you have supposed that I only offered to make you a partner in my business to induce you to remain, and then to deceive you. To prove the contrary, here is a deed drawn up by which you are a partner, and entitled to one third of the future profits. Look at it, you will find that it has been executed in due form before the cadi."

He had put the paper into my hand, and I was about to return it with a refusal, when a loud knocking at the door startled us both. It was a party of janissaries despatched by the aga, to bring us to him immediately. I knew well enough what it must be about, and I cursed my folly in having delayed so long; but the fact was, the wine proved so agreeable to the aga's palate that he had drunk it much faster than usual; besides which, the body of the slave took up at least a third of the cask, and diminished the contents in the same proportion. There was no appeal, and no escape. My master, who was ignorant of the cause, did not seem at all alarmed, but willingly accompanied the soldiers. I, on the contrary, was nearly dead from fear.

When we arrived, the aga burst out in the most violent exclamations against my master. "Thou rascal of a Jew!" said he, "dost thou think that thou art to impose upon a true believer, and sell him a pipe of wine which is not more than two thirds full,—filling it up with trash of some sort or another. Tell me what it is that is so heavy in the cask now that it is empty."

The Jew protested his ignorance, and appealed to me. I, of course, pretended the same. "Well then," replied the aga, "we will soon see. Let thy Greek send for his tools, and the cask shall be opened in our presence; then perhaps, thou wilt recognize thine own knavery."

Two of the janissaries were despatched for the tools, and when they arrived, I was directed to take the head out of the cask. I now considered my death as certain—nothing buoyed me up but my observing that the resentment of the aga was levelled more against my master than against me; but still I thought that, when the cask was opened, the recognition of the black slave must immediately take place, and the evidence of my master would fix the murder upon me.

It was with a trembling hand that I obeyed the orders of the aga— the head of the pipe was taken out, and, to the horror of all present, the body was exposed; but instead of being black, it had turned *white,* from the time which it had been immersed. I rallied a little at this circumstance, as, so far, suspicion would be removed.

"Holy Abraham!" exclaimed my master, "what is that which I see! A dead body, so help me God!—but I know nothing about it—do you, Charis?" I vowed that I did not, and called the patriarch to witness the truth of my assertion. But while we were thus exclaiming, the aga's eyes were fixed upon my master with an indignant and deadly stare which spoke volumes; while the remainder of the people who were present, although they said nothing, seemed as if they were ready to tear him into pieces.

"Cursed unbeliever!" as last uttered the Turk, "is it thus that thou preparest the wine for the disciples of the Prophet?"

"Holy father Abraham!—I know no more than you do, aga, how that body came there; but I will change the cask with pleasure, and will send you another."

"Be it so," replied the aga; "my slave shall fetch it now." He gave directions accordingly, and the litter soon re-appeared with another pipe of wine.

"It will be a heavy loss to a poor Jew—one pipe of good wine," observed my master, as it was rolled out of the litter; and he took up his hat with the intention to depart.

"Stay," cried the aga, "I do not mean to rob you of your wine."

"Oh, then, you will pay me for it," replied my master; "aga, you are a considerate man."

"Thou shalt see," retorted the aga, who gave directions to his slaves to draw off the wine in vessels. As soon as the pipe was empty he desired me to take the head out; and when I had obeyed him, he ordered his janissaries to put my master in. In a minute he was gagged and bound, and tossed into the pipe; and I was directed to put in the head as before. I was very unwilling to comply: for I had no reason to complain of my master, and knew that he was punished for the fault of which I had been guilty. But it was a case of life or death—and the days of self-devotion have long passed away in our country. Besides which, I had the deed in my pocket by which I was a partner in the business, and my master had no heirs—so that I stood a chance to come in for the whole of his property. Moreover—

"Never mind your reasons," observed the pacha, "you headed him up in the cask—Go on."

"I did so, your highness; but although I dared not disobey, I assure you that it was with a sorrowful heart—the more so, as I did not know the fate which might be reserved for myself."

As soon as the head was in, and the hoops driven on, the aga desired his slaves to fill the cask up again with the wine; and thus did my poor master perish.

"Put in the bung, Greek," said the aga, in a stern voice.

I did so, and stood trembling before him.

"Well! what knowest thou of this transaction?"

I thought, as the aga had taken away the life of my master, that it would not hurt him if I took away a little from his character. I answered that I really knew nothing, but that, the other day, a black slave had disappeared in a very suspicious manner—that my master made very little inquiry after him—and I now strongly suspected that he must have suffered the same fate. I added, that my master had expressed himself very sorry that his highness had taken away the pipe of wine, as he would have reserved it.

"Cursed Jew!" replied the aga; "I don't doubt but he has murdered a dozen in the same manner."

"I am afraid so, sir," replied I, "and suspect that I was to have been his next victim; for when I talked of going away, he persuaded me to stay, and gave me this paper, by which I was to become his partner with one third of the profits. I presume that I should not have enjoyed them long."

"Well, Greek," observed the aga, "this is fortunate for you; as, upon certain conditions, you may enter upon the whole property. One is, that you keep this pipe of wine with the rascally Jew in it, that I may have the pleasure occasionally to look at my revenge. You will also keep the pipe with the other body in it, that it may keep my anger alive. The last is you will supply me with what wine I may require, of the very best quality, without making any charge. Do you consent to these terms, or am I to consider you as a party to this infamous transaction?"

I hardly need observe that the terms were gladly accepted. Your highness must be aware that nobody thinks much about a Jew. When I was questioned as to his disappearance, I shrugged up my shoulders, and told the inquirers, confidentially, that the aga of the janissaries had put him *in prison*, and that I was carrying on the business until his release.

In compliance with the wishes of the aga, the two casks containing the Jew and the Ethiopian slave, were placed together on settles higher than the rest, in the centre of the store. He would come in the evening, and rail at the cask containing my late master for hours at a time; during which he drank so much wine, that it was a very common circumstance for him to remain in the house until the next morning.

You must not suppose, your highness, that I neglected to avail myself (unknown to the aga) of the peculiar properties of the wine which those casks contained. I had them spiled underneath, and constantly running off the wine from them, filled them up afresh. In a short time there was not a gallon in my possession which had not a *dash* in it of either the Ethiopian or the Jew: and my wine was so improved, that it had a most rapid sale, and I became rich.

All went on prosperously for three years; when the aga, who during that time had been my constant guest, and at least three times a week had been intoxicated in my house, was ordered with his troops to join the sultan's army. By keeping company with him, I had insensibly imbibed a taste for wine, although I never had been inebriated. The day that his troops marched, he stopped at my door, and dismounting from his Arabian, came in to take a farewell glass, desiring his men to go on, and that he would ride after them. One glass brought on another, and the time flew rapidly away. The evening closed in, and the aga was, as usual, in a state of intoxication:—he insisted upon going down to the store, to rail once more at the cask containing the body of the Jew. We had long been on the most friendly terms, and having this night drunk more than usual, I was incautious enough to say—"Prithee, aga, do not abuse my poor master any more, for he has been the making of my fortune. I will tell you a secret now that you are going away—there is not a drop of wine in my store that has not been flavoured either by him or by the slave in the other cask. That is the reason why it is so much better than other people's."

"How!" exclaimed the aga, who was now almost incapable of speech. "Very well, rascal Greek! die you shall, like your master. Holy Prophet! what a state for a Mussulman to go to Paradise in—impregnated with the essence of a cursed Jew! Wretch! you shall die—you shall die."

He made a grasp at me, and missing his foot, fell on the ground in such a state of drunkenness as not to be able to get up again. I knew that when he became sober, he would not forget what had taken place, and that I should be sacrificed to his vengeance. The fear of death, and the wine which I had drunk, decided me how to act. I dragged him into an empty pipe, put the head in, hooped it up, and rolling it into the tier, filled it with wine. Thus did I revenge my poor master, and relieved myself from any further molestation on the part of the aga.

"What!" cried the pacha, in a rage, "you drowned a true believer—an aga of janissaries! Thou dog of a kafir—thou son of Shitan—and dare avow it! Call in the executioner."

"Mercy! your sublime highness, mercy!" cried the Greek. "Have I not your promise by the sword of the Prophet? Besides, he was no true believer, or he would not have disobeyed the law. A good Mussulman will never touch a drop of wine."

"I promised to forgive, and did forgive, the murder of the black slave; but an aga of janissaries! Is not that quite another thing?" appealed the pacha to Mustapha.

"Your highness is just in your indignation—the kafir deserves to be impaled. Yet there are two considerations which your slave ventures to submit to your sublime wisdom. The first is, that your highness gave an unconditional promise, and swore by the sword of the Prophet."

"Staffir Allah! what care I for that! Had I sworn to a true believer, it were something."

"The other is, that the slave has not yet finished his story which appears to be interesting."

"Wallah! that is true. Let him finish his story."

But the Greek slave remained with his face on the ground; and it was not until a renewal of the promise, sworn upon the holy standard made out of the nether garments of the Prophet, by the pacha who had recovered his temper, and was anxious for the conclusion of the story, that he could be induced to proceed, which he did as follows:

As soon as I had bunged up the cask, I went down to the yard where the aga had left his horse, and having severely wounded the poor beast with his sword, I let it loose that it might gallop home. The noise of the horse's hoofs in the middle of the night, aroused his family, and when they discovered that it was wounded and without its rider, they imagined that the aga had been attacked and murdered by banditti when he had followed his troop. They sent to me to ask at what time he had left my house; I replied, an hour after dark—that he was very much intoxicated at the time—and had left his sabre, which I returned.

They had no suspicion of the real facts, and it was believed that he had perished on the road.

I was now rid of my dangerous acquaintance; and although he certainly had drunk a great quantity of my wine yet I recovered the value of it with interest, from the flavour which I obtained from his body and which I imparted to the rest of my stock. I raised him up alongside of the two other casks; and my trade was more profitable and my wines in greater repute than ever. But one day the cadi, who had heard my wine extolled, came privately to my house; I bowed to the ground at the honour conferred, for I had long wished to have him as a customer. I drew some of my best: "Thus, honourable sir," said I, presenting the glass, "is what I call my aga wine: the late aga was so fond of it, he used to order a whole cask at once to his house, and had it taken there in a litter."

"A good plan," replied the cadi, "much better than sending a slave with a pitcher, which gives occasion for remarks: I will do the same; but, first, let me taste all you have."

He tasted several casks, but none pleased him so much as the first which I had recommended. At last he cast his eyes upon the three casks raised above the others.

"And what are those?" enquired he.

"Empty casks, sir," replied I; but he had his stick in his hand, and he struck one.

"Greek thou tellest me these casks are empty, but they do not sound so; I suspect that thou hast better wine than I have tasted: draw me off from these immediately."

I was obliged to comply—he tasted them—vowed that the wine was exquisite, and that he would purchase the whole. I stated to him that the wine in those casks was used for flavouring the rest; and that the price was enormous, hoping that he would not pay it. He enquired how much: I asked him four times the price of the other wines.

"Agreed," said the cadi; "it is dear—but one cannot have good wine without paying for it—it is a bargain."

I was very much alarmed; and stated that I could not part with those casks, as I should not be able to carry on my business with reputation, if I lost the means of flavouring my wines, but all in vain; he said that I had asked a price and he had agreed to give it. Ordering his slaves to bring a litter, he would not leave the store until the whole of the casks were carried away, and thus did I lose my Ethiopian, my Jew, and my aga.

As I knew that the secret would soon be discovered, the very next day I prepared for my departure. I received my money from the cadi, to whom I stated my intention to leave, as he had obliged me to sell him those wines, and I had no longer hopes of carrying on my business with success. I again begged him to allow me to have them back, offering him three pipes of wine as a present if he would consent, but it was of no use. I chartered a vessel, which I loaded with the rest of my stock; and, taking all my money with me, made sail for Corfu, before any discovery had taken place. But we encountered a heavy gale of wind, which, after a fortnight (during which we attempted in vain to make head against it), forced us back to Smyrna. When the weather moderated, I directed the captain to take the vessel into the outer roadstead that I might sail as soon as possible. We had not dropped anchor again more than five minutes when I perceived a boat pulling off from the shore in which was the cadi and the officers of justice.

Convinced that I was discovered, I was at a loss how to proceed, when the idea occurred to me that I might conceal my own body in a cask, as I had before so well concealed those of others.

I called the captain down into the cabin, and telling him that I had reason to suspect that the cadi would take my life, offered him a large part of the cargo if he would assist me.

The captain who, unfortunately for me, was a Greek, consented. We went down into the hold, started the wine out of one of the pipes, and having taken out the head, I crawled in, and was hooped up.

The cadi came on board immediately afterwards and enquired for me. The captain stated that I had fallen overboard in the gale, and that he had in consequence returned, the vessel not being consigned to any house at Corfu.

"Has then the accursed villain escaped my vengeance!" exclaimed the cadi; "the murderer, that fines his wines with the bodies of his fellow-creatures: but you may deceive me, Greek, we will examine the vessel."

The officers who accompanied the cadi proceeded carefully to search every part of the ship. Not being able to discover me, the Greek captain was believed; and, after a thousand imprecations upon my soul, the cadi and his people departed.

I now breathed more freely, notwithstanding I was nearly intoxicated with the lees of the wine which impregnated the wood of the cask, and I was anxious to be set at liberty; but the treacherous captain had no such intention, and never came near me. At night he cut his cable and made sail, and I overheard a conversation between two of the men, which made known to me his intentions: these were to throw me overboard on his passage, and take possession of my property. I cried out to them from the bunghole: I screamed for mercy, but in vain. One of them answered that, as I had murdered others, and put them into casks, I should now be treated in the same manner.

I could not but mentally acknowledge the justice of my punishment, and resigned myself to my fate; all that I wished was to be thrown over at once and released from my misery. The momentary anticipation of death appeared to be so much worse than the reality. But it was ordered otherwise: a gale of wind blew up with such force that the captain and crew had enough to do to look after the vessel, and either I was forgotten, or my doom was postponed until a more seasonable opportunity.

On the third day I heard the sailors observe that, with such a wretch as I was remaining on board, the vessel must inevitably be lost.

The hatches were then opened; I was hoisted up and cast into the raging sea. The bung of the cask was out, but by stuffing my handkerchief in, when the hole was under water, I prevented the cask from filling; and when it was uppermost, I removed it for a moment to obtain fresh air. I was dreadfully bruised by the constant rolling, in a heavy sea, and completely worn out with fatigue and pain; I had made up my mind to let the water in and be rid of my life, when I was tossed over and over with such dreadful rapidity as prevented my taking the precaution of keeping out the water. After three successive rolls of the same kind, I found that the cask, which had been in the surf, had struck on the beach. In a moment after, I heard voices, and people came up to the cask and rolled me along. I would not speak, lest they should be frightened and allow me to remain on the beach, where I might again be tossed about by the waves; but as soon as they stopped, I called in a faint voice from the bunghole begging them for mercy's sake to let me out.

At first they appeared alarmed; but, on my repeating my request, and stating that I was the owner of the ship which was off the land, and the captain and crew had mutinied and tossed me overboard, they brought some tools and set me at liberty.

The first sight that met my eyes after I was released, was my vessel lying a wreck; each wave that hurled her further on the beach, breaking her more and more to pieces. She was already divided amidships, and the white foaming surf was covered with pipes of wine, which, as fast as they were cast on shore, were rolled up by the same people who had released me. I was so worn out, that I fainted where I lay. When I came to, I found myself in a cave upon a bundle of capotes, and perceived a party of forty or fifty men, who were sitting by a large fire, and emptying with great rapidity one of my pipes of wine.

As soon as they observed that I was coming to my senses, they poured some wine down my throat, which restored me. I was then desired by one of them, who seemed to be the chief, to approach.

"The men who have been saved from the wreck," said he, "have told me strange stories of your enormous crimes—now, sit down, and tell me the truth—if I believe you, you shall have justice—I am cadi here—if you wish to know where you are, it is upon the island of Ischia—if you wish to know in what company, it is in the society of those who by illiberal people are called pirates: now tell the truth."

I thought that with pirates my story would be received better than with other people, and I therefore narrated my history to them, in the same words that I now have to your highness. When I had finished, the captain of the gang observed:

"Well, then, as you acknowledge to have killed a slave, to have assisted at the death of a Jew, and to have drowned an aga, you certainly deserve death; but, on consideration of the excellence of the wine, and the secret which you have imparted to us, I shall commute your sentence. As for the captain and the remainder of the crew, they have been guilty of treachery and piracy on the high seas—a most heinous offence, which deserves instant death: but as it is by their means that we have been put in possession of the wine, I shall be lenient. I therefore sentence you all to hard labour for life. You shall be sold as slaves in Cairo, and we will pocket the money and drink your wine."

The pirates loudly applauded the justice of a decision by which they benefited, and all appeal on our parts was useless. When the weather became more settled, we were put on board one of their small xebeques, and on our arrival at this port were exposed for sale and purchased.

Such, pacha, is the history which induced me to make use of the expressions which you wished to be explained; and I hope you will allow that I have been more unfortunate than guilty, as on every occasion in which I took away the life of another, I had only to choose between that and my own.

ANTY BLIGH

JOHN MASEFIELD

One night in the tropics I was "farmer" in the middle watch—
that is, I had neither "wheel" nor "look-out" to stand during the
four hours I stayed on deck. We were running down the North-east
Trades, and the ship was sailing herself, and the wind was gentle, and
it was very still on board, the blocks whining as she rolled, and the
waves talking, and the wheel-chains clanking, and a light noise aloft of
pattering and tapping. The sea was all pale with moonlight, and from
the lamp-room door, where the watch was mustered, I could see a red
stain on the water from the port sidelight. The mate was walking the
weather side of the poop, while the boastwain sat on the booby-hatch
humming an old tune and making a sheath for his knife. The watch
were lying on the deck, out of the moonlight, in the shadow of the break
of the poop. Most of them were sleeping, propped against the bulkhead.

One of them was singing a new chanty he had made, beating out the tune with his pipe-stem, in a little quiet voice that fitted the silence of the night.

Ha! Ha! Why don't you blow?

O ho!

Come, roll him over,

repeated over and over again, as though he could never tire of the beauty of the words and the tune.

Presently he got up from where he was and came over to me. He was one of the best men we had aboard—a young Dane who talked English like a native. We had had business dealings during the dog watch, some hours before, and he had bought a towel from me, and I had let him have it cheap, as I had one or two to spare. He sat down beside me, and began a conversation, discussing a number of sailor matters, such as the danger of sleeping in the moonlight, the poison supposed to lurk in cold boiled potatoes, and the folly of having a good time in port. From these we passed to the consideration of piracy, colouring our talk with anecdotes of pirates. "Ah, there was no pirate," said my friend, "like old Anty Bligh of Bristol. Dey hung old Anty Bligh off of the Brazils. He was the core and the strands of an old rogue, old Anty Bligh was, Dey hung old Anty Bligh on Fernando Noronha, where the prison is. And he walked after, Anty Bligh did. That shows how bad he was." "How did he walk?" I asked. "Let's hear about him." "Oh, they jest hung him," replied my friend, "like they'd hang any one else, and they left him on the gallows after. Dey thought old Anty was too bad to bury, I guess. And there was a young Spanish captain on the island in dem times. Frisco Baldo his name was. He was a terror. So the night dey hung old Anty, Frisco was getting gorgeous wid some other captains in a kind of a drinking shanty. And de other captains say to Frisco, 'I bet you a month's pay you won't go and put a rope round Anty's legs.'

And 'I bet you a new suit of clothes you won't put a bowline around Anty's ankles.' And 'I bet you a cask of wine you won't put Anty's feet in a noose.' 'I bet you I will,' says Frisco Baldo. 'What's dead man anyways,' he says, 'and why should I be feared of Anty Bligh? Give us a rope,' he says, 'and I'll lash him up with seven turns, like a sailor would a hammock.' So he drinks up his glass, and gets a stretch of rope, and out he goes into the dark to where the gallows stood. It was a new moon dat time, and it was as dark as the end of a sea-boot and as blind as the toe. And the gallows was right down by the sea dat time because old Anty Bligh was a pirate. So he comes up under the gallows, and there was old Anty Bligh hanging. And 'Way-ho, Anty,' he says. 'Lash and carry, Anty,' he says. 'I'm going to lash you up like a hammock.' So he slips a bowline around Anty's feet." . . . Here my informant broke off his yarn to light his pipe. After a few puffs he went on.

"Now when a man's hanged in hemp," he said gravely, "you mustn't never touch him with what killed him, for fear he should come to life on you. You mark that. Don't you forget it. So soon as ever Frisco Baldo sets that bowline around Anty's feet, old Anty looks down from his noose, and though it was dark, Frisco Baldo could see him plain enough. 'Thank you, young man,' said Anty; 'just cast that turn off again. Burn my limbs,' he says, 'if you ain't got a neck! And now climb up here,' he says, 'and take my neck out of the noose. I'm as dry as a cask of split peas.' Now you may guess that Frisco Baldo feller he come out all over in a cold sweat. 'Git a gait on you,' says Anty. 'I ain't going to wait up here to please you.' So Frisco Baldo climbs up, and a sore job he had of it getting the noose off Anty. 'Get a gait on you,' says Anty, 'and go easy with them clumsy hands of yours. You'll give me a sore throat,' he says, 'the way you're carrying on. Now don't let me fall plop,' says Anty. 'Lower away handsomely,' he says. 'I'll make you a weary one if you let me fall plop,' he says. So Frisco lowers away handsomely, and Anty comes to the ground, with the rope off him, only he still had his head to one side like he'd been hanged. 'Come here to me,' he says. So Frisco Baldo goes over to him. And Anty he jest put one arm round his neck, and gripped him tight and cold. 'Now march,' he says; 'march me down to the grog shop and get me a dram. None of your six-water dollops, neither,' he says; 'I'm as dry as a foul block,' he says. So Frisco and Anty they go to the grog shop, and all the while Anty's cold fingers was playing down Frisco's neck. And when they got to der grog shop der captains was all fell asleep. So Frisco takes the bottle of rum and Anty laps it down like he'd been used to it. 'Ah!' he says, 'thank ye,' he says, 'and now down to the Mole with ye,' he says, 'and we'll take a boat,' he says; 'I'm going to England,' he says, 'to say good-bye to me mother.' So Frisco he come out all over in a cold sweat, for he was feared of the sea; but Anty's cold fingers was fiddling on his neck, so he t'ink he better go. And when dey come to der Mole there was a boat there—one of these perry-acks, as they call them—and Anty he says, 'You take the oars,' he says. 'I'll steer,' he says, 'and every time you catch a crab,' he says, 'you'll get such a welt as you'll remember.' So Frisco shoves her off and rows out of the harbour, with old Anty Bligh at the tiller, telling him to put his beef on and to watch out he didn't catch no crabs. And he rowed, and he rowed, and he rowed, and every time he caught a crab—whack! he had it over the sconce with the tiller. And der perryack it went a great holy big skyoot, ninety knots in der quarter of an hour, so they soon sees the Bull Point Light and der Shutter Light, and then the lights of Bristol. 'Oars,' said Anty. 'Lie on yours oars,' he says; 'we got way enough.' Then dey make her fast to a dock-side and dey goes ashore, and Anty has his arm round Frisco's neck, and 'March,' he says; 'step lively,' he says; 'for Johnny comes marching home,' he says. By and by they come to a little house with a light in the window. 'Knock at the door,' says Anty. So Frisco knocks, and in they go. There was a fire burning in the room and some candles on the table, and there, by the fire, was a very old, ugly woman in a red flannel dress, and she'd a ring in her nose and a black cutty pipe between her lips. 'Good evening, mother,' says Anty. 'I come home,' he says. But the old woman she just looks at him but never says nothing. 'It's your son Anty that's come home to you,' he says again. So she looks at him again and, 'Aren't you ashamed of yourself, Anty,' she says, 'coming home the way you are? Don't you repent your goings-on?' she says. 'Dying disgraced,' she says, 'in a foreign land, with none to lay you out.' 'Mother,' he says, 'I repent in blood,' he says. 'You'll not deny me my rights?' he says. 'Not since you repent,' she says. 'Them as repents I got no quarrel with. You was always a bad one, Anty,' she says, 'but I hoped you'd come home in the end. Well, and now you're come,' she says. 'And I must bathe that throat of yours,' she says. 'It looks as though you been hit by something.' 'Be quick, mother,' he says; 'it's after midnight now,' he says.

"So she washed him in wine, the way you wash a corpse, and put him in a white linen shroud, with a wooden cross on his chest, and two silver pieces on his eyes, and a golden marigold between his lips. And together they carried him to the perry-ack and laid him in the stern sheets. 'Give way, young man,' she says; 'give way like glory. Pull, my heart of blood,' she says, 'or we'll have the dawn on us.' So he pulls, that Frisco Baldo does, and the perry-ack makes big southing—a degree a minute—and they comes ashore at the Mole just as the hens was settling to their second sleep. 'To the churchyard,' says the old woman; 'you take his legs.' So they carries him to the churchyard at the double. 'Get a gait on you,' says Anty. 'I feel the dawn in my bones,' he says. 'My wraith'll chase you if you ain't in time,' he says. And there was an empty grave, and they put him in, and shovelled in the clay, and the old woman poured out a bottle on the top of it. 'It's holy water,' she says. 'It's make his wraith rest easy.' Then she runs down to the sea's edge and gets into the perry-ack. And immediately she was hull down beyond the horizon, and the sun came up out of the sea, and the cocks cried cock-a-doodle in the hen roost, and Frisco Baldo falls down into a swound. He was a changed man from that out."

"Lee for brace," said the mate above us. "Quit your chinning there, and go forward to the rope."

THE BELL-TOWER

HERMAN MELVILLE

In the south of Europe, nigh a once frescoed capital, now with dank mould, cankering its bloom, central in a plain, stands what, at distance, seems the black mossed stump of some immeasurable pine, fallen in forgotten days, with Anak and the Titan.

As all along where the pine-tree falls, its dissolution leaves a mossy mound—last-flung shadow of the perished trunk; never lengthening, never lessening; unsubject to the fleet falsities of the sun; shade immutable, and true gauge which cometh by prostration—so westward from what seems the stump, one steadfast spear of lichened ruin veins the plain.

From that tree-top, what birded chimes of silver throats had rung. A stone pine, a metallic aviary in its crown: The Bell-Tower, built by the great mechanician, the unblest foundling, Bannadonna.

Like Babel's, its base was laid in a high hour of renovated earth, following the second deluge, when the waters of the Dark Ages had dried up, and once more the green appeared. No wonder that, after so long and deep submersion, the jubilant expectation of the race should, as with Noah's sons, soar into Shinar aspiration.

In firm resolve, no man in Europe at that period went beyond Bannadonna. Enriched through commerce with the Levant, the state in which he lived voted to have the noblest Bell-Tower in Italy. His repute assigned him to be architect.

Stone by stone, month by month, the tower rose. Higher, higher; snail-like in pace, but torch or rocket in its pride.

After the masons would depart, the builder, standing alone upon its ever-ascending summit, at close of every day, saw that he overtopped still higher walls and trees. He would tarry till a late hour there, wrapped in schemes of other and still loftier piles. Those who of saints' days thronged the spot—hanging to the rude poles of scaffolding, like sailors on yards, or bees on boughs, unmindful of lime and dust, and falling chips of stone—their homage not the less inspirited him to self-esteem.

At length the holiday of the Tower came. To the sound of viols, the climax-stone slowly rose in air, and, amid the firing of ordnance, was laid by Bannadonna's hands upon the final course. Then mounting it, he stood erect, alone, with folded arms, gazing upon the white summits of blue inland Alps, and whiter crests of bluer Alps off-shore—sights invisible from the plain. Invisible, too, from thence was that eye he turned below, when, like the cannon booms, came up to him the people's combustions of applause.

That which stirred them so was, seeing with what serenity the builder stood three hundred feet in air, upon an unrailed perch. This none but he durst do. But his periodic standing upon the pile, in each stage of its growth—such discipline had its last result.

Little remained now but the bells. These, in all respects, must correspond with their receptacle.

The minor ones were prosperously cast. A highly enriched one followed, of a singular make, intended for suspension in a manner before unknown. The purpose of this bell, its rotary motion, and connection with the clock-work, also executed at the time, will, in the sequel, receive mention.

In the one erection, bell-tower and clock-tower were united; though, before that period, such structures had commonly been built distinct; as the Campanile and Torre del 'Orologio of St. Mark to this day attest.

But it was upon the great state-bell that the founder lavished his more daring skill. In vain did some of the less elated magistrates here caution him; saying that though truly the tower was Titanic, yet limit should be set to the dependent weight of its swaying masses. But undeterred, he prepared his mammoth mould, dented with mythological devices; kindled his fires of balsamic firs; melted his tin and copper, and, throwing in much plate, contributed by the public spirit of the nobles, let loose the tide.

The unleashed metals bayed like hounds. The workmen shrunk. Through their fright, fatal harm to the bell was dreaded. Fearless as Shadrach, Bannadonna, rushing through the glow, smote the chief culprit with his ponderous ladle. From the smitten part, a splinter was dashed into the seething mass, and at once was melted in.

Next day a portion of the work was heedfully uncovered. All seemed right. Upon the third morning, with equal satisfaction, it was bared still lower. At length, like some old Theban king, the whole cooled casting was distinterred. All was fair except in one strange spot. But as he suffered no one to attend him in these inspections, he concealed the blemish by some preparation which none knew better to devise.

The casting of such a mass was deemed no small triumph for the caster; one, too, in which the state might not scorn to share. The homicide was overlooked. By the charitable that deed was but imputed to sudden transports of esthetic passion, not to any flagitious quality. A kick from an Arabian charger; not sign of vice, but blood.

His felony remitted by the judge, absolution given him by the priest, what more could even a sickly conscience have desired.

Honoring the tower and its builder with another holiday, the republic witnessed the hoisting of the bells and clock-work amid shows and pomps superior to the former.

Some months of more than usual solitude on Bannadonna's part ensued. It was not unknown that he was engaged upon something for the belfry, intended to complete it, and surpass all that had gone before. Most people imagined that the design would involve a casting like the bells. But those who thought they had some further insight, would shake their heads, with hints, that not for nothing did the mechanician keep so secret. Meantime, his seclusion failed not to invest his work with more or less of that sort of mystery pertaining to the forbidden.

Ere long he had a heavy object hoisted to the belfry, wrapped in a dark sack or cloak—a procedure sometimes had in the case of an elaborate piece of sculpture, or statue, which, being intended to grace the front of a new edifice, the architect does not desire exposed to critical eyes, till set up, finished, in its appointed place. Such was the impression now. But, as the object rose, a statuary present observed, or thought he did, that it was not entirely rigid, but was, in a manner, pliant. At last, when the hidden thing had attained its final height, and, obscurely seen from below, seemed almost of itself to step into the belfry, as if with little assistance from the crane, a shrewd old blacksmith present ventured the suspicion that it was but a living man. This surmise was thought a foolish one, while the general interest failed not to augment.

Not without demur from Bannadonna, the chief-magistrate of the town, with an associate—both elderly men—followed what seemed the image up the tower. But, arrived at the belfry, they had little recompense. Plausibly entrenching himself behind the conceded mysteries of his art, the mechanician withheld present explanation. The magistrates glanced toward the cloaked object, which, to their surprise, seemed now to have changed its attitude, or else had before been more perplexingly concealed by the violent muffling action of the wind without. It seemed now seated upon some sort of frame, or chair, contained within the domino. They observed that nigh the top, in a sort of square, the web of the cloth, either from accident or design, had its warp partly withdrawn, and the cross threads plucked out here and there, so as to form a sort of woven grating. Whether it were the low wind or no, stealing through the stone lattice-work, or only their own perturbed imaginations, is uncertain, but they thought they discerned a slight sort of fitful, spring-like motion, in the domino. Nothing, however incidental or insignificant, escaped their uneasy eyes. Among other things, they pried out, in a corner, an earthen cup, partly corroded and partly encrusted, and one whispered to the other, that this cup was just such a one as might, in mockery, be offered to the lips of some brazen statue, or, perhaps, still worse.

But, being questioned, the mechanician said, that the cup was simply used in his founder's business, and described the purpose; in short, a cup to test the condition of metals in fusion. He added, that it had got into the belfry by the merest chance.

Again, and again, they gazed at the domino, as at some suspicious incognito at a Venetian mask. All sorts of vague apprehensions stirred them. They even dreaded lest, when they should descend, the mechanician, though without a flesh and blood companion, for all that, would not be left alone.

Affecting some merriment at their disquietude, he begged to relieve them, by extending a coarse sheet of workman's canvas between them and the object.

Meantime he sought to interest them in his other work; nor, now that the domino was out of sight, did they long remain insensible to the artistic wonders lying round them; wonders hitherto beheld but in their unfinished state; because, since hoisting the bells, none but the caster had entered within the belfry. It was one trait of his, that, even in details, he would not let another do what he could, without too great loss of time, accomplish for himself. So, for several preceding weeks, whatever hours were unemployed in his secret design, had been devoted to elaborating the figures on the bells.

The clock-bell, in particular, now drew attention. Under a patient chisel, the latent beauty of its enrichments, before obscured by the cloudings incident to casting, that beauty in its shyest grace, was now revealed. Round and round the bell, twelve figures of gay girls, garlanded, hand-in-hand, danced in a choral ring—the embodied hours.

"Bannadonna," said the chief, "this bell excels all else. No added touch could here improve. Hark!" hearing a sound, "was that the wind?"

"The wind, Excellenza," was the light response. "But the figures, they are not yet without their faults. They need some touches yet. When those are given, and the—block yonder," pointing towards the canvas screen, "when Haman there, as I merrily call him,—him? *it*, I mean—when Haman is fixed on this, his lofty tree, then, gentlemen, will I be most happy to receive you here again."

The equivocal reference to the object caused some return of restlessness. However, on their part, the visitors forbore further allusion to it, unwilling, perhaps, to let the foundling see how easily it lay within his plebeian art to stir the placid dignity of nobles.

"Well, Bannadonna," said the chief, "how long ere you are ready to set the clock going, so that the hour shall be sounded? Our interest in you, not less than in the work itself, makes us anxious to be assured of your success. The people, too,—why, they are shouting now. Say the exact hour when you will be ready."

"To-morrow, Excellenza, if you listen for it,—or should you not, all the same—strange music will be heard. The stroke of one shall be the first from yonder bell," pointing to the bell adorned with girls and garlands, "that stroke shall fall there, where the hand of Una clasps Dua's. The stroke of one shall sever that loved clasp. To-morrow, then, at one o'clock, as struck here, precisely here," advancing and placing his finger upon the clasp, "the poor mechanic will be most happy once more to give you liege audience, in this his littered shop. Farewell till then, illustrious magnificoes, and hark ye for your vassal's stroke."

His still, Vulcanic face hiding its burning brightness like a forge, he moved with ostentatious deference towards the scuttle, as if so far to escort their exit. But the junior magistrate, a kind-hearted man, troubled at what seemed to him a certain sardonical disdain, lurking beneath the foundling's humble mien, and in Christian sympathy more distressed at it on his account than on his own, dimly surmising what might be the final fate of such a cynic solitaire, nor perhaps uninfluenced by the general strangeness of surrounding things, this good magistrate had glanced sadly, sideways from the speaker, and thereupon his foreboding eye had started at the expression of the unchanging face of the Hour Una.

"How is this, Bannadonna?" he lowly asked, "Una looks unlike her sisters."

"In Christ's name, Bannadonna," impulsively broke in the chief, his attention, for the first attracted to the figure, by his associate's remark, "Una's face looks just like that of Deborah, the prophetess, as painted by the Florentine, Del Fonca."

"Surely, Bannadonna," lowly resumed the milder magistrate, "you meant the twelve should wear the same jocundly abandoned air. But see, the smile of Una seems but a fatal one. 'Tis different."

While his mild associate was speaking, the chief glanced, inquiringly, from him to the caster, as if anxious to mark how the discrepancy would be accounted for. As the chief stood, his advanced foot was on the scuttle's curb.

Bannadonna spoke.

"Excellenza, now that, following your keener eye, I glance upon the facen of Una, I do, indeed perceive some little variance. But look all round the bell, and you will find no two faces entirely correspond. Because there is a law in art—but the cold wind is rising more; these lattices are but a poor defense. Suffer me, magnificoes, to conduct you, at least, partly on your way. Those in whose well-being there is a public stake, should be heedfully attended."

"Touching the look of Una, you were saying, Bannadonna, that there was a certain law in art," observed the chief, as the three now descended the stone shaft, "pray, tell me, then—"

"Pardon; another time, Excellenza;—the tower is damp."

"Nay, I must rest, and hear it now. Here,—here is a wide landing, and through this leeward slit, no wind, but ample light. Tell us of your law; and at large."

"Since, Excellenza, you insist, know that there is a law in art, which bars the possibility of duplicates. Some years ago, you may remember, I graved a small seal for your republic, bearing, for its chief device, the head of your own ancestor, its illustrious founder. It becoming necessary, for the customs' use, to have innumerable impressions for bales and boxes, I graved an entire plate, containing one hundred of the seals. Now, though, indeed, my object was to have those hundred heads identical, and though, I dare say, people think them; so, yet, upon closely scanning an uncut impression from the plate, no two of those five-score faces, side by side, will be found alike. Gravity is the air of all; but, diversified in all. In some, benevolent; in some, ambiguous; in two or three, to a close scrutiny, all but incipiently malign, the variation of less than a hair's breadth in the linear shadings round the mouth sufficing to all this. Now, Excellenza, transmute that general gravity into joyousness, and subject it to twelve of those variations I have described, and tell me, will you not have my hours here, and Una one of them? But I like—"

"Hark! is that—a footfall above?"

"Mortar, Excellenza; sometimes it drops to the belfry-floor from the arch where the stonework was left undressed. I must have it seen to. As I was about to say: for one, I like this law forbidding duplicates. It evokes fine personalities. Yes, Excellenza, that strange, and—to you—uncertain smile, and those fore-looking eyes of Una, suit Bannadonna very well."

"Hark!—sure we left no soul above?"

"No soul, Excellenza; rest assured, *no soul.*—Again the mortar."

"It fell not while we were there."

"Ah, in your presence, it better knew its place, Excellenza," blandly bowed Bannadonna.

"But, Una," said the milder magistrate, "she seemed intently gazing on you; one would have almost sworn that she picked you out from among us three."

"If she did, possibly, it might have been her finer apprehension, Excellenza."

"How, Bannadonna? I do not understand you."

"No consequence, no consequence, Excellenza—but the shifted wind is blowing through the slit. Suffer me to escort you on; and then, pardon, but the toiler must to his tools."

"It may be foolish, Signor," said the milder magistrate, as, from the third landing, the two now went down unescorted, "but, somehow, our great mechanician moves me strangely. Why, just now, when he so superciliously replied, his walk seemed Sisera's, God's vain foe, in Del Fonca's painting. And that young, sculptured Deborah, too. Ay, and that—"

"Tush, tush, Signor!" returned the chief. "A passing whim. Deborah?—Where's Jael, pray?"

"Ah," said the other, as they now stepped upon the sod, "Ah, Signor, I see you leave your fears behind you with the chill and gloom; but mine, even in this sunny air, remain. Hark!"

It was a sound from just within the tower door, whence they had emerged.

Turning, they saw it closed.

"He has slipped down and barred us out," smiled the chief; "but it is his custom."

Proclamation was now made, that the next day, at one hour after meridian, the clock would strike, and—thanks to the mechanician's powerful art—with unusual accompaniments. But what those should be, none as yet could say. The announcement was received with cheers.

By the looser sort, who encamped about the tower all night, lights were seen gleaming through the topmost blind-work, only disappearing with the morning sun. Strange sounds, too, were heard, or were thought to be, by those whom anxious watching might not have left mentally undisturbed—sounds, not only of some ringing implement, but also—so they said—half-suppressed screams and plainings, such as might have issued from some ghostly engine, overplied.

Slowly the day drew on; part of the concourse chasing the weary time with songs and games, till, at last, the great blurred sun rolled, like a football, against the plain.

At noon, the nobility and principal citizens came from the town in cavalcade, a guard of soldiers, also, with music, the more to honor the occasion.

Only one hour more. Impatience grew. Watches were held in hands of feverish men, who stood, now scrutinizing their small dial-plates, and then, with neck thrown back, gazing toward the belfry, as if the eye might foretell that which could only be made sensible to the ear; for, as yet, there was no dial to the tower-clock.

The hour hands of a thousand watches now verged within a hair's breadth of the figure 1. A silence, as of the expectation of some Shiloh, pervaded the swarming plain. Suddenly a dull, mangled sound—naught ringing in it; scarcely audible, indeed, to the outer circles of the people—that dull sound dropped heavily from the belfry. At the same moment, each man stared at his neighbor blankly. All watches were upheld. All hour-hands were at—had passed—the figure 1. No bell-stroke from the tower. The multitude became tumultuous.

Waiting a few moments, the chief magistrate, commanding silence, hailed the belfry, to know what thing unforeseen had happened there.

No response.

He hailed again and yet again.

All continued hushed.

By his order, the soldiers burst in the tower-door; when, stationing guards to defend it from the now surging mob, the chief, accompanied by his former associate, climbed the winding stairs. Half-way up, they stopped to listen. No sound. Mounting faster, they reached the belfry; but, at the threshold, started at the spectacle disclosed. A spaniel, which, unbeknown to them, had followed them thus far, stood shivering as before some unknown monster in a brake: or, rather, as if it snuffed footsteps leading to some other world.

Bannadonna lay, prostrate and bleeding, at the base of the bell which was adorned with girls and garlands. He lay at the feet of the hour Una; his head coinciding, in a vertical line, with her left hand, clasped by the hour Dua. With downcast face impending over him, like Jael over nailed Sisera in the tent, was the domino; now no more becloaked.

It had limbs, and seemed clad in a scaly mail, lustrous as a dragon-beetle's. It was manacled, and its clubbed arms were uplifted, as if, with its manacles, once more to smite its already smitten victim. One advanced foot of it was inserted beneath the dead body, as if in the act of spurning it.

Uncertainty falls on what now followed.

It were but natural to suppose that the magistrates would, at first, shrink from immediate personal contact with what they saw. At the least, for a time, they would stand in involuntary doubt; it may be, in more or less of horrified alarm. Certain it is, that an arquebus was called for from below. And some add, that its report, followed by a fierce whiz, as of the sudden snapping of a main-spring, with a steely din, as if a stack of sword-blades should be dashed upon a pavement, these blended sounds came ringing to the plain, attracting every eye far upward to the belfry, whence, through the lattice-work, thin wreaths of smoke were curling.

Some averred that it was the spaniel, gone mad by fear, which was shot. This, others denied. True it was, the spaniel never more was seen; and, probably, for some unknown reason, it shared the burial now to be related of the domino. For, whatever the preceding circumstances may have been, the first instinctive panic over, or else all ground of reasonable fear removed, the two magistrates, by themselves, quickly rehooded the figure in the dropped cloak wherein it had been hoisted. The same night, it was secretly lowered to the ground, smuggled to the beach, pulled far out to sea, and sunk. Nor to any after urgency, even in free convivial hours, would the twain ever disclose the full secrets of the belfry.

From the mystery unavoidably investing it, the popular solution of the foundling's fate involved more or less of supernatural agency.

But some few less unscientific minds pretended to find little difficulty in otherwise accounting for it. In the chain of circumstantial inferences drawn, there may, or may not, have been some absent or defective links. But, as the explanation in question is the only one which tradition has explicitly preserved, in dearth of better, it will here be given. But, in the first place, it is requisite to present the supposition entertained as to the entire motive and mode, with their origin, of the secret design of Bannadonna; the minds above-mentioned assuming to penetrate as well into his soul as into the event. The disclosure will indirectly involve reference to peculiar matters, none of, the clearest, beyond the immediate subject.

At that period, no large bell was made to sound otherwise than as at present, by agitation of a tongue within, by means of ropes, or percussion from without, either from cumbrous machinery, or stalwart watchmen, armed with heavy hammers, stationed in the belfry, or in sentry-boxes on the open roof, according as the bell was sheltered or exposed.

It was from observing these exposed bells, with their watchmen, that the foundling, as was opined, derived the first suggestion of his scheme.

Perched on a great mast or spire, the human figure, viewed from below, undergoes such a reduction in its apparent size, as to obliterate its intelligent features. It evinces no personality. Instead of bespeaking volition, its gestures rather resemble the automatic ones of the arms of a telegraph.

Musing, therefore, upon the purely Punchinello aspect of the human figure thus beheld, it had indirectly occurred to Bannadonna to devise some metallic agent, which should strike the hour with its mechanic hand, with even greater precision than the vital one. And, moreover, as the vital watchman on the roof, sallying from his retreat at the given periods, walked to the bell with uplifted mace, to smite it,

Bannadonna had resolved that his invention should likewise possess the power of locomotion, and, along with that, the appearance, at least, of intelligence and will.

If the conjectures of those who claimed acquaintance with the intent of Bannadonna be thus far correct, no unenterprising spirit could have been his. But they stopped not here; intimating that though, indeed, his design had, in the first place, been prompted by the sight of the watchman, and confined to the devising of a subtle substitute for him: yet, as is not seldom the case with projectors, by insensible gradations, proceeding from comparatively pigmy aims to Titanic ones, the original scheme had, in its anticipated eventualities, at last, attained to an unheard of degree of daring. He still bent his efforts upon the locomotive figure for the belfry, but only as a partial type of an ulterior creature, a sort of elephantine Helot, adapted to further, in a degree scarcely to be imagined, the universal conveniences and glories of humanity; supplying nothing less than a supplement to the Six Days' Work; stocking the earth with a new serf, more useful than the ox, swifter than the dolphin, stronger than the lion, more cunning than the ape, for industry an ant, more fiery than serpents, and yet, in patience, another ass. All excellences of all God-made creatures, which served man, were here to receive advancement, and then to be combined in one. Talus was to have been the all-accomplished Helot's name. Talus, iron slave to Bannadonna, and, through him, to man.

Here, it might well be thought that, were these last conjectures as to the foundling's secrets not erroneous, then must he have been hopelessly infected with the craziest chimeras of his age; far outgoing Albert Magus and Cornelius Agrippa. But the contrary was averred. However marvelous his design, however apparently transcending not alone the bounds of human invention, but those of divine creation, yet the proposed means to be employed were alleged to have been confined within the sober forms of sober reason. It was affirmed that, to a degree of more than skeptic scorn, Bannadonna had been without sympathy for any of the vain-glorious irrationalities of his time. For example, he had not concluded, with the visionaries among the metaphysicians, that between the finer mechanic forces and the ruder animal vitality some germ of correspondence might prove discoverable. As little did his scheme partake of the enthusiasm of some natural philosophers, who hoped, by physiological and chemical inductions, to arrive at a knowledge of the source of life, and so qualify themselves to manufacture and improve upon it. Much less had he aught in common with the tribe of alchemists, who sought, by a species of incantations, to evoke some surprising vitality from the laboratory. Neither had he imagined, with certain sanguine theosophists, that, by faithful adoration of the Highest, unheard-of powers would be vouchsafed to man. A practical materialist, what Bannadonna had aimed at was to have been reached, not by logic, not by crucible, not by conjuration, not by altars; but by plain vice-bench and hammer. In short, to solve nature, to steal into her, to intrigue beyond her, to procure someone else to bind her to his hand;—these, one and all, had not been his objects; but, asking no favors from any element or any being, of himself, to rival her, outstrip her, and rule her. He stooped to conquer. With him, common sense was theurgy; machinery, miracle; Prometheus, the heroic name for machinist; man, the true God.

Nevertheless, in his initial step, so far as the experimental automaton for the belfry was concerned, he allowed fancy some little play; or, perhaps, what seemed his fancifulness was but his utilitarian ambition collaterally extended. In figure, the creature for the belfry should not be likened after the human pattern, nor any animal one, nor after the ideals, however wild, of ancient fable, but equally in aspect as in organism be an original production; the more terrible to behold, the better.

Such, then, were the suppositions as to the present scheme, and the reserved intent. How, at the very threshold, so unlooked for a catastrophe overturned all, or rather, what was the conjecture here, is now to be set forth.

It was thought that on the day preceding the fatality, his visitors having left him, Bannadonna had unpacked the belfry image, adjusted it, and placed it in the retreat provided—a sort of sentry-box in one corner of the belfry; in short, throughout the night, and for some part of the ensuing morning, he had been engaged in arranging everything connected with the domino; the issuing from the sentry-box each sixty minutes; sliding along a grooved way, like a railway; advancing to the clock-bell, with uplifted manacles; striking it at one of the twelve junctions of the four-and-twenty hands; then wheeling, circling the bell, and retiring to its post, there to bide for another sixty minutes, when the same process was to be repeated; the bell, by a cunning mechanism, meantime turning on its vertical axis, so as to present, to the descending mace, the clasped hands of the next two figures, when it would strike two, three, and so on, to the end. The musical metal in this time-bell being so managed in the fusion, by some art, perishing with its originator, that each of the clasps of the four-and-twenty hands should give forth its own peculiar resonance when parted.

But on the magic metal, the magic and metallic stranger never struck but that one stroke, drove but that one nail, served but that one clasp, by which Bannadonna clung to his ambitious life. For, after winding up the creature in the sentry-box, so that, for the present, skipping the intervening hours, it should not emerge till the hour of one, but should then infallibly emerge, and, after deftly oiling the grooves whereon it was to slide, it was surmised that the mechanician must then have hurried to the bell, to give his final touches to its sculpture. True artist, he here became absorbed; and absorption still further intensified, it may be, by his striving to abate that strange look of Una; which, though, before others, he had treated with such unconcern, might not, in secret, have been without its thorn.

And so, for the interval, he was oblivious of his creature; which, not oblivious of him, and true to its creation, and true to its heedful winding up, left its post precisely at the given moment; along its well-oiled route, slid noiselessly towards its mark; and, aiming at the hand of Una, to ring one clangorous note, dully smote the intervening brain of Bannadonna, turned backwards to it; the manacled arms then instantly up-springing to their hovering poise. The falling body clogged the thing's return; so there it stood, still impending over Bannadonna, as if whispering some post-mortem terror. The chisel lay dropped from the hand, but beside the hand; the oil-flask spilled across the iron track.

In his unhappy end, not unmindful of the rare genius of the mechanician, the republic decreed him a stately funeral. It was resolved that the great bell—the one whose casting had been jeopardized through the timidity of the ill-starred workman—should be rung upon the entrance of the bier into the cathedral. The most robust man of the country round was assigned the office of bell-ringer.

But as the pall-bearers entered the cathedral porch, naught but a broken and disastrous sound, like that of some lone Alpine land-slide, fell from the tower upon their ears. And then, all was hushed.

Glancing backwards, they saw the groined belfry crashed sideways in. It afterwards appeared that the powerful peasant, who had the bell-rope in charge, wishing to test at once the full glory of the bell, had swayed down upon the rope with one concentrate jerk. The mass of quaking metal, too ponderous for its frame, and strangely feeble somewhere at its top, loosed from its fastening, tore sideways down, and tumbling in one sheer fall, three hundred feet to the soft sward below, buried itself inverted and half out of sight.

Upon its disinterment, the main fracture was found to have started from a small spot in the ear; which, being scraped, revealed a defect, deceptively minute in the casting; which defect must subsequently have been pasted over with some unknown compound.

The remolten metal soon reassumed its place in the tower's repaired superstructure. For one year the metallic choir of birds sang musically in its belfry-bough-work of sculptured blinds and traceries. But on the first anniversary of the tower's completion—at early dawn, before the concourse had surrounded it—an earthquake came; one loud crash was heard. The stone-pine, with all its bower of songsters, lay overthrown upon the plain.

So the blind slave obeyed its blinder lord; but, in obedience, slew him. So the creator was killed by the creature. So the bell was too heavy for the tower. So the bell's main weakness was where man's blood had flawed it. And so pride went before the fall.

ROSE ROSE

BARRY PAIN

Sefton stepped back from his picture. "Rest now, please," he said.

Miss Rose Rose, his model, threw the striped blanket around her, stepped down from the throne, and crossed the studio. She seated herself on the floor near the big stove. For a few moments Sefton stood motionless, looking critically at his work. Then he laid down his palette and brushes and began to roll a cigarette. He was a man of forty, thick-set, round-faced, with a reddish moustache turned fiercely upwards. He flung himself down in an easy-chair, and smoked in silence till silence seemed ungracious.

"Well," he said, "I've got the place hot enough for you today, Miss Rose."

"You 'ave indeed," said Miss Rose.

"I bet it's nearer eighty than seventy."

The cigarette-smoke made a blue haze in the hot, heavy air. He watched it undulating, curving, melting.

As he watched it Miss Rose continued her observations. The trouble with these studios was the draughts. With a strong east wind, same as yesterday, you might have the stove red-hot, and yet never get the place, so to speak, warm. It is possible to talk commonly without talking like a coster, and Miss Rose achieved it. She did not always neglect the aspirate. She never quite substituted the third vowel for the first. She rather enjoyed long words.

She was beautiful from the crown of her head to the sole of her foot; and few models have good feet. Every pose she took was graceful. She was the daughter of a model, and had been herself a model from childhood. In consequence, she knew her work well and did it well. On one occasion, when sitting for the great Merion, she had kept the same pose, without a rest, for three consecutive hours. She was proud of that. Naturally she stood in the first rank among models, was most in demand, and made the most money. Her fault was that she was slightly capricious; you could not absolutely depend upon her. On a wintry morning when every hour of daylight was precious, she might keep her appointment, she might be an hour or two late, or she might stay away altogether. Merion himself had suffered from her, had sworn never to employ her again, and had gone back to her.

Sefton, as he watched the blue smoke, found that her common accent jarred on him. It even seemed to make it more difficult for him to get the right presentation of the "Aphrodite" that she was helping him to paint. One seemed to demand a poetical and cultured soul in so beautiful a body. Rose Rose was not poetical nor cultured; she was not even business-like and educated.

Half an hour of silent and strenuous work followed. Then Sefton growled that he could not see any longer.

"We'll stop for to-day," he said. Miss Rose Rose retired behind the screen. Sefton opened a window and both ventilators, and rolled another cigarette. The studio became rapidly cooler.

"To-morrow, at nine?" he called out.

"I've got some way to come," came the voice of Miss Rose from behind the screen. "I could be here by a quarter past."

"Right," said Sefton, as he slipped on his coat.

When Rose Rose emerged from the screen she was dressed in a blue serge costume, with a picture-hat. As it was her business in life to be beautiful, she never wore corsets, high heels, nor pointed toes. Such abnegation is rare among models.

"I say, Mr. Sefton," said Rose, "you were to settle at the end of the sittings, but—"

"Oh, you don't want any money, Miss Rose. You're known to be rich."

"Well, what I've got is in the Post Office, and I don't want to touch it. And I've got some shopping I must do before I go home."

Sefton pulled out his sovereign-case hesitatingly.

"This is all very well, you know," he said.

"I know what you are thinking, Mr. Sefton. You think I don't mean to come to-morrow. That's all Mr. Merion, now, isn't it? He's always saying things about me. I'm not going to stick it. I'm going to 'ave it out with 'im."

"He recommended you to me. And I'll tell you what he said, if you won't repeat it. He said that I should be lucky if I got you, and that I'd better chain you to the studio."

"And all because I was once late—with a good reason for it, too. Besides, what's once? I suppose he didn't 'appen to tell you how often he's kept me waiting."

"Well, here you are, Miss Rose. But you'll really be here in time to-morrow, won't you? Otherwise the thing will have got too tacky to work into."

"You needn't worry about that," said Miss Rose, eagerly. "I'll be here, whatever happens, by a quarter past nine. I'll be here if I die first! There, is that good enough for you? Good afternoon, and thank you, Mr. Sefton."

"Good afternoon, Miss Rose. Let me manage that door for you—the key goes a bit stiffly."

Sefton came back to his picture. In spite of Miss Rose's vehement assurances he felt by no means sure of her, but it was difficult for him to refuse any woman anything, and impossible for him to refuse to pay her what he really owed. He scrawled in charcoal some directions to the charwoman who would come in the morning. She was, from his point of view, a prize charwoman—one who could, and did, wash brushes properly, one who understood the stove, and would, when required, refrain from sweeping. He picked up his hat and went out. He walked the short distance from his studio to his bachelor flat, looked over art evening paper as he drank his tea, and then changed his clothes and took a cab to the club for dinner. He played one game of billiards after dinner, and then went home. His picture was very much in his mind. He wanted to be up fairly early in the morning, and he went to bed early.

He was at his studio by half-past eight. The stove was lighted, and he piled more coke on it. His "Aphrodite" seemed to have a somewhat mocking expression. It was a little, technical thing, to be corrected easily. He set his palette and selected his brushes. An attempt to roll a cigarette revealed the fact that his pouch was empty. It still wanted a few minutes to nine. He would have time to go up to the tobacconist at the corner. In case Rose Rose arrived while he was away, he left the studio door open. The tobacconist was also a newsagent, and he bought a morning paper. Rose would probably be twenty minutes late at the least, and this would be something to occupy him.

But on his return he found his model already stepping on to the throne.

"Good morning, Miss Rose. You're a lady of your word." He hardly heeded the murmur which came to him as a reply. He threw his cigarette into the stove, picked up his palette, and got on excellently. The work was absorbing. For some time he thought of nothing else. There was no relaxing on the part of the model—no sign of fatigue. He had been working for over an hour, when his conscience smote him. "We'll have a rest now, Miss Rose," he said cheerily. At the same moment he felt human fingers drawn lightly across the back of his neck, just above the collar. He turned round with a sudden start. There was nobody there. He turned back again to the throne. Rose Rose had vanished.

With the utmost care and deliberation he put down his palette and brushes. He said in a loud voice, "Where are you. Miss Rose?" For a moment or two silence hung in the hot air of the studio.

He repeated his question and got no answer. Then he stepped behind the screen, and suddenly the most terrible thing in his life happened to him. He knew that his model had never been there at all.

There was only one door out to the back street in which his studio was placed, and that door was now locked. He unlocked it, put on his hat, and went out. For a minute or two he paced the street, but he had got to go back to the studio.

He went back, sat down in the easy-chair, lit a cigarette, and tried for a plausible explanation. Undoubtedly he had been working very hard lately. When he had come back from the tobacconist's to the studio he had been in the state of expectant attention, and he was enough of a psychologist to know that in that state you are especially likely to see what you expect to sec. He was not conscious of anything abnormal in himself. He did not feel ill, or even nervous. Nothing of the kind had ever happened to him before. The more he considered the matter, the more definite became his state. He was thoroughly frightened. With a great effort he pulled himself together and picked up the newspaper. It was certain that he could do no more work for that day, anyhow. An ordinary, commonplace newspaper would restore him. Yes, that was it. He had been too much wrapped up in the picture. He had simply supposed the model to be there.

He was quite unconvinced, of course, and merely trying to convince himself. As an artist, he knew that for the last hour or more he had been getting the most delicate modelling right from the living form before him. But he did his best, and read the newspaper assiduously. He read of tariff, protection, and of a new music-hall star. Then his eye fell on a paragraph headed "Motor Fatalities."

He read that Miss Rose, an artist's model, had been knocked down by a car in the Fulham Road about seven o'clock on the previous evening; that the owner of the car had stopped and taken her to the hospital, and that she had expired within a few minutes of admission.

He rose from his place and opened a large pocket-knife. There was a strong impulse upon him, and he felt it to be a mad impulse, to slash the canvas to rags. He stopped before the picture. The face smiled at him with a sweetness that was scarcely earthly.

He went back to his chair again. "I'm not used to this kind of thing," he said aloud. A board creaked at the far end of the studio. He jumped up with a start of horror. A few minutes later he had left the studio, and locked the door behind him. His common sense was still with him. He ought to go to a specialist. But the picture—

***

"What's the matter with Sefton?" said Devigne one night at the club after dinner.

"Don't know that anything's the matter with him," said Merion. "He hasn't been here lately."

"I saw him the last time he was here, and he seemed pretty queer. Wanted to let me his studio."

"It's not a bad studio," said Merion, dispassionately.

"He's got rid of it now, anyhow. He's got a studio out at Richmond, and the deuce of a lot of time he must waste getting there and back. Besides, what does he do about models?"

"That's a point I've been wondering about myself," said Merion. "He'd got Rose Rose for his 'Aphrodite,' and it looked as if it might be a pretty good thing when I saw it. But, as you know, she died. She was troublesome in some ways, but, taking her all round, I don't know where to find anybody as good to-day. What's Sefton doing about it?"

"He hasn't got a model at all at present. I know that for a fact, because I asked him."

"Well," said Merion, "he may have got the thing on further than I thought he would in the time. Some chaps can work from memory all right, though I can't do it myself. He's not chucked the picture, I suppose?"

"No; he's not done that. In fact, the picture's his excuse now, if you want him to go anywhere and do anything. But that's not it: the chap's altogether changed. He used to be a genial sort of bounder—bit tyrannical in his manner, perhaps—thought he knew everything. Still, you could talk to him. He was sociable. As a matter of fact, he did know a good deal. Now it's quite different. If you ever do see him—and that's not often—he's got nothing to say to you. He's just going back to his work. That sort of thing."

"You're too imaginative," said Merion. "I never knew a man who varied less than Sefton. Give me his address, will you? I mean his studio. I'll go and look him up one morning. I should like to see how that 'Aphrodite's' getting on. I tell you it was promising; no nonsense about it."

***

One sunny morning Merion knocked at the door of the studio at Richmond. He heard the sound of footsteps crossing the studio, then Sefton's voice rang out.

"Who's there?"

"Merion. I've travelled miles to see the thing you call a picture."

"I've got a model."

"And what does that matter?" asked Merion.

"Well, I'd be awfully glad if you'd come back in an hour. We'd have lunch together somewhere."

"Right," said Merion, sardonically. "I'll come back in about seven million hours. Wait for me."

He went back to London and his own studio in a state of fury. Sefton had never been a man to pose. He had never put on side about his work. He was always willing to show it to old and intimate friends whose judgment he could trust; and now, when the oldest of his friends had travelled down to Richmond to see him, he was told to come back in an hour, and that they might then lunch together!

"This lets me out," said Merion, savagely.

***

But he always speaks well of Sefton nowadays. He maintains that Sefton's "Aphrodite" would have been a success anyhow. The suicide made a good deal of talk at the time, and a special attendant was necessary to regulate the crowds round it, when, as directed by his will, the picture was exhibited at the Royal Academy. He was found in his studio many hours after his death; and he had scrawled on a blank canvas, much as he left his directions to his charwoman: "I have finished it, but I can't stand any more."

BERENICE

EDGAR ALLAN POE

Dicebant mihi sodales, si sepulchrum amicae visitarem, curas meas aliquantulum fore levatas.—Ebn Zaiat.

Misery is manifold. The wretchedness of earth is multiform. Overreaching the wide horizon as the rainbow, its hues are as various as the hues of that arch,—as distant too, yet as intimately blended. Overreaching the wide horizon as the rainbow! How is it that from beauty I have derived a type of unloveliness?—from the convenant of peace a simile of sorrow? But as, in ethics, evil is a consequence of good, so, in fact, out of joy is sorrow born. Either the memory of past bliss is the anguish of to-day, or the agonies which *are* have their origin in the ecstasies which *might have been*.

My baptismal name is Egseus; that of my family I will not mention. Yet there are no towers in the land time-honoured more than my gloomy, grey, hereditary halls. Our line has been called a race of visionaries; and in many striking particulars—in the character of the family mansion—in the frescoes of the chief saloon—in the tapestries of the dormitories—in the chiselling of some buttresses in the armoury—but more especially in the gallery of antique paintings—in the fashion of the library chamber—and, lastly, in the very peculiar nature of the library's contents, there is more than sufficient evidence to warrant the belief.

The recollections of my earliest years are connected with that chamber, and with its volumes—of which latter I will say no more. Here died my mother. Herein was I born. But it is mere idleness to say that I had not lived before—that the soul has no previous existence. You deny it?—let us not argue the matter. Convinced myself, I seek not to convince. There is, however, a remembrance of aerial forms—of spiritual and meaning eyes—of sounds, musical yet sad—a remembrance which will not be excluded; a memory like a shadow, vague, variable, indefinite, unsteady; and like a shadow, too, in the impossibility of my getting rid of it while the sunlight of my reason shall exist.

In that chamber was I born. Thus awaking from the long night of what seemed, but was not, nonentity, at once into the very regions of fairy-land—into a palace of imagination—into the wild dominions of monastic thought and erudition—it is not singular that I gazed around me with a startled and ardent eye—that I loitered away my boyhood in books, and dissipated my youth in reverie; but it *is* singular that as years rolled away, and the noon of manhood found me still in the mansion of my fathers—it is wonderful what stagnation there fell upon the springs of my life—wonderful how total an inversion took place in the character of my commonest thought. The realities of the world affected me as visions, and as visions only, while the wild ideas of the land of dreams became, in turn,—not the material of my every-day existence—but in very deed that existence utterly and solely in itself.

Berenice and I were cousins, and we grew up together in my paternal halls. Yet differently we grew—I ill of health, and buried in gloom—she agile, graceful, and overflowing with energy; hers the ramble on the hill-side—mine the studies of the cloister—I living within my own heart, and addicted body and soul to the most intense and painful meditation—she roaming carelessly through life with no thought of the shadows in her path, or the silent flight of the raven-winged hours. Berenice!—I call upon her name—Berenice!—and from the grey ruins of memory a thousand tumultuous recollections are startled at the sound! Ah! vividly is her image before me now as in the early days of her light-heartedness and joy! Oh! gorgeous yet fantastic beauty! Oh! sylph amid the shrubberies of Arnheim! Oh! Naiad among its fountains!—and then—then air is mystery and terror, and a tale which should not be told. Disease—a fatal disease—fell like the simoon upon her frame, and, even while I gazed upon her, the spirit of change swept over her, pervading her mind, her habits, and her character, and, in a manner the most subtle and terrible, disturbing even the identity of her person! Alas! the destroyer came and went, and the victim—where was she? I knew her not—or knew her no longer as Berenice.

Among the numerous train of maladies superinduced by that fatal and primary one which effected a revolution of so horrible a kind in the moral and physical being of my cousin, may be mentioned as the most distressing and obstinate in its nature, a species of epilepsy not unfrequently terminating in *trance* itself—trance very nearly resembling positive dissolution, and from which her manner of recovery was, in most instances, startlingly abrupt. In the meantime my own disease—for I have been told that I should call it by no other appellation—my own disease, then, grew rapidly upon me, and assumed finally a monomaniac character of a novel and extraordinary form—hourly and momently gaining vigour—and at length obtaining over me the most incomprehensible ascendancy. This monomania, if I must so term it, consisted in a morbid irritability of those properties of the mind in metaphysical science termed the *attentive*. It is more than probable that I am not understood; but I fear, indeed, that it is in no manner possible to convey to the mind of the merely general reader, an adequate idea of that nervous *intensity of interest* with which, in my case, the powers of meditation (not to speak technically) busied and buried themselves, in the contemplation of even the most ordinary objects of the universe.

To muse, for long unwearied hours with my attention riveted to some frivolous device on the margin, or in the typography of a book; to become absorbed for the better part of a summer's day, in a quaint shadow falling aslant upon the tapestry, or upon the door; to lose myself for an entire night in watching the steady flame of a lamp, or the embers of a fire; to dream away whole days over the perfume of a flower; to repeat monotonously some common word, until the sound, by dint of frequent repetition, ceased to convey any idea whatever to the mind; to lose all sense of motion or physical existence, by means of absolute bodily quiescence long and obstinately persevered in;—such were a few of the most common and least pernicious vagaries induced by a condition of the mental faculties, not, indeed, altogether unparalleled, but certainly bidding defiance to anything like analysis or explanation.

Yet let me not be misapprehended.—The undue, earnest, and morbid attention thus excited by objects in their own nature frivolous, must not be confounded in character with that ruminating propensity common to all mankind, and more especially indulged in by persons of ardent imagination. It was not even, as might be at first supposed, an extreme condition, or exaggeration of such propensity, but primarily and essentially distinct and different. In the one instance, the dreamer, or enthusiast, being interested by an object usually *not* frivolous, imperceptibly loses sight of this object in a wilderness of deductions and suggestions issuing therefrom, until, at the conclusion of a daydream *often replete with luxury,* he finds the *incitamentum* or first cause of his musings entirely vanished and forgotten. In my case the primary object was *invariably frivolous,* although assuming, through the medium of my distempered vision a refracted and unreal importance. Few deductions, if any, were made; and those few pertinaciously returning in upon the original object as a centre. The meditations were *never* pleasurable; and, at the termination of the reverie, the first cause, so far from being out of sight, had attained that supernaturally exaggerated interest which was the prevailing feature of the disease. In a word, the powers of mind more particularly exercised were, with me, as I have said before, the *attentive,* and are, with the day-dreamer, the *speculative.*

My books, at this epoch, if they did not actually serve to irritate the disorder, partook, it will be perceived, largely, in their imaginative and inconsequential nature, of the characteristic qualities of the disorder itself. I well remember, among others, the treatise of the noble Italian Coelius Secundus Curio, *De Amplitudine Beati Regni Dei;* St. Austin's great work, *The City of God;* and Tertullian, *De Carne Christi,* in which the paradoxical sentence, *"Mortuus est Dei filius; credibile est quia ineptum est; et sepultus resurrexit; certutn est quia impossibile est,"* occupied my undivided time, for many weeks of laborious and fruitless investigation.

Thus it will appear that, shaken from its balance only by trivial things, my reason bore resemblance to that ocean-crag spoken of by Ptolemy Hephestion, which, steadily resisting the attacks of human violence, and the fiercer fury of the waters and the winds, trembled only to the touch of the flower called Asphodel. And although, to a careless thinker, it might appear a matter beyond doubt, that the alteration produced by her unhappy malady, in the *moral* condition of Berenice, would afford me many objects for the exercise of that intense and abnormal meditation whose nature I have been at some trouble in explaining, yet such was not in any degree the case. In the lucid intervals of my infirmity, her calamity, indeed, gave me pain, and, taking deeply to heart that total wreck of her fair and gentle life, I did not fail to ponder frequently and bitterly upon the wonderworking means by which so strange a revolution had been so suddenly brought to pass. But these reflections partook not of the idiosyncrasy of my disease, and were such as would have occurred, under similar circumstances, to the ordinary mass of mankind. True to its own character, my disorder revelled in the less important but more startling changes wrought in the *physical* frame of Berenice—in the singular and most appalling distortion of her personal identity.

During the brightest days of her unparalleled beauty, most surely I had never loved her. In the strange anomaly of my existence, feelings with me *had never been* of the heart, and my passions *always were* of the mind. Through the grey of the early morning—among the trellised shadows of the forest at noonday—and in the silence of my library at night, she had flitted by my eyes, and I had seen her—not as the living and breathing Berenice, but as the Berenice of a dream—not as a being of the earth, earthy, but as the abstraction of such a being—not as a thing to admire, but to analyse—not as an object of love, but as the theme of the most abstruse although desultory speculation. And *now*—now I shuddered in her presence, and grew pale at her approach; yet bitterly lamenting her fallen and desolate condition, I called to mind that she had loved me long, and, in an evil moment, I spoke to her of marriage.

And at length the period of our nuptials was approaching, when, upon an afternoon in the winter of the year,—one of those unseasonably warm, calm, and misty days which are the nurse of the beautiful Halcyon[1]—I sat (and sat, as I thought, alone) in the inner apartment of the library. But uplifting my eyes I saw that Berenice stood before me.

Was it my own excited imagination—or the misty influence of the atmosphere—or the uncertain twilight of the chamber—or the grey draperies which fell around her figure—that caused in it so vacillating and indistinct an outline? I could not tell. She spoke no word, and I—not for worlds could I have uttered a syllable. An icy chill ran through my frame; a sense of insufferable anxiety oppressed me; a consuming curiosity pervaded my soul; and sinking back upon the chair, I remained for some time breathless and motionless, with my eyes riveted upon her person. Alas! its emaciation was excessive, and not one vestige of the former being lurked in any single line of the contour. My burning glances at length fell upon the face.

The forehead was high, and very pale, and singularly placid; and the once jetty hair fell partially over it, and overshadowed the hollow temples with innumerable ringlets now of a vivid yellow, and jarring discordantly, in their fantastic character, with the reigning melancholy of the countenance. The eyes were lifeless, and lustreless, and seemingly pupil-less, and I shrank involuntarily from their glassy stare to the contemplation of the thin and shrunken lips. They parted; and in a smile of peculiar meaning, *the teeth* of the changed Berenice disclosed themselves slowly to my view. Would to God that I had never beheld them, or that, having done so, I had died!

***

---

[1] For as Jove, during the winter season, gives twice seven days of warmth, men have called this clement and temperate time the nurse of the beautiful Halcyon. SIMONIDES.

The shutting of a door disturbed me, and, looking up, I found that my cousin had departed from the chamber. But from the disordered chamber of my brain, had not, alas! departed, and would not be driven away, the white and ghastly *spectrum* of the teeth. Not a speck on their surface—not a shade on their enamel—not an indenture in their edges—but what that period of her smile had sufficed to brand in upon my memory. I saw them *now* even more unequivocally than I beheld them *then*. The teeth!—the teeth!—they were here, and there, and everywhere, and visibly and palpably before me; long, narrow, and excessively white, with the pale lips writhing about them, as in the very moment of their first terrible development. Then came the full fury of *monomania*, and I struggled in vain against its strange and irresistible influence. In the multiplied objects of the external world I had no thoughts but for the teeth. For these I longed with a phrenzied desire. All other matters and all different interests became absorbed in their single contemplation. They—they alone were present to the mental eye, and they, in their sole individuality, became the essence of my mental life. I held them in every light. I turned them in every attitude. I surveyed their characteristics. I dwelt upon their peculiarities. I pondered upon their conformation. I mused upon the alteration in their nature. I shuddered as I assigned to them in imagination a sensitive and sentient power, and even when unassisted by the lips, a capability of moral expression. Of Mad'selle Salle it has been well said, *"que tous ses pas étaient des sentiments"* and of Berenice I more seriously believed *que toutes ses dents étaient des idées. Des idées!*—ah here was the idiotic thought that destroyed me! *Des idées!* ah *therefore* it was that I coveted them so madly! I felt that their possession could alone ever restore me to peace, in giving me back to reason.

And the evening closed in upon me thus—and then the darkness came, and tarried, and went—and the day again dawned—and the mists of a second night were now gathering around—and still I sat motionless in that solitary room; and still I sat buried in meditation, and still the *phantasma* of the teeth maintained its terrible ascendency as, with the most vivid and hideous distinctness, it floated about amid the changing lights and shadows of the chamber. At length there broke in upon my dreams a cry as of horror and dismay; and thereunto, after a pause succeeded the sound of troubled voices, intermingled with many low meanings of sorrow, or of pain. I arose from my seat and, throwing open one of the doors of the library, saw standing out in the ante-chamber a servant maiden, all in tears, who told me that Berenice was—no more. She had been seized with epilepsy in the early morning, and now, at the closing in of the night, the grave was ready for its tenant, and all the preparations for the burial were completed.

***

I found myself sitting in the library, and again sitting there alone. It seemed that I had newly awakened from a confused and exciting dream. I knew that it was now midnight, and I was well aware that since the setting of the sun Berenice had been interred. But of that dreary period which intervened I had no positive—at least no definite comprehension. Yet its memory was replete with horror—horror more horrible from being vague, and terror more terrible from ambiguity. It was a fearful page in the record of my existence, written all over with dim, and hideous, and unintelligible recollections. I strived to decipher them, but in vain; while ever and anon, like the spirit of a departed sound, the shrill and piercing shriek of a female voice seemed to be ringing in my ears. I had done a deed—what was it? I asked myself the question aloud, and the whispering echoes of the chamber answered me, *"what was it?"*

On the table beside me burned a lamp, and near it lay a little box. It was of no remarkable character, and I had seen it frequently before, for it was the property of the family physician; but how came it *there*, upon my table, and why did I shudder in regarding it? These things were in no manner to be accounted for, and my eyes at length dropped to the open pages of a book, and to a sentence underscored therein. The words were the singular but simple ones of the poet Ebn Zaiat, *"Dicebant mihi sodales si sepulchrum amicae visitarem, curas meas aliquantulum fore levatas."* Why then, as I perused them, did the hairs of my head erect themselves on end, and the blood of my body become congealed within my veins?

There came a light tap at the library door, and pale as the tenant of a tomb, a menial entered upon tiptoe. His looks were wild with terror, and he spoke to me in a voice tremulous, husky, and very low. What said he?—some broken sentences I heard. He told of a wild cry disturbing the silence of the night—of the gathering together of the household—of a search in the direction of the sound;—and then his tones grew thrillingly distinct as he whispered me of a violated grave—of a disfigured body enshrouded, yet still breathing, still palpitating, still *alive!*

He pointed to my garments;—they were muddy and clotted with gore. I spoke not, and he took me gently by the hand;—it was indented with the impress of human nails. He directed my attention to some object against the wall;—I looked at it for some minutes;—it was a spade. With a shriek I bounded to the table, and grasped the box that lay upon it. But I could not force it open; and in my tremor it slipped from my hands, and fell heavily, and burst into pieces; and from it, with a rattling sound, there rolled out some instruments of dental surgery, intermingled with thirty-two small, white and ivory-looking substances that were scattered to and fro about the floor.

SREDNI VASHTAR

"SAKI" (H. H. MUNRO)

Conradin was ten years old, and the doctor had pronounced his professional opinion that the boy would not live another five years. The doctor was silky and effete, and counted for little, but his opinion was endorsed by Mrs. de Ropp, who counted for nearly everything. Mrs. De Ropp was Conradin's cousin and guardian, and in his eyes she represented those three-fifths of the world that are necessary and disagreeable and real; the other two-fifths, in perpetual antagonism to the foregoing, were summed up in himself and his imagination. One of these days Conradin supposed he would succumb to the mastering pressure of wearisome necessary things—such as illnesses and coddling restrictions and drawn-out dullness. Without his imagination, which was rampant under the spur of loneliness, he would have succumbed long ago.

Mrs. de Ropp would never, in her honestest moments, have confessed to herself that she disliked Conradin, though she might have been dimly aware that thwarting him "for his good" was a duty which she did not find particularly irksome. Conradin hated her with a desperate sincerity which he was perfectly able to mask. Such few pleasures as he could contrive for himself gained an added relish from the likelihood that they would be displeasing to his guardian, and from the realm of his imagination she was locked out—an unclean thing, which should find no entrance.

In the dull, cheerless garden, overlooked by so many windows that were ready to open with a message not to do this or that, or a reminder that medicines were due, he found little attraction. The few fruit-trees that it contained were set jealously apart from his plucking, as though they were rare specimens of their kind blooming in an arid waste; it would probably have been difficult to find a market-gardener who would have offered ten shillings for their entire yearly produce. In a forgotten corner, however, almost hidden behind a dismal shrubbery, was a disused tool-shed of respectable proportions, and within its walls Conradin found a haven, something that took on the varying aspects of a playroom and a cathedral. He had peopled it with a legion of familiar phantoms, evoked partly from fragments of history and partly from his own brain, but it also boasted two inmates of flesh and blood. In one corner lived a ragged-plumaged Houdan hen, on which the boy lavished an affection that had scarcely another outlet. Further back in the gloom stood a large hutch, divided into two compartments, one of which was fronted with close iron bars. This was the abode of a large polecat-ferret, which a friendly butcher-boy had once smuggled, cage and all, into its present quarters, in exchange for a long-secreted hoard of small silver. Conradin was dreadfully afraid of the lithe, sharp-fanged beast, but it was his most treasured possession. Its very presence in the tool-shed was a secret and fearful joy, to be kept scrupulously from the knowledge of the Woman, as he privately dubbed his cousin. And one day, out of Heaven knows what material, he spun the beast a wonderful name, and from that moment it grew into a god and a religion. The Woman indulged in religion once a week at a church near by, and took Conradin with her, but to him the church service was an alien rite in the House of Rimmon. Every Thursday, in the dim and musty silence of the tool-shed, he worshipped with mystic and elaborate ceremonial before the wooden hutch where dwelt Sredni Vashtar, the great ferret. Red flowers in their season and scarlet berries in the winter-time were offered at his shrine, for he was a god who laid some special stress on the fierce impatient side of things, as opposed to the Woman's religion, which, as far as Conradin could observe, went to great lengths in the contrary direction. And on great festivals powdered nutmeg was strewn in front of his hutch, an important feature of the offering being that the nutmeg had to be stolen. These festivals were of irregular occurrence, and were chiefly appointed to celebrate some passing event. On one occasion, when Mrs. de Ropp suffered from acute toothache for three days, Conradin kept up the festival during the entire three days, and almost succeeded in persuading himself that Sredni Vashtar was personally responsible for the toothache. If the malady had lasted for another day the supply of nutmeg would have given out.

The Houdan hen was never drawn into the cult of Sredni Vashtar. Conradin had long ago settled that she was an Anabaptist. He did not pretend to have the remotest knowledge as to what an Anabaptist was, but he privately hoped that it was dashing and not very respectable. Mrs. de Ropp was the ground plan on which he based and detested all respectability.

After a while Conradin's absorption in the tool-shed began to attract the notice of his guardian. "It is not good for him to be pottering down there in all weathers," she promptly decided, and at breakfast one morning she announced that the Houdan hen had been sold and taken away overnight. With her short-sighted eyes she peered at Conradin, waiting for an outbreak of rage and sorrow, which she was ready to rebuke with a flow of excellent precepts and reasoning. But Conradin said nothing: there was nothing to be said. Something perhaps in his white set face gave her a momentary qualm, for at tea that afternoon there was toast on the table, a delicacy which she usually banned on the ground that it was bad for him; also because the making of it "gave trouble," a deadly offence in the middle-class feminine eye.

"I thought you liked toast," she exclaimed, with an injured air, observing that he did not touch it.

"Sometimes," said Conradin.

In the shed that evening there was an innovation in the worship of the hutch-god. Conradin had been wont to chant his praises, to-night he asked a boon.

"Do one thing for me, Sredni Vashtar."

The thing was not specified. As Sredni Vashtar was a god he must be supposed to know. And choking back a sob as he looked at that other empty corner, Conradin went back to the world he so hated.

And every night, in the welcome darkness of his bedroom, and every evening in the dusk of the tool-shed, Conradin's bitter litany went up: "Do one thing for me, Sredni Vashtar."

Mrs. de Ropp noticed that the visits to the shed did not cease, and one day she made a further journey of inspection.

"What are you keeping in that locked hutch?" she asked. "I believe it's guinea-pigs. I'll have them all cleared away."

Conradin shut his lips tight, but the Woman ransacked his bedroom till she found the carefully hidden key, and forthwith marched down to the shed to complete her discovery. It was a cold afternoon, and Conradin had been bidden to keep to the house. From the furthest window of the dining-room the door of the shed could just be seen beyond the corner of the shrubbery, and there Conradin stationed himself. He saw the Woman enter, and then he imagined her opening the door of the sacred hutch and peering down with her short-sighted eyes into the thick straw bed where his god lay hidden. Perhaps she would prod at the straw in her clumsy impatience. And Conradin fervently breathed his prayer for the last time. But he knew as he prayed that he did not believe. He knew that the Woman would come out presently with that pursed smile he loathed so well on her face, and that in an hour or two the gardener would carry away his wonderful god, a god no longer, but a simple brown ferret in a hutch. And he knew that the Woman would triumph always as she triumphed now, and that he would grow ever more sickly under her pestering and domineering and superior wisdom, till one day nothing would matter much more with him, and the doctor would be proved right. And in the sting and misery of his defeat, he began to chant loudly and defiantly the hymn of his threatened idol:

Sredni Vashtar went forth,
His thoughts were red thoughts and his teeth were white.
His enemies called for peace, but he brought them death.
Sredni Vashtar the Beautiful.

And then of a sudden he stopped his chanting and drew closer to the window-pane. The door of the shed still stood ajar as it had been left, and the minutes were slipping by. They were long minutes, but they slipped by nevertheless. He watched the starlings running and flying in little parties across the lawn; he counted them over and over again, with one eye always on that swinging door. A sour-faced maid came in to lay the table for tea, and still Conradin stood and waited and watched. Hope had crept by inches into his heart, and now a look of triumph began to blaze in his eyes that had only known the wistful patience of defeat. Under his breath, with a furtive exultation, he began once again the paean of victory and devastation. And presently his eyes were rewarded: out through that doorway came a long, low, yellow-and-brown beast, with eyes a-blink at the waning daylight, and dark wet stains around the fur of jaws and throat. Conradin dropped on his knees. The great polecat-ferret made its way down to a small brook at the foot of the garden, drank for a moment, then crossed a little plank bridge and was lost to sight in the bushes. Such was the passing of Sredni Vashtar.

"Tea is ready," said the sour-faced maid; "where is the mistress?"

"She went down to the shed some time ago," said Conradin.

And while the maid went to summon her mistress to tea, Conradin fished a toasting-fork out of the sideboard drawer and proceeded to toast himself a piece of bread. And during the toasting of it and the buttering of it with much butter and the slow enjoyment of eating it, Conradin listened to the noises and silences which fell in quick spasms beyond the dining-room door. The loud foolish screaming of the maid, the answering chorus of wondering ejaculations from the kitchen region, the scuttering footsteps and hurried embassies for outside help, and then, after a lull, the scared sobbings and the shuffling tread of those who bore a heavy burden into the house.

"Whoever will break it to the poor child? I couldn't for the life of me!" exclaimed a shrill voice. And while they debated the matter among themselves, Conradin made himself another piece of toast.

CALLED TO THE RESCUE

HENRY SPICER

The salient features of the following narrative have formed, the writer believes, the basis of a "sensation" story in a popular serial, but nevertheless in the latter differ so materially from the actual facts, that nothing but the *sequence* of circumstances suggests the identity of the two histories. This, then, divested of embellishments, is believed to represent the matter:

A young undergraduate of Cambridge, Mr. D——, had been reading, during the long vacation, at the quiet little town of Exmouth, at which place, as many readers are aware, the river Exe is crossed by a ferry, communicating with the Starcross station on the Great Western Railway. For this purpose a boat remains in constant attendance from dawn till dusk.

One night, between twelve and one o'clock, the young man suddenly awoke, with the impression of having been addressed by an imperative voice, saying, with such distinctness that the last word still rung upon his ear—

"*Go down to the ferry!*"

Thinking it an ordinary dream, he composed himself again to sleep, when a second time the command was repeated, with this addition—

"*The boatman awaits!*"

There was something in this second voice which it seemed to the young man's mind impossible to disregard. He did, however, combat the inclination, and sat up in bed for some minutes, wide-awake, reasoning with himself on what he tried to consider the absurdity of rising in the dead of night, at the bidding of an imaginary voice, to go to a ferry where no boat would be found (for the ferryman resided at Starcross), upon an errand of which he knew nothing. His efforts to dismiss the idea were, however, unsuccessful. He felt, at all events, that sleep was impossible. Then, at the worst, it was but a walk to the ferry and back, and none but himself need be aware of that little excursion. Finally, he sprang from the bed, dressed rapidly, not to leave time for more useless self-argument, and set forth.

He had not reached the ferry when, to his astonishment, the boatman's hoarse voice was heard through the darkness hailing him impatiently—

"Well, you've kept me waiting long enough to-night, I think. I've stopped nigh an hour for you."

The ferryman had, it appeared, received his summons also, but did not attribute it to any unusual source. Finding no passenger waiting on his own side of the river, he probably concluded that he had been hailed by a passing boat, and directed to go over.

By the time Mr. D—— had arrived on the Starcross side, a further idea or impulse, which seemed to have its origin in the former, had gained possession of his mind.

"Exeter!" "Exeter!" "Exeter!" was the word that kept continually reverberating, as it were, in his mental ear, like a summoning bell. His impression *now* was that at Exeter would be fulfilled the purpose, whatever it might prove to be, of this strange nocturnal expedition. To Exeter he accordingly proceeded by the first opportunity, and, it being only eight or ten miles, reached that good city about dawn.

Now, for the first time, he felt at a loss. All impulse or impression had departed. Wandering aimlessly about the streets, he blamed himself severely for the readiness with which he had yielded to what he now regarded as an idle fancy, and only comforted himself with the idea that at that early hour none of his acquaintance were likely to be abroad to question him as to his untimely visit. Mr. D—— resolved to return home by the next train; but, meanwhile, the shops and houses began to open, and passing an hotel the young gentleman thought he could scarcely do better than while away the hour that must necessarily intervene by ordering some breakfast.

The waiter was very slow in bringing the repast, but when at length he did so, apologised for the delay on the plea that the assizes, then proceeding, had filled the house to overflowing.

Mr. D—— had heard nothing of the assizes, and took but little interest in the subject. Seeing, however, that the waiter regarded it as an event of considerable importance, he goodhumouredly encouraged him to continue the theme, and was rewarded with a very amusing history of such cases as had been already disposed of, as well as with the waiter's own views concerning those yet remaining to be tried. Upon the whole, the man's entertaining volubility ended by inspiring young D—— with a portion of his own interest in the matter, and, accordingly, instead of returning to Exmouth by the next train, he strolled about until the court opened, and then took his place among the spectators.

The case just commencing seemed to create unusual excitement. The prisoner at the bar, who was in the dress of a carpenter, was arraigned on a capital charge. The chain of evidence against him, though circumstantial, was complete, and a conviction seemed inevitable. There was, in fact, no opening for a defence, unless the prisoner were in a position to prove the witnesses, one and all, mistaken in his identity, and establish an *alibi*.

When asked what he had to say, he quietly replied:

"It is impossible that I could have committed this crime, because, on the day and at the hour it took place, I was sent for to mend the sashline of a window at Mr. G——'s house, at M——. There is *one* gentleman," he added, after a pause, "who could prove that I was there, but I don't know who he is, nor where to have him looked for. Yes, I *know* he could prove my innocence, for a particular reason, that would remind him of me; but, there, I can't help it, the Lord's will be done," and the poor fellow, with a sigh, appeared to resign himself to his fate.

All this time Mr. D—— had been listening with profound attention to the progress of the trial, and when the prisoner concluded his sad and hopeless address, he started, and looked earnestly at him. As his eyes still dwelt upon the gloomy, toilworn face—one by one, link by link—a chain of circumstances, trivial enough at the time, but now important as bearing upon the liberty, if not the very life, of a fellow-creature, came back to his remembrance.

He had gone, some months before, to pay an early visit to a friend at M——. The latter was from home, but, wishing particularly to see him, D—— had decided to await his return, and, for that purpose, had gone up to his friend's library, meaning to beguile the interval with a book. Here, however, he found a carpenter, making some repairs about the window, and, in place of reading, he stood for some minutes watching the man, and conversing with him about his work. While doing so, something was said that he was desirous of noting down, and he took out his memorandum-book for the purpose, but found that he had lost his pencil, when the carpenter, observing his difficulty, handed him his own (a short, brown, stumpy article, with square sides), saying that "if he might make so bold, Mr. D—— was welcome to it."

All this came back to the young man's mind, as clearly as if it had occurred but the day before. Hastily turning to his pocketbook, he there found the very entry he had made, date included, written in the thick but faint lines produced by the carpenter's pencil. He instantly made known to the court his wish to be examined on the man's behalf, and, being sworn, deposed to the above facts, clearly identifying the prisoner, as well as the pencil, which the man produced from his pocket. The jury were satisfied, and returned a verdict of acquittal.

It is difficult to meet a sufficiently authenticated case of this description, otherwise than with the simple confession that God's ways are not as our ways, and that it may be His pleasure, as unquestionably it is within His power, to suffer his ministering angels to speak in this mysterious tongue to the souls of those whom He has selected as the earthly instruments of His divine will.

THE INEXPERIENCED GHOST

H. G. WELLS

The scene amidst which Clayton told his last story comes back very vividly to my mind. There he sat, for the greater part of the time, in the corner of the authentic settle by the spacious open fire, and Sanderson sat beside him smoking the Broseley clay that bore his name. There was Evans, and that marvel among actors, Wish, who is also a modest man. We had all come down to the Mermaid Club that Saturday morning, except Clayton, who had slept there overnight—which indeed gave him the opening of his story. We had golfed until golfing was invisible; we had dined, and we were in that mood of tranquil kindliness when men will suffer a story. When Clayton began to tell one, we naturally supposed he was lying. It may be that indeed he was lying—of that the reader will speedily be able to judge as well as I. He began, it is true, with an air of matter-of-fact anecdote, but that we thought was only the incurable artifice of the man.

"I say!" he remarked, after a long consideration of the upward rain of sparks from the log that Sanderson had thumped, "you know I was alone here last night?"

"Except for the domestics," said Wish.

"Who sleep in the other wing," said Clayton. "Yes. Well—" He pulled at his cigar for some little time as though he still hesitated about his confidence. Then he said, quite quietly, "I caught a ghost!"

"Caught a ghost, did you?" said Sanderson. "Where is it?"

And Evans, who admires Clayton immensely and has been four weeks in America, shouted, "*Caught* a ghost, did you, Clayton? I'm glad of it! Tell us all about it right now."

Clayton said he would in a minute, and asked him to shut the door.

He looked apologetically at me. "There's no eavesdropping of course, but we don't want to upset our very excellent service with any rumours of ghosts in the place. There's too much shadow and oak panelling to trifle with that. And this, you know, wasn't a regular ghost. I don't think it will come again—ever."

"You mean to say you didn't keep it?" said Sanderson.

"I hadn't the heart to," said Clayton.

And Sanderson said he was surprised.

We laughed, and Clayton looked aggrieved. "I know," he said, with the flicker of a smile, "but the fact is it really *was* a ghost, and I'm as sure of it as I am that I am talking to you now. I'm not joking. I mean what I say."

Sanderson drew deeply at his pipe, with one reddish eye on Clayton, and then emitted a thin jet of smoke more eloquent than many words.

Clayton ignored the comment. "It is the strangest thing that has ever happened in my life. You know, I never believed in ghosts or anything of the sort, before, ever; and then, you know, I bag one in a corner; and the whole business is in my hands."

He meditated still more profoundly, and produced and began to pierce a second cigar with a curious little stabber he affected.

"You talked to it?" asked Wish.

"For the space, probably, of an hour."

"Chatty?" I said, joining the party of the sceptics.

"The poor devil was in trouble," said Clayton, bowed over his cigar-end and with the very faintest note of reproof.

"Sobbing?" someone asked.

Clayton heaved a realistic sigh at the memory. "Good Lord!" he said; "yes." And then, "Poor fellow! yes."

"Where did you strike it?" asked Evans, in his best American accent.

"I never realised," said Clayton, ignoring him, "the poor sort of thing a ghost might be," and he hung us up again for a time, while he sought for matches in his pocket and lit and warmed to his cigar.

"I took an advantage," he reflected at last.

We were none of us in a hurry. "A character," he said, "remains just the same character for all that it's been disembodied. That's a thing we too often forget. People with a certain strength or fixity of purpose may have ghosts of a certain strength and fixity of purpose—most haunting ghosts, you know, must be as one-idea'd as monomaniacs and as obstinate as mules to come back again and again. This poor creature wasn't." He suddenly looked up rather queerly, and his eye went round the room. "I say it," he said, "in all kindliness, but that is the plain truth of the case. Even at the first glance he struck me as weak."

He punctuated with the help of his cigar.

"I came upon him, you know, in the long passage. His back was towards me and I saw him first. Right off I knew him for a ghost. He was transparent and whitish; clean through his chest I could see the glimmer of the little window at the end. And not only his physique but his attitude struck me as being weak. He looked, you know, as though he didn't know in the slightest whatever he meant to do. One hand was on the panelling and the other fluttered to his mouth. Like—SO!"

"What sort of physique?" said Sanderson.

"Lean. You know that sort of young man's neck that has two great flutings down the back, here and here—so! And a little, meanish head with scrubby hair—And rather bad ears. Shoulders bad, narrower than the hips; turn-down collar, ready-made short jacket, trousers baggy and a little frayed at the heels. That's how he took me. I came very quietly up the staircase. I did not carry a light, you know—the candles are on the landing table and there is that lamp—and I was in my list slippers, and I saw him as I came up. I stopped dead at that—taking him in. I wasn't a bit afraid. I think that in most of these affairs one is never nearly so afraid or excited as one imagines one would be. I was surprised and interested. I thought, 'Good Lord! Here's a ghost at last! And I haven't believed for a moment in ghosts during the last five-and-twenty years.'"

"Um," said Wish.

"I suppose I wasn't on the landing a moment before he found out I was there. He turned on me sharply, and I saw the face of an immature young man, a weak nose, a scrubby little moustache, a feeble chin. So for an instant we stood—he looking over his shoulder at me and regarded one another. Then he seemed to remember his high calling. He turned round, drew himself up, projected his face, raised his arms, spread his hands in approved ghost fashion—came towards me. As he did so his little jaw dropped, and he emitted a faint, drawn-out

'Boo.' No, it wasn't—not a bit dreadful. I'd dined. I'd had a bottle of champagne, and being all alone, perhaps two or three—perhaps even four or five—whiskies, so I was as solid as rocks and no more frightened than if I'd been assailed by a frog. 'Boo!' I said. 'Nonsense. You don't belong to *this* place. What are you doing here?'

"I could see him wince. 'Boo-oo,' he said.

"'Boo—be hanged! Are you a member?' I said; and just to show I didn't care a pin for him I stepped through a corner of him and made to light my candle. 'Are you a member?' I repeated, looking at him sideways.

"He moved a little so as to stand clear of me, and his bearing became crestfallen. 'No,' he said, in answer to the persistent interrogation of my eye; 'I'm not a member—I'm a ghost.'

"'Well, that doesn't give you the run of the Mermaid Club. Is there any one you want to see, or anything of that sort?' and doing it as steadily as possible for fear that he should mistake the carelessness of whisky for the distraction of fear, I got my candle alight. I turned on him, holding it. 'What are you doing here?' I said.

"He had dropped his hands and stopped his booing, and there he stood, abashed and awkward, the ghost of a weak, silly, aimless young man. 'I'm haunting,' he said.

"'You haven't any business to,' I said in a quiet voice.

"'I'm a ghost,' he said, as if in defence.

"'That may be, but you haven't any business to haunt here. This is a respectable private club; people often stop here with nursemaids and children, and, going about in the careless way you do, some poor little mite could easily come upon you and be scared out of her wits. I suppose you didn't think of that?'

"'No, sir,' he said, 'I didn't.'

"'You should have done. You haven't any claim on the place, have you? Weren't murdered here, or anything of that sort?'

"'None, sir; but I thought as it was old and oak-panelled—'

"'That's *no* excuse.' I regarded him firmly. 'Your coming here is a mistake,' I said, in a tone of friendly superiority. I feigned to see if I had my matches, and then looked up at him frankly. 'If I were you I wouldn't wait for cock-crow—I'd vanish right away.'

"He looked embarrassed. 'The fact *is*, sir—' he began.

"'I'd vanish,' I said, driving it home.

"'The fact is, sir, that—somehow—I can't.'

"'You *can't?*'

"'No, sir. There's something I've forgotten. I've been hanging about here since midnight last night, hiding in the cupboards of the empty bedrooms and things like that. I'm flurried. I've never come haunting before, and it seems to put me out.'

"'Put you out?'

"'Yes, sir. I've tried to do it several times, and it doesn't come off. There's some little thing has slipped me, and I can't get back.'

"That, you know, rather bowled me over. He looked at me in such an abject way that for the life of me I couldn't keep up quite the high, hectoring vein I had adopted. 'That's queer,' I said, and as I spoke I fancied I heard someone moving about down below. 'Come into my room and tell me more about it,' I said. 'I didn't, of course, understand this,' and I tried to take him by the arm. But, of course, you might as well have tried to take hold of a puff of smoke! I had forgotten my number, I think; anyhow, I remember going into several bedrooms— it was lucky I was the only soul in that wing—until I saw my traps. 'Here we are,' I said, and sat down in the arm-chair; 'sit down and tell me all about it. It seems to me you have got yourself into a jolly awkward position, old chap.'

"Well, he said he wouldn't sit down! he'd prefer to flit up and down the room if it was all the same to me. And so he did, and in a little while we were deep in a long and serious talk. And presently, you know, something of those whiskies and sodas evaporated out of me, and I began to realise just a little what a thundering rum and weird business it was that I was in. There he was, semi-transparent—the proper conventional phantom, and noiseless except for his ghost of a voice—flitting to and fro in that nice, clean, chintz-hung old bedroom. You could see the gleam of the copper candlesticks through him, and the lights on the brass fender, and the corners of the framed engravings on the wall,—and there he was telling me all about this wretched little life of his that had recently ended on earth. He hadn't a particularly honest face, you know, but being transparent, of course, he couldn't avoid telling the truth."

"Eh?" said Wish, suddenly sitting up in his chair.

"What?" said Clayton.

"Being transparent—couldn't avoid telling the truth—I don't see it," said Wish.

"*I* don't see it," said Clayton, with inimitable assurance. "But it *is* so, I can assure you nevertheless. I don't believe he got once a nail's breadth off the Bible truth. He told me how he had been killed—he went down into a London basement with a candle to look for a leakage of gas—and described himself as a senior English master in a London private school when that release occurred."

"Poor wretch!" said I.

"That's what I thought, and the more he talked the more I thought it. There he was, purposeless in life and purposeless out of it. He talked of his father and mother and his schoolmaster, and all who had ever been anything to him in the world, meanly. He had been too sensitive, too nervous; none of them had ever valued him properly or understood him, he said. He had never had a real friend in the world, I think; he had never had a success. He had shirked games and failed examinations. 'It's like that with some people,' he said; 'whenever I got into the examination-room or anywhere everything seemed to go.' Engaged to be married of course—to another over-sensitive person, I suppose—when the indiscretion with the gas escape ended his affairs. 'And where are you now?' I asked. 'Not in—?'

"He wasn't clear on that point at all. The impression he gave me was of a sort of vague, intermediate state, a special reserve for souls too non-existent for anything so positive as either sin or virtue. *I* don't know. He was much too egotistical and unobservant to give me any clear idea of the kind of place, kind of country, there is on the Other Side of Things. Wherever he was, he seems to have fallen in with a set of kindred spirits: ghosts of weak Cockney young men, who were on a footing of Christian names, and among these there was certainly a lot of talk about 'going haunting' and things like that. Yes—going haunting! They seemed to think 'haunting' a tremendous adventure, and most of them funked it all the time. And so primed, you know, he had come."

"But really!" said Wish to the fire.

"These are the impressions he gave me, anyhow," said Clayton, modestly. "I may, of course, have been in a rather uncritical state, but that was the sort of background he gave to himself. He kept flitting up and down, with his thin voice going talking, talking about his wretched self, and never a word of clear, firm statement from first to last. He was thinner and sillier and more pointless than if he had been real and alive. Only then, you know, he would not have been in my bedroom here—if he *had* been alive. I should have kicked him out."

"Of course," said Evans, "there *are* poor mortals like that."

"And there's just as much chance of their having ghosts as the rest of us," I admitted.

"What gave a sort of point to him, you know, was the fact that he did seem within limits to have found himself out. The mess he had made of haunting had depressed him terribly. He had been told it would be a 'lark'; he had come expecting it to be a 'lark,' and here it was, nothing but another failure added to his record! He proclaimed himself an utter out-and-out failure. He said, and I can quite believe it, that he had never tried to do anything all his life that he hadn't made a perfect mess of—and through all the wastes of eternity he never would. If he had had sympathy, perhaps—He paused at that, and stood regarding me. He remarked that, strange as it might seem to me, nobody, not any one, ever, had given him the amount of sympathy I was doing now. I could see what he wanted straight away, and I determined to head him off at once. I may be a brute, you know, but being the Only Real Friend, the recipient of the confidences of one of these egotistical weaklings, ghost or body, is beyond my physical endurance. I got up briskly. 'Don't you brood on these things too much,' I said. 'The thing you've got to do is to get out of this get out of this—sharp. You pull yourself together and *try*.' 'I can't,' he said. 'You try,' I said, and try he did."

"Try!" said Sanderson. "*How?*"

"Passes," said Clayton.

"Passes?"

"Complicated series of gestures and passes with the hands. That's how he had come in and that's how he had to get out again. Lord! what a business I had!"

"But how could *any* series of passes—?" I began.

"My dear man," said Clayton, turning on me and putting a great emphasis on certain words, "you want *everything* clear. *I* don't know *how*. All I know is that you *do*—that *he* did, anyhow, at least. After a fearful time, you know, he got his passes right and suddenly disappeared."

"Did you," said Sanderson, slowly, "observe the passes?"

"Yes," said Clayton, and seemed to think. "It was tremendously queer," he said. "There we were, I and this thin vague ghost, in that silent room, in this silent, empty inn, in this silent little Friday-night town. Not a sound except our voices and a faint panting he made when he swung. There was the bedroom candle, and one candle on the dressing-table alight, that was all—sometimes one or other would flare up into a tall, lean, astonished flame for a space. And queer things happened. 'I can't,' he said; 'I shall never—!' And suddenly he sat down on a little chair at the foot of the bed and began to sob and sob. Lord! what a harrowing, whimpering thing he seemed!

"'You pull yourself together,' I said, and tried to pat him on the back, and . . . my confounded hand went through him! By that time, you know, I wasn't nearly so—massive as I had been on the landing. I got the queerness of it full. I remember snatching back my hand out of him, as it were, with a little thrill, and walking over to the dressing-table. 'You pull yourself together,' I said to him, 'and try.' And in order to encourage and help him I began to try as well."

"What!" said Sanderson, "the passes?"

"Yes, the passes."

"But—" I said, moved by an idea that eluded me for a space.

"This is interesting," said Sanderson, with his finger in his pipe-bowl. "You mean to say this ghost of yours gave away—"

"Did his level best to give away the whole confounded barrier? *Yes.*"

"He didn't," said Wish; "he couldn't. Or you'd have gone there too."

"That's precisely it," I said, finding my elusive idea put into words for me.

"That *is* precisely it," said Clayton, with thoughtful eyes upon the fire.

For just a little while there was silence.

"And at last he did it?" said Sanderson.

"At last he did it. I had to keep him up to it hard, but he did it at last—rather suddenly. He despaired, we had a scene, and then he got up abruptly and asked me to go through the whole performance, slowly, so that he might see. 'I believe,' he said, 'if I could *see* I should spot what was wrong at once.' And he did. '*I* know,' he said. 'What do you know?' said I. '*I* know,' he repeated. Then he said, peevishly, 'I *can't* do it if you look at me—I really *can't*; it's been that, partly, all along. I'm such a nervous fellow that you put me out.' Well, we had a bit of an argument. Naturally I wanted to see; but he was as obstinate as a mule, and suddenly I had come over as tired as a dog—he tired me out. 'All right,' I said, '*I* won't look at you,' and turned towards the mirror, on the wardrobe, by the bed.

He started off very fast. I tried to follow him by looking in the looking-glass, to see just what it was had hung. Round went his arms and his hands, so, and so, and so, and then with a rush came to the last gesture of all—you stand erect and open out your arms—and so, don't you know, he stood. And then he didn't! He didn't! He wasn't! I wheeled round from the looking-glass to him. There was nothing. I was alone, with the flaring candles and a staggering mind. What had happened? Had anything happened? Had I been dreaming? . . . And then, with an absurd note of finality about it, the clock upon the landing discovered the moment was ripe for striking *one*. So!—Ping! And I was as grave and sober as a judge, with all my champagne and whisky gone into the vast serene. Feeling queer, you know—confoundedly *queer*! Queer! Good Lord!"

He regarded his cigar-ash for a moment. "That's all that happened," he said.

"And then you went to bed?" asked Evans.

"What else was there to do?"

I looked Wish in the eye. We wanted to scoff, and there was something, something perhaps in Clayton's voice and manner, that hampered our desire.

"And about these passes?" said Sanderson.

"I believe I could do them now."

"Oh!" said Sanderson, and produced a penknife and set himself to grub the dottel out of the bowl of his clay.

"Why don't you do them now?" said Sanderson, shutting his pen-knife with a click.

"That's what I'm going to do," said Clayton.

"They won't work," said Evans.

"If they do—" I suggested.

"You know, I'd rather you didn't," said Wish, stretching out his legs.

"Why?" asked Evans.

"I'd rather he didn't," said Wish.

"But he hasn't got 'em right," said Sanderson, plugging too much tobacco in his pipe.

"All the same, I'd rather he didn't," said Wish.

We argued with Wish. He said that for Clayton to go through those gestures was like mocking a serious matter. "But you don't believe—?" I said. Wish glanced at Clayton, who was staring into the fire, weighing something in his mind. "I do—more than half, anyhow, I do," said Wish.

"Clayton," said I, "you're too good a liar for us. Most of it was all right. But that disappearance . . . happened to be convincing. Tell us, it's a tale of cock and bull."

He stood up without heeding me, took the middle of the hearthrug, and faced me. For a moment he regarded his feet thoughtfully, and then for all the rest of the time his eyes were on the opposite wall, with an intent expression. He raised his two hands slowly to the level of his eyes and so began. . . .

Now, Sanderson is a Freemason, a member of the lodge of the Four Kings, which devotes itself so ably to the study and elucidation of all the mysteries of Masonry past and present, and among the students of this lodge Sanderson is by no means the least. He followed Clayton's motions with a singular interest in his reddish eye. "That's not bad," he said, when it was done. "You really do, you know, put things together, Clayton, in a most amazing fashion. But there's one little detail out."

"I know," said Clayton. "I believe I could tell you which."

"Well?"

"This," said Clayton, and did a queer little twist and writhing and thrust of the hands.

"Yes."

"That, you know, was what *he* couldn't get right," said Clayton. "But how do *you*—?"

"Most of this business, and particularly how you invented it, I don't understand at all," said Sanderson, "but just that phase—I do." He reflected. "These happen to be a series of gestures—connected with a certain branch of esoteric Masonry. Probably you know. Or else—*how?*" He reflected still further. "I do not see I can do any harm in telling you just the proper twist. After all, if you know, you know; if you don't, you don't."

"I know nothing," said Clayton, "except what the poor devil let out last night."

"Well, anyhow," said Sanderson, and placed his churchwarden very carefully upon the shelf over the fireplace. Then very rapidly he gesticulated with his hands.

"So?" said Clayton, repeating.

"So," said Sanderson, and took his pipe in hand again.

"Ah, *now*," said Clayton, "I can do the whole thing—right."

He stood up before the waning fire and smiled at us all. But I think there was just a little hesitation in his smile. "If I begin—" he said.

"I wouldn't begin," said Wish.

"It's all right!" said Evans. "Matter is indestructible. You don't think any jiggery-pokery of this sort is going to snatch Clayton into the world of shades. Not it! You may try, Clayton, so far as I'm concerned, until your arms drop off at the wrists."

"I don't believe that," said Wish, and stood up and put his arm on Clayton's shoulder. "You've made me half believe in that story somehow, and I don't want to see the thing done!"

"Goodness!" said I, "here's Wish frightened!"

"I am," said Wish, with real or admirably feigned intensity. "I believe that if he goes through these motions right he'll *go*."

"He'll not do anything of the sort," I cried. "There's only one way out of this world for men, and Clayton is thirty years from that. Besides . . . And such a ghost! Do you think—?"

Wish interrupted me by moving. He walked out from among our chairs and stopped beside the table and stood there. "Clayton," he said, "you're a fool."

Clayton, with a humorous light in his eyes, smiled back at him. "Wish," he said, "is right and all you others are wrong. I shall go. I shall get to the end of these passes, and as the last swish whistles through the air, Presto!—this hearthrug will be vacant, the room will be blank amazement, and a respectably dressed gentleman of fifteen stone will plump into the world of shades. I'm certain. So will you be. I decline to argue further. Let the thing be tried."

"*No*," said Wish, and made a step and ceased, and Clayton raised his hands once more to repeat the spirit's passing.

By that time, you know, we were all in a state of tension—largely because of the behaviour of Wish. We sat all of us with our eyes on Clayton—I, at least, with a sort of tight, stiff feeling about me as though from the back of my skull to the middle of my thighs my body had been changed to steel. And there, with a gravity that was imperturbably serene, Clayton bowed and swayed and waved his hands and arms before us. As he drew towards the end one piled up, one tingled in one's teeth. The last gesture, I have said, was to swing the arms out wide open, with the face held up. And when at last he swung out to this closing gesture I ceased even to breathe. It was ridiculous, of course, but you know that ghost-story feeling. It was after dinner, in a queer, old shadowy house. Would he, after all—?

There he stood for one stupendous moment, with his arms open and his upturned face, assured and bright, in the glare of the hanging lamp. We hung through that moment as if it were an age, and then came from all of us something that was half a sigh of infinite relief and half a reassuring "*No!*" For visibly—he wasn't going. It was all nonsense. He had told an idle story, and carried it almost to conviction, that was all! . . . And then in that moment the face of Clayton, changed.

It changed. It changed as a lit house changes when its lights are suddenly extinguished. His eyes were suddenly eyes that were fixed, his smile was frozen on his lips, and he stood there still. He stood there, very gently swaying.

That moment, too, was an age. And then, you know, chairs were scraping, things were falling, and we were all moving. His knees seemed to give, and he fell forward, and Evans rose and caught him in his arms. . . .

It stunned us all. For a minute I suppose no one said a coherent thing. We believed it, yet could not believe it. . . . I came out of a muddled stupefaction to find myself kneeling beside him, and his vest and shirt were torn open, and Sanderson's hand lay on his heart....

Well—the simple fact before us could very well wait our convenience; there was no hurry for us to comprehend. It lay there for an hour; it lies athwart my memory, black and amazing still, to this day. Clayton had, indeed, passed into the world that lies so near to and so far from our own, and he had gone thither by the only road that mortal man may take. But whether he did indeed pass there by that poor ghost's incantation, or whether he was stricken suddenly by apoplexy in the midst of an idle tale—as the coroner's jury would have us believe—is no matter for my judging; it is just one of those inexplicable riddles that must remain unsolved until the final solution of all things shall come. All I certainly know is that, in the very moment, in the very instant, of concluding those passes, he changed, and staggered, and fell down before us—dead!